UNBURIED
DARK BRILLIANCE DUOLOGY BOOK TWO

GLORIA BOTTELMAN

Copyright © 2026 by Gloria Bottelman

All rights reserved. No part of this publication may be reproduced, distributed, or transmitted in any form or by any means, including photocopying, recording, or other electronic or mechanical methods, without the prior written permission of the publisher, except as permitted by U.S. copyright law. For permission requests, contact the author.

The story, all names, characters, and incidents portrayed in this production are fictitious. No identification with actual persons (living or deceased), places, buildings, and products is intended or should be inferred.

Cover Design by Charlotte Slegers

Edited by Aurion Edits

First edition: April 2026

Published in the United States of America by Ravenwood Books. LCCN: 2026901448

ISBN: 979-8-9906910-5-6 (ebook)

ISBN: 979-8-9906910-6-3 (paperback)

Also by Gloria Bottelman
Untethered
Potions & Peculiarities

For those who have ever felt broken.

Before you begin, this story contains elements that may be difficult for some readers, including:
body horror, death and murder, depictions of anxiety and panic attacks, psychological abuse.

Chapter One

The cabin at the bottom of the mountain stunk of sour berries and dead things, and inside, Lux Thorn held out a twig. It was black and curled, knotted like a crone's finger, and it came from a devouring tree.

The gallow, she'd only recently learned.

The man who told her of it lived in the mountainside cabin. He was old. So old, his pallid skin was spotted, and his eyes were filmy. He had calloused, cracked fingers thickened with gout, and he used them now to relay an animated story. As his excitement grew, Lux's horror did the same.

"—and yes, my grandfather traded them. A fair trade for the woman, I was told. An appendix for that last seed and two means to contain it. I still remember the jar it was kept in. How it was so thick, it didn't move when you'd tap the glass." He bent to peer closer at the rotting twig. His expression collapsed into awe. "Gallows are certainly one of the rarest and most unique species in the world."

His fingertips barely pinching, he took the branch from her cold hand and promptly threw it into the hearth.

"No! *Why—*" She almost lunged for it, that last remnant of a devouring tree, but it went up in a blaze. She supposed that after having been detached from its frozen host for so long, it didn't hold further moisture to delay it.

"Plants hold power—even the rotted ones—as they live and grow, same as you. I apologize, but we do not desecrate the dead by carrying about their *fingers.*"

A muted cry of outrage left her lips. "As you keep a collection of...*this!*" Lux couldn't help but splutter as she gestured wildly to the shelves behind him. Snow tumbled from the folds of her cloak.

The man shuffled around to look as if he didn't know what he would find.

The horror. Lux hadn't journeyed far into the mountain range known as Barnabus Pass before she'd come upon her destination. With an excellent ear for indecent conversation, she'd learned a week ago of a man who offered the wildest and rare flora in all the land. She sprang upon the news as the twig she carried had started stinking. But what the gossip uttered next had unnerved her.

"He's a nattering recluse, that Edgar Dosem. Why, I heard he'll only barter for your parts!"

Lux herself had been on the receiving end of rumors and twisted tales; she knew they couldn't always be believed outright. But as it turned out, in this case, they could.

Assorted glass jars filled with liquids lined the narrow shelving before her. And inside—human things floated. Lashes and locks of curls. Various items of pink and beige and a single eye that rotated when Edgar reached up and rapped upon it.

"You are not a botanist, and it shows, young lady. Did you happen to bring a seed along with you too? Or do you only cart around dead things?"

Her lip curled. "No, I didn't bring a seed! How does someone even fetch a seed from a devouring tree? Nothing falls from them."

The old man couldn't have looked more disappointed in her. "The roots, the roots! There're pockets of them. Surely, you must have seen it? Fine then. Dangle the carrot. I see that's all you're good for. You know my knees are too bad to leave the mountainside and you're taunting me with it." His so-named bad knees bent slightly as he meant to lower himself onto the stool. He collapsed upon it instead. "It's just as well." His sigh filled the cabin.

"It *is* just as well. I've seen what those things are capable of. We should chop them all down and be rid of them for good."

Edgar whipped his head toward her, abrupt disgust in his eyes. "How dare you. So ungrateful. So self-centered. So *immature!*" He took a healthy swig of tea, muttering into his cup. "You are not good for my heart, girl." He sighed again, patting his chest and appearing to calm. "Balance. The living world is a beautiful work of *balance*. Demolish a species at your whim and you begin a landslide. It might take more than your lifetime, but it'll come, mark my words. Of course, a lot of you young people are too shortsighted for all that."

"Your so-called *gallows* consumed more than half of my city!"

"Nature only fights back if it's been wronged for too long. What'd you do to aggravate it?"

Lux's mouth opened and closed without comment.

"*Precisely.*" His stare swept her up and down. He harrumphed. "It's good you're traveling. Maybe it'll give you some perspective."

But her mind conjured the terror of what she'd witnessed in Ghadra, blocking everything he'd said.

We have been cheated, Lucena. We will take them all.

Goosebumps rose all over her skin. Truth be told, she was relieved he'd burned the twig. Carting it all this way had felt too much like pressing at a mouth sore with her tongue; it was better to be rid of it. She glanced at the pile of dark ash. Already, the dead smell was dissipating.

"As enlightening as this has been," she said. "I think I've gotten what I came for."

The botanist did not have any further seedlings, nor did he know of any around. His grandfather had been the only one to have ever held one, and he was long dead. It was a great relief to discover that truth, even if he was upset about it.

"Wait, wait, wait." A cane rapped against her knees. Lux turned back. "You came all this way but not to trade for *anything?*"

She stepped over the cane. "I have no interest in your cutting out my organs in exchange for a vine. Even if it promised to reach through the clouds or grant wishes."

"Well, those things are preposterous. Almost as preposterous as the first part of what you said. I don't *cut* anything. Except for flowers. And dead trimmings."

And now curiosity hooked her. She couldn't very well leave without knowing. "All right. How do you manage it, then? Because those aren't all found on our outsides." She gestured again to the jars. Particularly the pink, soft parts.

"Good eye, good eye." As if it'd been summoned, the eyeball specimen swiveled toward her. "It's actually quite extraordinary what nature can do." He shuffled away from her, his cane thumping against the weathered wood floor. He stopped before a small cabinet on the wall, and opened it.

Lux peered around him, but all there was to see were several tins and nothing more. She landed back on her heels.

Edgar balanced his cane against the wall in order to remove a rectangular tin. He worked the lid, and when it came free, a plume of powder puffed along with it. Lux stepped back.

"Oh, don't worry yourself. You have to chew them, not breathe them. It's only sugar." His thick fingers reached into the tin and withdrew the tiniest cake she'd ever seen. A dusting of white powder sat atop it.

He held it out for her inspection, which she gave, albeit nervously.

"It's a recipe handed down for generations. Gooseberries, juniper berries, and bayberries. Chew this and I can call up any organ I wish! Only one we agreed upon, of course," he added after observing her look of utter terror.

Lux swallowed against a tight throat. "She vomited up her appendix?"

"In exchange for a lot, I'd say. More than fair." He snapped the lid back into place. "And I have just the thing for you."

Though she was relieved to see the cakes hidden away again, Lux didn't want anything to do with whatever he had in mind for her. She backed away. "No. I need nothing." Her fingers tightened on the hidden handle of Shaw's knife.

"Two things," he muttered, puttering over to a potted plant with large violet leaves and little else. But when he pried them from one another, she saw a separate stem inside, overgrown with plump purple berries. "Two..." he grunted. A single berry pulled free. "Things." The second came away into his grasp. "They do *not* like to be plucked."

He held them out to her.

"What am I supposed to do with those? What even *are* those?"

"Gorga seeds. Fantastic plants. Their leaves clear toxins from the air, but the berries themselves are interesting. The juice is sour; if you swallow it, you'll lose your voice for hours. Ingest the seed, however, and you'll lose your voice until the end of your days. Did I say they were fantastic?"

Quicker than she knew he could move, the botanist snatched her hand. He turned it over as she struggled to free it. "All it'll cost you is a fingernail. That one."

Lux seethed through gritted teeth.

"Absolutely not."

Chapter Two

Her pinky finger throbbed still.

It'd been two days.

Lux adjusted the pack draped against her hip and stared into the looming city. *Loxlen*, read the arched iron letters foisted over the road. She swallowed, her throat gone dry. "Crowds," she muttered. "The bane of my existence."

Nevermind that she had multiple banes, and crowds were only one of them.

In the four weeks since she'd left Ghadra, she'd managed to avoid anything larger than a village. She'd taken meals from street vendors or small cafés, and she'd slept in little roadside inns that boasted the same number of rooms as they did stalls for animals. And all the while, she'd kept her ears trained for very particular words. Words like "lifeblood", "immortal", and "Bartley Tamish". So far, she'd encountered nothing.

Edgar Dosem and his cabin of horrors was a detour that some might not have deemed necessary, but to her, was a question written in a diary and in want of crossing off. Because even after everything that'd happened in Ghadra, she still yearned to understand why it did. Only, she wasn't sure it had been worth the fingernail.

Lux pulled at the tail of her bandage with her teeth, tightening the cloth until her finger smarted. "Here goes." Because nothing said "potential buyers of souls" quite like a bustling trading city.

She passed beneath the overlarge iron name and forced a slow breath. The late mayor of Ghadra, Bartleby Tamish, would have argued with her purpose.

Per his reasoning, he hadn't been selling his people's souls, but rather their souls' tether to their bodies. Something, she believed, he thought quite a lot less evil.

It didn't matter to him that without it, not a single one of those bodies would ever have a chance of revival. That to then *drink* it was another atrocious thing. It was irreversible and unforgivable what he had done. And though he was dead, his own over-aged body providing a slow, steady nourishment for a gallow tree, she felt justified in still loathing him for it all.

Lux tugged back the hood of her new cloak. Enough that she could absorb everything, her periphery unobstructed. A warning from Shaw rattled in her head—that she should never leave herself vulnerable to attack. Her hand rested on the handle of his knife as she walked.

The road had been dirt outside the city. Now, it was cobblestone. Her boots made a soft clack that was quickly overrun by the rumble of wheels, and she moved out of the way on instinct to make space for a death-cart. But these weren't the streets she'd grown up with. There were no death-carts here. Lux's attention swung instead to a carriage as it passed her by. Black, sleek, with twin lanterns, a dour driver, and a stack of leather-bound luggage.

The mayor's voice returned to her from the Beyond. *"The world outside pays very well for the gift of time."*

"Rich for certain," she grumbled. Then she stepped back onto the road and followed it.

Loxlen wasn't like Ghadra at all. For one, it wasn't comprised of shades of grey. The sun shone brightly upon beige, slate roofs and paler stone walls, and though there were shadowy places and plenty of alleyways, they didn't give her that sense of foreboding the town she'd left always did. She would even hazard a guess that if she were to walk through them, she wouldn't even step in anything unsanitary.

And then there were the people.

She hadn't seen many yet, as it seemed most were either tucked in their homes on the autumn day, or hidden away in carriages. A few were on horseback or sat on wagons, and only several walked as she did now. None, she noticed so far, possessed the shifting eyes of Ghadra's Dark. Nor even the upturned noses of Ghadra's Light.

Even the smell was pleasant: brisk air rather than burning hair.

She continued to trail the carriage. It followed the main road, and though there were many streets nearly as wide, it didn't turn. There was a common destination at the center of town, and that was where she was sure it headed.

Edgar, the mountain recluse, said Loxlen was a hub of trade. That, though it was some distance yet from the sea, being at the base of the range caused it to be near enough to offer itself as a prime location for all manner of people to sell and barter and buy. Lux didn't know how much stock she could place in a man who never left his own four walls, but she supposed he dragged enough details out of the people who found him. It seemed he was correct in this.

Not a single person cast a furtive glance or a scowl her way the entirety of the time she walked. With her cloak, pack, and dirt-splattered boots, she supposed she looked like any other traveler come to trade. But her hand didn't leave the knife anyway.

She passed by a woman and child, both wrapped in thin capes and white gloves. The woman smiled warmly at Lux, and Lux, so unused to strangers offering anything of the sort, blinked back at her. It went on far too long. The woman's smile faded, and her stare turned hard, and as quick as she was to offer Lux welcome, she hauled it back the same. The pair crossed the road to continue walking on its opposite side.

"Devil below. I'm forever doomed to be socially strange." She watched them turn, and only when she spun back did she realize the carriage had stopped.

She smacked headlong into it.

"Son of a—"

"My apologies, Miss."

Lux clutched at her nose with both hands, tilting her head back on the chance it bled. She didn't know if it did. It felt like it should.

"No. 's my fault," she mumbled from beneath her palms. Risking one hand, she waved his apology away.

Her watering eyes cleared a few moments later, and she saw the man hadn't left after all but stared at her with a stoic expression that her pessimistic self labeled "boredom". He was of average height, middle-aged, with a hat brim so wide, it'd likely keep his shoulders dry in a drizzle, and he held a leather bag at his side.

A second man's gloved hand reached out and took it from him.

"Will you be all right?" the driver asked her. "Or do I need to see about a healer or physician or an apothecary with a poultice?"

"No apothecaries, thank you," she replied, releasing her nose. "They're all quacks."

"As you say, Miss."

Her gaze narrowed on him for all of a moment before she remembered why she'd followed this particular carriage to begin with. While she'd been keeping her ears open for gossip and dealings, she'd also been keeping her eyes open for deep pockets—and a carriage and luggage this fine surely bespoke deep pockets.

Only, she'd gone and ruined it all by hurting herself. Now, whoever was in that carriage was lost to the crowd. She scanned the market, but it was bustling beyond belief. She'd never seen anything so large—not even Ghadra's Festival of Light could rival it. And this was a regular Noxday at noon, not even a holiday. Her eyes widened as far as they could.

What a hellscape this is.

People were quite literally *everywhere*. They ate mushrooms from skewers and bought ale from barrel-minders. They haggled over fabrics and exchanged coin for trinkets. And all the while, Lux's nose throbbed, and her head ached.

She did not love markets, and she did not enjoy most people. This was, in every sense of the word, a nightmare.

But she would suffer it anyway.

She must.

"Where did your charge go?" she asked of the driver before he could return to his perch.

"My *charge?*"

"Your passenger."

The driver's mouth pinched. "Do you have business?"

"Yes," she lied.

The man's gaze swept her up and down. "He's gone to meet Mistress Farrentail." He pointed to a large booth angled several stations down from the carriage. "I pity you if you're lying."

Lux sneered, but she said nothing else. Wiping at her swollen nose and finding nothing to be ashamed of, she pushed her way farther into the crowd.

She discovered the man easily enough after the driver's direction. He wore a tall bowler hat and a fine black coat, and his shoes seemed impeccably polished. He hadn't had to walk nearly as far as she had, sliding down mountainsides.

He appeared to already be in an intense discussion with a woman. One who wore more feathers than fabric, and whose hair was not any shade found in nature. Lux pretended to inspect a pail of wrinkled apples while the man gave up his entire leather bag in exchange for a vial.

Lux's insides grew heavy. She tried to see the color of the contents in that small bottle, but it disappeared within his coat before she could manage it. When he turned around, she slid from his path.

Because she *had* been lying. And because the driver's warning had unnerved her a little.

She realized she wasn't the only one to behave in this way. Several market-goers gave him room. Some, she noted, cast down their eyes and folded their shoulders. Some offered smiles. Others stared from the safety of the crowd, wary. The man climbed back into the carriage and, for the first time, Lux noticed the emblem on the door. An ornate, silver 'M'. She had no context for it and spun away before the driver could catch her stare. She made instead for the vendor.

"Hello."

The woman blinked back at her from behind thick spectacles. "Good day. Interested in business or pleasure?"

Lux did a precursory sweep of the vendor's display. All sorts of feathers were available for purchase; most were from creatures she'd never seen in her life. She recognized a crow feather, and that was all. "Business. I'm in the market for rare things. What do you sell that is most obscure?"

"Most obscure?" The woman peeled at the flaking rouge on her lips. "Well, now. I've not been asked *that* in an age." She raised a tinted eyebrow. "Obscure in what way?"

"Rare. Taboo. Expensive."

A second eyebrow joined the first. "Are you good for it?"

Lux could see the leather bag partially exposed behind the woman's stall. If it was full with goldquins, then she was certainly not. She reached into her pack. A handful of coins—and two seeds.

"I'm good for it."

The woman crouched at once. When she rose, she held a vial identical to the one before. Lux's heart beat in her ears. "Made from smoked phoenix feathers, though I won't tell you more details than that. They're drops for the eyes. Drip them on the dead and they'll tell you how they died."

It isn't lifeblood. A relieved lightness swept through Lux—only to be followed by an odd, bitter disappointment.

"Interesting," she said, and she meant it. It could be useful during a revival, for those invisible deaths. Not that it mattered much to her, but to those commissioning her for their loved ones? She could add the diagnosis for a small fee. Just enough to cover the cost. "How much?"

"Thirty goldquins."

"Devil's tits!"

The vendor reeled back. "Language, girl! This is a respectable market!"

But Lux had already clapped a hand over her mouth to avoid allowing anything else out. When her shock ebbed, she said, "Why so much?"

"Did you miss the part where I said *phoenix feathers*? Those birds are as elusive as the devil and twice as cunning."

"Sakes. I've never come across anything for such a high price before." She released the coins in her purse and held onto only the seed. "What can I get for a gorga seed?"

"A gorga seed?" The vendor's face fell as she replaced the vial. "I'm not sure I know anything about them, so I'll say nothing, thank you."

"A botanist called Edgar Dosem said if you swallowed the whole thing you'd lose your speech forever."

"Dosem? Dosem...the mountain trader? Saints above, does it really? Well." A devious gleam entered the woman's eyes, and Lux felt abruptly sorry for whomever had wronged her. "It's not worth the tincture, but I'll trade you this." She pulled at a feather in her scalp and winced when it came away. She held it out.

Lux stared at the narrow, yellow thing. At the white tip, tinged scarlet and wet. "Did you—"

"It doesn't work if you don't bury it under your skin, but once you do, it'll stay until you pluck it out. It's a canary feather. If you wear it, you can never be duped." When Lux didn't immediately take it, the vendor waved it beneath her nose. "Well? Do we have a deal?"

"Fine," said Lux. She placed the seed on the counter. "But wipe the blood away first, won't you?"

In the Loxlen market, Lux purchased everything she needed for a revival. Everything save marsh snapper eyes. Who knew such a thing would be nearly impossible to find? She'd never thought of the creatures as scarce, but there were no marshes here and not a lot of other uses for them.

Her money dwindled. All this time away, she'd not recited a single incantation and not told a single soul of her brilliance. At this rate, she would need to change her circumstances very soon, and she didn't have a clue how. In Ghadra, her occupation and whereabouts were known—or at least speculated. Out here in the wide world, she could be anyone. How did a traveling necromancer advertise?

She'd just finished eating her lunch, shouldering her heavier pack out the establishment's door, when she encountered the sleek carriage again.

The "M" was stark on its side, and it was parked across from the pub she'd stepped from. The man who'd served her had followed her out, trimming shears in hand for the wicked-looking shrub beside the entry.

"Do you know who that carriage belongs to?" she asked.

The man lifted his eyes to where she gestured, and his jaw hardened. "Mothlock." Then he snipped at the air and went back inside.

Mothlock. A person? A rival establishment? A town? The name didn't sound familiar to her. Unsurprising, though, as nothing sounded familiar to her anymore. She hadn't even seen a full map of the country in all her life until she'd bought one off a peddler on the road. With one eye on the carriage, she dug for that map now. Her fingers encircled a roll of thick paper, and she pulled it free.

She found Loxlen easily enough. It wasn't small, and her eyes roved a circle around it, spreading wider and wider—but there was nothing. To the north were the mountains, Ghadra to the west, a winding river cut across the south, and to the east was the sea.

Her thumb brushed along the vast body of water. An image filled her head of Shaw's immersive painting before it'd been shredded to pieces, the scent of salt and brine and the rhythmic roll of waves. Of all the things, of all the places that called to her, this shouted the loudest. She wanted it so badly it caused pains in her chest.

If only she didn't have to travel through a saintforsaken *forest* to get there.

The rich man in the tall hat emerged from the building across the street, and Lux held the map a little higher in front of her face. She peered at him from over its top. She guessed he was a similar age to his driver, and he carried a new bag this time. One that was large and long, oddly shaped, and not made of leather but fabric.

He didn't strap it to the back but attempted to wrestle it inside the carriage. The driver helped, shoving the bag through once the other man had climbed in.

The driver glanced her way when it was done, and Lux flung the map up even higher. Behind it, she waited until she heard the snap of reins and the crunch of wheels. Only then did she look again.

The carriage ambled away, and there had been a body in that bag.

She was sure of it.

Chapter Three

THE CARRIAGE ROLLED TO a stop outside a pale-stoned storefront. Lux caught her breath against a building while her eyes narrowed upon the fixed placard. *Mothlock's Manuscripts.* And in smaller print below: *May Your Mastery Be Limitless.* The hatted man climbed from the carriage holding a parcel and went inside.

And now he leaves the body behind...

She kept her face angled away to better act the strolling visitor. Only when she saw another person making for the door, did she hurry. This man didn't bother to glance behind him, either, and when he opened the door and released it immediately afterward, she grabbed it before it could swing closed. It was a heavy door. An entirely black door. And up close, it too, displayed the same emblem as the carriage at her back. Cold crept up her arm; she stepped warily inside.

Lux's eyes widened. First to better see because the shop was darkly decorated, but then at what she discovered. Lit by blue-flame lamps protruding from the wall, shelves lined either side—and they were filled from floor to ceiling with books. Her survey began at one end and skipped to the other, and by then, she decided not only had she never before seen so many books at once, but she'd never seen so many *well-appearing* books in all her life. They were glossy, their covers thick, and every spine held silver lettering bearing their titles. Lux forgot the men momentarily and stepped sideways to better view the volumes. Like the carriage, like the door, the spines had been stamped as well. The now-familiar silvery 'M' of Mothlock.

Her hand reached toward the shelves and swiped. She eyed her finger in shock. Not only were the shelves free of dust—a feat which she'd not seen managed in any establishment—but they were crafted entirely of stone. She squinted at the silver flecking and thought, *Cold colors.* The green shade of her cloak did not fit in here.

She would have, though—the past her, at any rate. The girl who'd understood long ago that to wear black in Ghadra was an asset in remaining unseen, and she'd grown to love it because of that. Because it had kept her safe.

"Apologies," mumbled a voice, a hand stretching out to grasp a book from beside her head.

Lux didn't have time to see its title before it was pulled free. She moved over to be out of his way and realized he was the customer she'd followed in. She didn't reply, and he didn't meet her eyes. Instead, he flipped open the book until he came to an illustration. From there, he began muttering to himself, his finger roving over the page. Both of them startled when a second man said, "I regret that this is not a lending library."

"Oh. I understand, Sir. I was only browsing."

But even Lux could hear the waver in his voice. She pressed herself nearly against the shelves and wondered where the man she'd *actually* cared to be near had suddenly vanished. There wasn't anyone but them three in the main room.

The nervous customer closed the book with a snap, and Lux could see the spine now. *Petrovno's Musical Assortment.* He pushed it back onto the shelf.

The clerk—or perhaps the proprietor, for his stare did seem severe enough to own the building—watched the action closely. When it was done, his lips lifted into a smile that could have been almost kind—if it weren't for his eyes. "If you're interested in browsing, I would suggest you visit one of our many libraries; they're all about the country. You'll know you're in the correct place by the insignia, and the copies there are not so expensively bound. Fine to be tarnished by the touch of so many...hands."

"I did plan to purchase—"

"Which did you plan to purchase? These shelves are catalogued. Give me the title, or at least the subject."

At this, the other man grew increasingly ruddy. Lux guessed he hadn't planned to purchase anything but had come to memorize what he could as quickly as possible. His embarrassment coaxed hers to the surface. She wanted to be gone from here, but she was trapped now in the corner.

"I... Only the..." And with his next breath, the man was gone, bolting through the door.

"Hmph," grunted the clerk. Then he turned his assessing gaze upon her. "And you?"

Lux floundered for several heartbeats until— "Art."

"Art."

"Painting...specifically."

The clerk managed a perfunctory glance down her person before turning on his heel. "Okay, then. This way."

She followed him along the deep bookcases. While she did, she stole glances around her. The blue light cast a cold, eerie glow, reflecting off the shelves and silver titles. There was still no sign of the bowler-hat man.

"Here we are," said the clerk. She stopped a single step before smacking into his side. "The arts. Painting, as you said. But in what capacity?"

"Oh. Maybe—"

The clerk sighed. "History. Catalogues. Journals. The brilliant technique itself..."

Lux, her teeth grinding, promptly said, "The technique."

He climbed up two rungs of a ladder before reaching toward the elegant bindings. "*Brilliant Brushstrokes.*" He descended again with the book in hand, but when he went to hand it over, he paused. "Now, I know you heard the exchange I held before. These books are extremely well-preserved. They are meant for *ownership*. Not for thumbing through. Do you agree?"

Lux felt her lip begin to curl and quelled it. "I cannot even look inside?"

"No."

She opened her mouth but found no rebuttal would come. She'd never heard of such a thing in all her life. But then again, they did not have bookshops in Ghadra, and maybe this was how things were done? It *was* an exceptionally beautiful binding.

"And the price?" she asked.

"Only a single goldquin."

Only. Lux rubbed her forehead. *Is everything priced beyond comprehension in Loxlen?* "Saints above…"

A hiss left the clerk. "None of that. We are not to invoke the Saints in anything but blessings and prayer."

Lux's hand dropped away. Her brow rose. "May I say, 'devil below'?"

"Do you wish to invoke the Devil instead?" The man's stare narrowed to a sinister level.

"No. If such a creature exists, I prefer they stay where they are."

"If such—*creature.* Bah." The clerk rolled his eyes, and his unyielding glare finally granted her a reprieve as he looked instead to the shadowed rear of the shop. "Do you wish to purchase the book or not?"

"It's a book of instruction? It will further this particular brilliance?"

The man stared at her, unblinking. "Yes."

And Lux, thinking of the only painter she knew, of the crow currently flying an endless journey in her pack, said, "I will take it."

"A worthy choice. I'll see it wrapped. You may wait here. Peruse if you must, but *do not browse.*"

Her stare narrowed on his straight back as he turned it to her, and once he began to walk, she noticed he hardly bent his knees either. *His outsides match his insides, I see.* She scoffed. He turned at the rear of the shop and vanished. Lux craned her neck back.

Two ladders, one for each side, rested on either wall. They were curious: rather than a sawed clean edge, their tops were curved and slung over a rod to match the bookcases. All of these books, a goldquin each...

History. Journals.

Her body tensed as she swung toward the shelves. What if...? Could there be...?

The smack of boots yanked her attention away. Her lips parted as the rich man from the carriage stalked the length of the store. He didn't so much as flick his gaze to her even though he must have felt her stare. His arms were divested of their parcel. He walked straight toward the door and out.

Lux bit at her cheek. She wanted to follow him. But she wanted that book just as much.

She could see from the window that he'd already climbed in alongside the body. And when the driver snapped the reins, her heart stuttered. The carriage moved onto the street.

She'd the goldquin clutched and ready in her fingers by the time the clerk reappeared. The book's wrapping was black, tied with a black, satin ribbon, and when he held it out toward her, she saw it was stamped with a silver wax seal. She traded the coin with hardly a wince, the idea of gifting such a book to Shaw suddenly a beating wing's worth of excitement in her chest.

Other than his life, she'd not gifted him anything, she realized. And even that had been bought by his sister, and as such, couldn't likely qualify. Her fingers traced carefully over the seal.

"Mothlock is a bookseller, then?"

The clerk peered down his nose. "Mothlock provides enlightenment to Malgorm."

Lux blinked back at him. *How pretentious.* She wanted to tell him they'd missed Ghadra in their "enlightenment" but didn't want to give such details of herself away.

"Are you in search of anything else?" he continued.

Yes. Lux nearly glanced out the window again. "Do you have much on the subject of necromancy?"

The clerk sucked a quick breath. But he gathered himself quickly and said, "We do."

His response ricocheted about in her skull.

"In what capacity?" she breathed; she didn't care she'd turned his own question on him. She *did* care, however, at how desperate she sounded. That emotion was the perfect opposite of what she needed. She made a show of nonchalance to make up for it, easing the book into her pack.

"Two separate volumes of history have minor mentions of necromancy. And one personal account."

Lux's breaths grew erratic; she noticed his calculated stare and fought to maintain her composure. "A personal account. How much?"

"Twenty goldquins."

She couldn't even curse this time. Really, a part of her had expected it. That it would be outside her reach. Her disappointment sharp, she said, "I suppose it will have to wait. Thank you for your time."

Only once she'd fully made it to the door, did the clerk say, "It's a dark brilliance anyway. Cursed, some would say." Lux pivoted and discovered him retreating. "May your mastery be limitless. Do come again."

The carriage left Loxlen by the east road. Lux stood at the edge of town and watched it go. There were some things she'd learned about herself in the past few weeks. For one, when it felt like her words were biting into her tongue, she must consider why—thoroughly. For two, pessimism had permeated her nature, but sometimes people were kind without want of anything in return, and she should consider that. And three, if there was a rich man in a rich carriage buying expensive, obscure drops and carrying a body like a bag of grain, she simply *must* know why.

"Oy, Gorga Girl. On your way already? You know there's plenty of places to sleep or stay in Loxlen." Mistress Farrentail, breeze rustling through her feathers, pushed open a rusted garden gate. "But not here," she added at Lux's stare. "My birds don't like strangers."

"What birds do?" Lux muttered and rolled her map.

"Some do. Crows do."

Lux's eyes snapped to the woman's. Her stare narrowed. And she tested the words to see if they would come. "Have you heard of anyone peddling lifeblood?"

"I don't even know what that is, dear. But please, don't follow the zealots." Then the woman walked through her decaying garden, opened her door, and went inside.

"Worth the ask, I suppose."

Gorga Girl. How hideous. She should tell Shaw. He could never complain of being called "Prowler" again.

Lux's chest hollowed, and she flattened her hand against it. It'd been doing that for at least a week now—whenever she thought of him. It was so different, missing someone who lived. She couldn't say she'd had any real experience with it until now, and she disliked it just as much. There were so many things she longed to tell him, she'd taken to writing them down.

She would have been embarrassed if she also didn't want to cry.

The autumn sun beamed down on her head, and Lux pulled her hood forward to shield her eyes. Already, she'd learned the clouds in Ghadra had both created a problem and protected her. Her pale skin reddened within minutes of exposure.

GLORIA BOTTELMAN

She tracked the vague blot of the carriage all the way to the blurred canopy it headed toward. The road to the sea meant a road first through the trees. And trees—well, she and they didn't have a history of getting along.

Chapter Four

Ravenwood, said the weathered sign staked into the dirt. At the forest's edge, Lux could see the bark of the trees was red and not black. That the moss was green and lush, not dark and putrid. It was another of Shaw's paintings here before her own two eyes, and she'd wanted to be here, experiencing it, for so long. But she couldn't go in.

Lucena. Lucenaaa.

She shivered with the memory.

She'd not touched a single tree since abandoning Ghadra; she'd not even gone into more than a grove. A massive part of her wanted to—begged to, even—but she couldn't force her feet to move. Today seemed to be no different.

No, today must be different. Because what was the point in testing if she could grow if she didn't give herself the room?

"You can't exchange fears," she scolded her head. "Besides, you've been through worse."

The bandage on her finger loosened again, and again, she pulled at the tail with her teeth. Riselda would have been perfectly horrified by her wrapping. The thought only made her grin. *Good riddance, you wicked hag.*

"I guess trees are not all bad," she said to the wood. "Your relatives did eat mine and saved me a lot of trouble."

Lux leveled her shoulders and straightened her spine. *Look at the difference in them. They even smell like they're good.* She glanced to her left, into the distance. Barnabus Pass wished her well on her journey, the snow-topped mountains glistening beneath the sun. And that Edgar Dosem, for all his oddness, had told her she would find no greater welcoming than Ravenwood.

"Those trees cherish their travelers. Stroke one and see. Tell them Edgar says 'hello' while you're at it. They'll know whom you mean, even though it's been so long."

Lux stepped one foot beyond the forest's edge and, ever-so-slowly, stretched out her hand—

Something whistled past her head.

She whipped around.

"Next one will stick if you move more."

Lux took one lingering look at the stranger, from his worn hat to his battered boots, and snarled, "You wouldn't *da*—"

A twang was her only warning. A second arrow snagged the folds of her cloak before ripping free.

She shrieked and leapt and heard him say, "Third one will *really* stick if you speak again too."

Movement caught at her periphery; she didn't dare look away from the man with an arrow nocked and aimed. Given the situation, whoever else came upon her was likely on his side and not hers.

A bandit was not a worthwhile—or even plausible—occupation in Ghadra's marshland. But here? On the traveler's road? Lux transferred her weight to her toes.

"Good girl. Now kindly hand over—"

She bolted into the forest.

"Hey!" screeched the voice at her back, but she'd already dodged behind a tree and kept running.

Remembering Edgar's words, her hand whipped out and brushed a curled, green leaf, the velvet feel startling even as she ran for her life. "Please," she huffed, her laden pack banging against her hip with painful slaps. "I came all this way."

She leapt over a fallen log. Then promptly slipped.

She wasn't on the road anymore, and fleshy toadstools carpeted the vast forest. Lux slipped again. If she died because of them, she'd carry her humiliation into the Beyond.

The bandits were relentless—because there was indeed more than one. She could hear them shout to one another in the reddened afternoon light, and she could do nothing but hope she was faster. She risked a glance backward and—

Devil's tits, there are four of them!

Four of them and only one of her. And unlike howlers, they didn't need to be upon her to snuff her life; they could do so easily from a distance.

They sprinted after her, and judging by their quick leaps and easy dodges, they were familiar with the terrain.

How many people do they chase through here?

Somebody could have *warned* her.

Lux ducked beneath a thick branch, more curled leaves trailing soft against her temple. If she could only outrun them—

A third arrow whistled by her cheek. A choked sob worked its way up her throat.

"Aim for her legs!"

No! She clutched Shaw's knife with every modicum of strength she had, because she knew if she did end up with an arrow embedded somewhere, she would happily cut down as many of them as she could before Death called her away. She leapt over another fallen log.

"You flopping idiot! Not her legs! Aim for her—"

Lux didn't register what else the bandit said. Because the road reappeared. And not only a road but a bridge loomed ahead. Wooden and arched and overgrown with thick green moss. It crossed a rushing, narrow river, the sides of which were steeped with boulders. She ran straight toward it.

She'd obviously done something wrong on her way here. Made some big mistake. The crone had told her there were dangers. Shaw had warned her to watch her dealings. But she'd shrugged at them. She'd thought she *knew*. She was a frequenter of Ghadra's Dark Market, for saints' sake—how worse off could anywhere else be?

Her first step onto the warped wood saw her slipping again. This time it was the combination of moisture and moss. And this time, when she pitched forward, an arrow ripped at her cloak—and stayed there. Lux grabbed at it, but it'd dug too deep. She couldn't see the head of it at all, buried as it was in the wood. She whipped backward.

"Stay away from me," she growled, brandishing the knife like a sword.

Angry, exhausted tears clouded her eyes. The bandits formed a blurred crescent in front of her, marking the knife's threatening wave and keeping an appropriate distance. One woman. Three men.

I'll skewer them all.

The reediest of them stepped forward, his speckled, white beard extending long past his chin. He waggled a finger in front of her knife. She knew it was the same finger with which he'd loosed those arrows. "Nah, don't cry, pet."

That *name*. He barely dodged the swipe of her blade, but still, he did dodge it, and Lux found herself pinned bodily to the bridge in the next breath. A rough hand brushed her tears away.

"Shh. We only want that bag of yours. Goldquins you have in there, hmm? We saw you in Loxlen." His hand reached for her pack.

But that was where she drew the line. Pushing forward, Lux used her free hand to slap the expression from the bandit's face. Grooves of red lined his cheek in the aftermath. Her pinky finger stung as the bandage flew free.

"Why, you *little*—"

The man's irises rolled upward.

"Viktar! What's the matter?"

Lux scrambled backward until her back met the bridge wall. She clutched the pack to her, her knife pointing out—and she watched as the three remaining bandits crowded the fallen man where he lay unmoving on the bridge. He'd keeled over.

Dead, she thought confidently, the feel of it stealing through her. Not even a shallow breath marked his chest now.

"He knew he had a bad heart! What was he thinking, wrestling with a girl spry enough to be his daughter?" The man dropped to his knees beside Viktar, swiping tears from his own scarred cheeks. "Come back!"

"He's not coming back, Sven," said the woman, her hand on the man's heaving shoulder. "Can't bring back the dead."

Lux's teeth clacked together. *Don't say a word!* her head demanded, and so she tried again to free herself instead. Her cloak only ripped further. The tearing drew the attention of the woman, whose hard eyes ground against Lux's.

"Best lash the girl up," she said.

"*No*," growled Lux.

The woman's gaze dropped to the knife. "Then give us the coin."

"Absolutely not. I'll starve."

"No, you won't. You'll get a job. Or married."

"Or you could do either of those things yourself and leave me be. I earned what I have; I didn't steal it like a coward."

The remaining sets of eyes focused on her.

"I'm married already," said the woman, in the same tone Lux had once heard someone mention their rotted tooth. "And this is my job."

Lux hacked a horrible laugh. "*This* is a crime."

"What do *you* do then?" said the youngest of them.

Lux's glance slid to the body slumped on the bridge. If her only options were to be tied and stolen from or threatened then stolen from—

Don't even think of it.

Too late.

"I bring back the dead."

Sven's mouth fell wide, his nose and eyes running yet. "What'd you say?"

"Sure you do," snorted the youngest bandit, his mouth twisted arrogantly beneath his crooked nose. "How convenient for you to suddenly possess some rare brilliance right as we're about to rob you."

"Believe me or don't. But I've the book I use to perform the enchantment, and nearly all the ingredients. Though Loxlen is alarmingly short of marsh snapper eyes."

"What the devil is a marsh snapper?" asked the crooked-nosed bandit, his attention traveling to his companions. "Any of you heard of that?"

"Me," said Sven, wiping his eyes on his sleeve. "Big-beaked turtles."

"Me," said the woman. Her voice was quiet but stern, and when she leveled her gaze at Lux, it was the same. "Say you can revive the dead, girl. That'd be a mighty sought after service. What were you doing out by Ravenwood all alone?"

Lux surveyed the bedraggled trio, the dead man at their feet. Their worn boots were each coated with forest debris, bits of mushroom clinging to the toes, their shirts faded and stained. The woman's skirt had a tear down one side, crudely sewn.

"Why do you care to know?"

The woman's stare sharpened. "Because it's helpful in assessing threats: a skill we need to survive."

"Will you get this damned arrow out without tearing it all the way through if I tell you?"

The bandit inclined her head.

"I'm making my way to the coast."

Lux didn't add further details. There was no possible way the bandit could think she would. That she would reveal how she'd spent her entire life in a miserable city, that she'd lost the only family she'd had and then lost the one she'd thought had returned. That she'd always wished to see the natural wonders of the world but had never allowed herself the dream.

That she'd gone from one quaint village and bustling city to the next, keeping her eyes sharp in search of bottled silver or whispers of ageless beings.

The bandits couldn't think she'd share all of that.

"What for?"

Or maybe they could.

Lux huffed. "I told you all I'm willing to. Now get this arrow out of my cloak. If you want him revived, I have twelve hours to do it, and none if we don't find those eyes."

She directed her demand to Sven, the only one who seemed to be truly in mourning. The man needed no further push; he scrambled forward and yanked the arrow free.

"What!" shouted the youngest of the three.

"Shut your fat mouth, Lars! Did you hear what she said? She'll bring him back for us! If it were your family lying here, you'd do the same." Sven reached out and gripped Lux's forearm, hauling her to her feet. "We shouldn't be going after children, anyway. Viktar's been getting too desperate."

Lux didn't bother arguing over being called a child. So long as they didn't shoot her full of arrows and steal *The Risen*, they could think of her as a toad. Sneering at the two holes marring her cloak, she looked up to catch the woman staring at her with a thoughtful tilt to her head.

"I know where to get you the eyes you need," the woman said. "We'll take you to Verity."

"Verity!" whined Lars, a second before he doubled over from an elbow to the gut.

"I'm Magda." The woman held out her hand, and Lux looked from it to her wrinkled hazel eyes and back again. "The coast, you say? Let's get you there."

Lux put her hand in the woman's.

It wasn't cold.

But it wasn't warm, either.

Chapter Five

Ravenwood forest smelled perpetually wet. It was a different sort than what Lux had grown up with. She breathed in the scents of bark and dirt and did not lament the absence of Ghadra's underlying hint of marsh mud. *Here,* she thought, *I would tolerate the rain.*

According to her reluctant company, they'd at least a few hours more to reach the forest town of Verity.

"*Unusual,*" Magda had called it.

"*The people love the trees more than each other*", had griped Lars.

Lux could see why. She'd been too desperate in her fleeing to pay attention to the details of the wood, but now that she walked a steady road, she admired the striated trunks and lofty heights. The canopy was thick, and the leaves were lush. She reached upward and dragged a finger along one, slowing to a stop when it unfurled.

Drops of captured water dripped onto her palm.

"They're like little clenched fists," said Sven, passing her by.

Sven and Lars carried Viktar between them, and every so often, Lars would walk too quickly, folding the dead man up like a book until his bottom dragged on the ground. Sven hated this and would shout so loudly each time, Lux had to block her ears. She watched them move on ahead. She didn't know how these four had ended up together, and she didn't care. So long as they saw her safely to the town as promised and didn't attempt a second robbery, she would be genuinely ecstatic to be rid of them.

Magda led their party. Short and grim, with greying hair and harsh hands, she seemed their leader. Which irritated Lux more that the woman hadn't reined Viktar in when he'd gone after her. Maybe it'd actually been Magda's idea.

She admonished herself harshly over her predicament. *Twenty-eight days you've not gotten into trouble. Now here you are one less fingernail and following a dead man.*

She glanced at the body ahead of her and rolled her eyes before hurrying to catch up.

Four weeks. It'd been only four weeks since she'd left the shattered city of Ghadra to make out on her own. And while the towns and cities had felt like a blink, here in a different forest, it felt like a decade gone. Already, she'd seen landscapes she'd only dreamt of.

Lux groaned over her aching finger. She'd aggravated it while clawing at Viktar's face. *If only Riselda were here, she would—*

Lux scrunched her eyes closed, disgusted with herself. Where had that thought even come from? Of course she shouldn't wish for Riselda, the woman who'd brought a plague upon Ghadra only to immorally revive those fallen and set them against the living. Her proclaimed *aunt* may have been a healer, but she was mostly a monster.

Lux lifted her left hand, examining the pointed nails she kept filed into miniature daggers, and to the one appendage now left bereft and reddened. The botanist had applied a salve. When he'd wiped it clean a moment later, it'd come away easily—the salve and the fingernail both. She shouldn't have refused his bandage. Her attempt had been amateurish and was now lost.

Her fits of pride didn't often benefit her. Maybe someday she'd learn.

They followed a winding road through the wood. Not wide, but it did seem well-traveled. She supposed it made sense for the town of Verity to remain connected to Loxlen by a maintained route. That city had been her first large one since leaving Ghadra, and it was the opposite of what she'd grown up knowing.

Rather strange, perhaps, when considering the bookshop, but strange did not mean corrupt.

Now, if she'd known she was being observed. If she'd known she'd been followed...

"What's that sour face for?" asked Sven, his own wrinkled with effort.

She turned the full force of her scowl upon him until his eyes widened and he glanced away.

Lars huffed behind them. "Uppity city girl, are you? Well, let's see what you think of Verity."

"*Lars—*" came Magda's warning growl.

"Verity isn't so bad," argued Sven. "It's got a nice air to it."

"It gives me the jeepers, is what it does," muttered Lars. "But maybe if you have enough *goldquins—*"

Lux could take no more. "You blathering idiot," she snarled. Spinning on her heel, she stomped over to him. "You know quite literally *nothing* about me. Keep what little thoughts are in your head to yourself, or I'll pry it open so you'll never have another."

A burbling sound drew her attention from Lars's paled features. Sven's face wrinkled further beneath her scrutiny, his attempts at stifling his reaction a struggle.

"How much farther?" she demanded of Magda.

The older woman glanced down the twisting road. "Not far at all."

Deep in the wood, sat the forest town of Verity. Or maybe "sat" was the wrong choice. Now that they drew closer, it might make more sense to say, "Here grows the town of Verity."

Wooden buildings rose red from the leaf-strewn ground, camouflaged with green moss having crept to seal the cracks. Whoever had built them had taken the natural curves of a forest as inspiration, being as the thatched roofs were quaint and sloped and covered by as many leaves as the forest floor. Even the doors were rounded at their tops.

Viktar's body rested amongst the sparse toadstools at the roadside—a reprieve for both Lars and Sven, who'd carried him the entire way. Magda perched silent beside them, though Lux wasn't oblivious and could tell from her periphery the woman watched her.

"They'll have marsh snapper eyes? Here?" Lux surveyed what she could see of the town. The evening light cast everything into shadow, and the trees were extraordinarily tall.

"They should," said Magda. "I told you it's an unusual mix."

Lux huffed a dismissive laugh. *More unusual than the Dark Market? I doubt it.* "There's about an hour yet until I can perform a revival," she said to the group. "We'll need to find a private place."

"What for?" said Lars.

"How private?" asked Sven.

"Somewhere he won't be bothered at having all his parts exposed." Lux darted a quelling look at them each.

"Oh, Viktar wouldn't care a whit. He's not a bashful sort."

Lux curled her lip. "Fine, then. A private place for me. I need to concentrate or else the attempt will be a failure."

She swiveled toward Lars's derisive snort.

"Serves. I wondered when you'd start hinting at not being able to do as you promised. Bring back the dead... No such thing."

Lux contemplated wringing his neck but instead pressed the heels of her palms to her eyes.

"Lars, my darling. If you cannot control yourself, I will leave you at home next. With your aunt."

Magda's threat had its desired effect as Lars shuddered. Lux looked between the pair of them and realized they did look quite alike. Same eyes, same mouth.

But where Lars's fractured nose had been clearly mismanaged at some point in his life, his mother's was straight and upturned at the tip.

"Up he goes then," said Sven. He groaned, hauling the body into his arms. Lars grabbed at the feet.

"He's getting stiff!"

"That's the point, imbecile," Lux griped to herself. She pulled her cloak tighter around her. The hood came up and over, hiding her hair and her irritated expression both. Then she said louder, "Not for long."

Chapter Six

Lux trailed Magda and Lars as they entered Verity. Sven had stayed behind with the body in a thick shadow of low-hanging branches and leaves.

There weren't cobblestones here, but dirt-packed streets, and she wondered how a town's appearance could be so like that of its surroundings. Many of the buildings were more than two stories tall. They sprawled upward, rather than outward, mimicking the reach of the trees. Magda had mentioned the town was supremely old, and most of those who were born here remained. While that fact, along with the stretched buildings, could remind her of Ghadra, nothing else was the same. The city she'd left behind had begun rotting long before Riselda's plague had descended upon it; if she looked at Verity any closer, she might see it breathe.

"The apothecary's shop is the next street over," said Magda.

"The apothecary? I need eyes, not a serum to lengthen my lashes."

Magda cast her a withering side-eye. "You're a haughty one, aren't you? He sells loose ingredients too—along with his lash serum."

Lux scowled. *Haughty?* Her? She didn't think she'd ever been called that in her life. "Fine. And where will we go afterward? It's nearly dark." She was tired and hungry, and she would be more so by the time she was through with the enchantment. The idea of laying out her bedroll on the outskirts of town was abysmal. She couldn't fathom how frozen she'd be come morning. Maybe she'd burrow into a fairy ring. At least the abundant leaves could be mounded around her.

"Maidenway Inn," was all Magda said, and if Lux was not mistaken, with a healthy dose of long-suffering.

As if this whole thing is my fault. As if I want to be doing this at all.

Lux surveyed the few people moving about their business in the waning hours. Noticed how they were bundled warmly with coats and cloaks, caps and thin gloves. But all of it was brown as dirt. She didn't comment on the observance, however. The word "haughty" still stung.

Wold's Apothecary had been painted in black lettering on a wooden sign as red as everything else. It was tacked to the storefront, and Lux climbed the three steps to enter the front door. Magda had gone in ahead, and Lux thought briefly of letting the door fall closed behind herself, but in the end, held it out for Lars to take.

The single room was unfortunately cool. Lux hadn't realized how much she'd hoped for a dousing of warm air until it'd been withheld. She tucked her hands tighter against her as she scanned the shop.

Shelving lined three of four walls, and it appeared to hold all of the annoyances she expected. Displays of vials and jars were labeled with every sort of inane promise. Candlesticks were interspersed between them in puddles of yellow tallow. Lux thought the entire room smelled terrible. Like molded herbs and salt.

She turned toward the counter last, to the tallest flickering candlestick of all, and the thick, tree of a man standing leery behind it.

Magda spoke to him in hushed tones—a sight which twisted Lux's insides in an irritating way. She hoped the woman wasn't doing business on her behalf. She moved to the bandit's side to catch the final bits of conversation.

"...Alesso. He's in town? Good. Later tonight." Magda offered Lux a semblance of a smile when she neared. "He has marsh snapper eyes."

To prove her word, the apothecary plunked a tin onto the counter. Lux leaned forward to examine his offering. There were plenty, and she only needed a pair for Viktar's revival, but she figured she may as well buy more while she could.

"I'll take them all."

"Oh...no. They're not all for sale. In fact, I can only sell you a set."

Lux's eyes widened. "Whyever could you only sell me a pair when you have twenty sets?"

She replaced her expression with one more determined—of a customer prepared for the uphill battle of a haggle, but rather than the glimpse of fierce welcome she'd become accustomed to in the Dark Market, this man's face grew closed and angry.

"For that, I'll sell you none. Leave."

A sound somewhere between a scoff and a cry of disbelief left Lux's lips at the same moment Lars declared, "I knew it. She's blasted useless," and Magda muttered, "Devil below. Must I do everything?"

The older woman shoved Lux belly up to the counter. "She'll take the set, and she'll pay you double."

"I will *no*—" But she didn't finish. Magda's hand slipped almost imperceptibly from the pocket of Lux's skirt, heavier now than it'd been moments ago. Her glance slid sideways to the woman's satisfied smirk. "*Double*," she ground out instead.

"That's a girl," said the apothecary, and Lux decided then in that moment the apothecary above her old apartment was not a singular, loathsome figure, and all apothecaries were loathsome and despicably the same.

She focused on steadying her breaths as he spooned the eyes into a black sachet, tightening the end, before holding out his hand, palm up. She sprinkled the coins on the countertop instead. Snatching the sachet, she didn't glance at either Magda or Lars to see if they followed, and on her way out, she saw all she needed to know about whom she dealt with. Not lash serum, but a concoction for growth, nonetheless.

"Here you are, Lars. Compliments of Mr. Wold and his generous business." She tossed the vial from the display, and Lars—to his credit—caught it. She chuckled over his cry of outrage all the way to Maidenway Inn.

Chapter Seven

"They're a suspicious lot to begin with, this close to the sea. And your attitude didn't help any."

"My attitude." Lux snorted. They stood on the inn's porch, their conversation the only thing keeping them from entering. These bandits had been discussing her attitude ever since they'd met her. As if they weren't the ones to pepper her cloak with holes and chase her like prey through the wood. If anything, she thought herself remarkably even-tempered for what they'd put her through. "Apologies for my misunderstanding that items in a shop were for purchase."

Magda cast her a disapproving look, her eyebrows harsh. "Those were stores from his own supply. You shame yourself with your entitlement."

"*My—*" Lux seethed. Dropping her voice, she said, "*You're* the one who stole from him to match the cost. Oh, don't deny it now; I know the money in my pocket didn't come from one of yours. Really, I shouldn't have been there at all. This is *your* doing."

Magda shrugged off that prickly truth. "I would say you aren't doing too well out on your own." The woman stared pointedly at her raw finger.

Lux fantasized briefly over what Magda's eyes would look like, unseeing and fixed. A pause which, apparently, the woman took to mean the argument had been won. "Inside now. There's not a speck of daylight left."

Glaring, Lux shouldered through the door.

She wasn't a frequenter of taverns, and Ghadra, with its nigh impossibility of visitors, did not have much in the way of inns. But Lux didn't think they should ever be this quiet. She scanned it quickly, and would have stepped back, if Lars hadn't come through behind her and knocked his bony shoulder with hers as he passed.

"Move over, City Girl. I need a drink."

Lux gritted her teeth. "We're here for a *room*. Sven is still—" But she spoke to empty air as Lars was already well on his way to the bar.

"Leave him be. We'll secure a room for your service, and then I'll send him off to collect Sven."

Lux glanced over at Magda surveying the room. If she wasn't mistaken, the woman did so with the eye of someone looking for another. "Do they always take to outsiders like this?" She looked away from the bandit to absorb the hard stares and keen suspicion above the rims of mugs and around bites of food.

Irritation welled within her at the perusal of her form, the clothing draping it, and the pack at her back. Lux's confidence in such company was still only a sapling hardly grown. This situation was about to pluck it out by the roots.

"An unusual group. They've lost plenty and think anyone unfamiliar is out to grab at the rest."

Some of the bite left Lux's voice. "Lost what?"

But Magda, too, had chosen to abandon her. She snagged at the sleeve of a passing woman carrying a tray; a hushed conversation ensued in which the matron nodded a curt agreement at its end. Magda returned to her.

"We've got three rooms for the night. Unless you plan to nest with the crows?"

"If it's that or share a room with someone who tried to shoot my legs from under me, I choose the birds."

"Girl, nobody was out to actually injure you. We herded you toward that bridge on purpose. And rest easy, you get a room all to yourself." When the oil-splattered matron appeared before them again, this time with three keys in hand, Magda handed her one. "Head up. I'll send Lars out."

AT HIS SIXTH HOUR of death, Viktar lay upon what would soon be his bed. Lux refused to perform the revival in her own room, on her own bedding.

Naturally, she'd not allowed anyone to watch, and though Lars muttered, and Magda stared, Sven ushered them from the room easily enough. She set to work.

She felt like Riselda on that night her imposter of an aunt had returned. Lux pulled forth all sorts of tins and vials, a mortar and pestle, and a jug of distilled rainwater—travel size, of course. Looking back at it now, Riselda's assortment had a much more sinister air. Lux only had the one weapon, and it lay strapped to her waist.

She took the knife out now, and once laying the bat wings flat, sliced them into thin strips. They were easy to tear by hand as they'd been dried, but Lux liked the feel of the handle in her palm. She turned over the blade when she was through.

When she looked at it, she could easily imagine another hand in place of hers. And then not only a hand but an entire body, warm skin and eyes like melted copper. A wave of homesickness crashed over her, a wrench of her heart leaving her doubled over and gasping.

She didn't yearn for Ghadra—not at all. But there were as many different meanings of the word "home" as there were shades of bat wings.

She rubbed at the space over her chest before tossing the readied ingredient into the bowl. "Who would guess my first revival in weeks is for a man out to rob me." She wiggled out a sprig of mint and crushed it beneath her nose.

A twinge of nerves beat a rapid tempo within her, but she ignored it and left *The Risen* wrapped inside. True, it'd been the longest she'd ever gone between enchantments, but that meant nothing. She could close her eyes and see every line of the incantation etched behind her lids. If she concentrated, that was. Lately, every time she closed her eyes all she saw was *him*.

You could have asked him along.

No. *No*, she couldn't have. His family's home had been nearly as devastated as his own. He had a mother and sister to look out for—she had no one but herself. She hadn't been about to cause him to feel torn over a difficult decision. The only logical answer was to dash it before it could ever form. She'd told him she wanted to go alone.

Lux continued to paint whorls onto Viktar's narrow chest, using her intact pinky finger to blend the lines. Another image rose from her memories with her movements: of a broader chest, one peppered with stab wounds rather than an invisible attack. She didn't think of it often—that night she'd met Shaw dead upon her table—but when she did, it caused a visceral reaction. The idea of him taken from her forever... That he nearly had been...

It vexed her that she'd lost the way of the carriage, but maybe someone downstairs would know something. With each passing day, she became more determined to discover who had purchased the horrific harvests of the late Bartleby Tamish. Not only discover them—but destroy them.

The lifeblood itself. And the deep pockets behind it.

She pressed her fingers to Viktar's fixed eyes.

"You'll apologize when this is done, mark my words."

Chapter Eight

Lux batted at the hands shaking her awake. "Devil's *tits*, get off!"

"Wake up then, would you?"

Lux squinted open one eye. "Sven?"

"What happened to you? Is this regular?"

Lux glanced about the room: Sven standing worriedly above her. Lars staring slack jawed. His mother's mouth pinched. She lurched upward when she spied Viktar in the corner, buttoning his shirt with shaking fingers.

Her head spun.

"I—" But she didn't know how to answer. Not even when she was a child, not even when consumed with fear and grief over her parents' deaths, did she *faint*.

"I can't believe you can really do it." Lars couldn't take his eyes off her. "Sorry for thinking you were a lying fraudster only out to hoard your coins because you're an uppity pile of—"

His strangled cry came about by Magda's hand slapping the back of his head. "That's quite a gift you have," she said.

"It has its uses." Lux pushed to her feet, waving Sven away. She decided immediately she wouldn't tell them. Not about how this was quite *irregular*. And certainly not about how strange her insides felt at the moment. She flicked her gaze to Viktar's.

And the man promptly broke down in tears.

Not gasping sobs, but cries, nonetheless. His puddled eyes locked with her own. "I'm awfully sorry, girl. I wasn't thinking. I mean I *was* thinking, but not about you. You were only a purse. And now here you've gone and brought me back." He breathed a ragged breath. "I can't help but feel I don't deserve it."

Lux began to reply when he cut her off, his confession incomplete. "Devil take me. You weren't the first I've done this to. I keep doing it. But I can't seem to stop. I can't quit seeing the possibility of help, only the money or whatever they can give me, and not the person. I don't care if they're old, infirm or a little girl. I've got ten children! Four of mine and six of my sister's who's disappeared and probably gone for good, and I've got a bad heart. A bad heart chopping lumber. Who will take care of them when I'm dead?"

His cries did turn to heaving sobs then, and he collapsed to his knees, head buried in his hands. Sven rushed to his side. "I didn't know. Saints above, I didn't know it was so bad. I've been wondering why we weren't picking our marks a little cleaner lately." Sven glanced at Magda, and Lux could plainly see the accusation he failed to hide.

"Viktar, I need to speak to you. In private."

Four sets of eyes found Lux's.

"Sure as anything," he said. "You can do anything you want."

She could sense they all were loath to go, save Lars, but she didn't give them any attention as they filed out.

"Could you sit?" she gestured to the bed when they'd gone, then turned back to the desk. She opened her pack to tug *The Risen* free.

Lux pulled at the leather cord, working the wrapping away. She still felt odd, her fingertips tingling and mind abuzz, but this seemed more important. She turned with the book tucked in her hands.

Viktar's glance flicked from her to it and back again.

"How long have you felt this way?"

"Like I'm drowning on dry land? I don't know. Ever since she left them behind, I suppose. Half a year?" He squinted at the book, bending forward to read the metal plate embedded in the cover.

She stopped him with a palm to his forehead. She winced at how similar to ice it felt. *Drowning on dry land.* She knew the sensation with terrible familiarity. "What if I might be able to ease it?"

He sat back. "Ease it? How?"

She flipped open the book, thumbing through its pages until she came to the enchantment she sought. An inked drawing of a bud near to opening had been marked beside the title.

Overcome

She turned it outward and held it for him to see. "I've been studying this ever since I—" She cleared her throat and pivoted from revealing more of her story. "For some weeks now. And I think I've started to understand what each of these incantations might do. You see here?" She tapped the line. "This alludes to despair, or a desperation. It's interesting, really, because—"

She glanced up in time to catch Viktar's perplexed expression. "Well. Anyway. I think it's worth a try."

"If you say so, Necromancer."

Lux's heart stuttered over the title, and though she cleared her throat immediately following and swore she'd ignore it, it didn't matter. She was still cast back.

Shaw's arm shifted beneath her body, his opposite draped across her waist. Her corset was gone, tossed to the floor, and now only a thin yellow silk separated his rough hands from her skin.

She pressed against his warmth, her fingertips trailing along the line of his bare shoulder. Her eyes closed when he feathered a kiss across one temple then the other.

"I won't ask you to stay, Necromancer. But know I'll be thinking of this moment every day you're not with me."

She sniffed, flipping the book back to face her. "It also might hurt some."

"Is that what sent you to the floor?"

"No." She scanned the pages, unfocused. "Exhaustion did that."

But the thing of it was she didn't feel exhausted—at all. The buzz in her fingertips quickened, an energy she'd not ever felt, and she laid the book upon the desk to distract herself. "I will need your hands," she said.

He complied at once.

Saints above, devil below. Allow me to—

It felt like sinking. Not in a suffocating sort of way, but in a weighted, languid, relax-in-the-bath way. And just as she could feel lifeblood during a revival, she could sense the soul the same.

It wasn't such a shock this time, since discovering her own soul that day, how overgrown and twisted its encasement had become, and Shaw's—the fresh absoluteness of his. If she must compare Viktar's to either of theirs, it would most be like that of the boy she'd left behind.

Outside, her eyes were closed, but inside, she scrutinized every clawed branch. She worked her nails into the minuscule spaces between, pitying Viktar's pained gasp; it couldn't be helped. When she'd enough of a hold, she began.

"Pressure builds in the time beneath. No rest nor reprieve, it will not sleep. A stone is strong and still it's worn. A yielding is to remain alone.
Reach for aid, surface slow.
To Overcome is to fight from below."

The buzzing in her fingertips now entered every part of her. Lux felt as if she were vibrating, unable to stay still no matter how she fought. And that energy seemed to pour from her, lighting the darkness, until that poisonous cage flamed its last. Until all that remained was unfettered brilliance and dissipating ash.

She recognized that terrible sensation seeping through her at its demise. *How awful*, she thought.

It was hopelessness.

Later, alone at her desk, Lux scrawled *hope* across the bottom of the enchantment's page.

Once, she would have never fathomed marking *The Risen*, and now she'd done it twice. She flipped the pages until she came to another. Beneath *Untether* she'd written *forgiveness*. Two enchantments now to pry away a consuming darkness. At least with this *Overcome* she didn't faint.

Her finger traced the word, and at the final letter, her hand lifted away. Mothlock's Manuscripts did not have a copy of *The Risen*. Was it because her brilliance was rare, and the book deemed unsellable? Or was the book itself rare? Maybe the bookseller didn't have a copy because none could be found. What had he even meant when he'd labeled it a dark brilliance anyway?

Lux reached down into the pack tipped at her feet. Her fingers skipped over the wrapped book of art until she pulled a frame free.

The crow's wings beat a steady rhythm, the sunshine lighting her face. Lux closed her eyes for several heartbeats to better absorb its warmth, and when she opened them, she felt lighter for it. No matter how far she'd gone away, she would never be without this piece of home. Her hands gripped its edges gently as she propped it at the desk's back. She'd been wary to bring it out in her travels, worried some sudden rain or wind would come and destroy its beauty, but here, it would be safe.

Next, she dragged out the map. She unrolled it and spread its edges flat, and then she leaned over Ravenwood. She'd not noticed a town between Loxlen and the sea, but she'd not thought to stare at the inked trees. She found Verity at last; it took much longer than it should have as it was written the same camouflaged way the entire town lived.

The candle near her arm flickered and spat a black cloud. Lux's nostrils flared. These candles were cheaply made, mostly fats, and it smelled of it. She didn't want more of its venting to tarnish her painting. With a huff of breath, it snuffed. She leaned back in the chair, where she stared instead out the window. A thin fog began to brush against the buildings, caressing lampposts and shutters. It didn't curl or creep, but still, it brought back memories of Ghadra she didn't wish to linger on while alone.

It was harder than she'd thought.

When she left, she'd been so intently focused on achieving her dream of escape, she'd not thought about what it would feel like in these moments. How, now that she'd carved away the darkness inside her, there'd be so much *space* leftover.

She'd forgotten. What it felt like to spend time with those she cared about. To talk about things that excited her. She'd become accustomed to her companionship with silence in all those years alone that trying to create a similar relationship with her voice now felt awkward and strained.

And now there was something else the matter with her, and she had no one to tell.

Her fingertips no longer buzzed, her body quieting nearly to normal. But two enchantments in a single evening would have had her trudging to her bed only a month ago.

What has happened to me?

Because she felt like she could walk all night.

Her stomach grumbled, and she placed a hand over it. The idea of going back downstairs to enter a common room full of sideways glances sounded like something worth starving for. But the smells... She smelled roasted things. Savory things. Things that were not travel food. And she did want to ask after that carriage.

"You've survived a plague and devouring trees to be scared off by a few suspicious townsfolk? Unacceptable." She shoved to her feet.

She opened the door and stepped out.

Her shoulder collided with another's.

"Blessed Saints! Apologies," said the stranger, righting her. "I suppose I should pay closer attention when walking a corridor of occupied rooms." Gloved hands left her shoulders to adjust the sharp cut of a black coat. "Are you hurt?"

"I'm fine," said Lux. "Yourself?"

The crude excuse of a lamp offered little light in the hall. The squat candle only lit one half of the man's face. A strong jaw, a straight nose, hair several shades fairer than Shaw's bothersome sister, and a grin stretching his mouth. "Never better. I've made it through worse." He stepped back from her. "After you."

Lux didn't like the idea of that. After being shot with arrows, she'd joined the rest of Verity's occupants as a suspicious sort. "No, I'll follow."

She watched his eyes widen, a pale frost-like blue. "If you insist," he said, and turned away.

She waited a few seconds until he disappeared down the stairway. She followed then, but slowly. Something had pricked at her while she had stood in his presence, but she couldn't describe it more than that. Lux flexed her fingers.

"You have to figure out what's the matter with you—and fast," she whispered crossly to herself. "You're about halfway to useless."

She headed down the stairs.

Chapter Nine

Lux couldn't help but watch him. Though he wore black, the man stuck out like moonlight in a barren landscape. He stood at the bar, his back to her, and while it couldn't be said the people of Verity dressed poorly, everything about him—from his perfectly swept hair to his polished black boots—shouted wealth.

But he was not the same wealthy man she'd encountered in Loxlen.

For one thing, he wore no bowler hat. For two, he was much younger.

Lux jolted when a body appeared at her elbow. She relaxed only a little when she realized it was Magda.

"Viktar told us what you did for him."

"Did he." Lux observed the man slide a few coins across the counter.

"What do you expect for payment?"

Lux finally tore her gaze from him. Her brow furrowed as she focused on Magda. "Payment? I would like the payment of you leaving me be. Of no longer targeting those just trying to live. Viktar's hopelessness clearly drove him to desperate crimes. Are you the same, that you'd condone it rather than help him?"

Magda's stare narrowed to match. "I've my own set of problems."

"So do we all! Steal from the rich then, if you must. Him, for example. A prime target if I ever saw one."

The fair-haired man turned around. Eyes locking with hers, he raised his mug in a toast.

Lux swallowed and lowered her voice. "Who is he?"

"The prime target?" Magda chuckled at Lux's glower. "That would be a collector." When Lux's expression softened to confusion, Magda continued, "Academics. They collect books, manuscripts. Things once lost to time. They're also philanthropists, but not for things that help me much. There's nothing I need from a library."

The Risen flashed in Lux's mind, lying wrapped and safe inside her pack. "Where do they keep them?"

The man had left his post, drawing closer to the rough-hewn fireplace. He draped an arm atop the mantle. No one approached him. They actively avoided even *looking* at him.

But Magda watched him closely. "The manor by the sea."

"A manor by the—"

"Sea. Yes. You have something of a rare text, right? Perhaps you might introduce yourself and solicit an invitation. Their Hallowed Banquet is nearing, after all." Her lips quirked into a suggestive smile. "You're young. He's young. I can't imagine what it must be like for him, spending most of his time with stuffed-up old men and dusty books."

Magda's expression left Lux's stomach in knots and the rest of her more flustered than she cared to admit. He *was* handsome. In a cold sort of way.

Because of it, she spat harshly, "I don't need your thoughts on my personal affairs. Or his, for that matter. Anyone who leads an attack four to one, when that one is alone and defenseless, is gutless and not worthy of any opinions in my mind."

"My, my, but don't you like to hold a grudge." Magda circled her before leaning in close. "You might have been alone, girl, but we all saw the knife. And you didn't look to be a stranger to its use. Defenseless? Bah." She retreated to the stairs. "Enjoy your time in Verity, Necromancer!"

Lux physically recoiled at the volume. *Witch.* She spun to absorb the intense stares now trained upon her. As if they needed any further reason to distrust her. And then there was that collector—who stared at her now most intensely of all.

Her feet rooted to the floor when he suddenly made for her.

He was tall, with a slenderer build than Shaw, and his eyes were indeed frost-like. The abundant lamplight made them appear like ice. *He should reside in a place of permanent winter*, she thought. But then he was standing before her, his lips pulled up in an incredulous half-smile, and she forgot everything else.

"Excuse me, Miss, but I don't think we've been properly introduced." He extended a gloved hand, and his smile transformed into the same grin she'd seen upstairs.

"Corvin Alistair, Collector of Mothlock."

Lux sat at the utmost edge of the bench, her fingers gripping the wood tight. Across the table sat a man of Mothlock. She didn't have much else to go on. Only that he was clearly wealthy, had a part in a philanthropic business connected to every corner of the country, and possessed an unnerving confidence. All things that sharpened her suspicious nature. He carefully adjusted the fit of his gloves while she stared.

If only a person's secrets could be revealed by staring…

"Two servings of the house stew and two pints of mead."

Lux startled at his sudden address to a barmaid. She forgot to protest the drink as the woman inclined her head, and only afterward did she notice the barmaid scurried as fast as the room's arrangement allowed. Lux's teeth clacked together.

But was the woman frightened of her or the man across from her? She leveled her gaze with the collector's. He grinned, and she added one more note to the list she'd begun to keep: His smile was awfully disarming.

Little did he know, though, she had grown up in a vile place; she wasn't easily disarmed.

"I don't mean to overwhelm you, Ms. Thorn. I only knew that soon, everyone would be vying for your attention, and I selfishly wanted it first. Thank you for allowing me to atone for my actions upstairs by buying you dinner."

She held back a snort as clearly *no one* wanted her attention, and said, "Consider yourself forgiven, Mr. Alistair."

"I'm relieved to hear it. Though Corvin will do."

She drudged up a smile. "Lux will do, too."

"A unique name—Lux." Corvin pulled his lower lip between his teeth and released it. "I rather like it. I wonder...is it a nickname?"

"No," she lied smoothly. "Is Corvin a nickname?"

His brow furrowed in amused confusion. "No." Pristine sleeves came to rest upon the tabletop, and that pricking sensation returned as her stare tightened on his gleaming coat buttons.

Mothlock Manor. That was where he was from. Not merely a group of lending libraries. Not a costly establishment. But the name for a manor by the sea. A place not on her map, she didn't think, but then again she'd also overlooked Verity.

The destination for a man in a bowler hat and a body in a bag. And though she'd lost that one, she'd found another just like him. How unusually lucky.

Lux did not trust luck. It felt like anytime she'd ever done so, something disastrous would follow shortly afterward. The universe righting itself after her accidental good fortune. She felt a little ill.

Regardless, she said, "Collector of Mothlock is an impressive-sounding title. What does it mean?"

His confusion morphed into incredulity. "Sincerely? You've not heard of us?"

"Why would I ask if I had?" *Damn it all.* Her annoyance with useless questions might just ruin all of this for her. She dragged her nails along the bench's woodgrain and lied again. "I only meant, I wish I had. But I haven't."

"Right." His confident smile faltered for the first time, and Lux, upon seeing it, reminded herself he hadn't done anything wrong. Yet. "Well, we're as our title says: collectors of the rare and important. Usually that means books, sometimes objects. All of which are brought back to our estate for the purpose of preservation."

"Preservation?" Lux immediately thought of her missing fingernail, floating now with others in an unmarked jar. "Whyever would books need to be preserved?"

Corvin eyed her thoughtfully, a perusal she found difficult to meet. "So many things are not cared for as they should be." His fingertips tapped solemnly upon the table. "You would be surprised, I think, at what was once at risk of being lost. But at Mothlock, we collect, study, print, and bind. Then we redistribute that knowledge back into the community. Can you imagine what this country would be like if we lost our history? Or the ability to strengthen our brilliances?"

Lux blinked, taken aback. "I... No, I suppose I can't imagine that." A crack slivered through her suspicions. "It sounds like a worthy cause."

Corvin's lips quirked. "And you sound surprised."

"Maybe I am."

It was strange—it being the pleasant kind for once.

"You know," he began, "I've only ever read of necromancers. I've always hoped to meet one in the flesh, but being as it's one of the rarer gifts, I never expected to."

In the *flesh*?

Suddenly, it was not Corvin who sat across from her, but the Mayor of Ghadra, Bartleby Tamish. His watery eyes and all his power-obsessed glory. Her defenses rose like hackles. She nearly bared her teeth.

"I'm not a collectible."

The collector's mouth dropped wide, aghast. "Of course not. Forgive me; I didn't mean to imply anything like that."

The deceased mayor dissolved before her. In his place were stark, clear eyes and a worried brow. Lux drew a deep breath. She stretched her fingers where they'd begun to sink again into the wood. *The mayor is dead,* she told herself. *He's dead, and you're not, and you will never be kept again.*

The words were the only sort of calming elixir she'd ever take. With her voice nearly normal, she tried to steer the conversation on. "You said you've read about people like me?"

Corvin's brow was slow to relax, but he did appear relieved to change the subject. "Very little, to my disappointment, but yes. Have you?"

"We didn't have many books where I'm from."

"Truthfully? We have lending libraries, if not booksellers, in nearly every city. A disservice for certain that we've missed yours. Tell me where it is, so I might pass it on."

Lux leaned away from the table as two bowls of stew and a plate of bread were placed before them. Matching mugs of mead completed the meal moments later. Lux thought the barmaid's hands were shaking as she did so but was too distracted to pay further mind.

The initial energy that had bombarded her with Viktar's revival had eddied only for the second enchantment to cause a resurgence. It still pulsed a faint, steady current in her core. She didn't know what changed within her aside from her own soul's recovery. And some lingering words from a cigar-smoking crone.

"You're free to be a great necromancer now, rather than settling for a mediocre one."

Except this didn't feel great. It couldn't be great to find herself returning to consciousness on the floor after performing an enchantment she'd done a hundred times before. The crone had been wrong.

She'd dug too deep.

She'd broken something.

But would any preserved book tell how it might be fixed?

Lux knew her brilliance was rare. Her parents, Riselda, the mayor, even this collector—they all told her so. But rare did not mean singular. Rare did not mean she was *alone*. Suddenly, this meeting felt fated rather than only lucky. An unfamiliar but blessed shift.

"You're quiet. Have I made you uncomfortable?"

Lux glanced up from her stew. She hesitated. Aside from the mountain trader, she'd told no one of where she'd come from. She'd wanted neither the questions nor the judgement. But she *did* want the reactions.

His, in particular.

"You've missed Ghadra," she said.

"Ghadra."

Her eyes tracked his carefully. She said nothing else.

Corvin grasped his chin. He huffed a laugh. Lux could pick out nothing but shock in his expression. "You cannot be from there."

She lifted the spoon to her lips.

"Blessed Saints." His forearms retracted as he sat straight. "This explains the lack of library. I've never met a soul out of that city."

Either he was very accustomed to acting, she was very poor at reading, or these collectors were not whom she sought. Not a drop of nerves seemed to alter him at her admission.

Lux wished she could claim the same. "I'm not surprised," she said.

And she wasn't. Ghadra was a secluded place, nearly never welcoming visitors. Those few who came never left. But perhaps now that its mad mayor was dead and a new order to be set, it could be different.

She hoped it would be different.

"I'll admit I tried to go there once."

"You did? *Why?*"

Corvin laughed outright. "Following a lead on a rare manuscript. But I couldn't manage the road. The marshes were impossible."

Lux swallowed at the idea of this man combing their city in search of his treasure. Of his gloved hands pawing through Riselda's dusty alcove filled with books and loose pages. "They were impossible."

She reached for a roll, but he took the bread from beneath her hand. Lathering it with butter, he held it out to her. "Were?"

Lux bit at her cheek but accepted his offering; butter oozed onto her fingers.

"Ghadra's under a new mayor." *It must be by now.* "I know one of the first changes was marking the marsh road."

Corvin wiped crumbs from his glove. "That's news I haven't heard yet."

She could tell he was interested, but she was in no headspace to elaborate on what happened behind that city's walls. She moved from the subject entirely.

"Do you live at Mothlock, then?"

"I do, along with the rest of my society. It's near here actually."

Her curiosity piqued. "How far?"

"Once you're out of Ravenwood, it's a half day's ride south. Why?" he asked, a tilt to his head. "Thinking of joining our cause?"

Lux's brow furrowed before she finally acknowledged the butter spilt over her hand and bit into the bread. "I didn't think—"

Her attention snagged on the staircase. Or rather the person descending it. With that dismal stare, he looked entirely too familiar.

The man bearing the body from Loxlen.

He wore the same black coat, but the hat was gone. His balding head glistened in the lamplight like he'd polished it. He descended the final stair, and when their gazes locked, Lux felt immediately trapped.

There weren't many people who'd ever made her feel that way. Those who had were dead. Her hand flew to the knife tucked at her waist when he made for them.

Corvin looked to see what had distracted her. Lux's gaze flicked to the younger man's profile in time to notice his jaw set. Did he not like this man either? Or did he condemn only the interruption?

The stranger reached their table, and though he'd stared at Lux the entire way over, he didn't look at her anymore. He glared at Corvin. "I need to speak to you." His voice was cast low, but if he thought to keep his words from reaching her, he should have gone lower. She'd a lot of practice in eavesdropping.

"I'm in the middle of dinner."

"It's *poison*."

"The dinner?"

"The body! It must be the same as the last."

Lux pretended not to pay attention as she absorbed every word. She scanned the room.

Wide stares connected with her own. Still bodies. Quick breaths. They gnawed at her, and her anger sparked. Once, she would have offered a sharp, grim smile—a dare to come closer. She nearly did so now, only…a gaunt man sat at the table nearest her. His nostrils flared and his fingers shook ever so slightly around his cup. It reminded her of someone. Of another man, brutalized and bloody, left broken outside a ruined trinket shop.

This was more than wariness.

What here has them so terrified?

Lux frowned as she glanced away, startling when she met two sets of eyes.

She raised an eyebrow. "Yes?"

Corvin inclined his head. "I know we've only just met, and you don't know much of anything about me, but this seems too blessed a meeting not to ask. Would you be interested in performing a revival? We're more than willing to pay."

"Oh." Lux stared at the man looming over Corvin's shoulder. At his once-rude expression now smoothed to blankness. His eyes were the strangest thing of all; she'd never seen such mixture of dark and light. "I cannot."

The older man scoffed. "Why not?"

Lux pulled her tongue from between her teeth. "Because this town won't sell me marsh snapper eyes."

"I have marsh snapper eyes."

"Why would you have marsh snapper eyes?"

"He eats them," said Corvin, smoothing his eyebrows.

Lux had heard of only one other person who'd make a snack of eyes; that person also created jewelry from raccoons and dipped apples in poison. What other depravities was this man up to? "My price is five goldquins."

Corvin's eyes widened. "That's all?"

"That's—" Lux floundered as an idea formed. "Wait. I'm sorry, I misspoke. *Twenty* goldquins. Unless, of course, you're wanting to bring back someone better off dead. I've decided I won't be reviving anymore villains."

"A lot of experience with that, have you?" questioned the older man.

"She's from Ghadra," murmured Corvin.

His jaw went slack. "Blessed Saints."

Before Lux's scowl could deepen much further, Corvin said, "Mistress Lefroy isn't a villain as far as I'm aware. She's an investor in Mothlock's mission, and while we'd thought it was only an accident or poor health, it seems it's something worse."

"Much worse," added the balding man.

"How long has it been since she died?"

The men shared a glance. "Coming up on twelve hours."

Lux groaned even as she'd guessed it to be close. She dropped her head and pinched the bridge of her nose, her eyes shut tight to drive the memories back. "Where is she? If she's been dead past twelve hours by even the smallest measure, this will end very badly."

"Let's be quick about it then." Corvin stood, their dinner forgotten. "She's upstairs and one room down from mine. And don't worry, Ms. Thorn. We can handle bad endings."

Lux pursed her lips, but she stood too. To the unnamed man, she said, "See that she's unwrapped and laid upon the bed." To Corvin, she added, "Wait for me outside my room. I need to gather my supplies, and I don't plan on knocking on a slew of doors trying to find you."

She didn't care that the older man glared at her abrupt directions. But she did care that Corvin looked at her the way he did.

His eyes hooded, he said, "Demand whatever you want of me," and gestured her on ahead.

Chapter Ten

When Lux stepped out of her rented room, Corvin had twenty gold coins in his palm. He slid them into a purse and motioned for her hand. When she obliged, he slipped it over her wrist.

"Thank you," he said.

"Don't thank me yet."

Several doors down, he knocked and then pushed his way in. Lux scanned the room quickly and found it to be a replica of her own. All except for the woman upon the bed, the bag enclosing her untied and pushed back from either side. Lux glanced toward the bedside table in time to see the balding man swipe a vial. He pocketed it while avoiding her eyes.

"How do you know it was poison?" she asked, because sometimes she liked to play games with rude people.

She began laying out her ingredients on the desk. Her nose wrinkled at the candle's smoke; it was larger than hers had been, and it smelled especially foul.

"I *know*."

Someone sighed behind her. "Silas."

"Corvin."

"It's a valid question for her work."

She looked over her shoulder in time to see Corvin gesturing toward her. She turned away and continued her grinding. It was not a valid question for her work, but she let him think what he liked.

These damned howler canines.

A heavy breath huffed somewhere at her back. "I have a tincture that give the dead a chance to tell you what killed them. She told me it was poison. Though I don't know how you know anything about that, since you weren't up here to hear it."

"I didn't need to be. Your whispering is not really..." Lux crushed the last bit of tooth with all her strength. "...*whispering*." She dumped the powder into the bowl.

A presence loomed beside her. "You have it memorized?"

She nodded and glanced up through her loosened hair to meet Corvin's intrigued expression. "It was my job. In Ghadra."

He stepped back, astonishment marking his features. "Very impressive."

"Thank you," she said, sticking her finger into the paste. "For this part, I'll have no one watch me work. For her privacy."

In this at least, Silas didn't argue. Together, he and Corvin stepped outside the room.

Lux was left alone with the woman. She stared down at the body, risking the waste of several seconds. The veins showed stark against sallow skin—starker than anything she'd ever seen before. It seemed like whatever had poisoned her had also caused the blood to blacken and congeal.

Lux made quick work of removing the heeled shoes and lace stockings and spent more time wrestling the thick, fine clothes from the body's frame. She began painting when she was through.

"What do you get from investing in a place like Mothlock?" she asked her. "Aside from an enemy apparently."

Except Silas had said "same as the last" while downstairs. So maybe the enemy was not just this woman's own, but an enemy to all investors. Maybe Mothlock in its entirety. Philanthropists with a nemesis? Did they defy someone even bigger than themselves?

When she was through, every line and whorl exact, Lux dragged the knife from her waist. She positioned it on the bedside table until its handle aligned with her hip. Then she pressed her thumbs to the woman's unseeing eyes and—

Devil's own...

Lux paused. Her fingers came away. She marched to the door, and when she opened it, Silas nearly toppled in atop her. He'd been listening.

"Grand," she said. "You're already eavesdropping. If you hear a thump, like a body falling to the floor, and your investor sounding strangely hungry, come in. Otherwise, wait for me."

She shut the door on their gaping mouths and returned to the bed. "All right. Let's see if that last revival was a fluke."

Again, she pressed her thumbs to the body's eyes.

"*Back from Death, we beckon. A guide between Life and Fate...*"

"Hello? Young lady!"

Lux blinked open her eyes and groaned. "*No.* Damn it all." Her insides vibrated alarmingly beneath her skin. She squinted at the face above her. Brown eyes, greying hair. The revived woman had already begun to dress, and the toe of her stockinged foot was buried yet in Lux's ribs. Lux shoved it away.

Her next breath drew ragged. She pressed her fists to her eyes right there on the floor.

You cannot break here.

But oh, how she wanted to.

She pushed herself up instead and stumbled to the door. She pulled it open and didn't meet the eyes of either man who came in immediately afterward.

"What—" The woman quieted at the faces entering the room. "Oh, Lord Corvin! Lord Silas?" She dropped to her knees. "What's happening here? That child won't tell me anything. I woke up *indisposed* on a strange bed with her splayed out on the floor. I thought I'd been kidnapped." Mistress Lefroy crossed herself before folding her hands in prayer, an incoherent mumbling pouring from her lips.

Lux's glance lifted from the woman's strange prostrating to see *Lord* Silas frown and say, "You were poisoned and died, Mistress Lefroy. I was taking you to be entombed."

"*What?*"

While the pair discussed the particulars, Lux returned to the desk and gathered her ingredients as quick as she could. She paused when the handle of her knife pushed into her vision. She looked up at Corvin.

"Splayed out on the floor?" he said.

Lux snatched the weapon from him. "It's nothing."

That same hand with which he'd held the knife now rested on her elbow. "If you're ill or something else, you can tell me."

"For what purpose?" She folded everything into her arms, and when he didn't have an immediate quip ready, said, "If you'll excuse me, I'm tired."

An absolute lie.

But he did not let her go. "I might be able to help."

The best way she'd ever found to keep tears at bay was to dig for anger—and she would not cry in front of strangers. Her lip curled as her eyes pricked. "Can you really? Are you a healer? Do you specialize in broken brilliances?"

"No, Lux. I don't specialize in anything hurt or broken. But I know someone who does."

She scrunched her eyes closed. Maybe she hadn't lied. Her mind was *exhausted*. "And you're volunteering their services?"

"I am. Aside from its mission in preservation, Mothlock finds value in helping those wherever it can. We're blessed by the Saints in employing the strongest gifts in the country."

More of that philanthropy Magda had mentioned. Was this another stroke of good luck? Or was it fate leading her? Lux peered up at him. She searched for pity, but he only seemed resolute.

She was not too proud, though, even if it had been pity. Not for this. "Suppose I am interested. How do I find this person? I have a map if it would be easier to show me."

"It would be easier to show you. Personally. Being as he's at the manor."

Behind them, Mistress Lefroy tied her boot with irritated yanks.

"You won't need to investigate the poisoner?"

"That's more Silas's expertise." His hand left Lux. "For what it's worth, it's rare for a brilliance to be broken."

Lux wedged the knife back against her waist, her pots and vials clinking. "I didn't realize your manor was open to visitors."

Corvin caught the sachet of bat wings before it plummeted. He placed it within her mortar. "Once a year on Hallowed Day's Eve and by invitation only. I'd gift you one officially, but it seems your hands are already full. The Hallowed Banquet brings in the most influential and powerful minds; you're welcome to attend it as well. Consider it an appreciation for all you've done here tonight."

There it was. The honey atop the teacake.

Her despair dwindled in wake of what he offered. A chance to fix what she'd broken... Powerful people who, in her seventeen years of experience, were often corrupt...

And the sea.

But she would have to be strategic. She might even have to be...*charming*. Lux glanced at Silas and found his hands folded as Mistress Lefroy's had been—and were now again. They murmured together, words she couldn't quite understand. There was something about him. The way he bent over the woman beside him. He'd been about to entomb her, he'd said. But where?

If it weren't for the fact that her body felt as if it held lightning inside it, Lux might have sat longer with these questions, but she could feel the opportunity Corvin presented like a freshly laid road. She could do this. She'd managed the Light in Ghadra on enough occasions and had even attended a masquerade with only minor mishaps. She could pretend to fit amongst this great manor, with its prayers and bookwork and renowned banquet of important people. Just for a short while.

But Corvin must have grown unsettled by her silence, as he said, "If this doesn't work into whatever plans you have for yourself, I understand. My invitation remains open indefinitely." He leaned in. "But my carriage leaves in the morning."

Lux stilled her tapping foot at once. "What time?"

Chapter Eleven

Lux had slept fitfully. While tiredness eventually came upon her, it was thoughts of Ghadra that kept her awake. Specifically, those whom she'd left behind inside of it. In the end, she'd dreamt of Riselda. Or rather, the tree into which the woman had been swallowed. She dreamt of the last time she stood before it. The day she'd left.

"*You were right. I can revive more than the dead.*" *Her eyes tracked up the massive trunk until she reached the silver-veined leaves.* "*How did you know? I wish you would have told me everything.*"

Outside the inn, Lux yawned and Corvin dipped his head toward her.

"Did you not sleep well?"

"No," said Lux, prodding at the purple splotches beneath her eyes. "Too many thoughts, and most of them contradictory."

The collector hummed his understanding. "I remember that feeling."

"How did you fix it?"

"By finally realizing my place in this world." He grinned at her. "It took a while."

Lux pulled her gaze away. She breathed deeply the scents of wet, growing things as she stared at the forest town. Realize her place in the world? Where did someone even begin? In Ghadra, every day felt like wading through a slog of marsh mud. Each one had been the same as the terrible day before; she'd been stuck fast. Now, here in the expansive world, she felt unmoored. How could anyone make the correct choice when there were so many choices to be had?

As if summoned by her thoughts, a black carriage rolled to a stop before them. Identical twin lanterns hung lit from either side, and the driver in front was dressed all in rich black, a wide-brimmed hat low over his brow. *Being in the business of preserving old things must be lucrative,* she decided, crossing her stained, yellow sleeves.

The one problem with colored silk, she supposed. It did not travel well.

When the second carriage ambled up behind it, Lux tucked her face away from its driver. She couldn't have her plans ruined now if he were to recognize her from Loxlen. Silas seemed a suspicious sort; he'd likely make sure she was entombed next.

This is the correct decision. It must be. And if it wasn't, well...she would be no worse off than now. Maybe she would still be better, because traveling to Mothlock meant traveling to the sea.

Corvin stepped forward and lifted the latch. He pulled the door open and gestured. "After you."

This time, she acquiesced and climbed in.

Only, the collector hadn't but placed one boot on the stair when a shouted, "Wait!" stilled his next step.

"*Wait!* Where do you think you're going?"

Lux leaned forward on the luxurious seat, her gaze riveted on the slivered space between Corvin and the door. On a frazzled Sven, hair a vast array of direction, barreling toward them.

"Please. *Miss.* Saints above, I never got your name. Where are you—"

"Sven!" Magda stood now at the inn's entrance, her stare severe. "Viktar needs you."

"But she's going with—"

"He needs *you.*"

Sven shifted backward, his expression torn. Corvin climbed in, and Lux said, "Take care," and nothing more, because neither did she truly know them nor wish to see them again.

But Sven's worried frown only deepened. "Please don't stay," he replied, entirely too solemn, before Corvin shut him out.

Lux parted the curtain as they lurched forward, giving her enough time to watch Sven arguing with Magda on the porch, his brown cheeks coloring a deep red. *Good riddance,* she thought, easing back.

"Friends of yours?"

Lux breathed a humorless laugh as she turned her attention to the man opposite her. While his gloves were in place and his coat buttoned, he went without a hat or hood. Away from the autumn air, it was a comfortable temperature in the carriage, and Lux lowered her own. His head tilted, studying her as if she were a portrait, which prompted her to raise her eyebrow and say, "They tried to rob me in Ravenwood. The oldest of them died of a bad heart, and when I revived him in exchange for my freedom, I received my being outed as a necromancer in a suspicious town in return. So no, not friends of mine."

"Death to the Devil," snorted Corvin, and his eyes appeared to lose some of their iciness. "Did you come from Loxlen? Someone should have warned you Ravenwood is filled with bandits. They're a lawless bunch preying on anyone they can, but our carriages are usually left alone."

"I did, and no one said anything of it." She scowled as her heart niggled at her to be fair. "I suppose I hardly spoke with anyone either."

His stare deepened, his gaze assessing. "It must be difficult to connect with the living when what calls to you most often is death."

Lux sucked a breath. When her throat constricted next, she tried to swallow but failed.

She didn't know what she should say. If she even wanted to acknowledge it at all.

How could he say such a thing to her?

She despised how he'd managed to verbalize her insecurity so simply; in fact, she could say she hated it. She'd become so good at masking herself, she wondered at what point she'd let it slide from her face. Or had it been plucked from her—weeks ago—by a boy in an alcove in a mansion far away? He was a thief, after all.

What she did know was if this collector kept staring like that, as if he could see beyond any shred of armor still intact from Ghadra, she would leap from this carriage, damning herself to bandits and whatever else.

Lux dragged her gaze away. "I'm trying," she managed.

"All we can ever do, correct? At any rate, you should be safe from further bandits or anything else while you're with me. Mothlock is well-known and widely respected for its work. We're not bothered."

"You must have collected a grudge from someone if your investors are being poisoned."

Corvin's nose wrinkled. "Right. That. That is new."

"Maybe your Mistress Lefroy will eventually remember who murdered her."

"She doesn't; I'd hoped for that too. But the victims have each had a mark." He lifted his finger to just below his ear. "A bloodied one. She remembers the prick and nothing else."

"I didn't even notice."

"It was small, so I'm not surprised."

Lux took a turn then in studying him as he had her. His eyes remained focused on her all the while she did. As if he wished to hide nothing from her. As if he'd never known masking. It was...unnerving.

"You aren't worried," she decided.

Corvin blinked at her, slow and deliberate. "It will be handled."

Lux bit her tongue to say nothing else. It slipped free anyway. "By that *Lord Silas*?"

She expected him to glare at her for her sarcasm. She did not expect a grin to spread across his face. "You take issue with our titles."

"No issue," she lied. "Only think it's odd." *And pompous.*

She couldn't deny her knowledge of Malgorm's running was vague at best while sequestered within Ghadra. She could have sought more, but she hadn't cared to. She'd barely survived each day. That had changed in her month of travel. She'd learned the country was not run by any singular person, but a large council far away. Though even they were not considered lords.

"Well, *I* certainly didn't choose it," said Corvin. "The title was given to me on my induction into the society. It's supposed to represent reverence or something—respect for the role we've carved out for ourselves in this world."

She hummed a noncommittal note. His grin grew.

"Tell me why you left Ghadra, Lux. Aside from the obvious fact you were meant for bigger things."

Lux ran her nail along the seam of the cushions. Over and over. "I left Ghadra because it was a part of my life that had run its course."

"A chapter ended. So you don't plan to return?"

"I—"

The carriage lurched.

Lux's hand reached out to steady herself just as pressure came down upon her leg. She stared at her fingers gripping the soft fabric over Corvin's forearm. At his own gripping the space above her knee. Their hands retracted at the same moment, and Lux straightened her skirt while Corvin did the same to his coat, his eyes looking anywhere but at her.

"Apologies," he said. "This road is rough with roots in places."

"No need. I'm relieved to be in a carriage rather than walking, for once."

That brought his gaze back, and it was horrified. "You've been *walking*? Why?"

"I never learned to ride, for one. The only horses in Ghadra were reserved for the death-carts or hired carriages. And my funds have been a bit dismal with my lack of revivals."

"Death—we will come back to that. You've been traveling alone, walking, this entire way? You're either very lucky or very skilled with that knife. Or both."

"It's honestly neither."

Corvin rubbed his smooth chin, and gradually, the shock faded from his features. "All right. What of these death-carts? I've never heard of such a thing."

Lux's gaze held his. "They were our means of transporting the dead out of the city and into the forest. There, the trees consumed them."

He sat forward, eyes impossibly wide and appearing younger than she'd yet seen him, hardly older than her. "A devouring wood? Now you must tell me everything."

Chapter Twelve

The solitary flame pulsed hungrily in the dark. It beat in time with her heart.

"Please, stop. Please. Don't."

Her ankles were strapped, her wrists too. She didn't know what would come, but she knew it would be terrible.

Struggling was useless. The bindings would not give. She smelled nothing. Heard nothing. The flame was the only thing she could see. The only thing—

A tortured face emerged from the void, dripping and insidious.

"What are you afraid of, Lucena?"

Lux's eyes sprang open to a hand jostling her knee. She flung herself backward at once, where she hit the cushioned seat. Her breaths heaved.

"I'm sorry to wake you, but we're nearly there. Blessed Saints, are you all right? You look like you saw the Devil."

The sweat on her skin began to cool and then grow outright cold. Goosebumps erupted on her flesh. Lux rubbed at her arms beneath her cloak. She'd been back in some nightmarish version of an already nightmarish place. Except, rather than the Shield mocking her from the shadows, the face had been her own.

The Devil? *Near enough.*

"I'm fine."

"I didn't mean to startle you. I only wanted to warn you before we arrive: Mothlock's garden is unusual. Though, for someone who has lived beside a hungry forest, maybe you won't think so."

She forced herself to relax into the seat and scrubbed the sleep from her eyes. "Unusual in what way?"

He cocked his light head, a smile pulling at his lips. "You're not frightened? Even as I compare it to your dastardly trees?"

"You implied it's not so bad as that, so now I'm only curious."

He chuckled. "No. Not so bad as that. But it's best to stay on the paths. The plants don't like to be disturbed."

"How much do they not like it?"

"Enough to weaponize themselves and inject a toxin."

"Deadly?"

"Debilitating. For a while."

It was Lux's turn to tilt her head. "You know this firsthand."

Corvin laughed outright, a flush of color highlighting his sharp cheekbones. "Yes. It's awful. I wouldn't recommend it. Especially as the timeline would interfere with the Hallowed Banquet, and you really cannot miss that."

"It's truly so great, is it?"

He shrugged. "I've always looked forward to it. To open the doors to like-minded individuals who wish to celebrate our work and that of brilliance itself? The Saints have honored us with the best night of the year. Once you've seen our healer and everything is right again, I think you'll enjoy yourself immensely."

Doubtful. Though Lux's confidence around the living had grown, it didn't erase her disdain for crowds. She *was* intrigued, of course. But she'd prefer to experience the event from a shadowed alcove or obscure balcony over answering questions from prying minds about a young necromancer from a city no one ever left.

But could she find the possible purchasers of lifeblood while hidden away in said balcony? Likely not.

She fiddled with the window's dark hangings. "Has your society been assembled a long time?"

"Over a century. Though Mothlock is a lot older. The estate used to house an impressive family before it was transformed into the philanthropic society it is now."

"Is the family still there?"

Corvin's brow furrowed. "What do you mean?"

Lux attempted a smile and couldn't tell if she succeeded. "Their descendants. Or did they move on?"

"Ah. No. No descendants. In fact, I was the last child to grow up there."

"You grew up in the manor? You've been there your entire life?"

And how long has that life been, exactly? she wanted to add.

"I have," he said and leaned forward, eyes bright. "I could show you all the interesting rooms, the terrace, the best corners of the estate. There's the garden and the path down the cliffsides to the cove. Have you been to the sea yet? No? Then I'll make it a priority."

It came upon her all at once, that utterly overwhelming feeling of a dream about to be actualized. Her fingers and toes tingled. Her breaths shallowed. She couldn't tell if her heart sped, galloping away, or if it'd slowed to a crawling thump. Either way, Lux pressed her palm over her mouth.

She'd climbed a mountain. Touched the bark of a red tree. Now, all she needed was to feel the waves lapping at—

A subtle roar began at the far reaches of her hearing. A few minutes more and it drove out the silence with its power. Lux's eyes grew wide.

"Is that...?"

"Prepare to meet it," answered Corvin, and grinned.

Chapter Thirteen

The gate outside the mayor's mansion in Ghadra had been tall and spired, the whorls of iron shaved sharp enough to cut. These gates put all of it to shame. Twice as tall, with spires needle-fine, and whorls that seemed off-putting to Lux's eyes—until she noticed what it read.

Mothlock

She pressed her face nearly upon the glass to better view the thick stone pillars supporting them, and how those pillars gave way to a wrapping iron fence, extending as far as she could see. And beyond it—

Lux sucked in a breath.

"It's really not so unfriendly as it appears." Corvin's voice resonated between their bodies, quiet and reassuring.

But she hadn't even glanced at the hulking residence spearing the sky.

She stared at the water.

It was far away and interrupted by fencing, but it was blue. A deep, dense blue. And it stretched on forever. Hardly a cloud marked the sky, and the sunset beamed upon the land unobstructed. It lit the sea last, its evening rays bathing everything in shades of orange. Then it all vanished.

Lux eased back as the carriage turned to face the manor. It was almost too impossible to fathom. That she was here and not *there*. That there was so much *space.* That she could look out on a clear day and see the very reaches of the horizon.

People live like this?

A jolt of envy skewered her at the thought, dousing her cold. How horribly unfair. To have been born in Ghadra. To grow up as she did and see what she saw. Her fists clenched around her hidden books.

Devil below, what I would do to change it. Her gaze met Corvin's and narrowed. *To have his life...*

"Are you well?"

His blatant concern only angered her. Because somewhere deep down she knew she was being irrational. One cannot help what they cannot control, and the circumstances of her birth fell into that category. But if she'd been brave enough to leave sooner—

"I think my lack of sleep is catching up with me." She massaged her temples in an attempt to lessen the tension.

She listened to Corvin's reply from behind closed lids.

"I'll secure you a room. The whole of Mothlock will be yours to explore come morning."

Her eyes snapped open. "All of it?"

"Fine. You've caught me out." Corvin ran a hand through his hair, a smile tugging at his mouth. "*Most* of it. There are, after all, a lot of dead spaces and ends in an old house like this."

"I didn't realize an invitation allowed so much." Lux studied the peculiar markings on the pillar as they passed it by. *Are those...faces?*

"It doesn't. That's what you have me for."

Lux turned back in time to catch his devilish grin and could well imagine the sort of child he'd been, with a clever, curious mind and a sprawling manor for a home.

She thought he might also be an orphan. But she didn't dare ask.

"And how quickly could I see the water?"

"Immediately?"

Her heart skipped before galloping ahead. "Please," she said, hoping it didn't sound as pleading to him as it did to her own ears.

Corvin's expression softened; she knew then she'd been begging.

"I cannot deny you," he said, and when the door swung open, he descended first. His hand reached between them, into the carriage. "Welcome to the great Mothlock Manor, Lux Thorn."

Lux slipped her hand in his—and promptly lost her breath.

They were too close. She couldn't possibly take it all in at once. Lux stumbled back against the carriage and stared, her gaze sweeping upward. Black stone stairs ascended to black doors, and onward, to cross-barred windows and a single, peaked tower. Sculpted creatures peered down at her from the highest vantages.

"This is…" Deep-green vines crept partly up the walls, their fingers digging in tight to any cracks. Blue blooms larger than her head were spread stark against the black.

"I know."

Lux afforded herself a quick glance and found him staring up at the manor's entrance with something akin to reverence. But the roar of the sea was louder now outside the carriage, and she couldn't be distracted for long. Her gaze swept the garden.

The rather…overgrown garden. Pale stone paths branched from either side of the courtyard she stood within, tunneling into the reddened briar. *But which one leads to the water?*

When she asked, Corvin huffed a laugh. "I've never met someone so singularly obsessed with the sea." She stared at him until he relented. "This one," he said, pointing to their right.

She immediately started toward it, but he gripped her arm. "Remember to mind the plants."

Lux breathed away the reactive wish to toss his hand off. Instead, she waited until he removed it on his own before nodding and heading into the thicket.

Corvin followed behind her—she could hear his soft footfalls—but she kept her eyes trained forward. To the growth lining either side of the pathway, but also on the roar ahead. She could smell the salt stronger here than before, the brine-scent of sea-grown things, and when the first dusting of water peppered her skin, she nearly wept.

So this is what it feels like to live your dream.

The path curved, and Lux stopped, an arched door of dark wood rising to meet her. She glanced over her shoulder, her hand outstretched toward the ring in question, but when Corvin only winked at her, she faced ahead once more and, mindful of the brambles, pulled.

There beneath the stone archway, Lux nearly sank to her knees.

Stone steps and a raging sea. They were so much higher above it than she expected, and it sapped the strength from her legs. She could see indefinitely. Dark cliffs dripped with seaweeds and sea-spray beneath her. Farther out, spears of rock rose from the waves, so drenched they appeared black. It was dramatic and wild—so far removed from any creek, lake, or river, it seemed unreal.

Corvin stopped beside her.

"The steps lead down to the cove. It isn't safe during certain times of day with the shifting tides, and you mustn't enter the water here, but otherwise, you can walk the shore. It's a good place to think and dream."

"I have no more dreams than this."

"None?"

She could feel his stare against her profile, but she couldn't pull her gaze away. *Maybe one more,* she supposed, and gasped when a great wave crashed below, the windswept spray coating one side of her face.

"What do you dream of?" she asked.

Corvin watched the waves with a thoughtful expression, his brow furrowed. "I've not had anyone ask me that, I don't think. Not for a long time anyway. I suppose I dream of accomplishments. To be the best I can be. To learn as much as I'm able to in this life. And I dream of dreams. I've slept without for too long."

"You can't dream?"

"No. Not in the traditional way. Not in the way I'd like to."

Lux studied him, at how well he seemed to fit upon this cliffside, with his hair as light as the sky and the rest of him blended into the dark seascape. To sleep without dreams? Rarely could she recall experiencing it herself.

Most of what's in my head are nightmares.

"Those are admirable," she said, just as another—larger—fissure cracked her suspicions.

"So is experiencing what you never have before. I apologize if I implied otherwise. I've come to take my home for granted."

"You didn't imply." She extracted her gaze from his and breathed in lungfuls of salt. "The mountains were breathtaking, but treacherous and cold. And the forests I came to, like Ravenwood, were calm and beautiful, nothing like what I'd grown up with. But this..." She shut her eyes a moment. "*This* speaks to my soul."

"Careful," murmured Corvin. "Or I might have to convince you to stay."

And before she could think of what those words could mean, she said, "I might let you."

Chapter Fourteen

Corvin stood outside Mothlock's front doors, his hand poised to level the knocker against their barred front. He glanced down at her beside him. "Don't mind the gruffness of the other collectors. The youngest of us do most of the traveling, and that leaves the old ones behind to mildew—and you're not made of paper."

"I'll try my best to seem interesting and worthy."

"Try? You already are those things."

The knock sounded against the door, and Lux swore she heard its echo in every direction behind it. She straightened her posture.

The doors swung inward to reveal a beanpole of a man all in black, save for his gloves, which were white. He inclined his head once he saw whom he addressed—a heartbeat before he sank to his knees. "Lord Corvin and guest. Welcome to Mothlock."

Lux's nose wrinkled, taken aback by the display. What was he doing, bowing before them like a sycophant? Her eyes snapped to Corvin, but the collector didn't seem the least bit put out. Mistress Lefroy—in her relieved resurrection—Lux had almost forgiven and forgotten, but this?

Corvin didn't move. Instead, he smiled at the man. "Manphry. I require a suite prepared for our guest. I think fourth floor, room seven would suit. Dinner, too, should be sent to our respective rooms as soon as possible."

The man blinked twice, his eyes a washed-away brown. Like aged wood. "Certainly."

When Manphry rose to allow them passage, Corvin gestured her in ahead of him. "And a message to Lord Kent. We will be needing his skill right away."

Lux caught the sideways glance of Manphry before he cleared his throat. "I will see it done."

The footman vanished on the heel of his words, and Lux stared at his vacated space. At the lacquered floors beneath her dust-spattered boots. She stepped back and noted her prints remained, marring the floor.

"Don't worry," said Corvin. "A place like this sees all sorts trekked through its halls. We keep a large staff for a reason. Soon, no one will have known you were here." He followed her gaze upward. "What do you think?"

Lux stared awhile more at the massive iron ring suspended above her head, where hundreds of candles flickered a yellow light. What did she *think?* She spun a slow circle.

There was too much to absorb. The deep, shadowed corridors. The intricate architecture. The way the dark banisters of the wide staircase rolled toward her like waves. The painting on the—

"Who is that?"

It was the largest portrait she'd ever seen. Larger even than Ghadra's dead mayor's, which she'd always thought had been inappropriately sized. It hung upon the wall at the top of the staircase. Bordered by ornate sconces, pointed arched windows, and twin ivory statues, her initial guess was that she gazed upon a shrine.

"That would be our founder. The Overlord of Mothlock's Society. Alixsander Osric Alesso."

Lux moved forward without meaning to, not stopping until her boots tapped the first stair. The dead founder stared down at her, his eyes the color of midnight and his hair the same. Even from her distance, she could see his features were expressive and maybe even kind.

But...*Overlord?*

"He looks like you," she said. A perfect inverse, really.

"You're not the first to say it. We're relations. You can look at it closer if you'd like."

Lux turned her head at the laughter in his voice. "Are you sure it won't swallow me up if I get any closer? How long did something like that take?" All she could think of was Shaw, painting for days—maybe weeks—on end.

"I couldn't say. But you'll be safe, I swear. I was told Alixsander didn't have a modicum of ill-will for anyone in life. I don't believe his portrait does either." Corvin gestured her up the stairs.

Lux acknowledged it and placed her hand on the banister. She began to climb. All the while, she kept her eyes trained upon the portrait. As it drew nearer, she realized how young he appeared. Older than her but probably no older than the man beside her. She reached the landing and stared up at his frozen features.

"He founded your society while so young himself?"

She glanced at Corvin and saw he studied it too. A tick had worked its way into his jaw, and she watched it feather until he noticed her stare. He returned his attention to her with a smile that wasn't quite happy. "He founded it young, and died young too."

"What happened?"

"Murder."

Lux blinked, caught off her guard. "Tragic."

"It was. A horrendous betrayal. When Mothlock began its transition into what it is now, there were some who didn't agree with his mission. He believed whole-heartedly in honoring the Saints while slighting the Devil, and that the best way to do so was to encourage one's mastery of brilliance. Mothlock was planned to be a place of learning in order to achieve this goal. He didn't consider there'd be those who would take advantage of his generosity. He was killed not a decade in."

Lux stepped back several paces to better view the portrait's features. Frustration filled her. "Why does everything good die young while evil lives forever?

I will never understand it." She scowled up at the painting. "Did they find his murderer?"

"They did not."

"Of course, they didn't." She was all too familiar with murderers being allowed to walk free. *Though, Shaw doesn't count.*

Her glance landed next on the ivory statues flanking the portrait. Full-bodied but vague, entirely without faces, and lit by the same flickering blue flames as the shop in Loxlen. Each were draped in long, flowing robes, both with crowns of thorns. Lux peered up at the one nearest her.

"What do these represent?" she wondered aloud.

"The Saints."

"But faceless? I've never seen them this way." Hardly any way, if she were being honest, but the sentiment was the same.

"It was purposefully done. So anyone might imagine themselves in their place." Corvin drew a deep breath. "Shall we continue up to your room?"

Immediate awareness over the cling of her worn clothes and the emptiness in her belly overcame Lux. And though she had many questions—and a fair few concerns—she said, "You'll get no argument from me."

BY THE THIRD FLOOR, Lux draped bodily over the protruded balcony.

"You climb this every day?"

Corvin chuckled, not the least bit winded. But then he didn't have the circles beneath his eyes like she did. "When I'm at home, yes. Your legs will adjust."

Lux stared down and down, skeptical of his confidence in her. Until her thoughts faltered. She saw something she hadn't before: Words in the lacquered floor. Burned or painted or carved in some way she couldn't fathom, it would have been impossible to discern up close, blending in with the natural whorls of wood. But up here?

May Your Mastery Be Limitless

When a figure, cloaked and hooded, tread slowly across them, she reeled back.

"A collector," said Corvin, following her stare. "Don't be alarmed when you find me in the same stuffy garb tomorrow."

She pressed a fist to her breastbone, willing the tightness away. She couldn't help imagining the phantom inside. Imagining *Riselda* inside. Lux shoved herself from the railing. That woman *haunted* her. Her nails cut into her palms only to keep the sudden fury at bay. Would she ever be free of the torment?

She cleared her constricted throat. "Seems bothersome while reading."

"Well, it isn't only reading that we do. But sure. I suppose it can be uncomfortable if it's not laundered properly. Ready for the final stretch?"

Lux eyed the last staircase and groaned. "You collectors must live healthy, long lives with this routine."

"Generally," said Corvin, humor still in his voice.

"Fine. If only for your Manphry's promise of dinner."

"One more floor," he said, coaxing. "I have faith you can make it."

Lux did, indeed, make it.

Or she would have—if the toe of her boot had cleared the final stair. She stumbled. Corvin reached, his arm wrapping firmly about her waist to right her, and her cheeks flamed when he released his grip.

"Are you all right?" he asked. "I should have offered you my arm from the start. I'm not used to escorting anyone, and especially not someone I admire so much. I think it's lapsed my judgement."

Lux bit back a scoff and shook free of her embarrassment. "You admire *me*? Why?"

"I can't believe you have to ask." His gaze searched her face. "You've mastered *necromancy*, one of the rarest and most difficult of gifts. And it's a feat you've managed all on your own. Of course I would admire you."

Lux moved farther onto the landing, breaking his gaze and putting distance between herself and his admirations. Her attention settled on the balcony ahead. There were no more floors after this one that she could tell—only a lit corridor. Strange, considering she'd eyed a tower outside.

She focused on those things so she could focus less on what Corvin said. And how he'd said it.

It *was* a mesmerizing view from here. In the mayor's mansion, the balustrades were trimmed in gold and often draped in ribbon in celebration of some frivolous event or another. The architecture of Mothlock Manor would not stand for that. It was comprised entirely of onyx, with sharp angles, blue fire, and dark woods, devoid of all frills. Though the detailing left her intrigued, it was unaccountably imposing.

"Where do you keep the things you've collected?" she asked while staring upward, the beams arching far overhead.

"In the vault, under lock and key."

Lux glanced over her shoulder at him, a bemused lift to her brow. "Why? You said the manor is only open once every year and by invitation."

Corvin shrugged. "Our society is careful with every original work. Those of us who don't take to the roads in search of new finds spend our days on the press, creating copies of what we already maintain. Hence the robes, to protect ourselves from the ink."

"Was this the compromise to your founder's vision then?"

Corvin traded his shrug for a beaming grin. "You've caught on. Yes. Alixsander wished the manor would be a place of learning. After his murder, a pivot was done to safeguard the society. We collect what would otherwise be lost and revive it."

"A necromancer of books." Lux found herself smiling back, though once she realized she did, it faltered.

"I don't think I can claim anything so accomplished as that." He winked at her. "Maybe a healer of books."

Lux's smile vanished entirely, thinking of what she'd tucked away only for herself. *The Risen* suddenly weighed heavily in her pack. "So they're kept safe from rodents and sea air in this vault?"

"It's more the stealing of them we're cautious over."

"That happens?" She turned from the balcony in surprise, facing him fully.

"Once. A long time ago. Before you and me."

"But why would—" Her stomach clenched. A sudden bout of nerves had her skin pricking with cool sweat. *It can't be.* "What sorts of books?" she managed.

Flames danced along the ice in the collector's eyes. "A rare book of necromancy. And an unbound manuscript. Arguably the most important discovery of Mothlock's time. One we've never found another edition of."

Devil take me. Lux rubbed her knuckles against her chest. Her pack grew heavier. "Who would do something like that?"

Corvin glanced at the shadowed wall behind him, and Lux followed suit. Paintings of a more respectable size hung unlit. There were no shrines for these. "The last member of the prestigious family of this estate. *Her.*"

Lux no longer sensed the pain in her stubbed toes. She didn't register Corvin near her side nor the remaining frames on the wall. Her vision tunneled instead to a single portrait. She crept forward.

It was of a young girl. Her expression fierce, her raven hair perfectly pinned. Her eyes were scorching, framed by thick lashes, her irises colored a vivid—

Lux's hip knocked against a pillar.

The portrait's eyes—the exact shade of Lux's own—watched her retreat. Seemed to judge her for it too. Inside that frame was a girl who would never consider abandoning a cause no matter what stood against her. No matter if that cause benefited her alone. No matter if it ruined others.

No matter if it was heinous to start.

Lux could *feel* the child's determination. She choked. "She did that?"

"So the story goes. Around that time, Mothlock was in the midst of being remade to better suit the society. And though her family had already surrendered the estate, she didn't approve of the vision. Of course, there was also the family's mind disease. No one should have been surprised when it surfaced in her too."

"Mind disease?" Goosebumps littered Lux's arms, her chest beginning to thrum.

"Talk of tragedy. That was a family of broken brilliances, driving them each to madness at different ages. I know I said to you back at the Maidenway it's extremely rare. Lord Artemis, our healer, says he's never seen it surface. He believes it's genetic—not caught or suddenly formed." Corvin sighed over the frames. "Their gradual fall brought about the biggest change in Mothlock. Sometimes that's the only way through though, isn't it?"

Lux's heart continued to beat as fast as a bird's; she worried it might pulse right out of her chest. "Yet you still display their portraits."

"Why wouldn't we? This was their home first, and regardless of their unfortunate ends, they were the catalysts for propelling our mission. Many of the oldest volumes housed here were first collected by them."

But this one stole and fled... And though the eyes weren't what she remembered, that meant little when it came to the woman Lux knew. She would recognize that expression anywhere.

Lux's desperate need grew until she couldn't bear it any longer; she had to hear him say it. Her chin quivered the smallest fraction when she asked, "What was her brilliance? What was her name?"

Corvin turned his back on the painting to face her. "Healing. Riselda Grimrook. Of the late House of Grimrook."

Chapter Fifteen

"This is a *room*?" Lux spun a slow circle, dropping her pack to the floor—where she immediately snatched it off, remembering how dirty it was from all she'd put it through. "This was my apartment in Ghadra."

Corvin's gaze flicked across the expanse, nonplussed. "A travesty."

She made her way around the draped four-poster bed to push into the washroom, squealing silently over what she found: a tub, copper and overlarge, with ornate, clawed feet. She'd not used one like it since her childhood, withering away in the late mayor's mansion. All at once, her skin itched to soak.

"There's a dressing room attached through that wall," Corvin said, coming up behind her. "Which you can also enter from a second door out here. These suites are kept stocked for the sake of rare guests, but if you should need anything in particular, you only have to ask. There's a bell pull beside the bed."

Lux surveyed her soiled sleeves. "A launderer, I think."

He chuckled at her back. "That can be arranged."

A gentle knock sounded against the main door, and Lux returned to the bedroom alongside Corvin. "That'll be Manphry with dinner," he said.

He strode to the door and opened it, but Lux knew in an instant it wasn't, because Manphry was shaped like a stalk, and this man was as broad as a wall.

"Lord Corvin."

"Oh. Lord Kent."

Corvin stepped aside until Lux could see the full size of the man entering the room. He lumbered forward, a black hood pulled low over his brow, and Lux's skin grew clammy—though his hands were clean of dirt and empty.

"And this is your guest, I presume?" With hands the size of meat pies, Lord Kent gestured to her person.

"This is Lux Thorn of Ghadra. A necromancer."

Lux bristled at the slew of details all laid bare in a breath. But before she could throw Corvin a glare, one of Kent's large hands reached within his robe and drew forth a measuring roll. "Ghadra? Well, well. And Ms. Thorn can bring back the dead, can she?" The tool unraveled and tumbled to the floor. He suspended the opposite end near the top of her head. "Average enough, for a woman."

"Excuse me?" She stepped back from him, outrage curling her lip.

"Height, Ms. Thorn." He picked up the opposite end, and with a flourish, roped her inside it. "Average again." The roll left her waist, and he looped it quickly. "The rest I've an eye for. No need to fret. I'll have you a wardrobe by morning."

"But I—"

"Thank you for your time, Kent."

"You're welcome. It's not often I'm allowed my brilliance its range. Tell me, Ms. Thorn, are you skilled at reviving the departed?"

"Of course," said Lux, still reeling with confusion.

"Praise to the Saints. What a find," he replied, but not to her.

To Corvin.

Her mouth parted over his final words, and when Kent ducked his covered head to pass through the door frame, Corvin rushed to shut him out. He turned back toward her, twin splotches of color reddening his cheekbones. "He's a tailor. Or was. His brilliance is in fabrics, rather. But he's a collector as well."

Lux's lips thinned over Corvin's rambling thoughts. She'd not yet heard him unpolished. In fact, she'd begun to think it was impossible. "So, because he works most often with objects, he treats people like them? I didn't ask for a wardrobe, let alone to be measured. '*What a find?*' I told you before and I'll say it again. I did not come here to be *collected*."

His color deepened. "Please accept my apology for his behavior. Remember what I warned you of while outside? His manners aren't what they should be after having been secluded so long. He's only eager and intrigued. We all are, really—it's our nature as academics. Of course you're not something to be collected."

He'd said she should be wary of gruffness from old men, not insults from one without so much as an age spot on his hands. But following Corvin's chagrined apology, Lux gathered her courtesy. She couldn't entirely abandon the role she had to play if she wished to unearth secrets.

She exhaled a slow breath. "I suppose it was a nice gesture. With the clothes. Only, I would have appreciated your asking. I don't know if I have the funds to cover it." In her head, her newly acquired goldquins were already spent on the book in Loxlen.

Corvin cleared his throat. "Consider it a gift." Lux pressed her fingers to her eyes and groaned, but he remained undeterred. "Please? You might not have sensed it, as you don't know him, but he is thrilled. You'll let him create something for you?"

Lux slowly lowered her hands. "Seems I haven't a choice in the matter, being as he's already left." Her finger slipped through the arrow-made hole in her cloak. "Traveling wasn't so easy as I thought."

"Did you find what you wanted, at least? In your travels?"

Her parting promise to Shaw and the mayor's daughter was ushered to her mind's forefront. That should she stumble upon any hint of lifeblood, any evidence of its inhumane extraction, she would put an end to its use. It morphed to conjured images of the child's portrait on the wall, of the girl touching the things Lux now touched. Of her short life here in a room just like this one.

You were rich beyond measure, Riselda, and you fled to Ghadra? Why? To live out your madness for decades to come?

But Corvin hadn't anymore answers, and Riselda was gone and devoured. That should have eased her mind, but instead she felt hovered over and watched. She peeked over her shoulder to be sure but found nothing.

"Nearly," she said, and that was true enough.

Lux's dinner did eventually arrive. But as she broke through the crust of the steaming dish, she realized her appetite had vanished. A hollowness gnawed at her breastbone in its place.

Only hours ago, she would have devoured something like this, but in her present state, the pie may as well have been a pile of ash. She forced a bite past her lips anyway; she could use the strength.

Lux swallowed hard.

"What is the matter with you?"

A massive mirror, tall enough to reflect even Lord Kent, showed her expression back to her from across the bedchamber. She'd seen a similarly sized mirror before, in her time in Ghadra's mansion, but that one had been propped on two feet. This had become part of the wall.

You miss him, replied her head. And it was true. She could see it in her eyes.

All at once, they filled, blurring her reflected image and then the food in front of her face. *Stop it,* she told herself. *You're only tired.* But the tears spilled anyway, dripping down her nose. She pushed the plate away.

Only a month. A single, solitary month, and she was already overwhelmed. By a chase through the forest. By Riselda's portrait and uncharted madness. By a second boy whose eyes seemed to bore straight to her core. Considering the poisonings, she might have embroiled herself in some murderous mess again, and the thought caused her fear of what transpired over Viktar and Mistress Lefroy's revivals to spike. A sob escaped her mouth before she could stifle it.

That was too much, too far. She couldn't hardly handle it.

Lux staggered to the huge bed. Nevermind her unwashed face and unclean teeth—she needed to sleep away everything she felt. Perhaps by morning her emotions would be in better control. She pulled back the thick coverings, climbed into the downy softness, and curled into herself. The bed was easily three times the size she was used to, and she arranged the excess of pillows around her.

When her eyes fluttered closed, Lux imagined the weight of an arm around her waist, the press of body heat against her back, and she imagined the sweet taste of honey, until she thought of nothing at all.

Chapter Sixteen

"DIDN'T YOU KNOW? WE *murdered our parents.*"

The rotted version of her whispered wetly in her ear.

"*Now, it's our turn.*"

Sunlight seared her eyes. Lux stood upon the curved balcony off her bedchamber and basked in it until the memory of her horrid nightmare burned away. Her bare feet were cold against the stones, the iron railing like ice beneath her fingertips, and she stretched to the tips of her toes, enough so she could see over and down.

All the way to the treacherous shore below.

Corvin had given her a room facing the sea.

The autumn breeze tugged against her nightgown and brought with it again the taste of salt; she inhaled it greedily. All the while the sun lifted farther above the horizon.

Never in her wildest imaginings. Never had she pictured something so beautiful, and never had she felt so small yet so perfectly suited. Aside from that nightmare near dawn, she'd slept soundly and woken with a new determination. She might have been lonely. She might have missed whom she'd left behind. But that didn't mean she would wallow away her limited time here. There were more important things to be done than all that.

A knock came upon the door, and she turned.

"Come in."

A dour-faced woman peered around the wood. Followed closely by a second face higher above it. Lux left the balcony and moved back into the room.

"Good morning. I'm here to deliver a message," said Manphry, and nudged the shorter woman through. The pair entered her bedchamber, and while Manphry inclined his head, the woman dipped with a quick bend of her knees.

"I'm assigned to your upkeep," said the woman.

Lux raised an eyebrow. "I'm confused. Is she the message?"

Manphry's obvious boredom was redirected to the woman beside him. "Mind your duties in silence."

Chastised, the woman hung her head and proceeded to lope toward the wide fireplace. Selecting the poker from the stand, she prodded the flames back into existence.

"My apologies." Manphry returned his hands to his back. "I've come to inform you Lord Corvin has invited you to breakfast with him in the morning room. If you wish to decline, however, that is at your behest, and I will send your meal up as soon as I am able."

"Oh..." She glanced at the washroom, where the tub caught her eye, tempting her in. "Immediately?"

Manphry, noticing where her attention landed, said, "It is early yet, and a delay is allowed. Shall I tell him one hour?"

Allowed? How magnanimous. She might have been truly irritated if she'd believed the wording actually came from the collector. This footman seemed as wooden as his eyes; she didn't doubt he chose the delivery himself. "Please do."

"Hildred will show you the way at that time." With a pointed glance to the woman now coughing over the smoke she'd stirred, he reached for the door. "Come, Hildred. You've other rooms to see to."

"Yes," said Hildred, and having returned the poker to its place, followed doggedly behind.

The door closed behind them, and Lux pulled in her lip. She didn't like this Manphry, she decided. She especially didn't like how he treated his peers. Or did he think the woman was beneath him in some way and so talked down to her? Her teeth sank harder into her flesh before their release.

Lux tugged the thick nightgown over her head. The air nipped at her skin, and she hurried into the washroom to the tub, gripping the handles until water spewed out. It didn't take long to warm—a marvel all its own.

Saints above, she'd never yearned for a bath so much as this one.

But no...she supposed that wasn't quite true. Because here, she was not coated in fear and the black grime of a devouring wood. Here, she could only complain of travel dust and salt, no matter the layers of it that had accumulated. The Maidenway Inn had balked at her request for bathing the night before.

When the water neared the tub's lip, she swung one leg over the edge. The rest of her quickly followed suit, and she sank like a stone beneath the surface. There, in the quiet dark, she allowed her consciousness to follow.

It was truly mesmerizing, the human soul. Contained within a perfect orb and made up entirely of light. Its warmth permeated her consciousness; she wanted to bask in it like she'd done beneath the sun outside. On cue, her lungs began an expected protest. She ignored it as best she could.

Lux knew the sight and feel of corruption, had slowly begun to study what sorts of things brought about its strangling reach, but she could see no evidence of it inside her now. By all appearances, it didn't *look* broken. So what had she unbalanced?

She ground her teeth at the lack of answers. Yes, she might have done something wrong, dug too deep, but she would never stay damaged. Even if she had to scour this place for more than lifeblood. Even if she had to break into locked vaults for a cure.

I swear I will if this healer turns out useless.

By now, her chest felt near to erupting; she knew she couldn't stay beneath the quiet anymore. Lux rose to the surface on a gulping gasp.

She opened her eyes—and screamed.

Her bathwater had turned black. Not dark with dirt, but midnight black and oil slick. She scrambled backward against the edge and watched it drip slow and rotten from her fingers. Her mind seized in paralysis; she couldn't comprehend what had changed. Of what she'd done to ruin the water.

The smell wafted around her. Fetid and sour, it stank of dead things long gone. It smelled like the devouring wood, the dark moss that had squelched beneath her step. Her hands shook as she raised them higher. And it was then a scratching came from the wall marking her dressing room.

Only the piping? But every hair on her body stood on end.

"To hell with this," she breathed and leapt from the tub.

Her feet slipped sharply from beneath her.

Lux landed hard on her side, her hip meeting the flagstones first, knocking out all her air. Not even the rug could prevent the bruise she knew would come. She pulled a slow breath, gritted her teeth against the throbbing pain, and pushed herself to her elbows.

She stilled.

Her hands. Her legs.

They were wet—dripping yet—but with water. Only water. She flung herself up to peer into the tub.

Perfectly clear. The room smelled of soap and nothing else.

Goosebumps remained all over her body, but because the water steamed yet and her pulse beat with fright, Lux shakily climbed back in.

"It's only your imagination running," she murmured to the stillness. Nevermind it'd never run to *that* extent before.

She sank until she could hardly see the seam of the wall. The scratching didn't come again. Nothing moved. She reached toward the tray standing beside the tub, her fingers enclosing around a random selection. Her palm grew sudsy at once.

"Just your imagination," she whispered, and though she didn't quite feel alone, she still hoped with everything it was true.

The repeated knock came upon her door as she finished rinsing the travel grime from her hair. Lux climbed from the tub into a puddle of suds and shouted, "Just a moment!"

In a hissed whisper, she added, "You rushing oafs." He'd told her she'd have an hour. It couldn't have been already that.

She reached for a towel and wrapped it about her body before noticing the dressing robe hung on a hook. It was ivory and long; when she donned it, it trailed on the floor. She padded to the door.

"Excuse me, but I'm not—"

Kent filled the frame. "Excellent timing, I see. Ms. Thorn, your clothing is ready."

Lux stared at the bundle in his arms. "Did you even sleep?"

A heavy pause blanketed the air. "No," he finally said and held the fabrics out to her.

Her fingers enclosed around their lush softness, and her eyes widened over the feel. "What material is this?"

"Why…it's velvet. A necessity this time of year. Ghadra does not have velvet?"

"Maybe. But not that I've ever owned." She ran her fingertips over the pale red skirt. "I should pay you."

"You shouldn't. You're not the first I've made garments for, nor will you be the last. Besides, you will need something to wear for the banquet."

Her brow furrowed. "Do you often receive guests as ill-prepared as me?"

"Are you ill-prepared?"

"I—" She swallowed at the intensity of his voice, of his eyes watching her from their shadowy recess. Of realizing they might be speaking of more than just attire. "Probably."

His posture lightened. "There's a remedy for that, and it comes in stages. Knowing you're ill-prepared is the first."

"And the next?"

"Put on the dress."

"Perfect," said Lux, full of long-suffering.

"It should be. Find me if it isn't."

"I will."

She wouldn't.

The collector inclined his head and turned to leave, but Lux interrupted his departure. "I have a question." He shifted back. "Have you ever been overwhelmed by your brilliance? Or in your years of using it, has it ever felt...changed?"

"In what way do you mean?"

That intense pitch in his voice had returned, and Lux struggled again beneath it. She yearned to be more open, more trusting, and she'd made heaps of progress. But in the end, she couldn't discount the main reason she'd come here. She certainly couldn't ignore the replay of his words. *What a find...*

"Nevermind. I'm running behind."

"Ah, yes. Lord Corvin is anxious for your arrival no doubt. I won't keep you two apart."

She reached to her throat at his words. The way he'd said it... The twitch of his half-hidden mouth... She glowered. "That's not what this is."

"What *what* is?" he replied and chuckled. Gripping the door knob, he gave her his back. "Do come to me with any adjustments."

Lux stared first at the closed door, then at the bundle of clothing in her arms. She tromped to the bed where she threw the garments atop it and proceeded to select the soft, red dress from amongst the pile. It appeared almost otherworldly. Like she should put it on and sit in a field of dense, dark blooms and mushrooms.

"How can a man like him make something like this?"

Her fingers strayed down the trailing sleeves before touching the round neckline. There was no adornment. No delicate stitching or ribbons or frills.

That was fine with her. She'd long ago buried her love of ribbons. In the center of the room, she shrugged off her dressing robe and pulled the dress on. A lacing tucked against either side cinched her waist as she tied it. It felt positively decadent against her skin.

Lux ran to the mirror.

Her hair was damp still and hung limp just beneath her shoulders, but the rest of her looked...*soft*. She couldn't remember ever having worn this color. She swished to the side to better view her back. Darting had been added to the base of her spine, accentuating her curves, and she blushed, imagining Shaw's expression with vivid accuracy. She must be sure to keep it and wear it upon her return.

If I return, interrupted her head.

Lux's breath caught as that hollow sensation in her chest returned. It'd been worse last night, as most things were, but she'd been doing better at burying it during the daytime. It was both unexpected and unwanted in how wide it suddenly yawned.

"Who would have guessed you'd grow so sick of being alone so quickly. That used to be all you knew." Her reflection revealed one eyebrow cocked in accusation until her eyes darted to something of greater interest.

She stepped forward.

The mirror upon the wall had been encased in dark wood, and that wood, she noticed now, had seen the hands of an artist. Lux brushed her fingertips along the carved vines and thorns, but it was only when the pad of her forefinger traced the familiar shape of a letter, that she realized this was similar to the gate outside. These carvings created words, and those words contained a message.

She leaned back to better view what it said.

May Brilliance Lead You To The Greatest Destination

"May brilliance—" Lux broke off and scoffed. "Literal or a riddle? Hmm, I hate it either way."

A soft tap interrupted her musings.

"I've arrived to escort you to breakfast," spoke a subdued voice outside the door.

"Damn it all!" Tripping on her skirt, Lux flew to the dressing room, where she pulled on hose and boots and combed her damp hair with her fingers. She caught sight of herself in a looking glass and couldn't help but laugh.

Let them see the wild-haired girl and her dirty boots and think she's off to ensnare a frost-eyed collector now.

Imbeciles.

Chapter Seventeen

Lux trailed her hand along the balustrade. Not a scratch snagged her finger.

She watched her serious escort discreetly. Hildred refused to connect her gaze with Lux's, but the woman didn't seem frightened, only unsure. Like she must be given directions at every turn. Maybe she was new here.

The staircase loomed as silence spread between them, and Lux slowed at the balcony's end. The portraits of the late Grimrook family would not be ignored. There were a fair few of them, and they all appeared similar with various shades of dark hair and light eyes. Before she realized, she'd stopped entirely and said, "Is the family buried here? Somewhere on the grounds?"

"In the garden."

"*In* the garden?"

"The Saints honor their sacrifice."

Lux swung her head around. "*Sacrifice?*"

"We do not honor that one."

Lux knew where Hildred would point before she did. "I suppose not. But what did you mean? About the rest of her family."

"Come. Breakfast is being served, and the lords won't like it if you're late."

Hildred continued down the stairs, but Lux was slow to listen and slower to follow. The remainder of Riselda's family all wore intense or severe expressions. Imagining them now in the manor she stood in caused a cascading sense of foreboding. It suddenly all seemed too…heavy.

She turned away with the same sense of turning her back on the Shield, sure she could feel Riselda's painted eyes watching her go.

"The morning room is through here," Hildred called up.

Lux made her way down. When she reached the second-floor landing, she peered along the corridor where the woman had pointed. "Where?"

There was no answer. Lux turned to catch Hildred scurrying away, the maid stopping only when she neared the painting of the murdered founder of Mothlock's Society. There, she curtsied so deeply, Lux thought she would surely prostrate herself beneath its frame. But after several moments, Hildred rose and loped down the final staircase. Lux turned back to the wide corridor, bewildered and at a loss of where to go next.

There are too many doors.

She paused beneath the arched frame marking the second floor's entrance, the stone walls beyond it black as everything else and extending seemingly without end. It was dim, almost ominous, and the sconces' blue cast could do little against it. Not even the sun allotted through the narrow windows brightened the expanse.

Her nerves pricked.

Enough of that. I've come here for a purpose and no dark corridor is going to deter me.

Bolstered somewhat, she walked to the first door, gripped the etched, silver knob, and turned.

"Lux."

Her hand lifted away at once. When she searched for who had called her name, she discovered a robed figure in a doorframe farther down. Corvin lowered his hood. His light hair, nearly white, stood out starkly. As did his grin.

"Wrong door."

Lux sucked her lip between her teeth for all of a second before she said, "I hope one of your preserved books has a map of this place."

Corvin continued to smile as she made her way toward him. Her boots echoed against the flagstones and the chilled sea air crept through the cracks of the window to remind her of her damp head.

"Well?" she said when she reached him.

Corvin's eyes flicked down her dress before returning to hers. "Well what?"

"A map? Does it exist?"

"I'm sure it does. But you won't need it." He made to return to the room behind him.

"I'm sure I will," she said, following. Her gaze swept over his long, black robe. At how it just brushed the floor, allowing for only a sliver of his polished boots to show.

He glanced over his shoulder. "I will be your map."

Lux narrowed her eyes at him. "Except when you leave me for some new collection."

"Oh." His words snaked around him to find her. "That won't be for some time now."

She hardly heard him. Instead, her attention had fixed upon the dining table. The sheer, imposing size of it. She stopped before the gleaming wood, her quick glance revealing a massive fireplace, beams arched like a blackened ribcage overhead and nothing but portraits of aged men and burning lamps on the walls.

"This is not quite..."

"I know. The old collectors like the dark here in Mothlock. They believe it protects the knowledge stored within. I'm sorry if you find it stifling; I suppose I'm used to it."

"Within the walls or within their heads?" Except it wasn't only dark. It was positively *gloomy*. She'd expected an area labeled as a morning room to contain a window to observe said morning, at least.

She'd rather breakfast in her bedchamber. On her windswept balcony.

Corvin didn't answer, and she turned to find him speaking with a man dressed similarly to Manphry. The person rose from the floor. When he disappeared beyond a revolving wall, Lux stared after him.

"Passage to the kitchen," explained Corvin. "Most of the common rooms have something similar for the attendants' easy access. You see? Morning rooms and hidden doors. Look at how well of a map I've become already."

She sat in the chair he pulled out for her. "I fear you'll not get anything else done."

Corvin only smiled. Another of his attendants entered the room from the inconspicuous door, hands ladened with a matching pair of covered dishes. Corvin took a seat across from her, and they waited in silence as the plates were set before them, lids removed with a flourish.

"That will be all, Godfrey. Return to the kitchen. Tea, Lux? Or coffee?"

Lux curled her lip at Godfrey's collapse to the ground. She waited for him to stand again before glancing across the table, to Corvin's gloved hand poised over a teapot, a taller carafe set beside it. "Tea, please."

He nodded and poured her a cup. She reached for it, tracing the peculiar depiction of a melancholic statue when it settled in her palms. It didn't move. "Your staff is...especially devoted."

"You speak of the attendants' homage I assume? It's a tradition of the society, to pay their respect to the role. Hardly *my* choice, but I won't deny them it. I hope you like honey, by the way. This particular batch is a specialty to the area."

Saints above. She took advantage of the cup in her hand and drank a slow sip. By the time she swallowed, she managed, "I do."

Drizzled overtop artfully toasted bread, with a poached egg and a light sauce, Lux wondered if she could even stomach it. The last time she'd breakfasted with someone, it had been with Shaw. Lux peeked through her lashes. Corvin poured himself a cup of dark liquid from the carafe and paid her no attention.

She pressed her thumb and forefinger to her eyes.

"How did you sleep?"

"Like the dead," she replied, only for her abdomen to tighten at his smirk. She hurried on. "I'd forgotten what a bed could feel like."

"It's true, inns are a far cry from our own. I'm happy to be home." He studied her a moment more. "And Kent has seen you?"

"You don't recognize his work?"

"Oh, I do." He lifted his cup again to his lips—slower, this time. Lux shifted in her seat. "I've spoken with our healer, Lord Artemis. He's very interested in your case. I'm told to escort you to him at midmorning."

"What did you tell him?"

"Only what you told me. I saw nothing for myself, so I didn't think I should speculate."

"Thank you," she said, and she meant it sincerely. Because even if it turned out she was only jaded and had followed the wrong money trail, at least she would have this.

At her first bite, the taste of honey bloomed across her tongue. Lux's fingers tightened on her fork. "Any news on your poisonings?" she asked.

Corvin leaned back in his chair. "Not yet. Silas planned to return Mistress Lefroy to her home in Loxlen, and while there investigate the situation. The only other death occurred in the city as well. I hope they find the culprit quick. It wouldn't bode well to have an active attacker on the loose, overshadowing a celebration."

"Would it be postponed? It's only two days from now, isn't it?"

"Not since its inception has that ever happened. I doubt it."

"Hmm," she replied. But really, she thought it odd he hardly considered it an option. Her attention shifted to the wall. "Those are former members of your society? Or current?"

"Current but passed to the Beyond. Once inducted, you're considered a part of it forever. Even in death." He didn't turn to look but continued with his meal. "The Lords of Mothlock. All have accomplishments worthy of honor. Like the one with the draping mustache—a brilliant stone mason. He built Mothlock into what it is today."

"It isn't all original to the Grimrooks?"

"Most of it is. But there were rooms we required that weren't present in its original state."

Lux sipped at her tea. "Like the vault?"

Corvin winked. "Like the vault."

He made to swallow the last of his coffee when a deep thrum pulsed through the manor. Lux jerked upright, her eyes sweeping the room. "What is that?" The sound continued to beat several more times before ceasing. When her bewildered stare met Corvin's, he appeared unphased.

"That would be our call to Invocation." He stood and tossed his napkin onto the plate. "Return to your room and rest. Exploring can wait. You've had an arduous journey, and this period won't be long. Excuse me."

He hardly spared the time to offer one of his smiles before leaving through the door.

Lux stared after where he'd gone and startled only a little when the wall opened, admitting the same man who had brought their meals from below-stairs. Lux nodded politely at Godfrey, who didn't return it. He ducked his head and began stacking their dirtied things.

Her jaw hardened. *The most unfriendly staff in existence,* she thought. And that included the mayor's mansion.

Her attention slid to the wall he'd come from, and her senses heightened with curiosity. She wouldn't be ordered about, and exploring couldn't wait. Lux slipped from her seat. She made a show of examining the portraits on her route, lingering slightly longer on the mustached collector. The seriousness of these men bled through the paint—they took to their career of books with great responsibility.

But at least they're actually dead, she thought.

With every breath, she eased nearer to that particular wall, and once she reached it, her fingernail traced the vague seam. She glanced over her shoulder. Godfrey was still occupied with balancing a teapot in addition to plates.

She only wanted to open it. To see how it functioned.

That was a lie, but it was what she would say if questioned.

Lux held her breath and pushed.

And cried out when she fell.

Chapter Eighteen

Her knees cracked against stone, her body tumbling down several stairs before stopping. Lux lay draped backwards on the staircase, gasping for air.

Devil take me.

Everything hurt, but her palms screeched loudest. She rolled off them, cradling her hands to her chest and biting her lip against a sob. Pained tears puddled in her eyes.

She'd *tripped* on her saintforsaken dress. "What sort of torturous climb is this for the help?" she cried. Because not only were the stairs sharply spiraled, but the steps were too narrow; she'd stepped down like they were normal, not deadly.

Lux climbed to her feet. Still cradling her hands, she looked toward the door to a seam hardly visible. Really, she could see nothing much in the scant light.

Her knees ached terribly. When she glanced at her palms, she found while they weren't bleeding, they were fiery red. "Devil's tits," she seethed.

Should she go down? The pain had bled the worst of her interest from her. She doubted the stairway led to the vault anyway. Probably only to a kitchen, as she'd been told. She sniffed away the remainder of her tears. The passage smelled the same as most dark, enclosed spaces: a musty mixture of dust and stone. She'd never liked such things and positively hated them now.

But you only have two days, the matter-of-fact side of her demanded she remember. Two days and only herself to count on.

She stepped forward and winced at the painful flare in her knees. Maybe it did only go to the kitchen—but it was better than obeying Corvin's direction to do nothing. She moved farther down the staircase.

"You're going the wrong way, Lucena."

Lux flattened herself against the wall. *That voice...* She waited, crouched like a thief, and didn't so much as breathe.

But no one appeared; the voice said nothing else. And as time ticked on, she wondered...there *had* been a voice. Hadn't there?

Her muscles protested loudly now. Lux tentatively peeled herself from the wall. *It was nothing. No one here knows my given name. No one here knows...* She pushed away until she stood in the center of the stairs, trembling as if she'd caught a terrible fever. Because while the trees had spoken to her, too, it had never sounded like this. Like her nightmares. Like the words had come from her very own mind.

She had no courage left for this. Goosebumps lifted along her skin.

"You're only having a conversation with your own head. You've done it all the time." It had been a habit since losing her parents young. With neither family nor friends, who else did she have to speak to other than herself?

Lux continued on her way. She rounded the next curve faster than the one before and nearly toppled down the stairs a second time. She caught herself on the stones—only to stumble backward.

Someone stood at the bottom.

Lux hurtled back around the corner and pressed herself against the wall, trying as best she could to quiet her breaths. Who the devil was down there? It couldn't be a collector.

Whomever it was dressed all in white.

"A buried girl. Let her out."

Be quiet! she snarled at the voice. The girl might be real. For all Lux knew, she might be an attendant.

Dressed entirely different from any of the others...

Lux edged along the wall. She would look again. If this was like the bathwater and thus a figment of her mind, the person would be gone. Or at least standing the same as she had been before. And if she were real, she must have moved by now.

Lux breathed a deep breath at the corner's curve before peering around—

Right into another's eyes.

She screamed.

The figure had come partway up the stairs, and though she'd moved as Lux had hoped she would, it was in the worst possible way. The steps were solidly beneath her; the girl's feet did not touch them. They somehow suspended above.

It can't be. Ghosts are not real.

But why wasn't the figure fading?

Why did it look just like Lux herself?

Lux's heart racketed against her ribs. Because—*saints above*—maybe ghosts *were* real. Maybe madness took over families and elixirs could make the dead speak and if her forgery of an aunt had to cough up her appendix for a seed what else could happen?

Really, what did Lux even know of the world?

She stared into the apparition's empty eyes. When it moved closer, she backed away. "If you can't even stand on the stairs, then you cannot hurt me."

Maybe that would be true too.

"Tell me who you are," she ordered when the figure floated only several stairs down.

The apparition's dark tresses hung curled but limp, wet over a nightgown, and its feet were bare and dirty. Aside from the soulless stare, Lux would have been positive it was human. But then the figure opened its mouth and revealed rows of pointed and blackened teeth.

Lux's head lightened. "Nevermind. I don't wish to know."

"*Lucena Thorn. Necromancer. Thief. Murderer.*"

Lux would go back. This instant. She'd obey Corvin and return to her room; she'd even lock herself inside.

"*Shine bright, little Lux. And do not forget your dreams.*"

"Enough," she hissed.

"*So hateful. So lonely.*"

Lux stepped up sideways, keeping the curved wall at her back. The apparition didn't move, but its stare followed her. "Leave me alone!"

"*Never alone. Not anymore.*"

"What in the devil's own hell are you?"

"*I am you.*"

Lux had taken two steps more before the apparition began to follow again. "You are nothing like me."

"*I am your darkness. I am your talent. Look at what you have made.*"

Lux was sure she would be sick. She turned to face the figure fully, her steps moving steadily backward. Meanwhile, the creature stalked her the same. Its lips pulled back into a menacing sort of smile, and she could see then its gums were rotted alongside its teeth.

This is a nightmare...

But aren't I awake?

She thought she was, but who knew for certain? She had seen this face while asleep. Perhaps this was a dream within a dream, and maybe—if she pinched herself—she would wake up. Lux did so, her nails nearly puncturing her skin, but other than gritting her teeth, nothing changed. She was still walking backward up the passageway. The apparition still mimicked her movements. If she ran, would this creature run too?

She found she didn't want to test the theory.

"If that's true, then I regret it. Tell me how to be rid of you."

The figure's smile morphed. Lux thought it looked terrifyingly pleased. "*Rid of me? I am innate. Your other half. Carve me out or keep me. Either way, I am yours.*"

"I don't want to do either of those things."

The blackened mouth bared into a snarl and shrieked, "*CHOOSE!*"

The creature's scream outpitched her own. Lux leapt backward before she sprinted.

Around and around, she ran.

She saw the door. It wasn't close enough. Her hand stretched before she even reached it. Until—finally—her fingers met stone. She spun for one last glance.

The apparition stood behind her. It smiled.

"You're. Not. Real." Lux whipped back and pushed. She jolted when the figure morphed beside her. When it bent to her ear.

"You're not real," she whimpered at the same time the creature murmured, "*We're a monster.*"

And stepped into her skin.

Chapter Nineteen

Lux flew.

Past Godfrey and his pile of broken dishes. Through the morning room door and along the dark corridor. She ran onto the landing, where an immortalized Alixsander Alesso could witness her heaving breaths, and then she ran down the staircase.

Lux sprinted right out of Mothlock.

Gravel shifted beneath her boots, and an autumn breeze cooled her damp scalp. She gulped heaps of fresh air and dappled sunlight before finally closing her eyes.

"You'll be all right. You'll be fine." And maybe it was the combination of sea air and sun that had her believing it.

Anxious thoughts. *Panic*. Sometimes her brain created alternate realities in which she'd get lost navigating. This could be like that. It could be—

Lux opened her eyes to the garden. On either side of the courtyard the brambles rolled red and wild, devouring the grounds. The only parts left alone were the stone paths and circular drive. Not even the iron fence was spared. She ran her tongue over her canines, then she turned and stared up at the manor.

It appeared as formidable as the day before, with its towering pinnacles and barred windows. The morning light hadn't reached the crawling vines, and the flowers were closed and pointed like arrows toward the ground.

Her brow furrowed over trying to imagine a family here. Children here. And she snorted aloud at her own judgements, because she'd grown up breathing thick air and smoke. 'Formidable' did not matter so much, she thought, when one had the sea.

I don't have to stay if I don't wish to, she told herself. *I can leave right now.* But the words didn't permeate her soul so much as they should. In fact, they didn't even scratch the surface. It almost felt like she told herself...a lie.

She frowned up at the stonework. Lux couldn't deny she felt drawn to it somehow. And maybe that would have bothered her, but it didn't feel the same as when she'd been drawn to the devouring gallow trees. It was softer. More embracing, less consuming.

"I feel entirely mismatched between my brain and body," she said to the air and brambles. "This cannot be my new normal."

But what if it is?

Her nightmares had never manifested before. The closest she'd come to anything similar was braving her early childhood home. But even then, it was only her traumatic memories growing bold; she could still blink those away.

She'd not been able to blink away the muck in the tub. Nor the apparition from the passageway.

She couldn't dispel the voice in her head.

Her finger reached to her neck. To where she'd once been injected with a solution that brought her insecurities to shadowed reality. But she'd not been attacked with any needle here. Had she drunk something she shouldn't? Eaten something toxic? Maybe the pressure had stressed out her senses.

Lux's true fear beat somewhere underneath, but she refused to dig that far right now.

Maybe she really should return to her room. Rest, as Corvin had so graciously directed. Wait for him to return for her.

The sea air urged her otherwise.

It promised a cure—albeit a momentary one—by standing at the edge again, absorbing the spray against her skin and relishing the feel of some sort of freedom. But...there was also a second path through the brambles. Where she'd chosen to go right yesterday, what would going left reveal now? It couldn't lead nowhere, she didn't think. What would have been the purpose of that?

Lux didn't think anymore on it.

She set off down the path.

Though it was cool, she didn't miss her cloak. The sun had finally severed the clouds, and now it shone unobstructed upon her head. The feel of it brushing against her temple did more than any cup of tea ever could. Out here, she thought, she might breathe every tumultuous emotion away.

Still, she kept darting glances from her periphery. The brambles shifted too much for her liking, and they were uncomfortably tall. Taller than most people she knew. Clearly, no one minded this wild garden.

And while the air did smell a little sweet, she now noticed it smelled a bit like iron too.

Like blood.

She tucked her elbows in farther when the breeze brushed them aside. Scarlet stems topped by a mimicry of teeth peeked from underneath. "Don't even think of it," she snapped at them. "I'm not some all-forgiving botanist—I'll rip you out by the roots."

The strange plants shrank back from her threat. Or it might have been the wind.

The path curved then, and a bench appeared, the seat hardly visible in its overgrown state. A short stone statue perched just beyond it. Lux slowed, stopped, and tilted her head.

The stone had been sculpted into a man, his face pulled into a grimace, the edges worn smooth. She frowned at it. A single vine had wrapped its way around the base, up and up, until it encircled his throat with a deep-blue bloom to match the manor's. The mayor's mansion hadn't anything but busts of the mayor himself lining its rich halls; she'd never seen a fully formed statue before. Unlike the saintlike style guarding Mothlock's shrine to its dead founder, this one had been intricately detailed and was quite smaller. She could see the man was made to be handsome, with a strong nose and jaw, and hair to his shoulders. But like the brambles, he was unkempt.

Forgotten, perhaps?

Lux shook herself free of his gaze before leaving it behind.

She curved immediately into a second statue and stumbled to a halt. Her hand clutched her throat. "You *scared* me," she scolded it. Or *her*. The form of a woman only stared back, her eyes sad and stone cheeks drooped in melancholy. She was not strangled like the man before, but her bare feet were covered in moss. Another bench was set beside it.

"No one is assigned to your upkeep, either, I see." The statue only pondered her in all its pitiful sorrow. Lux couldn't help herself. She knelt at its feet.

The moss was darkly green and soft to the touch. She pressed a finger against it to be sure, but nothing leached from it. It was regular, with hardly any scent at all. She pried it away.

The dirt beneath crumbled and blew in the breeze. What was left, Lux brushed aside. "There you are," she said, a moment before her fingertips snagged on an indentation. "What—"

Oh...

ROSAMUND GRIMROOK
The House of Grimrook

Lux shoved to her feet, her hands limp at her sides. She stared at the woman and then at what must be laid beneath. They'd been buried in the garden, Hildred had said.

"What a way to be remembered. Who carved you like this?" Then she glanced over her shoulder at the man.

Lux hurried back to him, and while she didn't need to clear any moss, she did need to shift the gnarled fingers of the vine. It was loath to let go, but once several of them broke, the remainder retracted. She lifted the vine above the statue's base.

GRANVILLE GRIMROOK
The House of Grimrook

Lux dropped the plant and backed away. She stared down the path. Because the sun had shifted, and her eyes knew what to search for, she found more pale outlines dotting the way.

Graves.

She did not stand in any garden.

She stood in the cemetery of Riselda's family.

And Corvin hadn't told her.

Chapter Twenty

At the end of the path rose a wooden door, arched the same as the one leading to the sea at the other side. Perched atop it was a crow.

"In all the—you do know this isn't the forest, Crow? There are hardly any trees out here, and there are cliffs." The crow cocked its dark head to better view her and listened. "So you think yourself as good as a seabird on this wind? That's bold."

She waited for the creature to caw its outrage at the comparison or, at the very least, to hop from one part of the fence to the other. But it did neither, and its direct stare began to unnerve her.

"This is a graveyard. You're disturbing the dead." The animal gnashed its beak. "You'll leave them alone. The statues, I mean. They're not for perching on. Or *worse*."

She wondered why she bothered scolding the creature. It would clearly do what it wanted, and especially did not need to listen to *her*. But she'd felt a fierce protectiveness build while making her way through the so-named garden. She did not know these people; really, she shouldn't have cared. Yet, as she cleared vines and moss and dirt away from a number of statues, she'd found, in fact, she very much did.

Lux scoffed at the bird, strode up to the door, and yanked.

The door did not budge.

She released the ring before gripping it a second time. This try she pulled harder, thinking it must be stuck—swollen from the salt. Still, it didn't give.

It's locked? Why? The same door existed at the other side. Why couldn't she also go through this one?

The crow cawed. Lux ignored it. It flew down, stirring her hair, only to return and land gracefully on the iron fence once more. It cawed again.

Her first instinct was to call the animal a bothersome beast and frighten it into flight. Except her second reminded her of the blood debt she owed a bird she could no longer pay. "Are you trying to help?" she asked. "The brambles are too thick over there. Did you see those flowers? They're made of *teeth*."

The crow didn't speak further, merely tilting its head again. It eyed her wary approach.

"What did you find?" she asked it.

She peered beneath the animal's perch, and realized she'd been wrong. The brambles had left a natural gap between their branches and the fence here. Though she'd been explicitly told not to, Lux stepped off the path. She crept carefully along the bars until she stood under the bird, and it was there she discovered it—the metal bent slightly off center. Not without tucking her long skirt, she couldn't fit, but maybe—

A deep thud came from outside her line of sight. It startled her; she dropped to a crouch at once. Leaning, she peered through the brambles, back to where she'd come from. She knew that sound; she wished she didn't. It was the thick noise of a blow to the gut. And it was much too close.

"If I hear another *whisper* of your grumblings... If I hear the name *Alesso* even leave your pruned mouth, I'll sew your lips shut myself. Turn them into a ribboned hem for your ugly face, what do you think of *that?*"

A volley of hoarse muttering proceeded to bombard her after that harsh visual, and Lux patted down her bodice before groaning inwardly. *You forgot the knife, you idiot!*

"...no, absolutely *not*. They're not for you to command until you've proven yourself. We have all bided our time and so will you. Have I made myself clear? Or do you need a second lesson to be sure?"

More hoarse muttering. A grunt of approval. Lux heard shifting and then nothing.

Good. They must have continued back down the walk.

She straightened. *Alesso?* What about the name of a dead man had them so bothered? Lux glanced behind her to the opening in the bars. Her hands shifted over her skirt. If she gathered them just right, she could slip through and see what lay on the opposite side. Even if Corvin missed her absence for a few minutes.

She looked for the crow, but the bird had flown.

An aggressive caw resounded from behind her. Her fingers fell away as she spun.

"Which circle of Hell is this?" shouted a voice in outrage.

Lux crept around the brambles' edge until she could make out what happened down the lane. Until she could see the crow circled a giant of a man in collectors' garb, his hands outstretched to swat it away. His hood fell back.

The crow descended again, and this time its talons made contact, scraping along the man's hairless head. He roared. Lux stepped onto the path, her back to the door. She'd never known a crow to behave this way outside of a singular time, and that crow's eyes had been murky, revived beyond what it should have. This one was not like that.

"Crow!" she shouted.

The bird paused its attack. It cawed again—rather irritated, she thought. Then it lifted higher into the sky and was gone.

The man didn't turn at first. With his back to her, Lux saw angry lines had been carved into his—rather unsightly—pale skull and his shoulders heaved. His gloved hands lifted to his hood as he shifted to face her, and Lux startled at the glimpse of his features before they were hidden. Sagging, mottled, and with grey undertones, his skin seemed to have forgotten it was alive. His gaze pierced her, a blue so light it could be called silver.

She watched his chest rise with a deep inhale, and then he laughed. "A necromancer and a friend to crows. What other beasts have you befriended?"

Lux recognized his voice. "Befriended is probably too strong a word. Tolerate, maybe. Are you injured, Lord Kent?"

His hood shifted, dipping down her person. "I've survived worse attacks in my lifetime, Ms. Thorn. Please don't worry over me." Finishing his assessment, he added, "The color suits you. I knew it would."

"Thank you."

"You're very welcome."

When he neither moved nor said anything further, she fought not to glance behind her. Toward the locked door she'd been about to force herself around. But she couldn't help asking, "Does the door on this end lead to another cliffside trail?"

Kent's hood shifted. "Indeed, it does. But that one is unusable due to erosion of the landscape. We keep it locked now. For safety."

"How sad. I would have liked to have seen it."

"Well, come along then," he said, and Lux's eyes widened. "I'll allow you a glimpse."

"You're serious?"

"You're wearing my dresses. I'd love for you to wear my *gown* come the banquet. A fair exchange?"

Fairer than I thought. "Yes, I think so."

He paused for a moment. "You're a serious one." A soft laugh left him as he made his way toward her. Then he passed her by.

Lux was slow to turn. Once she did, his exceptionally broad shoulders blocked her view of anything. She heard a click but couldn't see how it was made. She'd not noticed any keyhole when she'd stood in front of it before, but apparently she'd not looked hard enough. The door swung inward with a protesting screech.

"There you are," he said and stepped aside.

Lux moved to fill the space, her hand reaching reflexively toward the frame once she did. He'd been honest; the path crumbled sharply away. Her breath caught over the disconnect between the narrow lane behind her and the sudden openness outside the door. She felt strangely if she were to step through, she'd walk clean into another world.

A world of drowning waves and slow deaths, her macabre mind granted. If she'd even survive the fall first.

Her eyes snagged on something then. A protrusion from the cliff. A cone-shaped roof, black shingles in disrepair. She spun back to the collector.

"What is that?"

His hood shifted, and she knew he followed where she pointed. His voice rumbled, "That would be Grimrook House."

Her brow furrowed. "House? I thought the family lived in Mothlock."

"They did. Eventually. When the erosion worsened. Come back from there now. There's a chill in the air and we wouldn't want you uncomfortable."

He guided her away with a slight tug at her sleeve. Lux's lip curled, but otherwise she did nothing. Because she realized something staggering. The impressive and imposing Mothlock Manor didn't call to her at all. *That* house did.

Kent blocked her view once more, the door screeching a second time.

"But why build up a manor on an already crumbling cliff?"

"The wonders of a skilled mason, Ms. Thorn. Now, I think it's time we go back inside." As if urged by his words, the brambles shifted, arching over the path beside her. She stumbled away only to notice they did the same on the opposite side. "It doesn't help to linger," he added, his tone ominous.

Lux, carefully moving nearer to him, said, "They sense a person's presence?"

He turned away and began to walk. She couldn't share the path as she might have with Corvin, and so she fell in line behind him. When she glanced over her shoulder, the brambles had yet to return to their original place, still stretching high and menacing over the lane. The statues were gone inside them. All she saw were stems of teeth.

"Your heart," he answered.

She shivered, the chill he'd warned her of suddenly apparent. "And wish to do what with it?"

The collector remained silent for longer than she expected. "Such a question makes me wonder at your history, young Necromancer. But as for its answer: to siphon from it. The plant is called guardian's leech. In that it is both protective of its territory and consuming. Those tooth-like petals are hollow. In one moment, they may inject a toxin. In the next they might draw in. It is important you don't ever allow the latter."

Her face twisted behind his back. "Allow? And how does one go about dissuading a plant from drinking your blood?"

Kent glanced over his shoulder, his light eyes hidden in shadow. "By telling it so. Of course, once it has a taste, it will not stop. Not until it has taken its fill."

Her gut told her she knew the answer; she asked anyway. "How much is that?"

"All you have."

She stared at the brambles with renewed horror. "Corvin said nothing of that. Only about the toxin."

"Yes, well, they're usually kept well fed, I'll give him that. I'm sure he didn't want to frighten you off after just finding you. But you're here and out in the garden alone. I will not coddle anyone."

Well fed? Devil's own tits. "You feed them blood?"

"Are you being obtuse? He'd said you were bright. Of course we feed them what they need."

Lux's anger flared at once. Her lips parted to say something scathing. However, in that brief moment, she recalled exactly how the giant of a tailor had pummeled a man only minutes ago. And there was no one out here but them. Her teeth clenched. She ran her thumbs along each pointed nail.

Kent continued, "I'm sorry your breakfast didn't go as you wanted. I heard you'd run from the manor. You were reported as rather indisposed. Are you enjoying your time at Mothlock? It requires some adjustment for most."

Lux could outrun him, she knew. Barring the problem of being enclosed and unsure how to open a gate that looked as if it weighed more than a carriage. She bit down on her anger, but it wouldn't return to less than boiling.

"Too early to say. It hasn't even been a full day," she ground out.

"Hasn't it? My, how slow time goes when in anticipation for something."

Lux didn't answer. Instead, she focused on her breaths. Focused on forcing her heart rate to ease. She glanced again toward the melancholic woman as they passed her by, her stone features fraught.

She blurted, "What do you know of the madness of brilliance?"

The man slowed. He stopped, and when he turned around, she could feel his hard stare. "The madness of brilliance," he repeated.

Her nails dug into her wrist. She waited.

"It is very rare, what you mention." But before Lux could latch onto any small relief, he said, "Of those who have suffered, it is the dark brilliances that progress the quickest. The Grimrook family is the most notable for falling to it. Some faster than others."

Dark brilliances. Around and around the phrase went in her head. She wasn't sure she breathed. "I've heard that term before. I didn't know brilliances had categories."

"Anything and anyone can be categorized. Casting of curses. Manipulations. Necromancy. These sorts of enchantments feed on dark energies. You feed yours draughts of death. A necessary darkness, but darkness all the same. Tell me, have you fed it other things?"

She thought, belatedly, she should stop them, but for once the words tumbled out. She wanted too badly to be put at ease. "Guilt. Hopelessness."

He nodded, soaking in what she admitted. "They yearn to grow, our brilliances. Feed it more than it was accustomed to, even once, and it will stretch. I would proceed cautiously if I were you."

With that, he turned around, and when he continued down the path, this time, she did not follow.

Chapter Twenty-One

Corvin found her sitting on the stone walk, her back leaned against the overgrown bench. She couldn't risk sitting on it.

"There you are," he said, and after several moments without a reply, he settled beside her.

Lux didn't move. Her chin rested on her bent knees, her gaze upon the brambles. Her eyes were focused solely on the ground beneath. On a hand—it's pointed nails grey and cracked—raking in the dirt over and over. A slightly bent wrist was attached to it. The rest disappeared into the undergrowth.

"Do you see it?" she asked.

"See what?"

"The hand."

She waited for him to speak. Waited to see if the apparition would reveal more of itself. Waited for the nightmare's voice to return.

"No."

"But I do. It's the third time. Seeing something that isn't really there. But I've felt it before then. In my head. I've felt it growing bolder since Verity."

Corvin's palm cupped her far shoulder, his arm draping heavily along her back. "It'll be all right, Lux."

Her attention flicked to his touch, and when she looked again at the brambles, the corpse-like hand retracted until it was gone. "It doesn't feel like it."

"I told you I'd take you to see our healer. And I'm here to make good on that promise." His gloved fingers tightened on her shoulder before dropping away. He stood and stretched out his hand. "Come with me. He's waiting."

It felt like she'd only blinked, and she stood again before Alixsander's portrait. By the next they were down a third-floor corridor and standing at one of its black doors. Corvin knocked.

The door swung inward on Lux's next breath. A person stood behind it. Short and portly, robed and hooded.

"You're late," he said.

"My apologies," said Corvin.

"It was my fault," said Lux.

Lord Artemis, the healer, sniffed from beneath his hood and marched into the room.

Corvin indicated for her to go in ahead and she did, her eyes on the table and shelves and everything in between. Her heart clenched. It looked so much like her workroom—aside from the clearly nicer finishes—her grief rebounded. She did *not* miss Ghadra. But she missed that room a startling amount.

Dried herbs hung from strings slung along one wall while bottles and jars and vials made up another. Drawing farther into the room, Lux stared longest at the counter, where all manner of tortuous looking instruments were set. Her heart released as her jaw clenched instead. Now this was less reminiscent of her workroom and more the mayor's.

She stared hardest at the line of needles.

Her nerves jolted when the door snicked closed behind them.

"Now, Ms. Thorn. Lord Corvin tells me you're experiencing some unwanted symptoms related to your fascinating gift of necromancy. Do tell me more."

Lux eyed the healer warily. He skirted about the room until he found a stool beside his questionable counter whereupon he sat and propped his feet on the rung. Waiting.

She glanced at Corvin, who nodded his support. *Go on,* that gesture said.

Lux drew a long breath. "I performed a revival two days ago. I fainted immediately following. That's never happened, not once. Afterward—"

"How long have you been practicing?"

She frowned at the interruption. "Nearly a decade."

"Hmm. Okay. Continue."

Her stare narrowed. "*Then* I performed a smaller revival, for hopelessness. That one only left me with a strange buzzing, but I stayed conscious. Although for Mistress Lefroy—"

"Our investor?"

"For her, I fainted again."

"I see." His finger crept onto the counter where he began to toy with a syringe. "Have you ever exercised your brilliance so much in a single day?"

Lux worked quickly through her memories. "No," she said.

"It could be that you overtaxed yourself. Or you were ill from something else. A virus, perhaps, that only needed to run through your system."

"I don't—"

"Get up onto the table, Ms. Thorn."

"Excuse me?"

The healer rose from his stool. "I will need to perform an exam. You deny it could be a virus. Or that you were overtaxed. So I will have to assess for myself."

Lux scowled across the room at Corvin, who shrugged apologetically.

Old men, he mouthed and rolled his eyes.

She stepped toward the table.

"Up. Up." The healer patted the gleaming surface.

Lux's exhale was more a hiss, but she did as told. She climbed up and sat, facing him.

"Anything else I should know before I begin? Less guesswork is always best when it comes to healing."

Lux cleared her throat, acutely aware of Corvin behind her. She couldn't decide whether she preferred for him to stay or go.

I would prefer not to be here at all.

"Nightmares aren't new for me, but lately, I've been having them where the monster waiting for me is me. Only it's worsened, somehow. This morning, my bathwater turned black. By breakfast, I swore I saw myself in the dark. Even heard the thing speak. Just before I came here, I experienced it again. A hand in the garden."

"Hallucinations," murmured Artemis. "All right. Lie back."

Her muscles contracted at once. "Is that necessary?"

She'd never lain on her, or rather *Riselda's*, table—ever. Even when having her broken ankle set by that physician in Ghadra, she'd been propped. Just the idea felt abhorrently vulnerable.

"I'm afraid so. Here's a support." He reached beneath his counter to retrieve a flattened pillow covered in some sort of garden debris. He swatted it clean before laying it at the table's end. "Go on now."

Lux swung her legs onto the table and very carefully lay backward. She loathed every second; when her head hit the pillow, she choked on the scent of mildew.

"Very good," said the healer. "Corvin, come hold her hand."

Lux pushed to her elbows. "Why would he need to do that?"

"Because assessment can be disconcerting. I will need samples. Hair, to start."

Corvin came to stand beside the table. "He's assessed me before," he said. "It doesn't bother much."

Lux eased again to her back and searched for Artemis. He'd retreated to his counter. When he turned around, he carried a puffing beaker, a pair of tweezers, and the smallest blade.

He set them beside her head. "Hair first." He plucked a strand, and Lux scowled. He dropped it into the beaker where it sizzled to nothing. "And now blood."

Her insides seized. "I don't think so."

The healer's hood shifted toward her; he'd been reaching for her hand. "Why don't you think so?"

"Because I was told never to offer up my blood."

"Don't you ever, darling. Do you understand?" Riselda's hand lay atop Lux's head. "That's the main ingredient—in curses."

"Who told you that?"

Lux gritted her teeth. "Someone who didn't want me ever to be cursed."

"Well lucky for you, my dear, I am a healer, not a curse-wielder. And even if I were, curses are not all they're made out to be. Would you really suffer so much if I cursed you with two left feet or the inability to love?"

Lux swallowed hard. "Yes. I think I would suffer a lot actually."

"We don't need to agree. But you do need to believe me in that I won't harm you. That this *is* the only way."

"Go on, Lux," said Corvin. "He's telling the truth."

Her teeth pressed harder together. She didn't know to whom she should listen. She prodded at her instincts for some insight, but other than the fierce prick of nerves and a growing despair, she felt nothing distinct.

If she was broken beyond repair...

"Fine," she bit out. "Only a little."

Like it mattered.

"Excellent," said Artemis with entirely too much glee. He sliced the pad of her middle finger.

Lux hissed, but she didn't move. She allowed the healer to hold her finger over the beaker until several fat drops landed inside. They sizzled, same as the hair.

"Once more now," he said.

"Again?" She took the wrapping from his outstretched hand and wound it around her fingertip.

"The foot this time."

Lux immediately met Corvin's frost-like stare. "It was the same for me," he said.

"Of all the saintforsaken hells..." she grumbled.

Lux sat forward, and they gave her room. She unlaced her boot first then removed it. She stared at the stocking a moment before easing her skirt marginally higher. Her cheeks heated as she worked it free.

She lay back when she was through, staring at the herbs, and only winced a little when the sharp pain nipped through her toe. This time, the healer wrapped it for her.

"Perfect," he said. "Now drink."

Lux stared at the thimble he offered her. "Is that the elixir?"

"It is. An amount appropriate for the size of you. Drink up." She reached for the thimble and lifted her head, downing it in one swallow. "Her hand, Corvin," she heard him say, but already, it sounded far away.

Corvin's hand settled over hers.

At first, Lux didn't grip it back. While everything felt distant, it didn't otherwise feel abnormal. Then the pulsing started. She noticed it in her heart first, which made sense, she supposed, but she soon tightened every muscle as her every vessel came alive. They beat, fast and thudding, and once they began to squirm, she held onto Corvin's hand as if it were her only anchor to the real world.

"Oh. Oh dear," someone said.

Lux couldn't tell if the tremors were inside or out, but her vision warped. Things moved across her pupils. "Wait. It's too much," she seethed.

Corvin only squeezed her hand tighter.

"This is not good news."

Lux opened her mouth; she practically panted. She could feel the pressure of fingers on her temples but didn't know what they did. "*Please,*" she begged. "How much longer?"

"Just...a little...ahh. There. That's it."

The pressure left her forehead, and her veins stopped rioting at once. The pulsing remained elsewhere, but even that eddied with the next few beats of her heart. Lux allowed her eyes to fall closed, her hand to grow limp. She felt Corvin pull away.

"*Disconcerting?*" she said, low and murderous.

"Do you need a jolt?" said the healer. His voice, at least, had returned to its normal distance. "I keep a fresh carafe in my workroom."

"A jolt? That feels like what just happened!" Her eyes flew open, and in her next breath, her legs swung around to sit. Her wounded toe dangled, bandaged and throbbing. "You need to warn people beforehand. I wasn't at all prepared!"

Her entire chest *hurt*. Her time in the mansion's underground had left scars she hadn't fully realized until now. To be beneath someone's brilliance without means of escape... Her eyes welled with tears. She flung her hands up to stifle them.

"Would you still have done it?" he said.

"It depends if it worked." She heaved more slow breaths and then lowered her hands. "Well?"

Artemis inclined his head. "It worked precisely as it should, Ms. Thorn." He held a book out by either cover, its pages exposed to her. It revealed a figure, bent on their knees, a noxious cloud billowing from their head. A description she couldn't make out had been transcribed beneath it. "*Mania Malus*. Or rather, the madness of brilliance. Quite advanced, too, considering your hallucinations. I find myself dreadfully intrigued."

Lux heard Corvin's sharp inhale before losing her hearing entirely. A terrible whooshing sound had replaced all else. The young collector came around the table, his hand trailing along her frozen arm. When he stood in front of her, she stared up at him. She didn't know what he saw. Only that his face fell afterward. He said something, but she couldn't hear it. He slumped onto the healer's stool. His head dropped into his hands.

Lux noticed her vision tunneling. *What an odd thing.* She reached out to steady herself against toppling forward, but her fingers were numb. Her feet, too, in fact.

"I need... I'm..." she mumbled, and her lips tingled where they touched. *You cannot faint here,* she admonished herself. *You will not—*

"Breathe with me," echoed a memory. But it came too late.

Lux slumped forward as her vision went dark.

Chapter Twenty-Two

Cold pressed against her forehead. Her neck. Lux blinked awake. Her head throbbed, and it took too long to focus. When she finally did, she stared blearily at Corvin, watching as he adjusted his gloves.

"Blessed Saints. You fainted," he said.

Lux blew out a weak breath in reply.

"Can you stand?"

She nodded from her place on the floor.

Corvin gripped her beneath the arms, and she leveraged herself against him, pulling against his shoulders. "I'm sorry," she mumbled, as hot now as she was cold before. The flush swept her entire body. She refused to meet his eyes.

A steaming mug was shoved into her hands. Lux stared down at it. "Drink the coffee, Ms. Thorn," said Artemis, then he clinked his own cup against hers and sipped. "My apologies over my abrupt delivery of your diagnosis. I spend so much of my time now experimenting and studying. So many books, you'll understand; not even with all the time in the world, could I accomplish everything I want. Still, I should have been more tactful."

Lux didn't look at him. Instead, she leaned against the table behind her and stared into the mug of brown liquid. She didn't mind the smell, but it looked a concerning color. She lifted the cup to her lips and drank.

Her face twisted into a grimace. "Ugh! It's bitter."

"It won't jolt you enough if it's had any other way."

Against her better judgement, she braved a second sip. She didn't grimace this time, and when the bitterness doused her tongue, she embraced it. It matched the bitterness in her heart now. "What can be done?" she said.

Corvin's glance pricked at her profile, but she didn't turn toward him. She leveled her hard stare on Artemis.

The healer met it with a shadowed one of his own. "You have two options, and neither one has been practiced with any regularity."

Lux braced herself with another sip of the bitter drink.

"For the first: You do nothing. You learn to cope with your hallucinations and dysfunction as best you can. Eventually it will lead to your death, but at what age and by what means, it is impossible to tell. Most of the Grimrook family, for example, met their ends rather young and by secondary methods."

Lux felt as if she would never get the dark taste from her tongue. "Which sorts of methods?"

Artemis crossed his arms, revealing a paunch abdomen beneath the robe. "Accidents. Stabbings, drownings, being run over by a carriage. The mind can only handle so much."

"And the second option?" A sourness filled her mouth now, her stomach a riot.

"The second option is something I've been working on for quite some time. It's a means of removal. One I've had nothing but success with while in the experimental phase."

Lux straightened. "A removal of the madness?"

"Yes," said the healer and inclined his head. "Unfortunately, being as it is attached to your brilliance, that would have to come too."

"Attached to my—" She stared down at her fingers' grip on the mug. They were beginning to numb again.

"I've named it 'The Stripping'. It's a simple procedure but must be done with severe accuracy. Once completed, you should be returned to your rightful self. Sans necromancy."

Lux's balance shifted. She felt disembodied. "I need to sit down."

Corvin's hand was at her elbow, guiding her onto the table. "I'm so sorry, Lux," he murmured.

"This can't be all." Despair bloomed through her. "This can't be it."

"I feel I need to ask," began Artemis. "Considering the rarity of this. Does your family have any ties to this place?"

"No," Lux said immediately.

"Yet you look just like her. It's uncanny."

"I thought the same," said Corvin.

"Like who?" she asked.

You know who, her gut told her.

"Riselda Grimrook. Did you see her portrait? She was never found, you know. Perhaps you are a relation and were never made aware?"

"That's impossible."

"Impossible or undiscovered?"

Impossible or undiscovered...

Lux tumbled into a memory.

"Lucena is such a big name for her, Mads."

The man sitting beside her on the sofa reached across his thin frame to tweak her nose. Lucena scrunched her face and laughed.

"Only you would think so. No one calls me Mads, but you." Her mother came to sit at her other side.

Lucena squirmed happily. There was no better place than here, between the two people who loved her most.

"Hmm," hummed the man, undeterred. "What do you think, my darling? Your mother would keep your name as is. But I hear her every night. 'Shine bright', she says. Well, I'll call you Lux. That way you will never forget what a light you are."

Lucena grinned, nodding her agreement.

"She likes it," her father said.

"She likes everything," laughed her mother.

"It's better than Vesperine at any rate," he said, and her mother's face twisted and hissed, and Lucena grew frightened, because she didn't recognize that name as her own, only that it meant "before".

Before she was theirs.

Lux emerged from it choking. Her hand clutched at her chest as she hacked. Artemis began clinking glasses together while Corvin's palm met her back in sharp thwacks. She pushed him off.

"I'm fine," she wheezed. "I only swallowed wrong."

It wasn't a lie. The shock of a memory—only ever vague and mostly emotion—now clear as a mountain stream, had knocked the breath right out of her. She'd gasped haphazardly at its end.

The healer stilled in his preparations. "Death to the Devil, girl. What sort of bad luck are you carrying?"

"The eternal kind." Lux tipped her head back only to startle when the door slammed in.

"Oh! My apologies." A collector stood bewildered in the doorway. He came to his senses after a moment more. "There's...an ongoing incident with the staff. Someone's bleeding badly, and I'm not supposed to—"

"We'll see to it," snapped Corvin, which had Lux's eyes snapping to his in turn.

She'd never heard his tone so cutting. Her gaze raked his expression. He didn't return it but looked instead at Artemis. Some wordless agreement passed between them, one that had Corvin visibly relaxing.

"Lead the way, Lord Tobias," the healer said, and together the two men exited the workroom.

"What was that about?" she asked once they'd gone.

"Nothing you need to ever worry over," Corvin replied. "How are you feeling?"

"Numb." She stared in a haze at the closed door.

"You're in shock. Should I call for something other than coffee? I know you don't prefer it."

"I need nothing except to be alone."

Corvin grew quiet awhile. "All right. Let me walk you to your room."

Lux made her way around the table. Her attention shifted dazedly to the wall by the door, to the statue there. Another saint, intricate and crowned. A bowl of incense smoked at its feet.

Even faceless, she felt as if the saint watched her. That it judged.

She didn't know if she believed in Saints. But she could be swayed to believe in the Devil. What else would ensure she contracted some rare degeneration right as she planned to begin her life? What else would place these stepping stones directly in her path so she would end up beside the sea as she'd always wished, but also in Riselda's childhood home? That she would have to discover the woman's early portrait and be overwhelmed by the idea that maybe the mayor's daughter had been mistaken in that nameless wood. Maybe Riselda really had borne a child once upon a time and that child had become Lux's ancestor. That Riselda would then be tied to her too.

Lux did not know her birth parents. Her parents hadn't ever spoken of them. And aside from a strange feeling of isolation as her earliest memory, she had no further clues.

"She has no family," Morana had said.

"We are family," Riselda had said.

Lux climbed the staircases silently beside Corvin, and when she passed the Grimrooks' portraits, she could only glance and keep moving. Because those were not Riselda's eyes staring back at her today—but her own.

"Should I send up a meal for you?" he asked outside her door.

Lux stared at the engraved 7 until it blurred. "No, thank you."

"I feel like this is my fault."

Lux's vision sharpened as she turned toward him.

"I gave you false hope, speaking of the condition's rarity and praising Mothlock's healer. I shouldn't have. I know how much worse it is to raise your expectations only to have them dashed."

She absorbed every distraught line of his face. "You didn't give this to me. Someone else did." Her fingers closed over the knob. "Thank you for trying."

His hand settled atop hers before she could turn it. She stared at the contrast of dark leather against her pale skin. She didn't look at him.

"Will you consider the treatment?"

Lux shook her head. "I feel hollow enough. There'd be nothing of me left if you took my brilliance from me."

"I don't believe that. Not even for a moment."

Lux's eyes scrunched closed. "If nothing else, I was finally able to meet the sea outside of a daydream. That's something, at least."

Then she turned the knob and left Corvin behind.

Chapter Twenty-Three

She thought she would retch.

No, I won't.

Yes, I will.

Saliva pooled. She swallowed it away.

No, I won't!

She held a hand to her mouth, because maybe if she pressed hard enough, she wouldn't vomit her anger, her *despair*, over the bed's dark furnishings. But nothing prevented it from building inside her head like an overzealous tumor.

She'd been numb before. She wasn't any longer.

Feed.

Grow.

Madness.

"*You're free to be a great necromancer now. Rather than settling for a mediocre one.*"

Her whole life was a string of betrayals. Except this time, she had betrayed herself.

Lux had witnessed the consequences of madness. Riselda's voice, her laugh—they'd changed from one moment to the next. The effect had been chilling and jarring and Lux never wished to be in its presence again. But while lifeblood might have prolonged Riselda's years beyond any members of her family, it never did bring about a cure. Like the mayor's tumors, the disease began to eat again at once. The likelihood that the consumption of lifeblood hadn't been in practice with the remainder of the Grimrooks spoke to Lux's theory: It was not a family secret passed through the generations. It was knowledge Riselda had discovered all her own.

Knowledge she might have fled with.

Knowledge a burgeoning society might have wished to keep for themselves—

"Will you consider the treatment?"

Corvin's words burrowed into her like a thorn, and every time she shifted, she felt its sharp bite. All her life, her brilliance had elicited strong reactions. Poor or positive, it never mattered. She was rare. Powerful. She could do a remarkable thing. And for many years, it remained the only part of herself she was proud of. Her one source of confidence. It still was.

It is all I have. Who will I be if it's gone?

... no one.

Her grim thoughts were going to burn her from the inside out. Lux hid her head in the pillows. She'd never felt so broken in all her life.

Unfair. Unfair. Unfair.

The nauseous despair retracted, rootless, as her anger grew in strength. It licked at every part of her until her skin grew damp with it. And when she could take it no more, she bit into her knuckles until they cut—and screamed.

Only when it was done did she cradle her head in her hands. Her breaths were labored and loud in her ears.

"It isn't fair," she murmured, hoarse and aching. "None of it is fair."

How she wished she could have screamed for real rather than the voiceless imitation she'd allowed. But she didn't want to bring anyone running. Not when there wasn't a single one of them who could offer her comfort now.

Riselda had broken their rules and taken what they coveted. Why? Was it the madness that drove her to it?

You stole from them. And you were only a child. What did you see that I haven't? What did you know that I don't? Why did you run?

To Ghadra, of all places.

"My mind can't take anymore." But she knew it wasn't her mind at all, but her heart this time, causing her pains.

Before, those vulnerable words would never have left her mouth; they would have been swallowed by now. She'd become uncomfortably skilled at wallowing silently before burying her hurts deep. Except she'd lost that skill some time ago—purged it, rather—and then willingly left behind the person who had been there for her to practice speaking her feelings aloud.

Lux shoved to her feet.

She walked to the mirror, her steps heavy and slow, and when she neared it, close enough that she could read the words etched into the dark wood, a deep rage began to wrap around her anger, causing it to flicker and rise.

She couldn't reach the words; her nails scraped along the glass instead. Her teeth bared. She audibly seethed. The sound was the only one she heard.

"Brilliance is meant to be a *gift!*" Her fingers enclosed the body of a decorative gargoyle. She lifted it with both hands from its shelved perch. "And a gift should—not—lead—to—madness!"

She sneered at the statue—and swung it front-first against the wall.

The *crack* reverberated throughout the room.

Lux sucked a breath.

She picked through the pieces of the fractured figurine. She pulled at what gleamed. A silver ribbon, at the end of which hung a silver key. She frowned down at it before turning it over in her palm. Then she lifted the remains of the gargoyle once more. A bent hinge lay exposed on its severed neck. Now headless, she could see inside. It'd been hollowed out. She dropped it back onto its ruin.

"What do you unlock?" she asked the key and glanced afterward at herself in the mirror.

Something shifted in its reflection.

She stepped closer.

She raised her hand.

"It can't be."

But the lock reflected to her seemed as real as the key she held.

Lux raised it until it almost touched the glass. In the reflection, the lock remained instead. It didn't make sense that it should work, but she pushed the key forward and watched with widening eyes as it slipped through. She turned it, heard it click. And the mirror swung in.

She stared into a pitch-black abyss.

A hidden corridor.

"Saints above, devil below."

Who needs a boy for a map...

Not her.

Spinning away from it, she hurried to her desk where she gathered an unlit candlestick. Her match struck, and the wick flamed. She gripped its holder and moved toward the secret door.

"Please don't have any monsters," Lux begged of the gloom—a heartbeat before she stepped inside.

THE PASSAGEWAY SMELLED WORSE than the stairwell to the kitchen: like wet seaweed gone to rot. Lux could see nothing but her candle's glow in her first few steps.

"This seems a worthless place," she whispered. Though she also wondered if that was the point. Someone adept at breaking into places not meant for him had once told her if he ever found something that did not make sense, it meant there was something hidden. He'd said he hadn't yet been proven wrong.

A high creak met her ears. Lux swung back. She held out her meager flame. And she watched as the mirrored door swung fully closed all its own.

A ghost of a girl was reflected back at her when it was done; she could make out the candle in her tight grip. The dense dark wouldn't reveal her face, and Lux was glad of it—she didn't need to see the sheen of sweat forming on her brow or the terror in her eyes.

But she did need to be sure she could return to her bedchamber this way. She dug quickly for the key and audibly sighed in relief when a lock showed at once. "Least it seems to work from either s-i-de!"

The floor fell away from her feet.

Lux landed hard on her bottom, slipping then plunging into the pitch. She slid down a steep incline and could not stop. The meager flame guttered; she thought it'd gone out, but when her hand flew up to protect it, it flamed back to light.

Onyx walls whipped past. She curved first one way and then the other. She nearly toppled over twice. And then she did—the incline abruptly ending, expelling her onto flattened floor.

"Why?" she cried, groaning from her place on the ground.

Lux rose to her feet with a huff of breath. She still held the candle, its flame miraculously flickering yet, when she turned back the way she'd come. Toward an impossibly steep passageway, and no way to climb it.

"*Dead spaces,*" she mimicked, furious at Corvin, and accepting none of the blame herself. She spun around. "If this is also a dead end…"

But it wasn't.

Not yet.

Lux held her candle over the edge of a stone staircase coated in decades of dust. She teetered at the top. And ahead—

I can make it through this.

But suddenly, she didn't know if that were true. The path down was as dark as the rest, but this one felt as yawning as a void. Her entire body rejected the idea.

She swallowed. "There's something down there, isn't there…"

Lux recalled the first time she'd felt Death. She'd been outside Ghadra's fog-crept walls. Her mother had been beside her, bent double with a sickle to hack at marsh grass, and she'd been explaining the ways of the world to Lux.

"*You should never take more than you give. That's called greed.*" Then she'd handed off the bundle of grasses and dug inside her purse. She tossed a handful of seeds into the soggy soil.

When they landed, sinking into the muck at different depths, a pressure had tapped into Lux's chest the same.

A dead woman was recovered later that day.

Lux relived that memory now as she stared into the void. She didn't always notice such subtle premonitions, but today, right now, she felt the lurk of Death on this hidden staircase.

Soon. Soon. Soon, beat her heart, and she would have claimed it as true—if she could still trust it. Unfortunately, her systems were now diagnosed as a wreck.

"But even if there is something...that's the point, isn't it? To see if there's anything to hide?"

She'd thought speaking it might embolden her.

Her fear did not care.

She still didn't know what judgement could be passed on Mothlock and its cloaked society. On the surface, it seemed a good thing what they did—collecting books that might otherwise be lost, binding new copies, and distributing them throughout the country. But there was a current moving underneath.

One of old money, desolate monuments, targeted murder, and vague truths.

Lux could feel it beneath her skin.

Her fingers tightened around the key. She only wanted to find the vault. To put her suspicions to rest. Whatever else went on here didn't matter to her, so long as they'd nothing to do with Bartleby Tamish's bad business.

She only wished it would be above ground.

You're delaying, chastised her head.

I know, she replied, and understood there could be no turning back. If she must have some rare condition, the least she could do was see this one goal through to the end. Lifeblood might be here. It might not. But she would have an answer soon enough.

GLORIA BOTTELMAN

Lux stepped down—and her nightmare reached up from the dark.

Chapter Twenty-Four

She shrieked, dropped the candle, and the only light went out.

To run anywhere in the pitch black was a poor choice. One Lux had chosen to do twice before and once more. She counted on her body's instinct to propel her down the stairs without breaking her neck, and it mostly succeeded. She sprawled onto her front at its end.

"Of all the saintforsaken hells," she cried, clutching the candlestick to her like it mattered.

"Isn't it hard to be broken?" said the voice. *"We will never know peace."*

"I've never known peace anyway. Get out of my mind!"

It wasn't true, what she said. She'd felt peace. All-consuming. Twice in recent memory. In Shaw's arms in the hours before she'd left Ghadra, and in a merchant wagon, a butterfly on her palm. But if she thought of those moments, and the drastic difference to her present, she would collapse and never rise again. And she could not afford that.

She swiped out at the dark and met nothing but air. Lux continued forward on her knees, searching for any further surprises. She found nothing but flat stone. *Have I finally reached the bottom?* She pushed to her feet.

The voice came from behind her. *"We will not last. It's worse for us than any of the others. We've the darkest brilliance of all, and we will hurt everyone before we finally hurt ourselves."*

Ice burst inside her. "I won't hurt anyone," she hissed.

"We will hurt them terribly and thoroughly. We will again be the suffering of those we love before our end."

A weight collapsed on top of her at those severe words. Lux staggered forward without speaking. Her throat was too tight with a forced-back sob to manage it.

It isn't real. It isn't real.

But why did something not real bite so hard? She felt like she bled on the inside.

Her outstretched fingers met a wall ahead. Lux ran her hands over it desperately. *I must do something worthwhile.* Maybe then she could shed this newfound weight.

She swept along the seams of the stacked stones. Up then down, and once she reached the edge, she went back and ran her fingers horizontal across it.

They caught.

Lux fitted her fingertips into the crack, and though they couldn't reach all the way through, they reached something. Her middle finger snagged at a protrusion, and then the entire thing *clicked*, and swung in.

Blessed light doused her. Dim and far away as it was, the relief swept, palpable, in her chest. Lux spun, looking everywhere for the blighted apparition, but she found no one with her. Only the stone stairs she'd stumbled down and the small landing she stood upon. She turned again to the door.

To the tunnel beyond it.

Narrow and shadowed and comprised of black stone same as the rest of the manor; a torch shone blue in the distance. She huffed a fortifying breath. It no longer smelled of seaweed but of something cloying that she couldn't identify.

She stepped through.

It reminded her of the tunnels beneath Ghadra. The mayor's mansion, to be precise. All that needed to be traded was stone for brick and random screams of terror for weighted silence.

She'd not gone more than a few steps when this door, too, swung closed. It groaned rather than creaked, and when the latch clicked, Lux's heartbeat threatened to overwhelm her ears.

She stared after it.

At the silver image depicted upon it.

A robed figure, palms out and head wrapped in a tragic crown of thorns. Another faceless saint.

She'd never stepped foot in a church in all her life, but she swore walking by their steps hadn't felt so sinister as this. *It's only because you're down here alone in the dark,* she told herself.

Lux crept steadily away, not daring to turn until the light grew significantly brighter at her back. She glanced quickly at the torch and then to the tunnel that now forked. Both right and left were lit the same, with torches down their lengths until they curved out of sight.

She'd once come upon a fork similar to this one. That day, she'd chosen to run left because the right had frightened her. She'd learned later she'd been correct to be. A monster had lived there.

"This will not be all for nothing," Lux murmured into the heavy quiet.

Today, she must choose the wretched right.

THE WIDE ARCHWAY AT the passage's end rose tall, steeped in dense shadow. It was a dark unmoved by the twin torches perched on either side. The sight reminded Lux of another tortuous chamber. Immediately, she did not want to go farther. Her palms slicked with sweat.

"You're alone, you ninny. There's no one to strap your wrists and shove a needle in your neck."

There's no one here to save me, either.

No Riselda.

No Shaw.

The hollow pit in her chest pulsed. She shrugged it off. There wasn't any room for that here. Nor fear for that matter. Nevertheless, the latter made itself fit, and Lux practically shook in her boots when reading the inscription above the archway.

The Greatest Destination Is Beyond

She had no choice. No option but to push through her fright, ignore the pair of saints standing sentry, and pass into the gloom. For being sightless, the dreaded feel of watchful eyes pressed upon her, and she cursed herself for leaving the candlestick behind at the bottom of the stairs. If anything lurked in this dark with her—

Lux marched in before her mind could finish the thought.

If she didn't, she'd never go.

The archway—unnervingly—spat her out at its opposite side after only a few strides. The room flared to light; a pop and fizzle marked torch after torch leaping aflame. They lit a high-ceilinged room, shining onyx, circular and domed.

Lux teetered back on her heels.

"What in the saintforsaken *hell*..." she breathed.

There stood the most gargantuan statue she'd ever seen.

Ivory-pale, it stretched to the ceiling, and same as its smaller counterparts, this statue was robed and crowned and entirely without features. Its arms hung straight, its hands hidden, and at its feet rose a black throne set on a dais.

She could focus on none of it any further than that. Being as a body lay before her.

Lux's brow knit. She thought her heart slowed then halted entirely. Because this body was not lying upon a worktable or on a bed or within a box—but entombed in a grave of ice. She shivered at the frigid temperature of the chamber. Her fingers retreated beneath her arms.

Lux could feel her mind itching to work through the reasonings, but she couldn't gather a coherent thought. Someone had made a *grave* of *ice*.

Her legs began functioning again, and she moved toward the large encasement. Now that she could see beneath it, she saw it rested on a wooden beam, polished and thick and adorned with similar faces to the pillars outside. She straightened.

"Who is this?" A thin cloud left her mouth along with the question. The suspended body was unclothed, the opaqueness of the ice obscuring all fine details. Male, she guessed.

"What even *is* this?" Her attention pulled to the throne, to its many spires and imposing size. She skirted around the ice grave toward it, unaware until her arrival at its side of her entire body thudding with warning.

It was the all-consuming cold.

It was the cottage in the wood.

It was *wrong, wrong, wrong*.

A pedestal sat next to the throne, a silver basin with a depressed lip atop it. She frowned and reached for it, because it looked recently used. Wet. Her finger brushed along its edge; she lifted it to inspect what came away.

Nothing.

Her lips parted. She craned her neck, staring up and up. The saint didn't watch her back. If the sculptor had gifted it eyes, it would have stared instead at the man frozen in time. At the entrance too. Lux scanned the curved walls surrounding her, and realized there were recesses in them. Rectangular cutouts—and inside were familiar shapes resting in black shrouds.

Some were empty.

Most were not.

Lux stepped down from the dais. She stalked toward the first recess she could reach and peeled the shroud back.

Hollowed eye sockets in a skeletal face stared back at her. She pulled it farther, until a breastbone with a silver ribbon and a cross-shaped pendant flashed in the torchlight.

Collectors?

Had she actually found the resting place of the morning room's portraits?

Contrary to what her prior job might have indicated, Lux didn't wish to disturb the dead. She dragged the shroud back into place and stepped away. "A throne overlooking a room of corpses," she whispered and tucked her thumb between her teeth.

And one frozen body.

It was the strangest thing seeing a person buried in ice. She could pick out the faint, pallid line of leg and arm, and the barest profile. Lux crept forward and then crouched to better view the angles. A familiarity niggled at her. Her hand lifted.

"Saints above. Could you be Alixsander the Overlord?" she wondered, settling her fingertips on the coffin.

The cold shocked her straight through. Lux hissed at the burn. She jerked her fingers back only for it not to work on one. The pad of her thumb remained stuck fast. Lux gritted her teeth. She pulled again and yelped. It wouldn't release her.

"*Devil's tits*," she ground out. "You're the biggest idiot!"

Lux stilled on her next breath.

Beyond the coffin—

The sound of something being dragged. Her insides matched her outsides as everything within her froze. *No. No!*

She yanked again on her finger and a single tear slipped down her cheek from the pain. *Please don't come around. Please stay on that side.* Lux curled in on herself, and because she could see nothing, she listened as hard as she could.

She'd experience with the sound of a dragging body. Whatever was being hauled into the chamber was not that. It sounded heavy, wooden maybe, and whoever had been made in charge of it breathed like a bellows.

Lux wished she could do the same.

She kept her breathing minimal, and then stopped entirely when the dragging ceased.

"Open the lid," said a voice, harshly familiar. "Now lift him together. Do not drop him. Yes, place him there."

No muttering. No questions. Only direction. And heavy breaths.

Lux slapped a hand over her mouth when a different hand fell overtop the ice grave. She huffed away her startled yelp, her eyes wide as saucers. The limp limb was brown and uncovered. Snaking black veins lined the length. It could have been Mistress Lefroy's in death if the skin were powder white.

Poison, Lux thought as the hand settled in line with her vision. But why were they stacking a poisoned body above a frozen one? Was this standard process in their entombing?

In that moment, she realized to whom the voice in the room belonged. Silas—the collector she'd followed since Loxlen—had arrived at last. With a new body in tow.

"Prepare the basin."

Lux glanced quickly to the pedestal at her back in a panic. She hauled again at her finger and gritted her teeth at the sharp pain. She could hear footsteps coming around the left side of the coffin. If she were caught here, what would happen? There were too many possibilities to consider, and she already didn't like things as they were now.

Lux bared her teeth—and ripped her finger away.

Her mouth gaped in a silent scream before she stuck the damaged pad of her thumb inside it. She scurried around the opposite end just as boots and a black robe appeared in her periphery. Blood pooled in her mouth; she tried not to gag. Instead, she pressed her tongue to the wound and lamented the sting.

Around the coffin sat the source of the noise.

A wooden contraption. With two wheels, two handles, and a closed lid carved with another saint and words she couldn't spare the time to read. She crouched beside it until she could be sure the collectors' backs were to her. Except—they weren't all collectors. She'd guessed wrong. Only one was. The other two were dressed in Mothlock attendants' garb.

The body atop the ice was a strange sight. The opposite hand dangled on this side too. They'd allowed him his undergarments and nothing else, and she wondered how long he'd been dead. Beyond rigor mortis and so beyond her services for certain. On the dais the attendants were busy preparing the basin in whatever way Silas required. Lux heard the plink of something against it.

She glanced again at the chamber's entrance. Had it always been so far away? Would she make it?

She began to edge backward.

"Sweep the room for rodents. The torches were on when we arrived. Kill any you find and keep them for your dinner. Then return the cart to Lord Artemis."

Lux's muscles seized. *Devil take me...* Silas came around the coffin. She pressed herself against the cart, but aside from rapping on it in passing, he continued out of the room without a backward glance. Lux scanned the chamber for any new ideas but found none. When the attendants stepped from the dais, she used her last seconds of freedom to do the only thing she could think of.

She cracked the lid of the cart and climbed inside.

Chapter Twenty-Five

Little do they know they've already caught the rat, she thought, swaying with the cart's movements. Her mind, quick to conjure anything grotesque these days, brought about an image of Ghadra's overgrown alley rats, boiling away in a wide pot.

Silas. She shuddered. *There is something* wrong *with him. With that room. With...all of it.*

The cart lurched, and Lux winced as her head knocked against the side. The men pulling it were not in sync with their hauling, and her many bruises were about to be proof. She carefully lifted the lid again; she'd done it twice already.

A sliver of torchlight and black stone came into focus. They were still in the same underground passage. A welcome rush of air filled her nose before she allowed the lid to ease shut. It smelled pungent, a sharp scent she was unfamiliar with and wished she had remained so. The same, faint smell she'd noticed when entering the tunnel.

What had she gotten herself into?

Because this was certainly no good and honest business.

Think, she scolded. *What do you know for certain?*

Nothing, was her first instinct, but she ignored that one.

She knew there'd been poisonings of Mothlock investors but knew neither by what nor why. She knew her own brilliance had broken somehow, and a probable madness previously tied to Riselda's family had crept in. She knew there was a man frozen in an ice grave, and he looked near enough to the murdered overlord to unnerve her. She knew there were a lot more secrets here than she realized, and that chamber in particular felt like it housed an insidious one. But if buying up Ghadra's lifeblood was one of the manor's mysteries, why were there so many bodies gone to rot below ground?

If only she had also discovered the vault to be sure.

Lux bit at her cheek. She knew, of course, she must return to that chamber by whatever means. There was nothing else for it. She had to know what else they played at. Because she hadn't seen any books.

The cart slowed. Maybe this was her chance to leap out. But her hand only brushed the wood before she was biting back a gasp. A grunt had come from outside and now, she lay fully horizontal.

The attendants were *carrying* her.

Gravity gripped her, and she slid down to the foot. As they began their ascent upstairs, the attendants didn't speak to one another, not even an oath. Aside from heavy breathing, they made no noise. Lux knew she wasn't so heavy as that body had been; she'd hoped because of it they wouldn't think to check at the start, and they hadn't. But surely, carrying her would have been another thing. Did they not feel the difference?

"Should we just drown ourselves in the sea, Lucena?"

Lux sucked a gasping breath and shoved away from the face now peering down at her. Long strands of lank hair dripped on either side of the nightmare's features, draping atop Lux's own. It mimicked her every movement.

No, not here. Go away. GO AWAY!

The apparition—her broken brilliance—ran a bloated tongue over rotted teeth. *"Carve me out or keep me."*

Carve you— Lux couldn't bear to see her own face so twisted and gruesome. Though her mind begged her otherwise, she shut her eyes.

The Stripping.

The Stripping...

The healer's experiment flooded her mind. Her heart hammered in her chest, and she thought if it was *this* now or a permanent hollowness later—devil below, the attempt might be worth it. Her chin quivered in the dark.

"*Someone will die tonight. We've felt it before. Do we feel it now?*"

Lux held her breath in wait for her nightmare to solidify and run one of those cracked nails along her cheek. But if it did, she couldn't feel it. It was all in her head. None of it was real.

Sure, she'd felt Death coming to Mothlock. What did it matter?

"What do you want from me?" Her demand was whispered, so soft it might not have left her lips at all.

"*To choose.*"

Lux braved to blink and found the perverted version of herself so near, she could see nothing but its eyes. They weren't murky or grey but dilated to only black.

I've made my choice.

When she blinked next, the apparition was gone—and they'd stopped moving. Lux felt the wheels settle again to the floor.

She attempted to sort her thoughts into a semblance of something that might do her good. But that...monster. It terrified her to the marrow. And she did not have *time* to be terrified. Lux scrunched her eyes shut for one deep breath, and when she opened them again, they were narrowed and filled with fire. *I will not be undone by something rotted and better off buried.*

Lux settled her heels against the back of the cart. One palm rested beside her hip while the other rose to the lid. When they rapped on the door, she would sneak out.

Her hand fell away as she was jostled. Moving again?

"No, don't leave it in the middle of the room. Over there in the corner." The muffled voice eased through the cracks of the cart, and Lux's lips parted.

We are already inside. Her stomach plummeted. The healer's door had already been opened. Lux braced her hands on the walls as she was suddenly propped upright.

Artemis's voice came again. "Good. Be on your way."

A shuffling sounded and then a click of a latch. *Devil's own tits!* She was back in the damned healer's workroom. How would she ever get out? The pungent smell still lingered. Saints above...would he think to clean it?

"Now, child, I know it's frightening, but you won't be allowed to remain in here forever."

Ah. Lux rested her head back as her body went limp. Of course he knew. How he did, she didn't know, but then she supposed it didn't matter. Riselda had been gifted with the ability to feel the state of certain things with just a touch. Perhaps this healer had learned something similar and all without the need to place his hands on her. How inconvenient.

Lux could think of no lie that would make any sense. Why would anyone in their right mind sneak into a cart that had previously hauled the dead? Why would she have even been near that tomb of a chamber? Why had she—

Except I'm not in my right mind...am I?

It would have to do. She began to press at the lid, the words prepared on her tongue, when another answered, meek and pitched high. "I don't want to go back. Please don't make me."

Lux held onto her breath and let go of her plan at once. Her eyes widened over the unfamiliar voice.

"You'll feel better once you've had the elixir. I understand it can be hard, transitioning from a life in the forest to a life beside the sea. Your lungs need to adjust. Sip this."

Lux heard nothing for a short period and then a dainty cough. Whoever the meek voice belonged to seemed nervous to even clear her throat.

"Excellent," said Artemis. "Feel better?"

"A little."

"Give it more time."

"Sir...Lord. What about my holiday? I was promised two days."

"After the Hallowed Banquet."

"But Corvin said—"

"*Lord Corvin* must have told you it would be after the banquet. Besides, you're ill with the salt-sick. We cannot have you out wandering your way back toward Ravenwood with a respiratory ailment that urges you into the sea. These cliffs are perilous and so is the water. What sort of employer would Mothlock be if that were excused?"

Lux couldn't understand the girl's subsequent muttering.

"Yes," said the healer. "Exactly right. A bad one. And we are not a bad one. Who else would cultivate your brilliance while providing room and board? All for the mere exchange of your honest work."

"But the others—"

"Are content. Soon, you will be content too. Lord Tobias will return you to your bedchamber. The Saints have blessed you, Ms. Otterbee. A position here is a privilege. You'll realize that. One way or another."

There was no more argument. Lux could hear the barest footfalls of their leaving and then little else. Something burbled and glass clinked.

"There it is. Ah, that's beautiful, isn't it? Just the tincture for a transformation." A hacking cough followed.

Inside the cart, Lux narrowed her eyes. Sounded like apothecary nonsense to her. Or worse...

An alchemist.

She recalled that old woman puttering in her basement apartment in Ghadra. With her bubbling liquids and creation of a potion which had begun a plague. Mothlock didn't dabble in that, too, did it?

Another thing I do not know.

A soft knock. Lux swung her head toward the subsequent click.

"I took care of her," said Artemis. "She won't cause any more problems. For today, at least."

"I didn't doubt it," said a voice. It wasn't one she recognized. It was harsh and rasping. Like the person was ancient or fought a chest cold. "I appreciate your quickness in stitching the cook closed."

"Head wounds do tend to cause a mess."

"I don't understand how she broke through to begin with. I thought we had administered enough."

"It's the red hair. You have to double anything you would give anyone else. That is why it's the color of fire—warning you they burn through it all too quick. Hallowed Day will be blessed, indeed."

A hard chuckle descended into a cough and then, "All these righteous years, and I am still learning."

"The beauty of Mothlock."

"Praise to the Saints. As for the necromancer"—Lux caught her breath again—"she is the answer and must be cared for as such."

"I offered her all I could," said Artemis. "She is rather strong. Even in her current state."

"All the better," hummed the unfamiliar voice. "She is all I've ever wanted for Mothlock."

A drawn pause brought with it a wave of tension. "You cannot mean—"

The rasping voice said, "Think of it, Artemis. She is tied to the Beyond. She is tied to this estate. By Hallowed Day, she could become Mistress of Mothlock as it was meant to be. She could *soothe* it."

Lux's every muscle stiffened.

"You said nothing of this. I have already told her of her diagnosis. I have already recommended the Stripping."

"As you should."

A grumbled oath. "I see it is your plan to keep me in the dark."

"You must learn to thrive in it as I do—or risk being lost."

The healer snorted. "Good luck in your endeavor. When I said she was strong, I also meant her will."

"Your faith is lacking," replied the voice, and now it grew hard. "We must thank the Saints for their offering. It is by their design we have her at all, and so it is meant to be."

"Of course, Overlord. I didn't mean to falter. We will see it done."

A low noise resounded, vibrating from deep within the manor. Lux felt it in her bones.

"Second Invocation already, is it?" said Artemis. Something clattered onto the counter. "The days do fly by. Here you are, Overlord. Freshly brewed."

"Thank you, I've gone too long. After you."

Lux waited until she heard the door open and shut and then waited a little while more. Tentatively, she pushed from the cart. The workroom was empty. On the counter, a pot sat suspended above a small flame; a thick substance within was bubbling away. She was reminded of Riselda's brewing when she was a child, how some concoctions would take days to cure but then could do great things. Like heal bones. This entire room smelled earthy and herby and warm, and if it weren't for the conversation Lux had overhead, she might have been put at ease. As it was, she was sure every nerve of her body hummed.

No one had mentioned a living overlord before. And the only dead one she knew of had a portrait hanging in the hall. Why hadn't Corvin told her about him? It didn't make sense for a living leader to be kept secret.

Unless he isn't living...

She rejected the thought. No. Ghosts did not exist. She could feel souls and they never lingered, regardless of the manner of their deaths. She coaxed them back from the Beyond every time.

But the rasping in that voice didn't sound natural. It sounded like a nightmare. And that body entombed in ice *felt* like one.

Her fingertip moved carefully over the rim of Artemis's elixir. Lux was no stranger to aged men wanting her for some purpose or another. The mayor of

Ghadra had desired her rare power to ensure his longevity. But what could this mysterious Overlord of Mothlock desire her for, if not for that? What could she possibly soothe? Her brilliance was broken.

Mistress of Mothlock.

Ghadra's Necromancer.

Lux had no use for titles, and decidedly less for ones that tied her to something. And she would not be tied to something evil again.

They will never keep me here.

She would find out this night whether the lifeblood of Ghadra's people lined Mothlock Manor. She would destroy it if it did, and then she would leave.

Damn the overlord.

Damn the Hallowed Banquet.

And damn her draw to Grimrook House as it sat beside that enthralling, consuming sea.

She would find Corvin, and she would trick him into telling her everything.

Chapter Twenty-Six

Lux leaned over her balcony.

Night had come early, and all she could see were shades of grey. She listened to the waves crash upon the cliffsides, a hauntingly beautiful melody. She brought her chin down to rest on her arms where they lay folded atop *The Risen* on the balcony's edge.

To the sea air, she said, "I'm thinking it was a mistake, coming all this way alone." In response, the wind whipped against her, dragging her hair across her eyes. She pushed back to right the strands.

A flutter of wings jolted her, and Lux turned to see the crow from the fence. It landed on the railing and, in a single hop, neared her side. Lux knew it was not the crow from her old life. She reached out anyway. The animal didn't bolt or twitch, allowing her forefinger to run along its sleek crown.

"What do I do about the hallucinations?" she asked the bird and the world both. "I won't allow that lunatic to carve anything out of me. Does this mean I'm meant to live out my days as the necromancer who faints with her revivals and speaks to the nightmare haunting her even while awake? That didn't work out well for Riselda."

She hissed a sudden breath of pain.

"What was *that* for?" Lux lifted her hand to see. A red streak marred the back of it. "You bit me, you cruel bird!"

She sank down to the floor, the book in her clutches. Between the sharp pain in her hand, and the hollowness of her heart, she suddenly had no strength left to stand. She glared out at the cliffside. The barest gleam of pale stone could be seen around the manor's onyx tower: the edges of Grimrook House she now knew.

The crow hopped onto her lap. Lux froze. The bird tilted its head, its beady eye searing her own. If ever an animal could look disappointed, this bird managed it.

Her teeth clacked together. Her jaw grew hard. She breathed a deep breath, and at its end, her face relaxed. "I won't give up so easily," she explained to the animal. "I was only grousing."

Again, she picked apart that conversation in the workroom bit by bit. From the treatment of the girl to their cryptic talk of Lux herself. Disgust filled her over their eager words. "Who in the saintforsaken hell is that overlord? I'm sure I have no idea."

This time, the bird pecked at her thigh.

"*Devil*—get away!" Lux shoved the bird off, where it immediately took flight and was gone. She hauled her skirt into her hands until the mark was revealed.

It didn't bleed, but it was certainly an ugly scratch. *Beast*, she seethed. She'd been told they were clever birds, but it seemed this one was just awful.

Her skirt pooled around her at the same time a knock came upon her door.

"Lux?" said the muffled voice.

Devil below. *Corvin*. Lux shoved to her feet and called, "Just a moment."

She'd told Hildred to invite him to dinner. She'd forgotten to also tell the woman to report back on his answer. The attendant was the most literal person she'd ever met.

Lux hurried from the balcony to deposit *The Risen*. She ran then to the mirror, and when she neared it, saw that though she'd become disheveled from the breeze, she wasn't entirely unpresentable. Her fingers worked quickly to twist windswept strands from her face, securing them with clips she'd purchased in Loxlen.

Not for the first time, Lux felt relief over her shorter locks. She could well imagine the state of her hair by this point had she kept its length. She wiped at the space beneath her eyes and admired the new pink in her skin.

She returned to the door and opened it.

Her joints stiffened.

Corvin held out a gloved hand. And following that gloved hand was a black shirt and black trousers. He'd changed into a similar ensemble as their first meeting.

He also had that familiar half-smile on his mouth, the coy one, and her eyes narrowed upon seeing it. His smile bloomed fully. "I've come to escort you to dinner. Thank you, of course, for your invitation, but I'd something else in mind than the small tables these rooms allow."

Lux raised an eyebrow. "Is there an evening room?"

His hand further bridged the distance. "Better. Please, allow me to distract you. I understand you've had the roughest of days, and I won't pretend you haven't. But the night is perfect, and I know you love the sea."

Distract her? Her perusal began at the top of his light head and didn't finish until she'd dragged it down to his well-crafted shoes. When she met his eyes again, she found his cheekbones tinged with color. *No*, she thought. *I will not be distracted.*

"All right," she said, offering a coy smile to match. "If you insist."

MOTHLOCK MANOR POSSESSED A secret terrace. One Lux hadn't been able to view from her balcony's position, jutting from the building's side. Attendants held the doors wide, and once outside them, she lost her breath.

"This is almost too beautiful to be real," she whispered.

Lux felt Corvin's glance for a moment before he proceeded to follow her gaze. From the intimate seating to the lit lampposts and all around the extended intricate railing. The lamplight wasn't blue, but warming and soft and in pleasant contrast to the moon. The sea's lullaby haunted her in a delicious way.

Now you are being distracted, admonished her head.

She snapped free of the trance.

"I've begun to relish seeing Mothlock through your eyes. It reminds me to be grateful for everything the Saints have bestowed upon me."

Lux sucked at her teeth. "I'd noticed the Saints seem to be a main feature of the manor." Even now she found them. Taller than the garden statues, they rose pale and stark on either side of the doors. "I didn't realize Mothlock was so devout."

His attention carried to where she looked. "We are. In a sense."

"In a sense," she repeated and noted him fidget. "Something your *overlord* commissioned then?"

Corvin glanced down at her. "Yes, actually. A long time ago."

"Because he died a long time ago."

He huffed a laugh, his stare turning bemused. "Precisely."

Hmm. She allowed him to lead her to the table, where he didn't have an attendant pull out her chair but did so himself. She sat. "Did you say who took over his position? At his death, I mean."

"No, I didn't." He pulled out his own chair and sat, beckoning at the doors with two fingers. An attendant swooped in. "Mothlock has had no leader since. We are all known as 'lords' and our voices carry equal weight. Everyone matters here."

Lux's goblet was filled with a deep red liquid, and once Corvin's was, too, she lifted hers. She ran her nail up and down its side and noticed when his eyes latched onto the movement and held there. *So. Either he does not know of this nightmarish overlord...or he's lying.* She chewed her lip as she assessed him.

"Is this wine?" she asked. And waited. "Corvin?"

"Mm, what? Wine? Yes. Verdinia."

She nodded like she knew of it and pretended to take a sip. Her eyes hooded now, she watched him as he watched her. His gaze dipped.

She couldn't blame him. The gown she'd dressed in was the color of emeralds and cut to her form exact. Kent, for all that she didn't like about him, was indeed brilliant in fabrics and threads. She'd stared at herself in the mirror for far longer than she ever had before.

Lux set down the goblet in time for their meals to arrive. Same as breakfast, the dishes were covered, and she waited until the attendant removed it with a silent flourish before she said, "You didn't tell me the garden is really a graveyard."

He stiffened with surprise in his seat. "Can it not be both?"

Maybe. If there were anything other than blood-sucking brambles occupying it. "Are the prior collectors also buried on the grounds?"

"Collectors, investors, and attendants. All our given rest here on Mothlock grounds when their time comes." He drank from his goblet. "Are you looking forward to the banquet tomorrow? I'm eager for you to experience it."

Attendants. Even the attendants are entombed below? But he'd changed the subject purposefully, and she didn't know how to steer it back. "I'm not sure I can stomach a crowd. I was never inclined to begin with, but after the healer's diagnosis...I would rather be left alone."

"Yet you sought out my company tonight."

"Well." Lux worried her lower lip. "You are different. I...feel different. Around you."

Like I might get you to tell me exactly what I need to know. His eyes were truly an unbelievable color. She watched them dilate beneath her scrutiny. His nostrils flared.

"I've come to realize the same thing," he said.

He hadn't touched his food. Nor had Lux, for that matter. She raised her fork now and made a slow show of selecting a bite and bringing it to her lips. She let it slide gently behind her teeth and did not speak.

He cleared his throat. "Kent will be disappointed."

"Kent? Whatever for?"

"He told me of the gown he had in mind for you. And now I feel robbed of seeing you in it."

Lux pressed her tongue sharply to her canine. "Maybe I will wear it. After the banquet is over."

But he didn't leap at the suggestive invitation.

"That would be very late, indeed," he said. "I didn't tell you before, but Hallowed Eve is a twofold celebration, really. One part is for our guests. The banquet, and the honoring. The second is a ceremony—for the collectors."

"A ceremony for Collectors only?"

"It's a sacred ritual. We call it the Hallowed Harvest—in respect to the season, the Saints, and all the abundance we've gathered and shared." He leaned forward conspiratorially. "Lux, Artemis didn't mention a third route you might take. Truthfully, maybe I shouldn't be mentioning it either. But after your adamance in saving your brilliance—to choose your gift over your sanity—it proved how serious you are in being your best version. If you'd participate in the Harvest with us—well, I believe you could be cured."

Lux lips parted; she needed to physically restrain herself from allowing her jaw to swing wide. *This* she did not expect. Another way? A way that would allow her to keep her brilliance but expunge the madness?

"How would a ritual fix me?"

The lamplight flickered behind him, highlighting the near-ivory strands of his hair. A breeze whistled up through the railings, and the hollowness in Lux's chest carved itself wide. *You're alone. You're alone. You're alone.*

She mentally shook herself free of the feel, then lifted her thumb to her mouth to lick the sauce from her skin. Corvin noticeably swallowed.

"Are you not religious, Lux?"

"Not overly."

His gaze left her to focus on the darkened sea. "Riselda Grimrook is said to have been a heretic."

Of course she was.

Lux knew of all ranges of beliefs in Ghadra, but the mayor had prayed over his spiked tea every morning. She did not think it mattered.

"Is that why she disappeared?" She pretended to take another sip of wine.

"So they say. Riselda wanted the benefits of the Harvest, but without any of the society's guidance. It's said she strived to master brilliance without yearning for the greatest destination of all: *perfection*. And that's the problem, isn't it? Someone cannot achieve anything close if they're also a heretic. Personally, I think that's why she ran."

Lux's eyebrows rose nearly to her hairline. "No one can achieve that."

Corvin's responding smile was soft. He traced the rim of his goblet with one gloved finger. "What do you believe in?"

Lie or tell the truth?

"I believe in the Beyond. I believe in people—in that we all have a brilliance embedded within each of us whether we choose to do anything with it or not. I believe in myself sometimes."

The truth. For what it was worth.

"You believe in all those things but not that there's something greater?"

She shrugged. "Maybe there is. Ghadra's mayor prayed over his drink for prosperity without fail, and he did die awfully rich."

Corvin's laugh didn't sound especially kind. In fact, it was almost smug. "That could have some correlation, for certain."

No, it couldn't. She'd said it with sarcasm, but Corvin had missed it. The mayor was self-serving and immoral. There was nothing holy about him. He certainly wasn't *saintlike*.

"What is it you pray for?" she asked.

"Enlightenment," he answered immediately. "The purge of mortal failings. Every Invocation, we pray for the mastery of brilliance."

"You—" Lux blinked incredibly slow. "Unless you're some sort of saint yourself, you can't be rid of failings."

"Precisely." An underlying current of confrontation propped up the word. Her own reared to match. "Corvin." She stared at him hard. "Be serious."

"Lux." He returned her stare. "I am."

She continued to watch him, wide-eyed, until the statue from the balcony corner beckoned her attention. Faceless. Looming. All of them.

So anyone might imagine themselves in its place...

Devil below. This was not religion as she'd heard it. This was something...beyond. She huffed a worried laugh and muttered under her breath, "Well, this has gotten out of hand."

Corvin continued, "Your way of thinking isn't isolated, of course. But it's another facet of what Mothlock is trying to achieve with its resources. Our books are distributed widely, and it's the spreading of that knowledge in which we place the hope of achieving further enlightenment of the country."

"I don't understand."

"The original works. They offer nothing about the true basis of Saints and the Devil. Real mastery isn't always about becoming the most competent in your brilliance—it's about knowing when to choose subservience. To realize there's a chance you may be called to kneel before those who've been blessed to become greater. It's a long, arduous journey for a collective achievement. Sometimes, I cannot believe I've been allowed a part in the cause."

Subservience! Lux had to duck her head so he'd not see her unpleasant reaction. The lending libraries. The bookshops. They'd tampered with them *all*?

"Corvin," she began once she could. "There are saints, if you believe in them, and then there are plain, mortal people. You can't be both."

He dipped his head. "You're right. You cannot be both."

Chapter Twenty-Seven

Lux could hardly speak the remainder of the meal. She'd been thwarted. Of course, she had been. She'd next to no experience in seducing answers out of anyone. It had been poorly done from the start.

Corvin rose from his side of the table, and Lux watched him with new eyes. *I followed the saintforsaken zealots, just as she told me not to.* She, of course, being Mistress Farrentail. But how was Lux to know this was whom the bespectacled, feathered vendor had meant? The woman certainly hadn't been specific. She hadn't even so much as pointed.

Lux felt herself pale as Corvin came around for her chair; she pushed it back on her own before he could grab hold.

"I'll return you to your room," he said.

"I know the way," she replied in a rush, standing.

"Lux." And then he was there, bending over her, his thumb at the corner of her mouth. Ever so softly, he dragged it beneath her lower lip, and she was too stunned, too frozen at his audacity, she did nothing but blink. "I realize," he began, his voice roughened, "you've been through unfathomable things in your past. Things that have stolen your trust and left you with scars." His hand dropped away. "But you would find you're not alone in that here. If you should wish to stay, I'm certain Mothlock would have you."

"I am nothing close to a saint." Even saying the words aloud felt ludicrous and even a little nauseating.

"You could be. A master of brilliance in this life. Sainthood into the Beyond." He straightened. "Just think of all the days we could spend together—I've shown you next to nothing yet." He grinned so boyishly an instant confusion came upon her.

"And I would be fixed?"

"More than fixed." His eyes shone with excitement. "Stronger than ever before. The greatest necromancer to have ever lived. All it takes is a minor adjustment, the smallest pain, and you will be free from any torment."

"But you're not."

The luster fled his eyes like a flame snuffed. "What?"

"You said you cannot dream." Lux caught her breath immediately afterward. His face—

"I..." He faltered. He would not meet her eyes. "You are correct." Suddenly, they lifted, and she felt frozen to the terrace floor. "I should have told you from the start. Maybe you wouldn't have felt so alone."

He cleared his throat. "I was born unwhole. And—well—if you are broken, Lux...I am certainly shattered."

By the time they stood outside her door, Lux knew this would be solidified as one of the worst days of her life. She gazed down the dimly lit corridor while Corvin spoke of the banquet tomorrow and the guests who would soon arrive. She stared at the apparition standing rigid in its center, and it stared back.

You did not tell me there was a third choice, she thought at it.

The nightmare only grinned.

All Lux wanted to do was scream. Instead, she said, "Why is there a tower but no way to it?"

Corvin's hand ceased its turning of her doorknob. "There was a way to it. It was blocked long ago." She raised an eyebrow, and his lips lifted. "One of those few places you rightfully inquired after in the carriage; I cannot take you there." He sobered, however, as he said, "The site of Alixsander Alesso's death."

Of course it was. "Corvin. This ritual—if I should agree to it and wish to join your society, what would they—"

"I'm sorry," he interrupted. "It's sacred and so we don't speak it. All I can say is it's a test of faith."

The door swung in by his hand, and when Lux moved past him, he murmured, "May we both be fixed by tomorrow's end."

That stopped her. "It will be your first time undergoing it too?"

"No." His eyes traced her face. "But I have faith it will be the time it succeeds in me."

A pit formed in her gut over his words at the same moment a deep bell resounded.

"What timing," he said.

"Where is it? That you assemble." She did not look at him again, choosing instead to stare at her reflection.

"The sanctum. A holy place. We will show you soon." A touch, featherlight, drew down her neck. "Now, get your rest."

The mirror revealed him turning on his heel, and Lux made no further effort to move into the room. She waited, her pulse spiking, nails nearly puncturing her palms.

Because she'd been to the sanctum. Knew from the moment she entered it was not holy, but wrong. And any acts done within its confines must be why.

Stop. You're to find lifeblood—or not—and that's it, she told herself. There would be no single-handed dismantlement of a zealot-fueled business. No convincing a shattered boy he was also being duped. If the vault was not in the underground labyrinth, then it must be in the sealed away tower. She would find it. She would avenge Ghadra's dead. She would—

She peeked beyond the doorway in time to see Corvin pass the balcony and begin his descent downstairs. Lux shut the door and ran.

Fumbling with the key in her bodice, she ripped it over her head. The lock formed, steadily growing more distinct, but she had no more use for the crypt. The entombing would have been long over, and she'd a tower to find. She tossed the key into her pack. Had nearly drawn the strap over her shoulder—when Death tapped. She shrugged it away; she did not care. But then a woman screamed.

Lux spun to face her balcony. She'd left the outer door unlatched, and now it swung in on the wind. She could hear all the sounds of the sea. She crept toward the landing.

It had sounded far away, that cry, but if—

She jolted at a sudden shriek. It felt different from the first, more severe. Lux lunged onto the balcony and stood on her toes at its edge. She scanned the drenched rocks far below before instinct drew her to the right.

On a cliff stood a person. Whether in skirts or a robe, she couldn't say, only that they wore white. And they were terribly close to the edge; closer than even she'd dared. Beneath the full moon's light, someone stalked toward them.

Lux stared at the dire scene. Made her choice. She picked up her skirt and sprinted.

Prior to her dinner with Corvin, she'd tied Shaw's knife to her outer thigh. It began to slip as she hurtled down the staircases. Lux gripped it along with her dress and used her opposite hand to propel her around the banisters.

She didn't meet a single collector. She wasn't sure what she would say if she did.

Lux shoved through the front doors and into the dark.

Gravel crunched beneath her boots, and she slowed only a little upon reaching the garden path. Another voice lifted on the air, more a shout than a shriek, and a word this time.

"*Stop!*"

"Don't even think of it," she spat at the parasitic stems. They swayed backward, scolded, and she resumed her fast pace. The air was cold; her dress whipped behind her. Lux felt her hair come completely undone. She arrived at the garden door and discovered it open.

I don't even know them. What am I doing, risking everything on the cliffs?

But that shriek had sounded petrified.

She went through the door and slowed at the edge. Steps led downward to the cove, but if she walked carefully, she could follow a narrow path along the cliffside instead.

She wanted desperately to grip the fence for security, but the brambles had claimed that section.

"*Please!*" screamed a high voice. "Don't come any closer!"

Don't fall, don't fall, Lux begged of her balance and hurried down the path as fast as she dared.

She noticed the white nightgown first, recognized its cut, and that led her to see the person grabbing hold of it. An attendant, or at least someone dressed in their uniform. The pair teetered on the cliff's edge, so close Lux's body pricked with fear.

"Let go of me! I only want to go home!"

The moonlight lit the person's face as they turned, and Lux's eyes widened as their gazes met. Red hair tumbled to the girl's waist—for she was indeed a girl, not a woman. She couldn't have been much older than Aline, and certainly younger than Lux herself. Lux's attention dipped at the resulting clank of iron. The girl's ankles were secured in shackles.

"Devil below, what is going on?"

The girl ripped at her nightgown. "Help me, please! She won't let me go!"

The attendant was quiet but strong. A topknot of greying hair bobbed as she was dragged forward by the girl and still, the older woman's grip would not yield.

"Hildred?"

The awkward attendant who'd tended her fire glanced at Lux for only a breath. "I cannot let you go," the woman said, sure and steadfast as any line she'd delivered to Lux earlier that morning.

As if they weren't all dangerously close to a perilous drop.

"You *will* let her go," said Lux loudly to be heard above the crashing waves. "You've no right to keep anyone here. What has she done?"

"She's disobeyed," said Hildred and yanked.

The girl toppled forward but didn't fall.

"I did not!" cried the girl, and though her voice was high and light, it wasn't as meek as it'd sounded while Lux was eavesdropping from the cart. Red splotches bloomed on her cheeks. "I quit! I don't want to work here anymore."

"There you have it," said Lux. "You can't force someone to work for Mothlock. You certainly can't chain them. That's not done."

"You must stay in your room until sunrise. Those are the rules."

Lux gaped at the woman. Because either she hadn't heard them, or she was too dense to understand.

"Hildred." Lux stomped up to her. Sea-spray lifted on the wind and coated her skin. *Saints above, we're too close to the edge.* "You're going to cause her to fall. Unhand. Her." Lux pried at Hildred's fingers without hardly any success.

She dug her nails into Hildred's damp forearm next. The older woman didn't so much as blink. *What the devil.* Lux seethed and dropped her hands, reaching for Shaw's knife.

"I only want to go home. I haven't done anything I shouldn't. I only want to go."

"Mothlock is your home. You will do as the lords say."

The girl screeched when Hildred's fist tightened in her hair.

"That's enough!" Lux shouted and ripped her blade free. "I will use this; I do not care where."

Hildred hardly glanced at it. Instead, she hauled at her prisoner. But the girl dug in her stockinged feet—and slipped. She fell, crashing to her side, and the momentum propelled Hildred backward.

The girl screamed with a voice full of pain; the attendant hadn't released her hair but used it as an anchor. Lux didn't think any further before her wrist whipped out. She cut through red locks of curl easy as butter.

It freed the girl on the ground.

It freed Hildred too.

The woman flailed her arms for balance. Once. Twice. Then she pitched straight off the cliff.

Chapter Twenty-Eight

Lux's body wound tight. She walked along the precarious edge. Hildred was dead for certain, but she needn't stay that way. Lux stared hard at the shore far below but could see nothing aside from jagged rocks and frothing waves. It was too dark.

"Where have you gone?" Lux asked.

What have I done?

"She's...dead?" stammered the girl. Lux almost missed the question as a wave crashed.

"For now. Maybe forever," Lux replied. Her dread intensified. "Are you all right? I'm sorry I cut your hair."

Clumps of red strands blew about the grass. The girl glanced at them and away again. "I can't go back there. They told me I would be better, that the drink would help the salt-sick, but I can't wait. There's so much *want* here, and it's making me sicker. You'll help me, won't you? You don't feel like them. That woman... She felt like nothing at all and that scared me the most."

Lux could hardly follow the girl's running thoughts. Her own were in too much turmoil. "I don't feel like them?"

"No. You feel lonely. And scared. And...very angry."

The girl's eyes had grown wide at her final assessment, and Lux had to indeed push down her anger. She was furious with herself. She hadn't thought through every consequence of cutting Hildred from the girl. She'd only been focused on the most obvious one. Giving the girl her freedom.

Because for Lux, freedom had always felt like the most important thing.

She surveyed the girl's attire. Her nightgown was a replica of Lux's own upstairs, gifted by Mothlock. "I can't help you yet. Wait for me if you can, but I must look for the body in the cove first."

"I'll wait by the garden door."

Lux nodded. That would do.

A few minutes later, she stood upon the first stone step and cursed her long skirt. This was why she'd always cut everything off at the knee. With so much fabric, she risked tumbling to her death the same as the body she sought. She adjusted her bodice and retied her knife, then she gathered her skirt in her fists. *Saints above, let me live.*

The first half of the path wasn't so awful: she slipped only once. But by the second half, she cursed and abandoned her grip on one part of her skirt to extend her arm for balance. To compensate for the drag, her opposite hand clutched her dress higher. Though her bare knees protested the exposure, it was infinitely better than falling.

The waves grew to a bellowing roar as she descended, and Lux almost lost her balance entirely at their sheer size. She'd been so focused on her feet, she'd not braved a glance. She paused now. A single step more and her boots would meet black sand.

She tried to remember what Corvin had said regarding this cove, what she should watch for. *The waves. I shouldn't swim in the sea.* Of course, she'd not told him at the time that she would never attempt it because she'd never learned how. Lux stepped forward. Her boots sank. She tried to hurry, but it was difficult. It reminded her of walking beside Ghadra's marshes—the strange feel of ground shifting beneath one's feet.

Rocks of various sizes littered the cove, the larger ones offering themselves as homes to blue crabs. She picked her way around two boulders dripping with seaweed and sea-spray, and a large crab sought immediate shelter at her nearness.

It was then she met the sea.

It came upon her quick, a collision rather than a meeting. A wave crested, the force of it peppering her face with drops, and when it rolled in, the water splashed over her more than she intended. It soaked her boots and a good amount of her hem. Immediately, she noted the added weight.

But she didn't care. It was breathtaking. Even in the moonlight.

So utterly, terrifyingly—

Lux's thoughts snagged. Because farther out was something decidedly not froth-like, but white all the same. A body. In a white apron. A wave caught it up, and for a brief moment, she glimpsed more than that.

Long hair. Sallow skin. Seaweed clinging to the length of skirt tangled about the legs.

Hildred.

Lux gasped when frigid water met her thighs. Except when she cast a surprised glance to the rock beside her, the one dripping and dark, it hadn't moved.

Which meant neither had she.

"It is the changing tides you must be wary of."

Her mind gifted her the remainder of her and Corvin's conversation, just as another wave crashed against her. Her dress hung heavy and limp from her hips. *Turn back,* demanded her head, but the woman had drifted closer. Enough that Lux could see the deep lacerations marring her legs. The body wasn't within arm's reach, not yet, but perhaps if she took one step closer.

Lux stepped—

And sank beneath the waves.

For several heartbeats of time the world was dark and serene. She was suspended in a place she'd never found herself before, and it might have been peaceful—if only she could *breathe.*

Lux found the barest foothold and pushed.

She hardly moved.

The dress. That lush, emerald velvet. She'd never worn armor, but she guessed it must feel something like this. The heaviness had dragged her down to the depths, and now she would die here. *Drowned*—in the very sea she'd longed for.

How poetic, crooned the chaotic part of her mind, as the larger portion screamed, *SAVE YOURSELF!* Her lungs began to harmonize with it.

Her boots brushed sand a second time—she would have wept if it were possible—and with better footing and arms outstretched, Lux shoved upward with all her strength. Her fingers reached the surface. But nothing else belonging to her did.

She was dragged down again.

The taste of brine swept into her mouth; she refused to open her eyes. *Please. Don't let me die like this.*

Her body smashed into rock.

Lux clenched her teeth against a cry and grabbed hold. Or attempted to; the edges had been worn smooth. Her fingers slipped against the slick surface, the rest of her at the mercy of waves and the dress' weight. But then her hand met something else—a cold, limp limb. She didn't think it through. Perhaps because her consciousness faltered, her lungs the only part of her capable of screaming now. She grabbed it tight.

Using the body as leverage, Lux hauled it down while she rose. Her head broke the surface. She dragged a frantic breath before another wave descended—and pulled her back under.

Lux did not know how to swim. Even if she could, she could never swim dressed as she was. And it was dark and cold, and she was too tired. Not even the small gasp of air had helped. The underwater sounds became a beckoning lullaby.

Her grip on the body loosened.

Then there was nothing.

Her chest *burned*. In the worst sort of way. There was too much pressure, and it came from both inside and out. She tried to gasp a breath, but nothing moved.

Then it all moved at once.

Water ran from her lips. She coughed, and it poured faster. She felt a pressure again, this time at her shoulders, then she was shoved onto her front, her forearms in the rough sand. There, she hacked until she vomited. Seawater poured from her mouth and nose.

It burned so terribly, Lux's eyes streamed from behind closed lids; she wanted to cry but couldn't. She couldn't do anything until it was done.

Her first true breath was agony.

Her second was a sob.

"Saints above!" exclaimed a small voice. "Please, you have to breathe not cry!"

Lux lowered herself to her side where she gasped like a fish, her injured thumb stinging from the salt and her lungs stinging from the same thing.

Her eyes fluttered open. Vague features blurred in her vision, her tears obscuring anything distinct. Lux still felt as if she were underwater. The world remained muffled.

"How"—she coughed and wheezed—"did you save me?"

"I almost couldn't. You were floating like the other woman, but knocking against the rock. Lord Artemis and Lord Corvin say I'm blessed by the Saints. Maybe you're not blessed?"

If Lux could have rolled her eyes, she would have. Instead, she pushed upward until she could sit. She coughed again and spat seawater into the sand. "Thank you," she murmured.

"You're welcome. The woman is over there. She's wedged in the rocks."

Lux's gaze tracked to where the girl pointed. The moon highlighted a single pale leg. A large wave crashed and receded, dragging the body back into hiding where it caught between a boulder and a cliff ledge. Lux shoved to her feet. She waded into the water, but only up to her knees; she wasn't about to repeat her near-drowning. When the next wave came, it crashed against the boulder, dousing her, but a torso emerged along with it. She gripped Hildred's upper arm.

She hadn't even managed to drag it before the girl's hand grabbed the woman's opposite side, urging her release from the rocks. Together, they plucked the body from the water, hauling it onto shore.

It was all Lux could do to simply breathe when it was done. Her chest ached with her efforts. The girl knelt beside the woman and stared down at what they'd held. Lux did the same.

Hildred was bruised beyond belief. Lacerated too. Lux didn't think there could be any blood left in her body; her skin was translucent. A portion of her hair remained in the topknot Lux had seen on the cliff, but the rest had been swept free by the wind and waves.

She stared at the attendant's bloodless face.

And—laying dead like this—a resemblance began to materialize in her mind. *Viktar's sister disappeared six months ago...*

"I should be able to revive her," Lux finally said, and her voice emerged rasping. She needed water. Preferably without salt.

"But she's dead."

Lux shifted her eyes to the girl. *She's not afraid of death. How interesting.* Relievedly so. Lux was sure she couldn't have managed another's hysterics in her present state. "What's your name?"

"Cecily Otterbee."

"Lux Thorn. My brilliance is necromancy."

Albeit a broken one.

The girl's eyes rounded. "I didn't believe necromancers were real."

"Real as this disaster I'm in." Lux reached down toward the dead woman. With two fingers carefully placed, she closed Hildred's eyes, and out of habit, felt for the lifeblood congealing within her.

Her fingers paused in their assessment. She frowned—then quick as a gallow root, shoved Hildred's eyelids back. Lux leaned forward, looked closer, and gently pushed against one fixed pupil. She stared at the result on the pad of her finger in the moonlight.

Perfectly ordinary.

There was no slit. No leaking lifeblood.

But the body...

It was empty.

Chapter Twenty-Nine

Cecily Otterbee was thirteen years old, and the girl could feel others' emotions. Blasted bad luck for her. When Lux had asked if she could also manipulate them, she'd said she didn't know. She'd never tried.

They tucked Hildred's body away from view as best they could, then Lux needed a reprieve. Her lungs were sore, and her muscles exhausted. Huddled and shivering on a rock, they stared out at the waves.

"It sounded like a dream to come here," lamented Cecily. "I have five siblings and I'm in the middle. Do you know what that's like? I feel forgotten a lot of the time. But Corvin—he made me feel unforgettable. He said he could see the blessing of Saints on me, and if I wished to work for Mothlock, he would ensure my education until I came of age to join their society. But when I arrived…"

Lux closed her eyes against a monstrous wave's violent crash. She absorbed what Cecily said in rapt silence.

"I feel ill here. Deep inside. I felt it right away, but I didn't know what it was from. Artemis is their healer. He said I was sensitive to change, that it was salt-sick and I would feel better soon, but the drink he gave me didn't last long. And the shackles to keep me from being lost hurt my ankle bones. When I injured their cook… I swear I didn't mean to."

The chain clanked as the girl shifted. Lux's hands twisted uselessly in her lap. They yearned to occupy something.

A knife. Or a throat.

"It isn't the salt-sick," Cecily whispered.

"I doubt it," said Lux.

"They want so badly. I don't think you can comprehend without feeling it yourself. It hurts me to feel it."

"But what do they want?" said Lux, mostly to herself.

"I don't know. But the attendants scare me. I told you about her." Cecily pointed toward the partially hidden body. "They don't feel like anything. And I don't want to be like that."

"Empty."

"*Empty.*"

Lux shook her head. She'd never known anything like it. The confusion overshadowed any guilt and any dread. *How could Hildred have been alive without lifeblood?* The old loose pages once belonging to Riselda's alcove said it couldn't be done.

"I need to go home. Even if I have to tell my parents they were right."

"They didn't want you to go?"

"They told me a story once. Of a person they knew. Who went to Mothlock and never came out again. They said it's a cursed place. And there are more of those stories."

"That didn't deter you?"

"Lord Corvin said they were lies spun by their enemies. That I couldn't trust the slanderers. It made sense to me...at the time." She rose from the rock. "And *you're* here. Why are you here?"

Lux followed her. Together, they made for the precarious steps cut into the cliff. "I'm sick too."

Cecily turned sharply toward her. "The same as me? I thought—"

"No. Not the same."

"But are you sure it's true? Artemis felt excited when he told me I needed his help."

Lux's memories retrieved an image of Viktar, cold and stiff upon his bed in Verity. "I wish it wasn't. My symptoms began before I ever met a collector."

"Well," said Cecily, beginning to huff in their steep climb. "I hope you get better soon."

"Me too." Lux pressed her knuckles to her chest. *Don't give out on me, you lumped organs.* But as they continued their ascent, she thought for sure she could hear the remnants of the sea she'd breathed sloshing around inside.

"I only have to get to the forest," muttered Cecily in front of her. "They won't be able to track me in there."

"Not to be pessimistic," Lux heaved. "But won't they make straight for your home?"

The girl tripped while sidestepping a crab, and Lux reached to steady her. *Ignore the pain,* she demanded of herself. Only, she saw how much farther they had yet and knew she might pass out by its end. Her sodden dress felt like it weighed five times as much.

"I didn't think of it."

"I have some money—a good amount. It should be enough to get you by for several weeks while you contact your family." Lux would have to say farewell to the necromancer's journal. The disappointment hurt. "Though, I'm not sure how far you're going to make it in those shackles."

Already, Cecily had to take each step with care. The chain between her ankles wouldn't allow her legs to stretch far enough to walk up the stairs normally. Lux didn't complain about the slow pace; she needed it badly.

The idea that they chained the girl nightly under the guise of safety... Lux clenched her teeth until they protested. "Maybe I can find something to cut through them."

Cecily remained silent, and when they crested the cliff, Lux realized why. She was crying.

Tears pooled in the girl's eyes and ran quietly down her cheeks. Every time she blinked, a fresh trail trickled.

"Cecily..."

"Why did I think I could go home? I'm so foolish."

"You're not. And maybe you can. Only, not yet. There's something I—" Lux's thought cut same as her words. Yes, there was something she needed to do. More than one thing now that she really considered it. But she didn't know how she could succeed. Sneaking through a dark manor in search of a single room with a singular goal was one thing. Doing something worthwhile about kidnapping and other unearthed atrocities was another.

Shaw had burned the mayor's experimentation room down with his sister's invention. What worthwhile thing could she do? She had no one.

"It's better this way. Lucena Thorn always destroys those we love."

Lux jolted at the voice in her head. At finding the nightmarish version of herself standing rigid at the garden door. It waited for her, wraithlike and dripping in the night.

"We killed another tonight. Because we did not think, only acted. We kill those we don't love too. We're an ugly, mindless monster. Lock us away and spare the world of our presence."

For the second time, Lux felt at a loss for air. She thought she heard another's voice but couldn't be sure. Waves bombarded her ears. Waves that weren't a part of the sea.

"Lux? Lux!"

Lux flinched as her upper arm smarted. She glared down at the sensation.

"I'm sorry! I didn't want to pinch you, but you looked—I mean you *felt*... What did you see?"

"I saw—" Lux blinked. Over and over. With each, the apparition faded a little more. When it finally vanished, her shoulders drooped. "It's gone. It's all in my head, at any rate."

"You were so terrified," said Cecily, her own voice shaking. "It scared me to feel it."

"I'm sorry I frightened you."

I shouldn't be around anyone, she thought. *Most of all, a girl like this.*

"And now you're angry and sad. I shouldn't have screamed and forced you to save me."

A bit of that anger flamed higher. What she didn't need was someone relaying her emotions back to her. But Lux bit back any scathing remark. Instead, she dragged a deep breath into her hurting lungs, and said, "You absolutely should have screamed. More of us should scream."

Cecily wiped at her eyes, blinking away tears. Then she nodded.

"Maybe I can trick that footman, Manphry, into finding me some sort of tool. He's been helpful."

"No! He's empty too."

Lux frowned, her hand on the rough door. "Who else?"

"Everyone I've met except the collectors."

Devil below.

"Okay. We'll manage on our own. There must be a carriage house outside the gate." Lux glanced along the iron fence, where it disappeared into darkened cliffs. There was certainly no going around.

Cecily sniffed. "Probably."

"Stay hidden in the garden. I'll gather the money and whatever else I can." Lux surveyed the girl's soiled and torn stockings. "Shoes for certain. It shouldn't take me long."

"And if it does?"

"Then wait a little longer. If it becomes really dire though, then I suppose go with your original plan. Make for the forest."

Lux pushed through the garden door. She hated that the girl absorbed every bit of the trepidation coursing inside her. *What a miserable brilliance. I would die from it.*

But she supposed that was why it wasn't gifted to her. She was perfectly suited to death: an emotionless state. For the one dead, at any rate.

They crept along the garden path. Lux gave up on her sodden skirt and spent her energy hauling up her drooping bodice instead. The moon was high now. It lit the tower's pinnacle and every beast's wing with a cool glow. And she decided she hated the look of Mothlock; its presence so like that of a hulking creature lying in wait in the dark.

Then its mouth opened.

The dim light of the courtyard's lampposts became overwhelmed at the manor's opening. Cecily stilled like a startled mouse when Lux dragged her knife free.

One. Two. Three. *Four.* Four collectors swept out onto the stoop. And she knew at once what they wanted. Their hoods shifted as they scanned the garden; both she and Cecily sank to a crouch.

Voices rose amongst them, growing louder. Two hurried down the stairs. One of those turned onto the far garden path. The other made straight for them.

"Devil's own *tits*," hissed Lux. Because there was nowhere, quite honestly nowhere, for them to go. "You're going to have to run for it, after all. As much as those shackles will allow you."

She heard Cecily's shuddering breath and felt the girl begin to rise.

"But give me five seconds first," said Lux.

She tucked away her knife. Then she burst to her feet and screamed.

Chapter Thirty

The collector screamed right back, and when Lux ran, barreling past him, he didn't react until she was already lengths ahead.

"Death to the Devil! What is going on?"

"Ms. Thorn!"

"Is she all right?"

"Grab her!"

Lux ran up the steps—where the other two men stood stunned—and grabbed hold of their robes. One was Kent; she could tell by the size. "Get this devil out of my head!" she cried. "It tried to drown me!"

"That can't be true. It wouldn't—there she is! Ms. Otterbee!"

Artemis.

Lux was flung off by Kent and into the arms of the healer. She shoved him away. Cecily moved as quickly as she could, her gait made awkward and slow by the shackles. She ran for the gate.

When the collectors from the garden paths moved to chase her, Lux leapt down the steps and shrieked again.

If I must be mad, let me be mad.

The pair whipped backward to see the reason for her cries, and she knocked into them both. One went sprawling into the gravel. The other latched onto her upper arm.

"That's enough of that!" he shouted.

Lux recognized his voice as Tobias, the one who had come to them with the cook's injury. "It's the *devil*. It tells me you've done evil things." She sneered at him. "It tells me you lock children away at night."

She kicked him in the shin with all her strength. The man howled and dropped her arm while the other struggled up from the ground. Lux lifted her eyes to the gate. To see Cecily heave against it without success. The girl began to climb.

"Saints, no," whispered Lux. The spires were many and so thin they glinted like they'd been layered in ice. No sane person would think of climbing over them. But there the girl was, scurrying up the gate anyway.

Cecily glanced back briefly, her eyes wide and panicked. Lux slipped through the collector's grasping hand, but his next, she couldn't dodge. The fallen one had risen to his feet, and now they both held onto her arms and would not let go. The girl reached the top.

"No, Ms. Otterbee! You don't understand, the salt-sick has hold of you! You have to fight it!"

But Lux met Cecily's eyes and shook her head. The girl ignored Artemis. She wedged her small foot in between the spires—and leapt.

The rip of fabric and a faint cry was all Lux heard before being dragged backward.

"Get your hands off me," she yelled. "I'm a guest here!"

"You're insane! You need to be medicated," said the collector on her left, meanwhile the other reached down for a palm full of gravel. Lux hardly acknowledged his muttering into the rocks as Kent and Artemis sprinted for the gate. *Please. Let her get free.*

Suddenly, she choked.

The collector's hand was over her mouth, gravel on her tongue, and it was tumbling down her throat.

Lux kicked and flailed. She saw shifting lights outside the gate. She heard a singular shout. The gate swung in at the same moment the man's hand fell away, and Lux spat at once. Dirt and rocks. She heaved a breath and coughed until she tasted blood.

Her head began to spin.

A carriage. There was a carriage outside the gate. And there was a collector climbing down from it, hauling a body draped in a white nightgown toward the vehicle's interior.

Lux's chest grew heavy. In fact, every part of her did. Her legs, her arms, even her torso—all seemed like it weighed ten times as much.

"What did you do to me, you wretched old man!" she shouted, horrified.

"I weighed you down. You think I don't know the tricks of stones? I practically built this manor on my own, girl. You will never be able to run now. You'll be lucky if you can walk without needing a respite."

"We cannot tolerate disobedience here at Mothlock," said Tobias, shaking her until her teeth clacked.

"Be careful," warned the other. "She's Alistair's latest project."

Lux's chest burned. There was blood in her throat and a heaviness throughout her. Not even anger would save her now, though it flared molten hot. Her chest had turned to stone; she was sure of it. She couldn't *breathe*.

"I... Wait..."

But they wouldn't. They didn't notice or they didn't care. They pulled her away.

"I...can't..."

"Do as I do."

For once, it was not the nightmare speaking. Lux pressed her eyes closed and clawed, frantic, into the memory. Outside it, the collector said something, but water had returned to her ears. She could not hear.

"Inhale with me."

She could see him so clearly. Could almost convince herself she could feel his skin against her own. His breath, warm and sweet, against her lips. And though he was so very far away, his heartbeat pulsed steady against her palm.

"...*know to find me.*"

She had. Through all the time and distance. She could hardly believe it.

Her lungs filled, full and—while not easy—decidedly less difficult. When Lux opened her eyes, she discovered Corvin bent to a knee beside her. His shadowed brow was etched in concern.

She'd been set on the foyer floor.

Corvin dragged his hood down, and she sucked a breath at the sight of his eyes. They were swollen—only slightly, and likely on par with her own—and that didn't draw her attention so much. The redness did; the state of every vessel marring the white.

"Lux." His hand reached out to cascade over her salt-damp hair. "What have you done?"

"I—nothing. I've done nothing. There was a girl. And then the tide. I nearly drowned." She couldn't collect her thoughts. She couldn't quit staring at Corvin's eyes.

"You've interrupted Invocation. Mothlock can only remain as successful as the obedience of its members. Are you sure I didn't mention it? I thought I would have."

"...what?"

"Did you help her escape? Did you know she's sick? She's one of our staff, and she could have been really hurt tonight. Is hurt, in fact."

"Help her *escape?* Is this place something to be escaped?"

"It is a place to be treasured. Venerated. The work we accomplish here will last through the ages. Of course it isn't a place to be escaped. But if you're ill. Not in your right mind..."

He let the sentence hang, and Lux didn't know if he meant Cecily's illness any longer or her own.

A collector came through the doors. *Silas.* She could tell by the walk. In his arms was Cecily, her face tucked against him, nightgown torn at her knees. A steady drip sounded in the silence. Blood splattered on the floor.

"Manphry," said Corvin, and Lux shifted to see the tall man emerge from a shadowed corridor. "Take the girl to Lord Artemis's workroom. Once he's through, return her to her room. Make sure the fire is built and extra blankets laid out."

Manphry acknowledged the command, and the transfer between him and Silas was quick. A soft cry came from Cecily at the movement.

I'm sorry, Lux said inside, because she couldn't say it aloud. Manphry made for the stairs and Artemis followed suit. Lux pushed herself to her knees, though it took a great deal of effort.

"Do you need healing too?"

"No," she growled. "I need your man to take his vile enchantment off me."

"I hate to see you so upset. Don't you think it's best if you keep the stones? You need your sleep, and this might be the thing to encourage it. Hildred!"

Lux's eyes bulged over the shouted name. She ducked her face.

Several silent moments passed. In which Silas left to return to whatever needed to be done about his carriage, and the other two collectors stood as barbaric sentries in the foyer. From here, Lux couldn't tell who'd turned their brilliance against her and so she offered murderous glares to both.

"Death to the Devil," grumbled Corvin. "I'll have to ask Manphry about her. Godfrey!"

Someone shifted and soon scurried down the lamplit corridor. "Yes, Lord Corvin?"

"Please assist Ms. Thorn to her bedchamber. Ensure she keeps the rocks inside along the way."

Lux's mouth fell wide as the attendant came to do as told. "No. *No.* Corvin, what are you doing?"

"What is best for you. For us both." His chin dipped, and suddenly his lips were a mere breadth from her own, his hand brushing back her hair. "Do this one thing for me. Have faith, Lux."

She sucked a stunned breath; Corvin's mouth brushed light and cold against her cheek.

Godfrey's touch was not gentle. He looped his arm beneath hers and hauled her up. Lux allowed the help as her legs were impossibly heavy. Once steady, she glanced at the attendant's profile. His eyes settled on hers before shifting away; they were hazel but muted. Dulled—same as Hildred's. Same as Manphry's.

Lux's stare narrowed. She used their closeness as an opportunity to grab hold of his wrist.

His temperature was strange. Cool, but like the way an inanimate object was at the whim of its surroundings. She dug deeper. Her eyes unfocused; she shifted to his insides.

She waited for light but found none.

She searched for corruption. She found none of that either.

Devil below.

He was *empty*. No lifeblood. No *soul*. No…

Nothing.

Her insides clenched and then roiled. She opened her eyes and thought she might be sick over her shoes.

It's wrong. It's so abhorrently wrong.

She swayed as she returned to herself.

"This way," said Godfrey.

He'd only shuffled her to the base of the first staircase when a pounding came against the doors. Lux glanced over her shoulder. She wanted to see if it was Silas, if he'd come with another poisoned investor for the basement crypt. She watched as Corvin moved toward the door, waving the other collectors aside to pull it wide.

Lux knocked into Godfrey.

"Up the stairs," he said.

She ignored him.

The man at the door was not Silas. Nor any collector for that matter, she was sure. This man wore a thick, brown coat and matching cap, brown trousers, and fine, black boots. The shirt snagged her eyes last and held them longest: a silken, jewel blue.

His arm was outstretched, and his bare grip revealed an ivory card.

"Ah, and so the guests of honor begin to arrive. Welcome to Mothlock Manor," said Corvin with a note of pleasant surprise. He took the card. His head snapped up after a short glance. "*Ghadra?*"

"Your invitation was well received by our newly elected mayor." The man stepped over the threshold where the lamplight discovered the sharp angles of his face.

He removed his cap and unruly, copper locks fell free.

"Shaw Roser, delegate."

His eyes lifted. Found hers. The warmest shade: the color of honey.

And Lux's body betrayed her. Or maybe it wished to save her.

She turned her head and vomited gravel all over Godfrey's boots.

Chapter Thirty-One

For the second time that night, Lux knew she was dying.

Her body had betrayed her, indeed. Blood pooled in her mouth—pouring down her throat and through her lips, both—and she couldn't bear it. The taste. The warm wetness. The painful parts shredded. The rocks that had been forced down her had torn her throat wide. They'd not wanted to be expelled.

Everything was red.

To die this way is worse than all the rest.

Lux slumped onto the stairs. She thought there might have been voices shouting, but like before, her hearing had gone. Her vision darkened at the edges, tunneling then blurring. Her eyelids fluttered.

The pressure on her body seemed to come from far away: hands on her torso, on her legs. She tried to breathe, to help them help her, but when she dragged a breath, only blood ushered in.

After that, she could not breathe anymore.

This was not poetic. This was her most heinous nightmare coming to pass.

Her body was moving. Someone held her. Ran with her. The muffled shouts wouldn't cease, and when she laid her head back, gasping for breaths that couldn't come, only darkness beckoned.

Close your eyes, it said. *It is peaceful here.*

Maybe it would be. She'd gone down that road so many times in her revivals, but she'd never reached its end. A wall, a veil, had always blocked her path, and from there she could only call a soul forward. She could not go on.

She could go on now.

Her eyesight was gone. Perhaps she'd closed her lids after all. A different pressure bit into her arm then, and it likely would have hurt—if her nerves hadn't been dulled to nothing. But she could feel the road beneath her feet. The veil at her fingertips. She could feel those two things plain.

Okay. I'll go, she decided—and reached.

Bright light burst in her vision.

Lux turned her head at once to hide from its shine. The veil vanished. The road disappeared. Her brow furrowed and her teeth clenched. And then a pricking sensation swept through every limb until it centered in her chest.

"She's not breathing."

"She will."

She did. A huge, gulping gasp and her lungs blessedly filled—with sweet air rather than blood.

From there, sensation returned. The hard surface beneath her horizontal body. The smell of iron and incense. She swallowed; her throat didn't hurt at all.

"Lux. Lux, can you open your eyes?"

"Slow your breathing now."

She *could* open her eyes. But she didn't want to.

I've hallucinated him. Logic said she must have, and she wanted to sob. She didn't truly hear his voice or feel the caress of his eyes. She didn't see him standing on that threshold: tall and broad and determined. Shaw could not be here. He was in Ghadra, and she was far away. Now, she was even farther. *This is madness, and he's not real.*

How quickly she'd spiraled into it.

Fingers gripped her jaw, and she could see no help for it. Lux blinked blearily upward. Her vision swam, the features indistinct for a moment. Then light eyes met hers. She jolted against the table.

"You swallowed too much," said Corvin, hovering above her. Like it was her fault. Her choice for enchanted rocks to be shoved mercilessly into her mouth. His finger swept her cheekbone. "I was so worried we'd lost you."

"It was a near thing."

The man at the edge of her vision moved into view. He was unfamiliar with his thick, grey eyebrows and full beard, his lips hardly visible. But his voice, she knew. A revealed Artemis stared down his hooked nose at her. She'd never felt more like a specimen. He said, "Tell me how you're feeling. I want to be sure you're comfortable and all has worked as it should."

"I feel..." Her gaze narrowed upon Corvin's pristine clothing. She'd been sure blood had poured from her like a fountain. Had it not?

Her head had been pressed against a hard chest. *Someone* had carried her.

Maybe I've imagined that too.

"I feel like I've vomited rocks."

"Yes. It is a bizarre enchantment, I'll admit. Of course, if you hadn't vomited, they would have dissolved naturally without discomfort. That aside, has the pain gone?"

Her eyebrows met. "I don't feel pain anymore."

Artemis seemed pleased at this, and she supposed he should be. He'd discussed her future as Mistress of Mothlock at length with his overlord; her death would have nullified that. Her rare, precious usefulness snuffed.

A sudden suspicion twitched through her. She lifted her arm.

"What did you give me?" she asked and examined the dried flakes of blood. A small puncture wound marked the bend of her elbow, already healed over.

"A mending tonic. You were losing too much of your blood volume out your mouth. It's a good thing I've managed a formula which can be administered in other ways."

"Nothing else?"

Her gaze flicked up to meet his. In time for an incredulous expression to sweep across his face.

"What else is there for the brink of death?"

Well, she certainly wouldn't know. He turned away, returning soon after with a burning lamp, which he placed beside her head.

"Allow me one last exam. No tonics or tinctures," he said with a hurry when she stiffened beside him. "Only looking."

Lux ground her teeth. Corvin touched her hand, his gloved forefinger rubbing a circular pattern atop it.

She didn't pull away.

She desperately wanted to.

"Only looking," she finally agreed.

She grimaced when the pads of the healer's leather-clad thumbs pulled at the sensitive skin beneath her eyes.

He leaned in.

Lux's lips parted. Her thoughts muddled, suddenly bewildered. Because the healer's eyes in the lamplight were not so dark as she'd thought. They were brown in places, yes, but hardly. The rest...

Silver as Corvin's. Silver as Kent's. And now that she studied these, she realized Silas's had also been shot through the same.

She didn't understand it. "Why are your eyes that way?" she whispered. Because not only were they silver, they were also red-lined and swollen. Like Corvin's.

The circle stopped on her hand.

"Corvin didn't tell you?" His unusual eyes roamed over hers. "Maybe he didn't wish to scare away something he's come to care for."

"*Artemis—*"

But the healer's expression only softened at Corvin's reprimand. "We have been cursed, Necromancer. All of us."

Lux was drenched in salt and blood; her skin itched and her chest felt tight. She stood beside the hearth, beside a cauldron suspended from a hook, and she sipped black coffee with a reluctant pleasure. They'd told her to sit. She would not.

Could not.

It was late. She'd nearly crossed into the Beyond twice. She was on the verge of hysterics. She could feel it bubbling away in time with the brew at her hip.

Too large a part of her wanted to run. She couldn't ignore it. She'd thought she was brave. That she was determined to see this to its end. That her life—all she'd gone through—would be worth something. But the hollow hole in her chest leaked a darkness she couldn't stopper.

Lux winced at the bitterness flooding her mouth.

"Can you not see she's been through enough tonight?" Corvin glared at the healer.

"I didn't tell her with any expectation. I merely told her because she asked. And because if she is to trust us, in what we're doing here, then she should know."

Trust. That single word encompassed a myriad of memories, emotions, and dreams.

Lux had no experience with curses. Only Riselda's instruction and the healer's own dismissal. It was the latter she addressed now. With a healthy amount of bite, she said, "Is it the dancing, then? Or the inability to love?"

"To sleep well," said Artemis while Corvin groaned into his hand. "To sleep at all."

"Let me guess. Riselda Grimrook's fault again?" Lux choked on a frightful laugh. She could hardly focus on the conversation, never mind all the other snapping threads.

Pay attention. You cannot give up or give in.

She wouldn't run—but she'd be damned if she didn't allow Cecily Otterbee a second try.

"Alixsander Osric Alesso."

Lux blinked dazedly at Corvin. "Your overlord?"

"He cursed us—using a mix of blood and fire and a healthy amount of intention. Unwittingly, we believe, assuming he meant to only harm his assailant. Distress distorted it." Artemis spoke while tidying his space. "But that is the risk of blessed blood pacts, connecting us all. Now, every day we plead for respite and receive very little."

"How? How can someone wield a curse so broad it spans decades of time? How can he still when he's dead?"

Corvin's expression turned pained. His tired eyes roved over her. Her stomach twisted. He said, "He cannot still. He could then." He drew a deep breath. "And because of it, our bodies have petrified."

"I don't—"

"We cannot age, Ms. Thorn," cut in Artemis. "We are stuck in a blasted worldly purgatory. To wield a curse requires the blood of the person you wish to lay it upon—you were correct. But to reverse such a thing requires the blood of the wielder themselves."

This cannot be true. Her cup sat upon the hearth, forgotten. Her stomach knotted so tight she didn't think it could ever be undone. It was...unfathomable.

"And he's dead," she finally said.

"And he's dead," agreed Corvin, picking at his sleeve.

Lux, lost for a moment in all the secrets and lies, suddenly snapped straight when Artemis murmured, "But he needn't stay that way."

Chapter Thirty-Two

She didn't require Cecily's presence to understand what emanated from the men standing before her now.

The want. It thickened the air.

"You cannot mean that," Lux whispered in horror.

Corvin's gloves followed several grooved etchings in the onyx wall. "The beauty of Mothlock is that it's always been ahead of its time. Where there are books and great minds, there are bound to be advancements. And Alixsander was not buried or burned." Frost-like eyes rose to ensnare hers. "His was never a permanent resting place, but a sacred preservation."

A preservation. A wash of dread swept down her spine. A pressure built in her chest, and her throat grew tight. *The ice.* "Corvin—"

"No, it's not what you think. I know the time constraints."

"Then—" She couldn't finish the thought. Her knuckles pressed to her chest, seeking to drive out the threatening sensation.

"It's not what you think, because none of that matters. Before the twelfth hour, his body was frozen. It hasn't aged."

Lux shook her head. It decidedly sounded *not* better, and inside, she fought a yawning panic. "You believe that makes the difference?"

Corvin stepped around the table. "Of course. Why wouldn't it? The alchemical process we put him through that night ensured his body would remain suspended. It would be no different than what you did for Mistress Lefroy in that inn."

Lux concentrated on her breathing. This was information she'd searched for all along—regardless of if she *wanted* it or not. But alchemy? The last alchemist she knew helped bring about a plague.

Corvin reached for her. His hand rested on her upper arm with a steady grip. "Lux. Knowing the book of necromancy was stolen, in knowing Riselda Grimrook had vanished, the hope we harbored for any future revival died. It was a drawn out, labored death. No amount of scouring the country turned up a necromancer. No amount of it turned up the book or Riselda either. Until you. Over a century later with more skill than we have ever beseeched the Saints for."

Now, he has both the book and the necromancer under his nose, and he doesn't know about The Risen.

Lux stared up at him. She tracked every broken capillary in his eyes and when she was through, knew the truth.

"I was something to be collected, after all."

Corvin's earnestness faded. "I did believe we could help you. Still do. And I've meant everything I've told you." His hand lifted to cup the nape of her neck, and she hardly flinched. "At dinner. When I said you could join with us—become so much greater. And here. When I said you've been through enough for one night."

How she'd managed not to jerk from his grasp she'd never know. But her arm lifted, her fingers grasping his at her neck, and when she brought it down, she pulled his hand along with it. She didn't let him go.

The healer cleared his throat with feeling. "We've not ever had a woman with strength enough to join our society. I think there is no one more suited. You belong here, Ms. Thorn. I believe you know it too."

A sudden cold sweat overcame her. She turned toward him, dreadfully slow. With affected sweetness, she said, "You didn't tell me there was something other than your experiment to cure me, Lord Artemis."

Artemis didn't blink. No guilt showed on his face. "I presented to you the options I had at the time."

The rage. The rage she felt could not be healthy.

"You realize, of course, that I nearly *died* because of your collectors."

"Forgive us, Lux." Corvin's thumb moved against her hand once more. "Forgive me. It's true, we must follow the order of things, but you will not be restrained that way ever again. Even it was only meant to keep you safe."

Damn you and your order, she thought. She would never forgive him, that was for certain. "The girl. Is she all right?"

"The child is fine," replied the healer. "Her laceration was deep and her ankles twisted, but she's been mended since and a calming elixir provided. She is lucky; the salt-sick can cause the most intense of yearnings. How *did* you come upon her?"

Lux became excruciatingly aware of every point of contact between her and the ageless boy beside her. "I followed the madness."

A strained silence stretched. Until Artemis cleared his throat and said, "You look chilled. Perhaps a soak before you retire."

Lux hadn't been near the tub since the water had turned thick and putrid on her. She dreaded it now. But she *was* cold. Inside and out.

They wanted her for her brilliance. One more revival to cure them all before the madness was siphoned from her in some sanctimonious ceremony no one would explain. Lux bit at her cheek to keep her nails from biting into the back of Corvin's hand. He held it still, the grip light but sure, and together they abandoned the healer's workroom for the darkened corridor.

Lamplight flickered along the black walls. A fierce whining wind buffeted the manor's exterior at odd intervals. The effect on her was an ominous one; she didn't feel as though the night was through.

"It seems you were right," he said.

Her mind careened off its path. "About what?"

"On Ghadra's decision to mark a path through the marshes."

Lux halted so quickly, Corvin's hand nearly slipped from hers. He stopped ahead of her. One light eyebrow rose.

"I'd..." She drew a shaky breath. But it was awful—why had tears sprung to her eyes? "I'm sorry. I thought I had imagined all of that."

No, she was going to fall apart. Right here, on this landing.

"Gallant for a delegate, carrying you that way. Tell me—do you know him?"

It *had* been Shaw. His hands. His arms. His chest. Her chin trembled, and quelling it was the hardest thing she'd ever done. Did she *know* him?

Devil take her.

Would Shaw have lied over this question? He'd come here dressed in finery, an invitation secured. Why would he have gone through the trouble? It did not make sense for him to do it.

Ah. There was her answer.

"No. No, I don't know him."

A slight tug on her hand brought her close. Corvin stared down at her. And she wondered, briefly, if he didn't believe her, if she had guessed wrong. A hardness entered his eyes. His lips curved.

"Well then, I'll see you introduced. You must be curious how your city is fairing in your absence."

Lux began to tremble in his grip. There was no earthly reason he wouldn't feel it. "I won't be managing anything other than sleep for tonight."

His gaze dipped. "Blessed Saints, you're shaking. I wish the stones had stayed put so you might have slept soundly. But since they didn't, I think you should rest the day tomorrow. I'll send Hildred to you for dressing come evening."

Goosebumps erupted on her arms at the mention of that name. "And your other plans?"

He *tsk*'d. "Artemis shouldn't have sprung this on you. Please worry over nothing tonight."

Lux didn't respond. Once they'd taken to the stairs, it was at the fourth-floor balcony that she gazed again upon Alixsander below.

"You said you were a descendant," she mentioned quietly.

Corvin followed her stare. His grip tightened on her hand for all of a breath before it relaxed. "I didn't want to frighten you off. People are already wary of us. There are rumors—of curses, entrapments, and unnaturally long lives. They're all true, of course, but not in the way they think. Forgive me the lie that day, Lux. He is my brother."

Chapter Thirty-Three

Lux forgot how long she'd soaked, but the water was cool.

The room blurred around her. She could not focus on any particular spot. Her hair hung over the lip and had begun to dry.

The Collectors of Mothlock were cursed. They collected books then redrafted those books to fit their beliefs. They believed they could achieve perfection. They believed they could become Saints.

They are older than Riselda.

Was the Grimrook family really dead from disease, or did they argue the point?

Lux ran her nail along her teeth. All of that, she could deal with—maybe—but not the staff. Empty, soulless, should-be-lifeless. What sort of brilliance managed something like *that*? Nothing she wished to partake in, and she bit down on her finger in sickened worry. Would Cecily be transformed next?

The nightmare creature crouched in the corner. Its head had turned at one point into an unachievable angle. It whispered to Lux in between her own spiraling thoughts.

About all the horrible things she'd done.

About all the horrible things she would yet do.

About what a monster she was.

Lux hated it so much, she wanted to drag her skin clean off. Wanted to snatch out her brain herself.

Lose my brilliance. Lose myself. Or become one of them.

Revive that man from the portrait, that Alixsander Alesso. Corvin's brother, murdered then frozen for well over a century—and save them...all?

Lux allowed her eyes to drift shut. All she saw was Shaw. Standing in the doorway. Draped in moonlight and fine clothes. An expression so intense, she'd nearly died upon seeing it.

He was *here*. In Mothlock. She did not know where. If they'd sequestered him for questioning or lavished him as a proper investor. If he were locked away somewhere or ensconced within a bed as large as hers. It'd better be the latter—for the collectors' sakes. She wanted to find him—would find him—only she didn't quite know how to start. How horrible was she that she'd not already begun, that she felt limp as a dish rag, her body and mind wrung dry?

"*Lucena Thorn, we are a selfish beast, doing nothing for anyone except to save ourselves.*"

Lux groaned aloud, the barbs sinking sure as any truth into her head. A soft creak sounded outside the washroom. She couldn't be bothered to raise her head, but she did tilt toward the sound. Soft candlelight and hearth-fire were all that lit her bedchamber; the deeper shadows revealed nothing. When she looked back to the corner of the washroom, the wraith was still bent and twisted as before.

When it cackled, she covered her ears. But she couldn't block it out. Same as it didn't block out a second creak. This time, much louder.

"Hello?" Her voice emerged, fragile and frightened. She hadn't meant for it to and remedied it immediately. "Tell me who is there this instant!"

Her hands were still clamped tight to her ears when he moved into the doorway.

Saints above.

Lux drank him in. From the disarray of tawny waves atop his head, to his ruined, blood-soaked shirt and fine, black boots. His gaze seared her in return. "You..." she whispered—and promptly burst into tears.

Fabric sank into the water, wrapping her up. In the next breath, his hands were beneath her underarms and hauling her upward, a sopping wet robe against her bare legs. His forehead pressed to hers before his arms came around her, crushing her to him. Lux's nose buried in the familiar hollow of his throat; her breaths filled with his scent.

When his thumb stroked her skin, she could hardly bear it. Her body flushed with a warmth she'd already forgotten the feel of.

"It's all right, love. I've got you."

She released an inadvertent gasp when he reached behind her knees. He lifted her up and over the rim.

"Shaw," she murmured against his chest. "Tell me I'm not dreaming." Her head was tucked beneath his jaw, and she decided it would never leave that space.

His fingers rose to grip her chin, then they swept back into her hair. He drew her closer until their brows touched once more. Her tears flowed freely; she could feel them mingling with the leftover bathwater, dripping from her jaw.

And that horrible, hollowed part of her chest...filled.

"You're not dreaming, and thank fate for it. I'd never been so scared in all my life." He pulled back. His lips pressed to her damp temple. He did the same to the other side. "They swore they would save you. If they hadn't—"

"Enough," she said, her voice thick. "It didn't happen."

There was a time in her life when she never would have dreamt of crying in front of anyone, let alone this boy. Now here she stood, sobbing in his arms, and she'd never felt more cared for. More—

Her thoughts refused to go any farther in that direction. "How did you find me?"

"Since it's late and I watched you nearly die against me, I'll save you the long version and say I will always find you."

Lux pressed her eyes closed, sending a new rush of tears down her cheeks. "Maybe I shouldn't ever have left."

"What are you saying? Of course you should have. But I should have gone with you."

"I should have asked you."

"I should have followed you when you didn't."

Weak as it was, a small laugh left her. "I suppose it doesn't matter now."

There was so much—too much—that needed to be shared. Lux could feel the events since her departure from Ghadra stacking themselves in order to be told. But she found she couldn't speak them.

It wasn't like with Riselda, where her heart had refused to fully trust her supposed aunt and her tongue had stilled in response. This was a wish for peace. A sensation she'd forgotten. All she wanted to do was pull a nightgown over her head, haul thick stockings on her feet, and crawl into bed with Shaw's arms wrapped around her just like this. To feel *warm*.

Surely, it could all wait for morning?

The apparition clicked its nails on the wall and said, *"Look, look who is here. He will die because of us, little beast. Slow. Painful. Irreversible. We cannot wait to watch."*

Lux startled and didn't think before she hissed, "I would die myself before that!"

She realized her mistake at once. Shaw's grip changed to her shoulders until he could take a single step back. He stared down at her.

"Lux," he began, and she couldn't help the wince. "Who are you speaking to?"

"Oh," she said. "Didn't they tell you? I've gone mad."

Chapter Thirty-Four

The story would not be stopped now. The tale of her descent into madness poured out of her. She thought she might have been ashamed to share it, mortified by the weakness, but Shaw's earnest gaze brimmed with compassion and concern. She *wanted* him to know.

At its end, she felt entirely wrung out again. Emptied of any energy she'd regained from Shaw having broken into her bedroom. For he had broken in. He'd picked the lock.

"Nothing about this sounds right."

"Of course it doesn't sound right," she huffed. "What madness would?" Lux rubbed at her temples to ward off the headache she could feel brewing. She hadn't realized how brutal the tension in her body had grown until she'd been mended by Artemis's injection. But already it returned.

They sat together on a thick rug before the hearth—her bedchamber only possessed a single armchair—and Lux couldn't help from leaning her weight against Shaw while they spoke. His arm draped over her shoulder, keeping her close.

It felt very much like...

Home.

"These collectors—Lux, they're the buyers. We discovered a bill of sale, between the mayor and some "Society of Saints". They'd labeled the product as 'Time' and the amount paid was beyond any amount of money I'll ever see, except it hadn't been fulfilled. Then the invitation arrived. The Tamishes weren't surprised. Morana said her uncle attended every year—until he was swallowed by a tree—but she swears she doesn't know more. Only that it was business dealings. And it was, I suppose. Just the worst sort."

Lux shoved upright, though she immediately lamented the loss of Shaw's arm. "But why? They're already cursed to never age."

Except somewhere between her question and Shaw's exclaim of disbelief, she thought of Mistress Lefroy. The woman she'd revived had known the collectors by name, had been intimate enough to be carted off for an entombing. To a sanctum below stairs and one of those shrouded beds. She had been labeled an investor.

And what greater thing to spend one's life's earnings on than a second lifetime.

Lux splayed her hands over her cheeks. "Devil's *tits*."

But it seemed Shaw hadn't yet recovered from what she'd said. "Curses are nightmare tales. Blood brilliances. I didn't think they existed."

"Maybe they don't. I certainly don't know real from fake anymore." She stared blearily into the fire. "This madness... Of course it would find me."

Shaw's fingers slipped through hers, dragging her hand from her cheek until it was tucked within his. "Tell me something."

Lux drew a deep breath and sighed with all her pent-up weariness. "What would you like to know?"

Her chest hitched when he didn't immediately speak, guiding the back of her hand to his mouth, instead. Rather than kiss it as she expected, he spoke against her skin. His breath warmed her through.

"Tell me why you are always so quick to believe you are broken."

"I—"

Except there were no more words after that.

Why did she?

Well…of course she would believe it. The label felt like slipping on her well-worn corset. She'd spent most of her life broken. It was the easiest thing to take up the mantle again once more.

"Because I've been before," she finally managed. "It's who I am, Shaw."

Shaw shook his head. Honey-gold strands tumbled into his eyes. "You weren't broken. Not even then. Everything I know you to be has always been there: that goodness, that loyalty. That desire for justice which matches my own. *That* is who you are, Lux. It doesn't mean you're broken if you're only buried."

Lux's eyes held his. Even though he did not blink. Even though hers welled. "I'm afraid," she whispered. "I don't like to say it, but I am."

"I know." Now he did kiss her fingers. "But you can't lose hope yet. I demand it, actually, and we both know you're always quick to do as I say. It doesn't make sense; the timeline is too suspicious."

She dug a retaliatory nail into his hand until his nose wrinkled. "But I told you about that bandit's revival."

"Yes. And you told me about how it energized you afterward. Tell me, what sort of madness makes a person feel alive? Where's that oversized book of yours? It must have some sort of note in there to explain."

"On the writing desk. You won't find anything. I already looked."

Shaw abandoned her side anyway, and she physically cringed at the loss of his warmth. Maybe she'd become accustomed to the coldness of these walls, or maybe it was the yawning loneliness she'd decided to embrace again, but regardless of how acclimated she'd grown, it was decimated now. She couldn't go back.

"What is this?"

"Hmm?" She glanced to where he stood near the balcony door, her pack open and a prettily wrapped book in his grip. "Oh! A gift. For you. I bought it in Loxlen. From the Mothlock booksellers."

Shaw's eyes remained on her as the wrapping came free. They dropped to the black spine. His finger ran carefully along the length and Lux bit into her cheek. "This is a book of art."

"I'd wanted to find you one. Something that would maybe teach you as mine taught me." *I hope he isn't offended.* She didn't think he would be.

And she was proven correct when his head lifted, grinning at her with wonder. "This is the best gift I've ever received. Or even imagined for myself. Thank you."

Lux couldn't help the small laugh that escaped over her triumph. *At least I've accomplished one thing.* Her smile was slow to fade, but it did fall away entirely when he added, "Your book isn't in here."

A distant buzzing echoed in her ears. Lux scrambled to her feet and raced to the bag where she dug through its depths. She flipped it over, shaking its contents onto the desk. Writing utensils. Flint. Twine. Paper and coins. They tumbled and scattered. A berry rolled free at the end. Followed by a feather. Lux watched it float to the lacquered wood below.

"*No*. It must be here."

"Maybe you stowed it in the dressing room?"

She shook her head. "No, I've left it in the same place for weeks. Since I left Ghadra."

She could feel Shaw's stare against her profile.

"Did any of them know?"

"They didn't. I never said a word about it. Maybe they assumed? But even so—oh, devil *take* her. That conniving wench!"

Shaw blinked in alarm. "Who?"

Lux tore at her hair. Her teeth clenched so hard she was sure they'd crack. She hissed, "That *bandit*. Their leader. *Magda*." She couldn't hear Shaw's response, and maybe it was for the best. She could make no room for anything but the roaring in her ears. "She knew of it. I stupidly told them of it. Why I did... *No*, I heard the name Alesso that night. I can't believe I didn't recall it until just now. She knew the name of their dead leader. She knew the name of—"

"He is my brother."

Devil take her. Their current one?

Corvin Alistair. Corvin *Alesso*? He could never be Mothlock's mysterious overlord…could he? The boy whom she'd assumed was hardly a man but had been cursed to never age. Their voices hadn't matched while she'd been sequestered within that cart in the healer's workroom, but of all the things she'd witnessed thus far, the ability to harness two distinct voices hardly seemed far-fetched.

"They're going to destroy it," she said.

"Why would they do that?"

"Because how else can they dole out their tampered copies if the real one still exists? Even if they don't destroy it outright, they will lock it away in their vault where it'll never again be opened. Where I will never—" Lux shoved her fingers into her eyes. "I can't believe he took it."

"Tampered copies?"

The cover of *Brilliant Brushstrokes* fell open in Shaw's hands. He scanned the pages long enough that Lux recovered. She came to peer curiously around his arm.

It really was a stunning work of art in itself. The pages were not regular paper but coated in thin gloss. *There will be no notetaking in this.* The script wasn't like anything she'd seen either. The letters were pristine, blocked, and while they were devoid of personality, the uniformity was simple to read and orderly. The character came instead from the illustrations: a mix of black and silver, all of them. Depicting everything from instructions to samples to nondescript flourishes she could find no meaning for. And saints.

Full pages were dedicated to them, faceless and sprawling. Lux curled her lip at the note beneath the illustration Shaw turned to.

"Dedication to the Saints will overcome all limits." She huffed. "That cannot possibly be in the original. I'm sorry. If I'd known it wasn't a true edition, I wouldn't have bought it for you."

She glanced at the opposite page.

To serve the Saints with one's brilliance is to be blessed into the Beyond.

Shaw thumbed through the pages, passing topics of portraits and poses, until he paused over an illustration with a sharp intake of air. Lux's mouth formed a perfect circle.

"What is *that?*"

But the answer came from the writing below and Shaw's mouth, both. "The devil."

The Devil will devour those who do not honor the Saints, casting them into a wretched ending.

Shaw brushed the pad of his thumb over a wide horn. A sagging, grotesque face. "It reminds me of what I painted during my worst nights. I burned them all."

Maybe we should burn this too, Lux thought.

She said, "What good does this messaging do? Is this what's to become of *The Risen*? For saints to be drawn into its pages, demanding some sort of hurdle be jumped before any successful revival? For the devil to make you fear any mistake? I can't allow it."

Shaw didn't answer her but flipped to the end.

Property of Mothlock
For the purpose of achieving a fulfilled enlightenment
"May Your Mastery Be Limitless"

"What is his brilliance? This Corvin Alistair." Shaw looked down his shoulder at her.

"I've not asked."

Shaw grumbled something she didn't catch. He returned to the fireplace, but this time he took the solitary chair. There, he sat in silence and worried his lip. His elbows rested on his knees, his fingers steepled beneath his chin. The book lay forgotten in his lap.

Lux watched him for a moment. How the firelight coaxed every strand of gold in his hair into shimmering. How his brow furrowed above a deepening scowl. She did not mind being alone, but she would gladly never feel loneliness again for the rest of her life. She didn't think she would—if she was able to keep Shaw in it.

She stepped near him and bent to take the book. She wanted to peruse it closer. To see what other messages might lurk inside. Shaw allowed it to leave with hardly a shift, and she turned away.

A strong arm looped around her waist upon her next step; her breath hitched. With her next heartbeat, Shaw dragged her backward and into his lap. He pulled her higher, situating her as he wanted, and only then did he lean back, stretching his long legs out before him.

Lux noted his fingers tracing slow patterns on her thigh.

"I have something to tell you," he said, the words rumbling against her back. "But I don't want to."

The statement should have seen her straightening, but she couldn't. Shaw's warmth permeated through her nightgown, and the fire flickered blessedly across her front. It would take more than words to move her now. But she did close her eyes. Her nails sank preemptively into her palms.

"Of course you do. What is it?"

His chest pressed against her back with his deep breath, and Lux's stomach twisted further. Shaw's voice softened as he said, "I left Ghadra for two reasons: to infiltrate the Society of Saints at their invitation, and to hopefully encounter you along the way. Before leaving, I checked in on the only two trees I cared to."

He paused.

Lux could feel his hesitation; it seeped into her. She shifted enough so she might scan his eyes. They were too anguished, she thought, and her stomach became a pit of fear. "And?"

"Riselda is alive."

Chapter Thirty-Five

Lux shook her head on instinct. *No. No, she is not.* "She was swallowed by a tree, Shaw. I watched it happen."

"I know. There were markings—all over the trunk. It looked to be from an axe, and once I could manage the light...they were done from the inside."

An axe.

The wretched, black-handled axe.

Riselda had taken it with her. She'd cradled it to her chest. But the woman had just administered a killing blow to Bartleby Tamish, and Lux then assumed it was affection that caused Riselda to take it to her living grave. *It shouldn't be possible.* But who knew the true meaning of impossible any longer? Lux certainly didn't.

Shaw shifted underneath her, his hand settling at the base of her neck as if he would keep her in place. "I picked up her trail outside the marshes. When I first found her, she looked like she should be dead. But between one town and the next, she was healthy as ever. I followed her nearly all the way here, but in Loxlen I lost her. I think she's looking for you."

Lux's body shook beneath his hand; her toes began to curl. A rage built within her, burning and burning. Shaw flinched when her nails relinquished her palms to dig instead into his thigh, but he didn't pull away. Her vision blurred in her fury.

How dare she. How dare she not die.

"If she comes here," she began, quiet as death. "If she thinks to touch me after all she's done—she *ruined* my *life!*"

Lux shoved from the chair, abandoning Shaw. She was heated enough with the rage within her now. In all honesty, she wondered how she didn't boil alive.

"Her death was my parents' justice served. Now what? She is just to…be *free?* To live for a thousand years, destroying whomever she decides is unworthy to be beside her and using those she finds interesting?"

Unfair. That word beat a tempo she couldn't outrun.

How was it Riselda could live two centuries having been turned a monster by her own vengeance, but Lux had gone mad before two decades? If anyone had done unforgivable things it was that imposter. She should be the one whose mind deteriorated. She should—

"Devil below." Lux turned her back on the mirror, where she'd been staring into it, unseeing. "I'd forgotten. She's mad."

"Her morals are certainly torched."

"It's not only that. They'd told me the Grimrook family, Riselda's family, all died because of this *Mania Malus*. That at its worst you can't distinguish reality from your dreams. What if Riselda feels she is in a dream? When really she is acting in reality." She shuddered, every fine hair standing on end. Sometimes in her dreams she did the most horrific things. Sometimes it wasn't her parents she stabbed, but others.

Then she woke with silent screams.

"What would they know of her family?"

"They lived here. You would have walked by their portraits. This was their estate. Then it morphed into—" Lux waved her hand about the room. "If she thinks to return here, there will be a reckoning for her, and it might not be me who gets the chance to deliver it. They say she stole from them, and they hate her for it." She glanced at the overturned pack, crumpled and deflated, and her heart felt like it must have done the same. She sniffed. "Now they've stolen it back."

In the background, Shaw murmured, "*Mania Malus?*"

"I have to find that vault."

"Lux."

"And we have to find where they keep their prisoners."

"*Pardon?*"

She caught his furrowed brow and parted lips and said, "Not like the mansion. Or...I don't believe it is. There's a girl they have chained somewhere. They diagnosed her with the salt-sick and say she can't be trusted to work in the manor until she is—" Lux met Shaw's intense stare.

He crossed his arms, the stained fabric straining against his shoulders. He outright glowered at her. "I'm rather good at discerning patterns, love. This is one. Tell me you see it? You're whisked away to some obscure landmark and conveniently diagnosed with a disease to render you scared and disbelieving reality. Why? Have they offered you a position? A treatment? Were you to stay on staff as Mothlock's own necromancer?"

"Except the girl has no real symptoms. None that she can discern, and I—" A flicker caught her attention. Lux turned fully toward the mirror. Her broken brilliance, manifested into a nightmare, hovered inside it.

"*Wishes. Hope. Wishes. Hope. All die in the end. Same as you. Same as him.*" It gnashed its teeth. "*And they die painfully.*"

She couldn't look away. The apparition's fathomless eyes captured her own and would not blink. *Maybe this is the true Devil, and it lives within me.*

"What are you looking at?"

"Myself," she whispered.

Shaw appeared in the mirror's reflection, and for a moment, there were three beings shown back to her. She watched his hand drift, catch her fingers, and the manifestation dissolved at once in a haze of false smoke.

"We've been apart too long," she said.

He lifted their hands, and his mouth brushed feather light across her knuckles. "I can't disagree."

Her eyes flicked upward to meet his. "So much has happened. Too much. I feel like I've so much more to tell you, but the only thing I want to say is that I've missed you a huge amount. More than I expected. It almost makes me angry."

It did make her angry, but she'd grown to bite her tongue a little now and then to ease her penchant for stings.

Shaw took one look at her scowling face in the mirror and laughed. He hauled her to him until she met his chest with a gasp. His opposite hand—the one that wasn't still holding hers—lifted to cup her face. "Is the lovely ice sculpture thawing for me?" He said it good-naturedly, chuckling, and Lux had hardly begun admiring the creases at the corners of his eyes when they disappeared. He sobered. "It hurt, watching you go that day. You wouldn't have seen, but I watched you until the marshes swallowed you up. I understood *eventually* why you set out on your own. I like to think I'm brave, but I realized then you're braver than me."

She shook her head against his hand. "That's because I haven't told you yet how many times I thought of running back."

"But you didn't so really that makes it even more true."

"Who am I to argue with your obviously sound logic," she said, rolling her eyes.

"Do you mean to start a quarrel with me? When we've only just been reunited, and you know I always win?"

A shout of laughter left her before she could stifle it, and Lux clapped a hand over her mouth, her eyes wide and focused on the door. She pulled her opposite hand from his to shove against his chest. "Look what you've made me *do*. We can't draw any attention to this room. Besides, you've not won—ever. And the one time I believe you're thinking of, you had a knife under my chin, and I hardly think that's fair or should be counted."

"You cannot call resourcefulness unfair. We will have to agree to disagree. Though I *do* agree with you on not calling attention to ourselves. At least for tonight."

"And tomorrow?" She could sense the minutes ticking closer to that official time. The clock upon the mantle confirmed it. Her dread was a rising, creeping tide. She held little doubt if she wanted to accomplish what she had set out to do that day from Ghadra, that it would be then or never.

"Cannot be avoided," he replied. "I fulfilled their order of *Time* when I arrived, so that part is settled, at least." At her cry of shocked outrage, he hurriedly added, "It's fake. It's paint."

Lux settled her hand over her throat for only a heartbeat before she reached and gripped his chin. "You might have *led* with that." A corner of his mouth lifted into a smirk. A shadow of growth pricked her fingers when it did—and Lux entirely forgot what she was irritated over.

She pulled him toward her, and he came willingly. His head lowered, his hand reaching to cover hers. But his finger landed atop her nail-less one. Though the skin had healed, she couldn't help but wince over the bare tenderness.

Shaw dropped his hand but snatched hers again right after. He turned it over while she grimaced.

"What are you doing?"

He answered with a question of his own. "What happened to your finger?"

"My nail? It was nothing."

"I didn't ask if it was something."

"I... Well, I traded it."

Shaw's eyebrows met. First in confusion and then in something else entirely. "For *what*?"

Devil's tits. No, I'm not brave at all.

She already knew this, of course.

"...berries."

He didn't appreciate her explanation. She knew he wouldn't. It did remind her, however, to clean up the mess she'd made in her search for *The Risen*.

Meanwhile, Shaw returned to the armchair where she'd discarded his book in her rage. She didn't care for it much anymore. Aside from the fact it cost an astonishing amount, its contents were tarnished and worthless as far as she was concerned. What else might they have changed?

Shaw stayed silent. He'd thought it was beyond foolish of her to offer up a piece of herself to someone she'd only just met, but she'd argued it wasn't blood, and at any rate, it hadn't even hurt...at first. He'd not argued after that. However, the tick in his jaw had yet to stop.

Whatever he held back, she was fine not hearing it.

She'd yet to tell him perhaps the biggest thread in this woven nightmare of a scene. That there was a man well over a century dead below them, and the society wished for her to reverse that. She'd not yet told him of the host of soulless people masquerading as attendants downstairs either.

She'd been selfish, complaining about her own ailment and the loss of her book before relaying all the ways in which they might be in real, imminent danger here. *The Risen* shouldn't matter nearly so much as those.

It shouldn't...but it did.

She sat upon the bed, the lush coverings pressing against her as she sank into the mattress. Her body begged for rest. But her mind—it couldn't be quieted. She'd survived on little sleep in those last horrific days in Ghadra, and she was certain she could again.

Also, she had an idea. Something which began as a feeling when she'd stared upon it but had slowly grown over her mind like a mold. Riselda had been tied intricately into the plot designed to destroy her city. Though she could not be the architect this time, Lux was surer than ever her false aunt had formed more than one knot in this wicked mess.

She must find them and unravel them.

She must go first to Grimrook House.

Chapter Thirty-Six

"These boots pinch like the damn devil itself."

Lux swung around to scowl at Shaw in the dark. "*Shh,*" she hissed between her teeth. Because she'd already told him—about what Kent had said regarding guardian's leech—and he'd acted properly horrified. Now, it seemed he was more horrified with his expensive new boots. She eyed the brambles with unease.

The collector had said they could sense a person's heart, but that didn't mean they should draw even more attention by tromping down the path, complaining. Lux eyed the first statue and then the looming manor itself. *Besides, who knows what else is listening?*

She stalked farther down the path. Shaw caught up to her in several strides and bent to her ear. "You've mastered the silent steps, I see."

Lux bit down on her tongue to keep from retorting. *Why he thinks he is the only one good at sneaking about...*

Her will was not strong enough, in the end. "I always have. You should take lessons from me. Considering it was *you* who nearly exposed us with your moaning and groaning in your climb over the wall that time."

"My climb...at the mayor's mansion? I did not *moan.*"

She snorted but otherwise didn't reply. They passed the statue of the distraught Granville Grimrook. The garden appeared infinitely more uninviting in the late night. It hadn't been inviting to start, but still, Lux was taken aback by the oppressive gloom. She adjusted the hem of her top, black to match the sky. She'd brought it along—that lace blouse she'd worn more often than not in Ghadra—though she hadn't pulled it on once throughout her journey. It felt familiar to wear it now, but in a strange way. The rest of the ensemble, though, she was quite content with. Her skirt fell to her knees, blessedly short.

They passed by the melancholy Rosamund Grimrook. Then those she hadn't memorized yet, but had dubbed the Miserly Lord and the Concerned Groom. More were too far buried in the overgrowth to discern, and she and Shaw came soon enough to the door.

Lux stepped up to it. The lamppost at this exit was unlit, and she could hardly see a thing. Still, she pulled the key from her corset. She glanced to Shaw, watched him nod, and said, "Why didn't you change your shirt before coming to find me?"

A cloud shifted to offer the barest glimmer of cool light. It lit upon his features and the dried stain both. "It's your blood," he replied with a tone of appreciation.

Lux wrinkled her nose. "How morbid."

He only grinned. "Put the key in the lock, Lux."

She crouched and prodded around for it. The lock was there, she discovered, only camouflaged. The key was a perfect fit. And Lux, grinning with triumph, turned it.

But a click didn't come. Scowling, she yanked it out and returned it. This time, she used more effort. Then she used both hands.

"Let me try," said Shaw, coming forward.

Lux was loath to release it—it had been her idea after all: to use the key she'd discovered in her fit of temper that had thus unlocked her mirror. But she did release it. Shaw's hand enclosed over the key in her absence.

He didn't use force, but a gentle pressure, and all the while, he bent his ear to the thing like it would speak to him and tell him what they'd done wrong. But Lux knew what they did wrong. It was the wrong key. Of course it was. Otherwise, it would have been too easy for the pair of them.

The universe never has luck to spare. She huffed an irritated sigh when he released it. "Can you pick it?"

He rose and tucked the key securely into her corset, his fingers dipping beneath the garment for hardly a second. It was, unfortunately, all that was needed to unravel her. Lux pressed her eyes closed when he turned away. His tools were already in hand, and she needed to restrain herself.

But he hadn't even *kissed* her yet.

Maybe...he didn't want to?

"It's an odd lock," was all he replied.

"Not as odd as the mayor's lifeblood cabinet, surely?"

"I can hardly see, but I don't feel any markings for directions. I think it's a regular lock, but also...not."

Lux's eyebrows met in her confusion, but she didn't ask anything else about it. He'd more experience than she in this. Instead, she listened to his tools scrape away. To the whisper of the sea breeze through the brambles and the waves crashing against the cliffs. She listened for anyone coming down the garden path. She listened to—a crow?

The creature cawed and startled Shaw enough that he dropped one of the tools. It startled Lux hardly at all. She stared up at it perched atop the stone arch, and she said in a heated whisper, "So you come back to gloat? Or did you come to peck at me some more?"

Shaw straightened from retrieving his lock pick. He glanced at the bird before returning his attention to her. "Enemy of yours?"

"*Yes,*" she said at the same moment the bird repeated its call.

"It seems one-sided."

"Does it?" Lux glared up at the animal. "Well, maybe it is. After all, I didn't bite *its* hand or peck *its* leg."

"It attacked you? It isn't—"

"No," Lux hurried to reply. "It isn't revived or even sick, I don't think. It's only mean."

Shaw stepped nearer to the door, his attention riveted on the bird and its lack of movement. It only watched them both. Calculating, she thought. But when it didn't launch an attack, he bent again to the lock.

Lux managed a short, shocked cry and nothing more when the crow flew down upon them both. She could feel wind. Wings. She crouched and covered her head, swatting at the air with her free arm. But she met nothing, and after several heartbeats, the bird had taken to the air again. This time, it landed farther along the fence line. She scowled fiercely at the animal and then looked at Shaw. Found him staring down at his one remaining lockpick.

The crow had stolen the other. It held it in its claws and cawed again—almost exasperated. And Lux could only shake her head.

"He won't fit," she said to the bird.

"Pardon me?" Shaw questioned.

"It's helping us. Or thinks it is. There's a bend to the bars in there, but it isn't much. I was even worried I—*wait.*"

Shaw stepped off the path.

He did so carefully, with his back pressed to the fencing and his front prepared for any movement of brambles. But when the shifting didn't reveal any teeth, and the bird continued its pacing, he moved quicker. Soon enough, Lux lost sight of him beyond the curve of iron.

"Fine," she huffed at the crow, and followed Shaw inside.

Lux tucked her hands beneath her arms while she watched.

Shaw gripped the bar a second time, and for the second time, he pulled hard against it. His entire body strained—she was close enough to see the pulsing tension in his neck—as he bent the bar further.

He stood to place his hands on his hips, breathing heavily. "That should be wide enough."

"For me, for sure. I don't know about you." She glanced him up and down.

"You'd be surprised at what I can get into."

Lux curled her lip at his tone but said nothing. She left him chuckling, and with the brambles' teeth swaying behind her, she crouched at the hidden opening. Then—very carefully—she squeezed through.

The fabric caught even with her slow maneuvers. She heard a short burst of ripping at her skirt and grimaced, but she'd made it. She straightened at the opposite side.

The cliffs were sheered near her feet, and the sea sent a brutal burst of wind against her bared skin. Lux shivered, goosebumps erupting over her body, but she didn't dare dwell on it.

There sat Grimrook House.

It was a quarter of the manor's size, pale stone, with a slated roof. The escaped moon highlighted one tower and two chimneys. She leaned as far as she dared, until she could see the house sat upon an outcropping, and that outcropping was large enough to contain a small garden with several trees and even a bench.

She straightened.

She shook her head.

Her entire body hummed with anticipation, leaving no room for nerves or fear. She didn't understand it, but there it was, rooted in her chest: that feeling of being on the right path. The feel of—

A grunted oath announced Shaw's arrival. She turned in time to watch his knee connect harshly with an iron bar. He hissed an expletive, and then he was through.

He staggered to his feet. "These trousers cost more than a month's rent in Ghadra." He limped toward her, the fabric torn wide over his thigh.

"Are you hurt?"

"Only if you want to tend to me."

She scowled up at him then pointed. "There it is. Riselda's childhood home. They'd said we can't get to it; that part of the path is crumbled away. But it seems every other thing they've told me has been a lie. That probably is too."

Now that Shaw stood beside her, she saw he bled; he did not appear to notice. Lux waited for the familiar sick feel in her gut, the tightening in her chest, but…it didn't arrive. Her eyes skipped from her own dried blood on his shirt to his trickling wound, and before she realized what she was doing, she'd pressed the torn portion of her skirt to his skin.

He stiffened in surprise against her, and she looked up. His pupils had dilated in the night until no warmth remained, but she could find it still in the line of his brow and the shape of his mouth. His lips parted. "Have you moved past your aversion to blood?"

Her fingers grew damp with it. "Only yours."

She blushed at his expression. Shaw's hand came around her back, fisting in the folds of her skirt. Her skin heated like a kettle beneath his grip. He cradled her face, his thumb tracing the line of her cheekbone.

Suddenly, he pressed his lips to hers, light and swift, and pulled back the moment he was through. She stumbled forward.

"No, I shouldn't focus on *that* right now. You've been manipulated by this deranged society, and we need to find out why."

She absorbed nothing after his first sentence.

What did it say about her that she would happily focus on it? Rather than the fact she'd tossed someone to a horrific death and had been tasked with reviving another. Rather than the possible deterioration inside her.

Rather than their discovery of the *buyers* of *lifeblood*—her most fervent goal.

He shouldn't have kissed her at *all*. She'd rather not get a taste if she'd be denied the rest.

"It's rather impressive, isn't it?" He stared from the cliff's edge at the sea. "I don't think I've done it justice."

"Yes. And you have." Lux sucked a salt-filled breath. "Have you—" She stopped, watching an immense wave crash against a jagged beast of a rock. Her brow furrowed.

"Have I…"

"It sounds far-fetched."

She glanced to find his eyebrow raised and an expression she took to mean, *"Really? After all we've been through?"*

She relented. "Have you ever felt like you've finally found it? The right path, or even the right choice? I don't know why, but ever since I saw the sea... When I glimpsed this house..."

Shaw's features turned thoughtful. It took him time to answer, but eventually he said, "That night in the prison. I knew we wouldn't make it. Letting you go was the only choice. I've never felt surer of anything than wanting you to live." He looked down at her. "Something like that?"

Lux's breath abandoned her in a rush. She stared up at him.

They'd never talked about it—what he'd said that night—but she still replayed the moment every time she closed her eyes for sleep. He'd confessed in that wretched hour. Finally admitted he'd come to like her as she'd come to irrevocably care for him. And then he'd hinted at more than even that.

Her chest felt heavy in a different sort of way. Heavy with words she *needed* to say.

"Something like that," she murmured.

His gaze roved over her face. "Let's see if this path has really fallen away or not."

Narrow, weather worn stone seemed to sheer sharply from the ridge. Ahead, Lux could see a bridge connecting their broken road to Grimrook House's garden. Her jaw clenched.

Shaw's sudden throw saw a rock landing perfectly suspended in air. "Looks like an illusion."

Lux sucked at her teeth. "It looks like the bridge outside Ghadra."

Chapter Thirty-Seven

The steps down to the cove had been more precarious than this, and factoring Shaw's steadiness and her shorter skirt, Lux felt nearly safe moving along it. Her uneasiness, however, couldn't be cured.

The bridge loomed before her.

It was like the other in that it was stacked stone and arched. But now that she stood at its end, she could see its cracks weren't crawling with moss, fog was not curling over its sides, and the garden beyond it did not whisper her name and hide several breeds of monster. Now that she was here, she realized instead of like Ghadra's, it looked as all bridges were meant to look.

Lux's gaze dipped through the narrow break in the cliff all the way down to the churning water below. Then she stepped onto the bridge.

"This is uncomfortable." Shaw peered over its side and straightened with a palm pressed to his mouth.

"No spiders. No high places," she said.

"And no weak tea," he added, lowering his hand.

"I was listing your fears."

"I do fear that," he replied, and with several long strides, hurried across the bridge.

But Lux paused partway. There was no gate at its end. There was, however, a garden wall. Waist-height, it matched the bridge and the house both, and in place of a gate, there were instead small pillars and a clear opening.

It invited her in.

She glanced all around. Could it be so simple?

The manor's tower loomed from its cliff. With the clouds dispersed, cool light lit the peak and transformed it from shining onyx to glistening silver. She looked for the yellow glow of candlelight but found none. Mothlock's monsters had entered their cursed sleep.

"This garden seems to have been tended to once." Lux shifted and found Shaw bent over crimson roses. Cradling a bloom between two fingers, he raised it to his nose. "There are paths cut through it and none of those saintforsaken statues."

"If Riselda's family was anything like her, then they also loved growing things. But not always for good, so I'd be careful what you sniff."

Shaw pulled away from the roses. A soft *snap* sounded between them. He held a long-stemmed bloom toward her, and Lux looked from the flower to him. To his slight smile.

"The thorns seem normal enough, but I would mind them anyway," he said.

She plucked the rose from his hand. "We don't have time for flower-picking, Shaw." But she inhaled its scent, and his smile grew.

"Look at that." Shaw snagged her corset. He dragged her to him, and only when the barest breadth was left between them did he say, "Thought this looked familiar."

Lux's skin flamed as he pulled the concealed knife from her clothing. When its blade caught the moonlight, she snatched it from him.

"You wouldn't *dare*," she said.

He clicked his tongue. "Trade you." He reached into the sheath at his belt and withdrew a black-handled dagger.

Lux turned his over, the worn, brown handle scraping lightly across her palm. She looked up. "Honest? I've gotten rather attached."

Shaw snorted, lifting her dagger to tap her twice beneath the chin. He flipped it after, so that the handle was presented to her, and she took it—along with all its memories.

Unwilling though she was, she offered his weathered one in exchange. *We meet again, you foul gallow blade.* Her lip curled. *Hopefully you can protect me from other vengeful things.*

It did fit better in her palm than Shaw's, it was true. And she had him entirely now—she didn't need his knife anymore. She tucked the rare dagger away.

"Devil below," he said, picking his way through the garden. "Look at that door."

Lux squinted into the darkness. The door was recessed, protected by a stone arch, and she thought he pointed out the tree that had grown around it, clinging gently to the overhang.

But then the light shifted, and a grotesque devil stared back at her.

She studied it as it studied her, and she realized then, in its life-sized rendering, while it did look similarly to the illustration in Shaw's book it also appeared like the nightmare of her recent days. It did not have her face. But the essence, the posture, the...teeth.

As the tunnel door below Mothlock showed a Saint, this door to Grimrook House showed the Devil.

Lux's nails dug into her wrists. "They're trying to frighten us away. We're on the right road. I know it."

"So long as one of us does." Shaw moved nearer, until he stood beneath the archway and the tree. "It's a good work of art, from that perspective."

Lux swallowed her unease. *If anything in Mothlock should be faceless to imagine oneself in its place, it should be this monster. The society are devils, not saints.* She asked, "Is it unlocked?"

Shaw glanced over his shoulder. "You'll send me in first?"

"What good is your size if you don't use it to brush away the webs?" When she could practically *feel* his responding shudder, her conscience pricked. "I'm not being serious. I'll go first."

But he was already at the door, bowing before the devil and inspecting the lock. A rattle sounded when Lux came up behind him. She held out the key.

"It's the same as the one before," he said, but he took the key anyway. After several tries, he returned it to her. "I think it's made to be opened by only one person."

Lux frowned. "Kent opened the other. Is he the only one who can open the house, then? The lock looks as old as the door, but he's not a Grimrook."

"It doesn't matter much now. We want to get in and we can't this way. The windows are barred in front, but maybe—"

They startled in unison at the crow's caw. "Devil's *tits*," she hissed. "That damn bird is trying to kill me."

The crow landed above them outside their line of sight. Lux heard plenty of rustling as it settled into the wayward tree. It cawed again.

She glanced toward the gnarled trunk beside her, following it up and overtop the stoop. "If you insist," she grumbled, and wedged her foot.

"What are you doing?"

"Climbing. Clearly that creature has a plan, and since we don't—"

"*I* had a plan," said Shaw, but when she looked down, he'd come to stand at the base. He tugged back his sleeves.

"Hurry up," she told him. "Or I'll explore without you."

She heard his scoff and indistinct mutter, because he likely thought she'd said it in jest. But she was serious. A surety grew in her chest, warm and reassuring, and it began to chip at the disgust leftover from the devil on the door. *I'm meant to be here.*

Lux reached the top of the tree, found footholds between its branches and the stone arch, and breathed a quick breath of relief. She peered up and over the roof.

She searched for the crow and found it—perched atop her cackling nightmare.

Maybe it was the suddenness of it. Or maybe it was the unexpected clashing of reality and not. But Lux screamed.

Lost her balance.

And toppled from the tree.

Chapter Thirty-Eight

"Hold onto me."

Shaw adjusted his footing, his free hand holding tight to the branch while his other splayed over her ribs.

Lux buried her face in his neck. Her heart hammered. She was sure her head was meant to be cracked open on the stones below, but Shaw had been higher than she'd known. He'd grabbed her straight from the open air.

"Place your foot above mine."

Trembling, Lux lifted her head to do as told. She wedged her boot.

"Good. Now grab hold of the same branch as me." She did that too. "I'm going to let you go now."

Her breath shuddered out of her. *It's fine. I'm fine. Quit shaking.* His hand released her waist only to come down on the branch beside her. She was caged fully by his body.

"I won't let you fall, love. Go on and climb."

"Is it too late to try your plan?" she asked with her eyes shut.

"This plan is just as good. Maybe better." His chest pressed her tighter against the tree and his lips brushed the shell of her ear. "Your bird is back."

Lux's eyes burst open, and she looked up—to the crow perched not far above her, its head tilted and appearing just as dissatisfied with her as earlier on the balcony. "So is the mad version of me."

"I'll be with you," he said. "No matter what."

She'd told him what it looked like. She'd needed to. And while speaking it aloud had drained some of the terror it held over her, it hadn't changed the fact the bird was still perched on *something*.

Lux gritted her teeth—and climbed up.

"Only a mannequin," said Shaw, after he'd walked across the archway, vaulting over the terrace railing.

Lux stood rigid as a pillar, her lip pulled up into a detested sneer as he righted the fallen figure. The window it had come from was broken; she hadn't noticed any of it before she'd fallen.

He pushed it back beyond the glass and said, "We have our way in."

Placing one leg through the opening, he turned back for her, his arm outstretched. Lux climbed over the short railing and gripped his hand, and then he disappeared into the house.

"Thank you," she said to the crow, a second before fingers tightened on her own, and she was tugged inside.

A puff of dust slurried around Lux's boots where she landed. She coughed into her sleeve. "Devil below."

Dresses littered the floor.

Two more mannequins stood fully dressed inside, and the wardrobe was thrown open. Lux's glance skipped from the four-poster bed to the mussed bedding stitched with dark florals and knew by the twisting in her gut this was not just any child's bedroom.

She lost her grip on Shaw as he made his way to the bed. To the nightstand and the frame standing atop it. He struck a tinderbox and lit a stub of a candlestick before he plucked the frame from the cobwebs. After several moments, he handed it to her. Lux took it warily.

A young Riselda stared back at her.

Alixsander stared back at her too.

"What the devil," murmured Lux, wiping the dust away. The pair sat shoulder to shoulder, a prim pose, and while Riselda did not smile, Lux could see the softness around her mouth. Alixsander, on the other hand, smiled hugely. He was older than her fraud of an aunt, likely around Lux's own age, his expression brotherly and warm.

They looked...happy.

"She grew up with the Alesso boys," said Lux. "She was close with the murdered one." Close enough that someone skilled with a brush had painted them to permanence. Had then framed it and gifted it.

Shaw kept himself busy pulling at drawers. He knelt now to peer under the bed. "Who killed him?"

"Corvin didn't say."

"Ah. Meaning he did it."

Lux huffed. "You're so sure, are you?"

"It makes the most sense to me. Your brother wants to run a school of learning. You want to hoard knowledge and alter the truth to better suit yourself. Kill the brother. Take his place."

Her brow furrowed. How quick he was to work through horrible theories. "If that were true, I don't see why he'd have kept him preserved for revival. Even with a curse—"

She realized her mistake then.

Shaw stiffened like her remark had fused a rod to his spine. He stared at her. In the candlelight, his eyes had turned molten.

His voice, however, was frigid. "*What* did you say?"

You twit! her head shouted.

She'd planned to tell him. Obviously. But not right now. Not when they had other things to uncover, and there'd already been so much leveled at them. Lux replaced the frame.

She drew a deep breath. "His body was preserved after his death. Some alchemical nonsense that supposedly will allow him to be revived. If I go through with it."

"If you go—*Lux*."

She threw her hands up. "I know! I won't. They said he unknowingly cursed them, and the only option for reversal is his blood."

Shaw's raised eyebrow bothered her more in the scant light. He looked at her like he couldn't believe she'd ever trusted a word they'd told her. Well, she knew now, didn't she?

"Maybe he did kill him," she growled.

Do I tell him about the Stripping experiment? About their other offering and the title she'd overhead them use for her? Her eyes raked over his irritated frown.

Definitely not. Besides, she would never have agreed.

Her inner voice writhed. *You didn't agree to the rocks,* it reminded her.

Lux eyed the dried flowers in their vases, the decayed plant matter in their pots. It seemed Riselda always held an appreciation for anything with roots. *Yet, you left them to wither in your escape.*

She wasn't surprised, only curious. After all, Riselda always chose herself in the end. She couldn't even die properly.

Another betrayal.

Her gaze flung to Shaw as a floorboard creaked. He held the loose board in one hand, the other holding the meager candle to the exposed space below.

"How did you find that?" she said incredulously.

"The edges were worn more than the rest—fingers have tugged on it often. But it's empty except for this."

He set down the board to show her a glinting coin—a silvdan.

"Riselda's childhood hiding place? She increased her scale by quite a lot, didn't she."

He fitted the floor back together and rose to his feet. "Seems so." He surveyed the room with one last practiced study. "I think this has been pretty well picked through. Apparently, they cared little for the clothes." He toed a skirt at his feet.

"She would have hated seeing them like this."

Lux hadn't cared for clothes in a long time; so much as they were practical, she was satisfied. Of course, she hadn't felt velvet on her skin then... She eyed the partially open door. "How much longer will that candle hold out?"

"Enough to get down the stairs." Shaw came up behind her, sliding the coin into her palm and continuing to the door. His hand splayed across it; he pushed it farther open. "Saints above," he muttered.

"What is it?" Lux hurried up to his back, her heart already thumping relentlessly.

Shaw pushed again on the door—it wouldn't budge. "Books," he said. "Everywhere."

Her heart continued its quick pace, but for another reason now. She bent to duck beneath his outstretched arm. Once she stood in front of him, he held the candle out from her chest.

"*Devil's...*"

Books were stacked in the hall. Flat on their covers and nearly to the ceiling on either side. A slim walkway had been created between the stacks, and Lux couldn't see where it led. She stepped amongst them, plucking the candle from Shaw's fingers as she did.

The hallway was mustier and held far more dust; it didn't have the fresh air pouring in from a broken window like the bedroom. Lux trailed the flame's light along the cobwebbed spines.

"Who would have thought," Shaw said, and when he lifted his eyes they were bright with triumph. In his hands, he held a book. "*Brilliant Brushstrokes.*"

Lux's eyes widened. Both at his luck and over the state of the book. It looked as if it would fall apart in his grip. "I can't believe you found it in all this mess."

"I hardly can either, but it feels real enough." He flipped it open, even though she was sure he couldn't read it in the shadows. "No devils. No saints," he said after a few moments.

"I'd guess none of these have them. They look as old as my alcove does."

Did, her mind corrected. That alcove was destroyed now, a tree root through its heart. And all the books and pages were gone. In the end, she'd only been able to save one. And in her biased opinion, it had been the most valuable. Regardless, the loss still smarted.

"Devil below, there are two of them." Shaw picked up a second volume of *Brilliant Brushstrokes* for her to see. But when he did, a tear sounded. Lux gritted her teeth as the cover pulled free.

The remainder of the book plunked to the ground.

He swore and scooped it up. "One is enough, I suppose."

"I think the collectors would agree." One manipulated volume, which was then multiplied by a cold, uniformed printing press. "This cannot be the vault...can it?"

"I doubt it," he said. "This seems more discarded than protected."

Lux pressed to Shaw's side in order to see the wounded book for herself. He gave it up, and it fell open to its middle in her palm.

This was how books were in her experience. Stained, wrinkled, torn, and with the unique script of whoever had written or replicated it. She couldn't trace the page with her hands occupied, but she could imagine the feel. She placed it carefully back in the stack.

"They're not collecting," she said, staring down the darkened hall. "They're stealing."

"But not destroying. Why keep them at all, I wonder."

"Corvin said the loss of any knowledge would be a travesty."

"Yet they keep them piled in this place to grow mold and dust."

Lux shrugged. She didn't understand it either. The manor was certainly large enough. Could they really have hoarded so many books and manuscripts to require overflow into Grimrook House?

Maybe their vault is reserved for hoarding only silver things.

Maybe they didn't care for books so much as they said.

"If you see a book of necromancy, grab that too," she told him as she picked her way through the hallway again.

"You forget you have the only light."

She yelped at his voice near her ear. He'd been well behind her just a moment ago. She swatted his arm, but he only smirked.

"Don't worry," he told her. "I'll find another." He set the book of art upon a random stack. Then he veered off through a door.

Lux huffed at his departure. His old skill in purloining rich trinkets and jewelry was on full display tonight, but she couldn't begrudge him any of it. In fact, she was jealous. The hidden ladder below her childhood home? The tunnel beneath the mayor's mansion? The manor mirror that was also a door? All were found by accident. While she was somewhat stealthy, she hadn't ever learned any skill in the art of details. She still couldn't fathom how she'd found the latch into Mothlock's underground.

Lux wasn't surprised when Shaw returned with more than a mere candlestick, but an entire candelabra. All five tapers were lit, and him grinning from behind it. She blew hers out and tossed it to the ground.

"A necromancy book, you say?"

She pursed her lips at him in response—only for her mouth to part when he grabbed her chin. He pressed another irritatingly fast kiss to them and made to let her go.

Lux gripped his wrist and held him there. Then she glared until his eyes widened with worry in the soft light. "That's enough. If you don't kiss me like you *mean* it, then don't do it *at all*."

Shaw's expression faded into unreadability. Lux didn't release him, and he didn't try. She waited to see what he would say; she couldn't even guess what it would be.

It was her turn for her eyes to widen, as he did not break her stare but set down the candelabra. His voice deepened. "That sounded remarkably like a dare, Necromancer."

She feigned nonchalance, but really her heart was hammering and even her damnable skin had flushed. She shrugged. "Maybe it was."

"I haven't been goaded into a dare ever. I have nothing to prove." His eyes dipped to her mouth. She could feel every point of pressure from his fingertips like a brand on her chin. "But I think I would like to argue this one."

She only managed a meager gasp before his lips came down on hers.

Immediately, she thought, *I've not kissed him enough.*

This kiss, again, was new. Not desperate with looming despair, but wild, nonetheless. He'd *missed* her. She could feel it everywhere. His hand remained on her jaw and hers on his wrist, but his other had flattened against her lower back and held her flush against him. She wrapped her own around his neck.

Everything burned: her skin, her lips, her heart. He nipped her lip, and she moaned, deciding nothing else mattered. Not the society nor the madness. Neither Riselda nor lifeblood. She would stay here in this moment and be perfectly selfish.

But Shaw, damn him, was the least selfish person she knew—and he began to pull away.

She growled in annoyance and felt him smile against her mouth, drawing the sound in.

"I will always *mean* it," he said, his lips brushing hers with the words. "Even if it's brief. Or seemingly random. I will always mean it with you."

"You're a better person than me."

He shook his head. "No. And you'll prove it to yourself before this is done." He leaned away at last, and also much too soon. His eyes delved into hers. "Shall we keep going?"

Lux opened her mouth to reply when a flicker caught at the edge of her vision. She turned toward it.

A second. A third.

A scraping—of a tinderbox.

At the end of the corridor, a wick burst aflame.

Lux's heart ceased its hammering. It might have ceased beating altogether. When the voice behind the candle said, "Welcome to my home, Lucena."

Chapter Thirty-Nine

"Well, well. Look at *you*, darling."

Lux slammed to an abrupt halt in the hall. Shaw's arm had extended across her body and the impact forced her back a step. She'd been charging forward without realizing it.

Toward Riselda, bathed in candlelight.

Her once-aunt lowered a draping violet hood lined with ivory fur, and when their eyes met, Lux felt like her present collided viscerally and horribly with her past. She could not breathe.

"Are those messy locks trimmed at last?" Riselda smiled. "You look just as I knew you could, nevermind the old, ruined skirt." Her gaze flicked to Shaw. "Hello, Cockroach."

Shaw's hand retracted to Lux's waist, his other coming to rest on her chest. He ignored Riselda's jibe. "In and out, love. She won't touch you."

But it wasn't so much the touching she couldn't manage. It was that Riselda was here. That Riselda was alive *at all*. Lux wanted to *strangle* her.

"Do it. Do it. Feed her blood to the thirsty mouths. The Grimrooks are meant for the ground."

Lux drew the dagger from her corset.

"Goodness." Riselda tracked the movement with a feral grin. "You reek of vengeance, darling girl, and I should know. I've smelt it on myself for a century."

"It isn't vengeance," Lux snarled. "Not anymore. It's justice I seek now. You destroyed Ghadra. So many people dead and all because of you. You deserve to be brought before them for your crimes."

"Ghadra is buried for me now. You have me on good faith I will never return to it."

Lux's laugh burst from her, cruel and dark. "Is that all you have to offer? You believe I should just let you go? To move from one town and city to the next, taking without a care for whom you harm?" The shock of Riselda's arrival had dulled into a heavy presence in her chest. One that was quickly being eaten by flames of rage. "How did you get *out*?"

Riselda shifted the fabric at her hip while the rest of her form remained hidden beneath the trailing cloak. She patted the axe resting there. "I was born by this sea, and I spent the greater part of my childhood here." Riselda's eyes lifted over Lux to the bedchamber beyond. "If there is one thing I've learned and has stuck with me, it is that we are not all just one thing. Sure, we have an affinity. A brilliance. But it is multi-faceted if you would only polish it enough. I am a healer. I failed to be a necromancer— I think because I am drawn to all that roots. To the living. I did not wish to harm the tree that devoured me, and I placated it enough with my wishes that it did not fight back as much as it could have."

"But you were inside it for weeks!"

"So they say. I would not know. Time doesn't pass the same when you're being digested alive."

Lux shifted, her fingers aching around the dagger. "Why did you come here?"

"It's the Hallowed Banquet, Lucena. And if there is one thing I love, it's a party."

"You forget I know you better now than ever before, Riselda. You don't love a party any more than I do. It's only about what you can gain from it."

Riselda chuckled. "Fine. I am here to *gain* the knowledge of your well-being. After that, I would like to gain access to Mothlock's vault. Then, I wish to gain you as a companion."

"Not that tired proposition. I will *never*, Riselda. I have no desire to traipse about this world for hundreds of years, watching all the deplorable things people do to one another and having no ability to stop it. And I'll certainly not desecrate the dead to do it. Good luck in your access. The society knew you. They've lived just as long, and I'm suffering from madness. My well-being is only 'being' at the moment. Do you wish to take your chances with them, or will you agree to return to Ghadra and face your penance?"

Riselda's brow dipped during Lux's tirade. Lux could see she had wished to interject multiple times but digressed. "What madness?"

"Well—the madness of brilliance," Lux stammered. "*Mania Malus.* They told me you suffered from it too. The entire Grimrook family."

"The madness of..." Riselda shook her head. "No, Lucena. *Mania Malus* did not afflict my family. I am certain it doesn't afflict you."

Lux ignored Shaw's agreeing exclamation. "But something does. I can tell you for certain, it does. I'm plagued by my brilliance manifesting as a nightmare." The apparition watched her now from the ceiling, clinging in the corner like a spider. Waiting. Always waiting. "It speaks to me. Urges me to do terrible things. It says"—Lux breathed a shaky breath—"it says soon, it will be all that I am."

Her lips pressed together when she finished. Because why was she telling Riselda all these things? Even now, after everything, why did Lux treat her as family who cared? Who would step in to lift some of the burden? Riselda was not family. Would never be.

She is a monster, Lux reminded herself. *I am surrounded by monsters. Even myself.*

"A nightmare, you say." Riselda licked her lips, and a little uneasiness stole across her features. "Darling, that is an Alesso boy's work."

Lux's brow furrowed, and Shaw stiffened at her side. "What do you mean?"

Riselda moved closer, the candlelight illuminating her face and nothing more. Shaw drew his knife. Her gaze flicked to it and returned to Lux.

"I mean that once upon a time there were two powerful boys growing up in Mothlock Manor, the orphanage sponsored by the great Grimrook family. One dark, with a brilliance of dreams. One light, with a brilliance of nightmares. Alixsander Osric and Corvin Alistair. They were thick as thieves, with me alongside. Until their games soured me to them."

"She's lying. I am innate. Your other half. Carve me out or keep me—"

Lux blocked her ears to no avail. "But he is not even here in this house with me!"

"You have been sheltered, Lucena, and it is not your fault. Not all brilliances require continued presence. Same as they don't all require sight or a voice. Corvin's close proximity has always been enough to set his horrid manifestations into someone's head."

Lux warily raised her chin to better see the ceiling. The nightmarish version of her scuttled closer. Its neck twisted and its knees bent inhumanly. It hissed.

Lux's insides seized. "You're sure?" she whispered.

"I'm sure," said Riselda. "Unless he's learned another new thing, it can only last the night until it must be redone the next. That is how it was when we were young." By now her former aunt stood just out of arm's reach. Her attention continued to be divided between Lux's heavy stare and Shaw's blade. "Now bring my father's candelabra and follow me," she said.

Riselda promptly turned on her heel, and with a flutter of her cloak, swept back along the deep corridor.

Lux's heartbeat returned as Riselda faded from view. Her breaths, while fast, weren't worryingly shallow. Her teeth ground together. "What should we do?" she said in a strangled whisper. "I don't trust her in doing what's right, but I feel..."

Furious, yet hopeful.

Devastated, yet terrified.

But determination beat louder than all the rest. She would never allow Riselda to choose her path. She would certainly not allow Corvin.

Which meant— "I need to talk to her. She knows more than anyone about what we're up against."

Even though she didn't have Cecily's talent, Lux could feel Shaw's irritation billowing around her. He said, "I suppose this means we're about to follow her into some unknown portion of this house."

"It does." She glanced upward to catch the muscle feathering in his jaw.

"Fine. But if she tries anything *at all*, it will be my version of justice she meets."

Lux drew a slow breath as he sheathed his knife with intent. "I think she knows."

"Good," he bit out. Then he snatched the book and candelabra both and said, "Let's see what the devil has to say."

Chapter Forty

The staircase curved, wide and scratched, the hardwood a warm, rich brown. It opened into a large room. One that sat steeped in darkness on one side and lit with firelight on the other.

Riselda perched in a high-backed chair before the hearth. Several more sat empty nearby. Dead plants claimed the windows, slumped in pots, and crumpled on the sills, while decaying vines draped from the walls. It smelled just as musty as the floor they'd come from, but now with undertones of earth and soot instead of paper. Lux rubbed at her nose.

"Decided the benefit outweighed the risk, Lucena?" Riselda didn't turn toward her but remained staring steadfast into the fire. It cast flattering highlights over her cheekbones. All it did for Lux was act as a reminder of the woman's agelessness.

"Your eyes are a different color entirely than your portrait in the manor." Lux came around a thickly cushioned armchair and sank onto it. "They used to be the same shade as mine."

"Yes." Riselda drank deep from a goblet. "Interested in a similar change?"

Lux curled her lip. "No." Shaw came to sit on a sofa near hers, but only on its edge, poised for any misstep on Riselda's part. Lux's heart warmed at the sight. Her mouth softened. "The collectors wondered that I looked like the Grimrook family. They used it as further reason I could be suffering from mind disease."

Riselda chuckled into her wine.

The sound boiled Lux's blood. "*Well?*" she demanded. "Am I a Grimrook or not?"

"How could you be, Lucena? You've already told me there is no possible way in which we would be family."

Lux's lips parted at Riselda's words. At the way she'd said them. And how she appeared afterward: accepting, but hurt all the same.

"Did you have siblings?"

"None that lived past infancy."

"Cousins?"

"Dead for more than a century."

Lux swallowed. "Did you…carry a child?"

Riselda drew a steady breath before giving into her drink again. "No."

Lux huffed. "So I am not."

"I did not carry a child. Someone carried you. For me."

"…*what?*"

But Riselda wasn't finished. "I am excellent at growing things, only not inside my own body. I'd no desire to sacrifice myself to childbearing. I traded for a gallow seed many years ago. I traded for something else that day too."

Lux hated this. Every word. Her chest tightened in its telltale squeeze when suddenly, her hands were enveloped in larger—warmer—ones. She focused on every point of pressure. Of every rough callous against her skin.

And Riselda said, "When I was ready, I called up what I needed from my body. And between me and an alchemist, we formed something marvelous. I lost my family by the society's design. I wanted one still. And when I sensed a womb ripe for growing, I used it. You were born early, yet somehow still fat and wailing. The loveliest thing I'd ever seen."

Riselda sighed while Lux tried to rein in her horror. It was *worse*. Worse than she'd ever thought. She didn't know it could be *possible*. But as she stared off into the aged room, abandoned and moldering, she knew if anyone would discover a way it would be the unyielding woman across from her.

Riselda could not be bent or deterred.

She'd wanted a child.

She'd done it.

And now Lux would vomit over her boots.

"Of course, *I* am not maternal," continued Riselda, as if the world hadn't fractured. "I realized my frailties quick in those first few months. I pushed through, because you were mostly sweet, and I don't wish to admit defeat in anything. But your parents... They'd wanted a baby and couldn't conceive. It was as good a compromise as I could make."

"I'm going to be sick," whispered Lux. Whimpering, she hung her head over the armrest.

"Lucena—"

"*Enough*," snapped Shaw, deep with rage.

Lux missed Riselda's reaction, and she didn't care. Shaw's palm moved slowly and steadily across her back, protective and comforting together. It was intoxicating.

And Lux could not love him more.

Devil's tits.

She scrunched her eyes closed to focus on breathing away the roiling in her gut. To focus on *anything* but how deeply she felt.

It was inescapable.

How long had she been in love with him?

Weeks, said her heart. *I tried to tell you.*

But she'd blocked it out. She'd a dream and a purpose and—even more important—she had a *promise* to fulfill. She did not have the capacity to also deal with something so altering.

Except now she'd gone and acknowledged it, and it could not be undone.

She, Lux Thorn, was in love with Shaw Roser, and damn it *all* she'd never felt so vulnerable in all her life. A yawning fear opened in her chest. She felt like she'd suddenly been turned to glass. If anything happened to him because of her...

Her eyes flew open when something met her clenched fist. Lux squinted at the biscuit pressing against her thumb.

"They're not so old," said Riselda. "I would whip you up a tonic, but I think you only need something in your stomach."

Lux hissed and swatted it away. It hit the fraying rug and collapsed into a mess of crumbs.

Another biscuit appeared, nudging her hand. Lux's stomach protested again, but this time, with food so near, she realized that while what Riselda had confided did sicken her...she'd also hardly eaten dinner.

Her jaw tightened as her hand unclenched. She took the biscuit from Riselda's outstretched fingers and didn't bother to thank her.

Nibbling at a corner, her nose wrinkled. It tasted like herbs and not the usual ones, but by the time she was halfway through, her stomach did settle. Despite everything. Her glance slid to Shaw, to the endearing furrow in his familiar brow and the concern in his beautiful eyes. She pulled her own away, flushing in an instant.

Yes, despite *everything*.

"*Lucena Thorn hurts those we love. Vesperine Grimrook will kill them.*"

Lux jerked so badly the remainder of her biscuit joined the first on the floor.

"Lux," said Shaw, gripping her upper arm. Even Riselda set aside her goblet.

"I'm sorry," she mumbled. "That name. *Vesperine*. It caught me off guard." She settled her head against the chair and forced slow breaths. Meanwhile, the horrifying version of herself swayed in the corner of the room. She could not see its eyes beneath the locks of limp hair—but its blackened teeth were bared and grinning.

When Lux managed to drag her attention from it, she caught Riselda's stricken look. One quickly shed from her face and replaced with thoughtful blankness as she said, "You remember that name?"

"I remember my father saying it once."

"Did he? Stupid man."

"He was not!" shouted Lux—so abrupt and harsh, Riselda startled. "Don't you *dare*. Don't you dare speak an ill word about either of them. Not when you've done what you did. Not when they're dead. Do you think I care we share blood, or that I will somehow be loyal to you? You never wanted a family; you wanted someone beholden to your cause. Well, I will *never* be."

Lux had to pack it away. Like she used to. Like she'd always practiced. Because if she didn't... If she thought of Riselda as her—

No. This cannot happen.

Lux didn't fold. She crushed. She stamped and pummeled the knowledge of how she'd come to this world deep into the void at the back of her head. It would try to get out—they always did—but that was fine in comparison to the alternative.

She would deal with it when she was ready; she was not ready yet.

Riselda watched her closely, and every few breaths her gaze would shift. To Lux's grip on Shaw's forearm. "What does he hope to gain, I wonder," she murmured.

Shaw stiffened underneath her, and Lux growled, "Who?"

"Corvin," Riselda answered. "I would not think, at his old age, he would be causing such pains for sport."

Chills swept up Lux's spine. And here now was the last information she'd kept from Shaw, wriggling to get free. This was not like what she'd just buried. This was something she'd always planned to divulge. He was going to hate it; he was going to hate her timing even more.

"He offered me a place in their society. To undergo some ritual and be named—" Saints above, she couldn't say it. "It was either that or a Stripping," she finished.

Riselda brow furrowed. "A what?"

"A procedure. One their healer suggested. He said it would prevent further decay"—Lux watched Shaw from the corner of her eye—"if I removed my brilliance."

Shaw, to her shock, did not react, and she couldn't help her curiosity. Lux turned fully to view him—and knew immediately she was wrong. Because though he hadn't physically moved or scowled or shouted the horror of it, his eyes revealed it all. Fury poured off him in waves. He stared at her—into her—but he didn't speak.

Riselda's voice crept like smoke between them. "Your brilliance is in your soul, Lucena. You cannot remove one without the other."

Lux braced her hands at once on the armrest, Shaw's reaction forgotten. "Pardon?"

Shaw fairly vibrated now beside her. She could feel him sure as if his skin was laid against hers. And strangely, that steadied her head when horror and rage began fighting for dominance.

"Saints above, devil below...he said it was an experiment."

And Artemis had been experimenting, all right—

With Mothlock's staff.

How many had been done?

Why had it been done?

Because what was the use of a discarded brilliance? Of an extracted soul?

And then her stomach plummeted so intensely she gripped her middle. "Riselda. You said the nightmares only lasted through the night, did you not?"

Riselda sat straighter at her tone. "I did. They would come while you slept, waking you enough to see them, hear them, but could not move..." Riselda's focus distanced into some memory.

"Then how is it I've seen them during the day?"

"The day?"

"While awake. It has been with me—this grotesque apparition—night *and* day."

"Darling, are you sure?" Riselda peered at her as though she could root out the chaos in Lux's mind. "Neither of the Alesso boys could force their brilliances outside the realm of sleep."

"But if they'd somehow claimed another's brilliance to ferry it out?"

"That is not—"

"*Don't* say it. Every time I have, it's been proven the opposite."

All that careened in Lux's head now were bloodshot eyes, dulled eyes, girls in shackles, and a basin doused in what she'd assumed was wet but had been dried and shimmering.

Silver.

"If these collectors aren't simply drinking lifeblood but drinking whole souls, then that entire manor needs to collapse. With every one of them inside." Shaw bit out the words like they were weapons themselves. Lux found him retreated to the front of the fireplace, his knife trailing shallow scratches in the mantle while he paced.

She scowled. Because using the word "simply" to describe such an awful act did not sit right with her. The rest, however, was too horrific to allow space in her mind. More so than her parentage, even.

Maybe that *was* the only solution. To destroy them all for good.

"Did you know about their curse?" she asked Riselda. "To petrify without sleep?"

Riselda shook her head. "I've heard nothing of a curse. Though, this Society of Saints did not emerge fully until my leaving—"

"And your thieving," interrupted Lux.

"Don't speak to me of thievery, Lucena. Grimrook House. Mothlock. *The Risen* and *The Essence*. Those things belonged to the Grimrooks long before the Alessos even existed. Before the minders of Mothlock Manor turned an orphanage into a harvest, murdered our family, and created a cult."

Our family.

The void yearned to unearth her hidden revelations. Lux gritted her teeth. "*The Essence*? Is that where the loose pages on lifeblood were from?"

"It was my legacy. This house, those books. It is *mine*. And they have claimed them falsely for long enough."

Lux stared at Riselda. At her perfect features and perfect sneer. She shifted, and Riselda's eyes immediately snapped to her own, a placating smile forming on her crimson mouth. Lux knew then—this was not a new web being strung together. This was an old one. With a very old and very capable spider minding its vibrations. And Lux had been stuck fast in it since birth.

"You knew about him."

"Be more specific, my dear."

"Alixsander's body. It was always your plan to come back here. To bring me along. Was I meant to revive him for you too?"

Riselda swallowed the last drops from her goblet and said, "It would have been an excellent bargaining token, you must admit. Dear Alix. Sometimes I wonder if I should not have left him to die."

Chapter Forty-One

Grimrook House possessed only a fraction of the rooms of Mothlock; Riselda left them behind for a different one. She didn't tell them where she went, but the candlelight slowly diminished down the main floor's corridor.

The light winked out of existence, and Lux frowned. Shaw had bodily blocked her sight. His knuckle nudged beneath her chin, and she obliged, tilting her face to meet his. "Yes?"

The intensity of his gaze, she expected. She didn't expect the compassionate sheen.

His eyes were glassy when he said, "You don't have to continue with this, I hope you realize. Not for me. Definitely not for her. She's put you through horrors, Lux, and she will again without a thought. You know anything she'd have you assist her in will benefit her and her alone."

Lux blinked up at him. More rapidly when she saw the tears gather despite his best efforts. They did not fall, but it was a near thing. Her heart tugged, tethered to his. "I know all of that."

"Do you? Because I know *you*. I've seen you despondent, struggling to remember your dreams. I watched the moment you went from wanting nothing but a brush of sunlight to realizing you deserved to try for it all. I can't allow you to fall back into old habits now. I will not allow it."

In response, Riselda's revelation rattled from the dark where Lux had forced it. It wanted to be freed. To overwhelm her. Her impulse was to bury it deeper.

But instinct told her that wasn't wise. That she had this boy—*man, he'd correct*—and he cared for her deeply. Would listen to anything she would tell him. He was opinionated, it was true, but not stubborn. Here was a person she could trust with everything she would otherwise shove into the darkest depths.

Lux drew a slow breath and cringed at its shaking. "That confession of hers felt like it wrecked something. Only, I'm not sure what yet, and I don't have time to check. I knew I wasn't born to my parents. But I never could have guessed *that*." Lux gestured wildly down the hall. "Whatever legacy her family has, I cannot survive being a part of it. I don't want to end up like her, but what if I have no choice?"

The quiet grew around them before Shaw spoke. "Even if your tendencies run the same, you always have a choice. Maybe it'll be hard. Maybe more than that. But you know what it feels like to come out on the other side. And you can lean on me. I might not have worthwhile advice to give each time, but I promise to always listen. I swear I'll never let you fall."

Lux stared up at him, her lips parted, a confession of her own on her tongue. But something clanged from deep in the house, and it shook her enough that she said instead, "I should have helped Aline that day. I shouldn't have left you to die."

"I didn't mind so much." Shaw wrapped her up against him. Her ear lay perfectly positioned over his heart; the steady beat lulled her at once. He was so solid—and she did not mean only physically. With his arms tensed and draped fully around her so she couldn't so much as slouch, she understood just how strongly he stood by his declaration.

His loyalty to his family and those who'd been wronged, she had witnessed. She was blessed indeed to realize it applied to herself too.

"*We're not good enough. Not for anyone. Definitely not for him.*"

Rotted nails snaked around Shaw's bicep from behind.

Lux shuddered in his embrace. *It isn't real. It's a nightmare. Only a nightmare.* But the words rang hollow in wake of what she saw.

Half her face, sallow and decaying, peered around him. *"Hear all that he promises to give us? What will we give him in return? Another Grimrook with greedy blood. We will only take. We will kill him a thousand ways. We will leave him with nothing!"*

Lux gasped in pain and terror both, burying herself in Shaw's chest.

"Devil below," she whimpered. "I can't do this."

Shaw's temple lowered to hers. "Do what?"

Lux's eyes scrunched closed. She did know what it was like on the other side. How *freeing*. To be back in that wagon, a butterfly in her palm. She yearned for that contentment desperately. That excitement for the days ahead.

She wanted to believe Shaw—that she wasn't broken. That she'd only ever been buried beneath the rubble of an unfair life. It had been easier to hope in her bedchamber, warm from the fire and the relief of seeing him. It was harder now, knowing such deep-rooted wickedness had also grown inside her since her conception. Though the nightmare plaguing her steps now was likely a twisted use of brilliance, it didn't negate the fact hers still was wrong.

This rotting version of her had only ever regurgitated her own fears. Granted, they were much harsher and infinitely more terrifying when delivered this way, but they were still familiar. Was she good enough?

She didn't know.

Lux's jaw clenched, a desperate determination building again within. She must be through with allowing fears to stand in her way of finding out. If she was not good enough, it would be proven before the end of this, and if she was unsalvageably rotten—well, she'd sever Shaw free.

Before she rotted him too.

"We must break into the vault," she and Riselda said in unison.

Riselda stared at Lux afterward, a tilt to her lips. Meanwhile Lux withered inside and wished for something to purge the connection between them. Perhaps there were curses to sever familial ties...

"It is late," continued Riselda. "We'll need something to keep us going." She spun away from them in the strange half-glass room and swished a decanter as delicately as a teacup. "How do you like my conservatory?" she asked.

Lux met Shaw's narrowed eyes. His jaw tensed and he scowled down his nose at her. They'd argued.

He wanted them to leave Riselda behind.

Lux wanted that too, but couldn't.

He'd contended they'd managed just fine as a pair in Ghadra.

She'd reminded him she had to leave him to torture, and the aftermath almost mentally murdered her.

She'd won—clearly. Because though he fumed, he couldn't deny her final point: Riselda knew where the vault was. They did not. And time, she'd learned long ago, wasn't something to be squandered.

"It's very..." Lux trailed as she caught sight of the same vines growing over the manor clinging to the rafters here. The blooms were many, more vibrant, and they hung nearly low enough to brush Shaw's head.

Half the ceiling above them was clear. Lux could see straight through to the moon and stars, and the cool light mixing with the assortment of candlesticks granted the room an eerie ambiance. The vast majority of the candles burned atop Riselda's workspace.

"...exposed," she finished.

Riselda's head lifted to gaze out the wide windows beyond her. The sea was especially wild tonight; the cresting waves glistened like ice. She said, largely wistful, "This was my favorite room of the house. It hurt to leave it."

Riselda whirled with the decanter in hand, and in the other, she held a short glass. She poured a small amount and held it to her nose. "For energy." Then she downed its contents.

She poured another and held it out. Not to Lux, but to Shaw. "Cheers, Cock—"

"*Enough*, Riselda."

Riselda bit back a grin. "To our resourceful Mr. Roser. A pretty face and a talent: quite an unheard-of combination. For a man."

Lux thought he would refuse it even as his eyes were begging for rest, but he surprised her. He accepted the glass and tossed the elixir back in a single swallow. He held it out to Riselda.

Who accepted it with a smile. The woman knew what she was doing, Lux must admit. If she'd offered it first to Lux, Shaw would have surely protested her drinking it. He didn't have the same sense of preservation for himself—she'd known this since discovering why he'd died.

"And lastly." A splash of liquid met the glass and extended toward her. Lux took it, but she didn't drink. She sniffed it instead.

"What do you smell?"

Lux stiffened at the question, as it was one Riselda had asked repeatedly when she had been considered family and tutor both. When they'd thought Lux's fascination with the body was a healer's mark rather than a necromancer's.

And same as then, Lux was not a discerning sort. "It smells sweet. Some sort of berry."

"Dried mulberries, yes."

In her periphery, she noted Riselda appeared to be her normal self, and Shaw too. He stood a little straighter, some of the tiredness leaving his posture. Lux swallowed the elixir. It was thin and light. She rid herself of the glass.

By the time she did, a fog she hadn't realized dulled her head had evaporated. Her eyes widened at the feel of it.

"Good. Now that we are all alert for the coming long hours, I have a key. Let's see if it still fits, shall we?"

Chapter Forty-Two

Lux had at first assumed the vault to be somewhere in the manor's dark underground corridors. She'd guessed later it was housed in the tower.

She was correct the second time around.

Behind Riselda's childhood portrait, the hidden passage to the tower was cold with stone on either side and nothing at all to heat the air. Lux held her hand to a torch as they passed it by just for the fleeting feel of its fire. Shaw kept pace behind her, Riselda in front, and every time she looked back her nightmare followed, silent to everyone but her.

She gritted her teeth against its relentless voice, ready to scream.

And she waited. She waited until they'd climbed to the very top and stood before the arched, wooden door, Riselda's heirloom key in its lock. She waited until the lock clicked open. Only then did she push the black-handled dagger into Riselda's back.

It didn't pierce the skin, she didn't think, and aside from stiffening, Riselda neither flinched nor made a sound. Her long-fingered hand held onto the key where it rested, and she said, "So it has come to this again."

Lux's nostrils flared, every muscle tensed. The nightmare barraged her, but she wouldn't be swayed.

"So it has. Self-preservation has always driven you, Riselda, and I know if it comes down to who should emerge from this unscathed, you'll choose yourself. So tell me—what's really in the vault? What do you want so badly?"

Riselda laughed, low and lovely. "My darling, you do not understand me so well as you think." She paused briefly. "But you do understand me better than anyone else alive, I will admit. You waited until I could get you in before you betrayed me. Dare I say I'm impressed?"

"I don't want to impress you," seethed Lux.

Push the dagger. Take back our power. She has siphoned from us long enough!

Lux flinched, and so did Riselda. She'd nicked her. "I *want* your answer."

"The deed to Mothlock's estate, Lucena."

"Why? You cannot think to take over this place. It doesn't need you here. The people nearby don't need you here."

"And yet, it shouldn't be left with this degenerate society, should it? You witnessed the remains of Grimrooks in that garden."

Lux's grip softened without meaning. Her memories propelled her backward. To the day Riselda enacted the last portion of her terrible plan in Ghadra.

"You planned for us both not just to come here," she murmured. "But to stay?"

"It's ours."

Lux stamped down the knowledge of their shared blood at once. *No. Don't think of it.* Riselda's goal could have been far more sinister, and while what Lux had said was true—those near Mothlock's estate would not thrive with someone like Riselda at its helm—it must be better than the harvests that occurred here now.

Another problem for the future; she was collecting them expeditiously now.

"Go on, then," said Lux, and stowed away her dagger.

"How kind," replied Riselda with the barest bite.

The door pushed in.

Unlike the cavernous crypt far below, this high room didn't flicker to light upon their entering. But there was something lit: A single lamp upon a desk.

And the room was aglow.

With a wide, glass-doored cabinet of lifeblood.

"We've found it," breathed Lux—at the same moment Shaw gripped her around the arm and dragged her behind him.

She didn't have time to question him or register the large contraption in the center of the circular room, when a new voice croaked, "*Intru—*"

An axe sank into the soft flesh of the person hunched over the bell pull; they hunched farther before slumping to the floor. A dark stain spread through the attendant's clothing.

He hadn't even protested.

"Riselda!" Lux hissed. "You could have knocked him unconscious instead of murdering him."

"No, Lucena. You're right. There is something wrong with their life force; we should cull them all."

Shaw moved toward the body, his fingers pressing to the man's wrinkled neck and coming away again. He was dead, Lux already knew. Shaw shoved his lids closed.

But she couldn't help her curiosity. She stepped forward herself, and when her finger pressed to his eye, she searched. "He's empty," she said. Her glance strayed around the room.

More ornate cabinets enclosed with glass. Stacks of blank paper and ink. The contraption in the center, which must have been the printing press, was larger than she'd ever expected. But what caught her attention longest was the scratched cup and tin plate scattered beside the dead man, empty of all but crumbs. "They kept him up here."

"And he more than likely managed to pull that rope," said Shaw. "We need to leave."

"I will have my deed first." Riselda spun away from the gruesome scene she'd created and, without bothering to wipe her axe, replaced it within the confines of her cloak. She began pulling open drawers at random.

Shaw's gaze found Lux's, and she could see precisely what he thought. *She cares for nothing but her own goals.*

Lux glanced at the body and immediately regretted having done so. The seeping wound would no longer be contained by any fabric and now puddled on the stone floor. She flung her eyes away. To the pages splayed out beside the machine, the contraption prepared for more.

Her heart told her what it was before she saw it up close.

"*Damn* them," she growled when she neared.

The finished pages were lying flat and unbound, her most familiar enchantment on display. The *Rise* incantation had been printed in uniformed letters—ruined by a depiction of the devil.

One that looked just like her own.

One that looked just like *her*.

With tortured eyes and a sinister smile, the nightmare wrapped around the detailed illustration of necromantic patterns to be painted, and Lux followed a trail of inked smoke down to a note printed across the bottom of the page.

To guide the dead risks leading an evil darkness home.
Beware those who venture this way.

"Oh, so now the devil found me outside the Beyond all those times and cursed me itself, is that it?"

Of course Mothlock's tweaked manuscripts would have it declared all her fault. Lux's teeth ground together. All that talk of dark brilliances. All that talk of madness. They sought to frighten others to bury their gifts or give them up, meanwhile pivoting only for her.

"Ah, at last. I don't like to confess my faults, but my memory is not what it once was." With her admission, Riselda dug into a drawer beneath a cabinet. A sharp *click*, and a drawer within a drawer popped free. She reached inside.

Lux bit down on her tongue when Riselda unrolled the scroll's copper edges. When she whispered, "The estate is *mine*."

Suddenly, Lux's fury over this vault—over everything in it—transformed into a singular mission. She pushed past Shaw's inspection of the wall, beyond the cabinet alight with lifeblood, until she came again to the slain attendant. To the lamp set beside him. She picked it up, stared awhile into its blue flame, and then she spun and threw it with all her strength.

Straight into the printing press.

"Lucena!"

But Lux could only grin. The freed flame leapt upon the newly printed parchment, the seeping oil dousing the contraption. All of it went up in a flare of fire and sweet smoke.

Riselda twitched when a shattering of glass sounded. Lux didn't. She watched Shaw stride toward her, *The Risen*—the original—in his grip. He said, "There's a second door, a hidden staircase I would guess. It probably shadows the one we came up on."

"Locked?"

"Not anymore."

Something wild grew inside her then. She couldn't explain it at first, hoping it wasn't hysteria, but as the printing press continued to burn, the manipulated version of her beloved book gone to ash, and Riselda looking on it all with outrage and disgust, she focused instead on Shaw.

The growing fire dragged every bit of gold to the forefront of his eyes. Highlighted the crimson splashed across his chest. Its heat licked her profile, and she knew they needed to leave or be burned along with everything else, but—

"I should tell you that I love you," she said.

The printing press bowed then crashed into a heap. Sparks leapt and caught at the edges of the room. Riselda squawked in protest, running to the cabinets housing memorabilia of an abandoned life.

Shaw hooked his fingers in the lace of Lux's collar. She expected him to drag her to him, but he didn't. He stepped forward instead. Until their chests met, and she was sure she would die both from the contact and the wait for him to speak.

She couldn't believe she'd found the courage to say it aloud. Finally.

She couldn't believe—

"I almost told you the day you left." He stared down at her, and though the fire had turned the color of his eyes into the warmest shade imaginable, the heat from his gaze belonged to something else entirely. Her lips parted, and he tracked the movement. "That night in the mayor's prison, Lux. When I told you—"

"I remember what you said."

His mouth shifted into a half-smile. "I love you too. I can hardly believe it."

She smiled to match. Her heart felt full to the brim. It remained so even as she asked, "Do you think we can survive this?"

"The fire or the society?"

"Caring about one another so much."

More glass cracked and a cabinet splintered.

Shaw bent until his nose just brushed her own and his lips were nearly against hers. "Does it matter?" he murmured.

Lux sucked in a breath full of smoke and him. "No."

"We need to leave, Lux."

"You said that already."

"Except now the entire room is burning."

"Learned it from you."

He laughed against her mouth, but she sobered on hearing it. Because she remembered—after the fire came the consequences. Consequences which nearly lost him to her forever.

Lux pulled back and found Riselda busying herself with gathering as many things as she could. Flames sparked all around her. The smoke shifted, and Lux noticed a long crack in the black stone of the wall. A tapestry lay in a crumpled heap at its base, already afire.

Shaw shifted to face it. "It's through there." Then he handed *The Risen* to her.

"I'll go first," she replied. "To clear the webs."

"Thoughtful." He glanced to Riselda, where another cabinet—the one containing scores of lifeblood—bowed then collapsed to smoldering bits beside her. Silver seeped to fill every groove in the flagstones. "And her?"

Lux sniffed and said nothing. She shoved her shoulder into the door, hardly stumbling when it spun. She huffed in the dark at its opposite side. Like the door in the morning room, this one led to a spiral staircase, but one much narrower and far more coated in dust. She didn't think it'd been used in a very, very long time.

She stepped down and into cobwebs. Grimacing, Lux swiped at them quick, not turning when a flare of light and warmth and smoke met her back. The door swung fully closed a second time, and Shaw held a flaming bit of wood aloft in the passageway.

The remaining webs burned away.

"What would a regular night with you be like, I wonder?" he said.

The passage muffled his voice strangely, and Lux looked up at him. "You making me tea. Sitting in comfortable chairs. You'll be painting. I'll be listening to the sea."

Even saying it aloud had her aching.

But abruptly, she realized there might not be more nights of any kind.

Because they'd reached the base of the hidden staircase.

And there was no door.

Chapter Forty-Three

"Devil's tits!" Lux cradled her shoulder, slumping to the ground.

"If it didn't work for me, I'm not sure why you thought it would for you." But Shaw rubbed at her shoulder with one hand anyway. With his other, he flipped quickly through *Brilliant Brushstrokes*.

Still.

He'd been at it for several minutes, crouched, his brow furrowed and chewing at his lips. But Lux couldn't handle more waiting. Thus, she'd propelled herself into the stone wall.

"What are we going to do?" The makeshift torch weakened, any breathable air slowly siphoning away. She shoved painfully back to her feet. "Should we go back?" When Shaw didn't answer, she nudged his elbow with her knee.

He pushed her away. "We can't go back. It'll be engulfed by now."

"We can't stay here until it finishes burning!" She heaved in a gulping breath. *Devil below. I feel it. The...air...*

Shaw cursed.

"What?"

He closed the book carefully, and then his eyes trained upon hers. "Do you remember when I told you I needed to mix blood with my pigments? This book says I was right."

Lux's mouth dropped wide, disgusted firstly and then confused. "That was a joke and blood is for curses. Are you saying your brilliance is...*cursed?*"

He cast her an exasperated look. "No, I'm not cursed. It doesn't have to be blood, but it does have to be a part of me. It could be hair. Or a fingernail." His expression turned pointed.

"And then?"

Lux sucked a sharp breath at Shaw pulling his knife free, slicing the tip vertically along his thumb.

"Shaw!"

"I have nothing else to paint with." He pressed his seeping finger to the stone.

His hand moved quickly, and Lux couldn't make out anything in the shadows. But once she stepped around to his opposite side, she held the torch out—lighting upon a quickly forming doorknob.

Flat and dripping. Formed entirely of blood.

Her stomach twisted.

When it was done, Shaw stepped away. She could tell his breaths, too, had shallowed.

"What did you do?" she asked. Streaks marred the stone where Shaw had wiped excess blood in the shape of a doorframe. Afterward, he twisted his wounded finger in the hem of his shirt. She stepped closer.

"It needs to dry. They always need to dry first."

He sounded as if he were willing to wait, but Lux couldn't stomach the feel of being robbed of air, and so she bent to the bloody work of art and blew.

She'd closed her eyes. She'd had to. But she could smell it still—the iron. She held herself back from heaving, though it was a near thing, and breathed out all that was left in her lungs. When she blinked open her eyes, a crimson knob sat directly in front of her face.

"Saints above," she gasped.

"Devil below," laughed Shaw. Then he grabbed the knob and twisted it.

The door swung outward into a flickering corridor.

They both stood in the stairwell; he didn't move, and she didn't either. Finally, Shaw peered around the newly formed doorway. "We're on the fourth floor, same as before," he murmured, low. "But Riselda's portrait…"

Lux was never one to starve her curiosity. She ducked under Shaw's arm to see what he saw.

Down the hall. The portrait. Melting. Riselda's piercing green gaze folding and falling.

A peculiar quiet doused the manor. She waited to feel Death's triumph. It didn't come.

She could have missed it—Riselda's long-awaited trip to the Beyond. Or Death was still lurking, and Riselda somehow still alive. Again.

The truest cockroach of them all, she thought.

The quiet was interrupted by a distant shuffling and muffled voices. Lux's body seized. She whipped back to Shaw, only for him to shove her farther out into the corridor. To then see him muscling the thick stone of the door closed, reopening his finger with his teeth and swiping it over the red doorknob.

He copied her earlier methods. He blew upon the crimson paint.

When it dried, the knob was gone. All that remained was a bloodied handprint.

How much time had passed, Lux didn't know. She blinked awake in the dark.

She couldn't see at all, not even the outline of the room. Her hand stretched outward, and of that, at least, she could note the vaguest outline. She pushed the four-poster's curtains aside.

She hadn't remembered drawing them.

She hadn't remembered climbing into bed to start.

It was dark, too, in the remainder of the bedchamber. The fire had guttered, leaving only blood-red coals, and the moon had vanished. Thick clouds must have gathered at some point in the night. Lux glanced down at her nightgown, picking at the silky material. Goosebumps littered her arms—the garment was thinner than anything she'd ever worn—and she searched for a robe. Her steps led her through the bedroom, the bath, and into the dressing room, but she found nothing.

Empty. Empty. Empty.

She returned to stand in the center of the room when she heard it. A soft wail. It seeped underneath the door. Her stare narrowed on the wood.

It tremored once, and then she was there, standing in front of it. Lux twisted the lock. The click reverberated throughout the room. She carefully turned the knob, and when the door creaked open, she fitted her eye to the crack and peered out.

A stray cloud had entered Mothlock. The entirety of the corridor was grey with fog and the lamplight had dimmed.

Inside it, a figure moved.

A woman. With ebony locks loose down her back and a nightgown the replica of Lux's own. Lux caught her breath. The wail came again, louder this time, even as the woman was farther away. Lux could see the glisten of tears on her cheeks when she turned to face a black door. It was odd, she thought, that they looked so much alike. Odder still that another girl came to be here, crying in the corridor, not more than two doors down—

The door swung open. A pale hand stretched from the dark. It grasped hold of the girl's wrist—and hauled her in.

The resulting scream froze the very blood in Lux's veins. She tumbled out into the hall.

In her hand was the gallow blade—she didn't remember grabbing it—and she was immensely thankful. She sprinted toward the door only to stumble and choke at its stoop. Death poured over her, soaking into her pores. The silence that followed was absolute.

"Too late," whispered a voice, and though Lux still clutched a knife, she clutched at her head too.

9, read the door. She reached and traced the curve of it. Her finger only just met the number's end when it was drawn away from her. Lux stumbled back.

Corvin filled the frame.

Though it wasn't him. Not exactly. Because instead of a collector's robe, he wore the black trousers and shirt same as when she'd first met him. And his hands—they were ungloved. Pale and elegant, he stretched his fingers toward her. The room behind him was black as midnight, but the lamp lit his eyes. A murky grey. A mark of the twisted revived.

"Welcome home, Vesperine Grimrook."

The walls began to throb. A tempo that first matched her heartbeat before exceeding it. And Corvin's hand cupped her cheek. It was cold; it burned like ice. His fingers gripped the base of her skull and only then did his thumb caress her, running along the fullness of her bottom lip. He dragged her to him. When he smiled, his teeth dripped, a red and silver mix.

"Little doll. Don't you want to stay?"

Lux jolted out of the vivid nightmare, her head cracking against stone. She cried out, cradling her skull, only to have another pair of hands claim that space. She blinked her eyes slowly open. To her darkened bedchamber. Her fireplace, the coals red and warm. To Shaw kneeling beside her, his nightshirt loose and open at his throat and his hair a mess.

She tried to orient herself but couldn't. Not until Shaw said, "Did you have a nightmare? I didn't even hear you climb out of bed."

Lux crashed back to the present. Her back was propped against stone and her head pounded. She glanced to her right to find the door, closed and locked, and her stockinged feet tucked back into the folds of her thick nightgown. "He wasn't real," she whispered. Only, her instinct rejected that line of thinking immediately. Hot then cold, a sickness in her gut—her mind had granted her a warning in the most horrifying way imaginable.

Careful hands worked the sweat-drenched hair from her brow. A bandaged thumb scratched her skin. "Let's get you back to bed."

Shaw scooped her up before she could form a reply, cradling her to him. He came to stand beside the bedframe and laid her gently down. "Do you need something to drink?"

Lux cleared her throat. "There's a pitcher of water—"

"I know where, love." He made for the table, and she watched him in the dim, red light.

"You need to go back to your room before they find you gone," she said.

He returned with a cup in hand. His glance strayed beyond the curtains, to the shut balcony door. "I can stay awhile yet."

His voice was gravel-rough from sleep, and Lux didn't protest when he climbed over her, settling himself against her back. She managed a single swallow from the cup before she had to set it down. She turned into his chest.

Her nose settled against the hollow of his throat. She drew a long breath.

"Do you want to tell me about it?" he rumbled against her ear.

She shifted and waited for his arms to tighten around her. She smiled when they did. "No," she sighed. "It's nothing I don't know or will ever allow to happen."

"Mmm, that's reassuring."

Lux's smile widened over his sarcasm. Really, she felt too safe and too warm to believe anything like that nightmare could come to pass. She would wait a few hours more. After that, she would ready herself for the Hallowed Eve celebration, and as the guests amassed, she would walk the many corridors. The flames had been hungry in the tower. She would see if the blue fire elsewhere had a similar appetite.

She would set the entire place ablaze.

Damn Riselda and any and all of her plans. Lux would burn it *all* down.

But first—her eyelids fluttered when Shaw's lips pressed to her hair—first, she would do only this.

Chapter Forty-Four

Her Hallowed Banquet gown was blood-red with silver stitching.

Lux finished securing the hooks of the corset while staring at the silken creation lying atop her mattress. She'd been gifted a note at midday, set amongst her luncheon tray, explaining the society's designs upon her for the evening.

Please allow me the honor of being your escort this evening.
-C

No mention of revival. Of curses. Not a single person had come to check on her, only an attendant with the delivery of her gown. No one mentioned the fire in the tower.

The silk slipped over her head and cascaded to the floor. Lux felt out of her skin. Shaw could not know her at the banquet. He was an investor and must be treated with all the dignity that allotted. And she...she must be aloof, acknowledged but otherwise ignored. Achievable, she thought. She'd plenty of practice.

If Corvin would let her go.

Rain tapped against the balcony door; a dreary sky met a fierce sea. Lux shifted away from it and caught her reflection in the mirror.

Purple crescents framed her eyes.

Her hair curled about her face.

Decaying arms wrapped around her middle.

Lux froze. She didn't move or shriek. But in her head, she screamed. She watched them move along her bodice, feeling nothing but seeing it all, and when those fingers arched into a clawing grip, she jolted when they disappeared inside her.

The apparition rested its chin on her shoulder.

"*Look at us: A proper monster. Who will we destroy next? The girl who feels too much? Do not fret, she is already dead.*"

Lux stared furiously into the mirror. "You're not real. You're made by someone evil. And all you say is lies."

"*Do we?*"

All at once, her veins felt coated in ice. Lux shivered, as the nightmare did not seem taunting, for once, but resolute. Her fingers reached into her corset—toward a key on a silver ribbon.

Corvin will be here at any moment, her head scolded.

Cecily is dead, her heart knew.

Death had come. Had looked over the slew of evil men and had taken a child, instead.

"*It is our fault,*" the nightmare claimed, and it vanished with a grin when the mirror swung in.

Lux anticipated the plunge and slipped down the hidden slope, faster now in silk. Her pack beat against the wall, and her hair fell from its pins. She held a lamp ahead of her.

The Risen made the bag heavy. She'd thought of hiding it somewhere in the room, but then she didn't know if she would return. She had no plan now other than seeing Cecily revived. After that, she would determine a new course.

The underground room's hidden latch was much easier to find in the light. Lux flung herself along the length of the revealed passageway, stopping only for a breath at its end. Nothing shifted, and so she barreled down the remainder until she stood before the mammoth archway, starved for air beneath looming statues. Lux curved her shoulders inward to be away from them and braced herself against the wall.

With a smidgeon of strength regained, she straightened. Adjusted the bag containing all she needed for a revival. And went through.

The torches flickered and lit.

Atop the grave of ice rested a body.

Same as the one before, it was clad in only undergarments, but Lux stared at the red braid. It hung limp. More so than the pale hand beside it.

Cecily lay dead before her.

Lux rushed forward and then around—away from the archway's opening. Grabbing hold of Cecily's rigid arm, she dragged the girl off the bed of ice. She did not waste time in searching for slit eyes—she delved straight for the gentle lull of lifeblood.

Lux huffed a breath in relief.

It was there, pooled within her, and under Lux's quick assessment, the body seemed to be around ten hours post mortem. She knelt beside the girl. Flinging open her pack, she dug inside. Howler canines, she had. Marsh snapper eyes, she'd pilfered from Silas's collection in Verity. She spread out all the rest beside her and worked as quickly as she could.

All the while, she listened.

For footsteps.

For her nightmare.

So far, she remained alone.

Lux painted Cecily and did not wait. Her first words of the incantation cast her onto the road to the Beyond. Lux had been here—on this shadowy path—so many times, she hardly registered it anymore. It was a plain road with plain earth beneath her feet, and once she reached the Veil, she reached out for the soul to cross.

"May your eyes become mine—"

Lux would lead Cecily home.

And there was no evil darkness to be found in it.

A human soul was light. Filled with energy. It seeped into Lux so she might carry it—the dead could not go back, only ahead, on their own. The girl's energy bloomed within her. It shot to her fingers, her feet. It pricked in her nose and behind her eyes.

Lux was nearly there. The enchantment nearly done. She could feel her: Cecily. But for the first time, she noticed something else lingering too. Another brilliance. A harnessing of emotions. Had such awareness during revivals always been a possibility? Had her own brilliance truly stretched?

Her consciousness flickered.

Contain it! her head shouted.

She...would. She *did*—

And slumped forward.

"Wake up! Oh, *please,* wake up."

Lux blinked dazedly upward. "Cecily?"

The girl was bent over her, braid tickling her jaw, and Lux didn't realize, until Cecily fell crying upon her, she was splayed out upon the cold flagstones.

Her body hummed.

Cecily's weight upon her was uncomfortable.

She gently shoved her off. "I'm fine," Lux mumbled, grinding her teeth over the lie.

She'd tried. She'd paid attention. She'd felt Cecily's soul overwhelming—*overtaking*—her, and she'd demanded her body to contain it. Souls had never fought her this way. They'd always been a welcomed warmth in her chest when her own had lacked that light. But now it seemed as though both her and another couldn't coexist. That it was too much for her to bear.

Maybe she wasn't broken—but she was certainly cracked. And she hated it.

Lux pushed to her feet and then hauled the girl up too. She bent to gather her things. "You died, Cecily. What do you remember?"

She glanced upward to see the girl shivering in her scant clothes, her eyes wide and alarmed, absorbing the eeriness of the sanctum. Lux had nothing to give her, but she glanced at the alcoves.

Moving to the nearest, she wrestled a black robe from its skeleton. Bones rattled, disturbed dust rising to meet her nose until she sneezed, but when it was free, Lux adjusted the pendant belonging to the dead.

"I'm sorry to bother you," she said.

Shaking the garment of anything that might yet cling, she presented the robe to Cecily. The girl took it with pinched fingers and pursed lips.

"I *cannot* wear this."

"I have nothing else to offer but a feather and loose parchment."

Cecily pressed her eyes closed. She noticeably swallowed. Then she donned the robe.

It puddled about her bare feet.

"You'll be their smallest collector," Lux said. "Make sure you raise the hood once we leave." She slung her pack over her shoulder.

"I remember dying."

Lux's fingers paused in their adjustment. She waited, terribly impatient, for what else Cecily would say.

"It was peaceful—once the pain faded."

Lux raised an eyebrow.

"The garden. The stems with teeth. He took me to them. I couldn't do much of anything after I drank the elixir for the salt-sick, and I still had the shackles."

"*Devil below.*" *He had her blood drained. Sentenced her to death in that graveyard garden.* Lux's insides were abuzz now with more than the revival's energy. She ground her teeth. "Corvin."

The name came to her tongue sure and resolute—but Cecily shook her head. "No. The large one. Kent."

"Kent?" Lux frowned. "Why would he?"

Cecily sniffed, her nose pink and running. She scowled immediately afterward. Lux knew the robe did not smell fresh. "After they struck, he told me I'm not worth the trouble I'll cause. That empaths are better off gone."

Lux could make no sense of it. "They wanted you badly back in the courtyard. They even mended you when you were hurt. Why would they turn around and sacrifice you hours later... How did he feel?"

"He was..." Cecily trailed off, her brow scrunched. "Not excited, exactly. Bitter and angrier than that. He felt like...retribution."

Retribution? Involving a girl who only wants to go home?

Lux shook herself free of trying to rationalize it; time was slipping, and they'd yet to plan any means of escape. She reached into her pack and removed every goldquin she could find. Then she shoved them within the pocket of Cecily's robe. "Let's get you to the gate."

Chapter Forty-Five

THE END OF THE underground corridor revealed a steep climb that spat them out behind Mothlock's grand staircase. Lux didn't push the hidden door fully open, but remained stuck partway between, assessing.

The foyer had filled with people.

The guests of the Hallowed Banquet were not dressed in bright colors as Bartleby Tamish's partygoers had been but in a sea of darkness and riches—deep jewel tones and silvers. Many were in black. The grim architecture surrounding them, coupled with flickering blue flames and lashing rain, had Lux thinking she shouldn't be surprised of any evil committed here tonight.

She could see the front doors.

She did not see anyone in collector's robes. Maybe they congregated elsewhere. Or maybe...they'd changed. Lux's eyes burrowed into the back of a thin man suited in black. She chewed at her lip. Her glance flicked to Cecily.

"Pull up your hood," she whispered.

A small alcove containing an urn wasn't far from them. Overfull with plum-colored dahlias, it would mark the safest hiding place. Lux shifted toward it slowly, and with a quick scan of the room, wedged her pack behind it.

"You're sure you can't come with me?" asked Cecily.

Lux shook her head. "I can't leave this unfinished." The doors opened beneath Manphry's hands. "Go. You will get through this time."

Lux strode with purpose toward the doors, her shoulders thrown back—a mask of indifference secured upon her face. Her hair was not done up as she'd planned, but perhaps that was for the better. She needed at least one thing to feel like herself.

"Manphry," she said. "Which way to the Hallowed Banquet?"

Eyes the shade of decayed wood met hers. Manphry focused only on her—not on the short collector rushing out into the rain. "You're not meant to be here, Ms. Thorn. Up the stairs."

"Why am I not meant to be here?" Her quick glance revealed a carriage slowing to a stop before the steps. An open gate beyond, another coming through.

The rain poured steadily. The clouds were low and grey.

Twilight.

Everything changes at twilight.

"You're not meant to be here," he said again.

So they hadn't told him. Thus this husk of a man was forced to repeat his instruction without any other thought. Lux glanced again to the courtyard—to a hooded figure darting beyond the gate.

Her entire body exhaled.

"Up the stairs, you said?" She turned away from the door. "Then I will just—"

A boy leaned casually against the banister on the second-floor landing. A goblet hung from his hand. He didn't smile or nod when their gazes collided but, instead, sipped from his cup. His eyes, however, could not be missed. A far cry from his current, confident slouch, they drank her in like they couldn't get enough.

Lux sucked in a breath. Her body felt as though it'd caught fire. Manphry had shut the doors to the elements but now she begged for the breeze. Shaw lowered the goblet when another addressed him. Achingly slow, his stare broke with hers.

Lux looked across the landing. Toward the person who'd come down the staircase and now spoke to Shaw so intently. A person she felt most sick to meet again. Corvin's icy coloring complemented the darkly intense feel of the manor.

He spoke fast, his arm gesturing back the way he'd come, and it was as Lux contemplated ducking away, that his glance strayed far enough—and ensnared her own.

Goosebumps lifted all along her bare arms.

Corvin stilled, almost startled, and then his lips lifted—a hard, slow grin. He crooked his finger at her.

Lux imagined herself snapping it.

Instead, she gave in to the gesture.

She wasn't alone on the stairs leading up toward the unfamiliar ballroom. But it felt as if she were. Two sets of eyes—one warm, one cold—watched her intently. Lux found she couldn't look at either of them, though for entirely different reasons. She stared instead just above them. Behind them.

At Alixsander's portrait.

Did Corvin really murder you because you were good?

Someone stepped to Corvin's shoulder—a woman in a black gown. It drew Lux's attention to his own attire. The fact it wasn't his customary color. Corvin wore a pin-striped suit of silver with a blood-red bow pinned to his lapel. Lux's mouth opened and closed, glancing down at once to her front. Had he taken a strip of her gown's fabric? Her stomach twisted when he offered a charming grin to the guest.

It remained so when he returned his focus to her.

Do not look at Shaw. Do not. You don't know him. He's no one—

Her gaze slipped.

She couldn't stop herself from raking her eyes down his form.

Shaw had combed his hair—though it was still unruly—and he'd shaved his chin smooth. He wore a black jacket with copper stitching and a deep-green waistcoat which brought out his eyes in a way that made her ache. His trousers were new and pressed, and his shoes were polished. He'd a gold watch in his pocket. He could have been a member of the Light. He could have been a man of industry. But he was none of those things, and all she thought was that if he could be anything, she wanted him to be hers.

She was about to lose control of the situation—she could feel it. Because how could anyone contain so much *feeling* without letting it be known? Corvin was going to see it in her eyes. How could he not?

With all her power, she turned away. She smiled. "You were right. It is as impressive as all that."

Corvin huffed a laugh, though Lux noticed his eyes didn't shift. "I love that you're so pleased. But a few well-dressed guests does not make the event."

She said nothing, and his gaze perused her slowly. "You are stunning in Lord Kent's creation. I'd come to collect you, but you were gone."

Collect. *What a choice of word.* Her mask nearly slipped. "The wait was too much. I was ready ages ago and wanted to miss nothing. I'm sorry to have inconvenienced you."

"No inconvenience," he murmured, and his fingers dipped into his waistcoat. The gesture bothered her tremendously, and for a moment she could not figure out why. Until she realized—

He has no gloves.

Her mind bombarded her with the reincarnated image of her dream. Of his hand appearing just as it did now, slim and pale, but reaching for her. A dream version of her. And the death she'd felt immediately afterward.

Corvin removed a watch, silver to match everything else, and clicked his tongue at the time. His attention lifted to the man across from them—one Lux had decided once and for all she would dutifully ignore.

"We should make our way in, but I suppose it would be rude to withhold an introduction. Being as this is your savior, after all." Again, his smile didn't touch his eyes. "Mr. Roser, this is Lux Thorn. A necromancer from your own city and Mothlock Manor's guest."

"Necromancer?" he responded, his voice low and lightly tinged with disbelief. One that descended quickly into smoke. "I've heard tales of you. In Ghadra. I can't deny I've always been eager to know more."

Lux blinked a moment longer than necessary, his voice cloaking her and setting her heart wild. She looked at him finally—and his eyes were brilliant with mischief.

"Are you well?" he wondered. "The last I was aware, you were bleeding heavily. It was concerning. But you look very"—color rose to his cheekbones—"healthy."

Lux wished she could know exactly what he thought of the dress Kent had created for her, but she could guess well enough.

Her arms were bare, her collarbones too. Shaw's gaze continued to dance along them, causing his nostrils to flare, his breaths coming quicker than his norm. His eyes traced her skin: from beneath her ear, down her neck, and along the line of her naked shoulder.

Remember Corvin's suspicions.

She mustn't rouse them further.

"Well enough," she said, her tone shifting to something formal and distant. "I didn't mean to mar your arrival with my display."

Shaw's eyes darkened. "You didn't."

Lux startled at Corvin's touch. His arm pressed against hers; his hand held flat to her low back. Cold seeped through the fabric of her gown. "Shaw Roser is an investor in Mothlock. New to the role, isn't that correct?"

"It is correct," said Shaw. "Though I'd venture to say I am your most anticipated?" Then he smiled at Corvin—and it was the most concerning smile she'd ever seen.

A flash of irritation swept Corvin's features. Lux might have missed it if she'd blinked. But she hadn't, and in the wake of the emotion, an artery pulsed blue in his pale temple.

If she were capable of discretion, she would have kicked Shaw in the ankle for his obvious baiting. She shifted instead. Until her skirt settled over the toe of his polished shoe. She poised her heel over it and stepped down. Hard.

His jaw tightened, his eyes narrowing briefly, but he didn't flinch or even pull his foot away. Instead, Shaw turned the full force of that smile upon her. At once, her insides heated, a flutter in her lower belly flaming to light. The smile that had looked so menacing toward Corvin now looked intentional in a different way.

Shaw reached and she offered her hand. He bent over it, low enough she couldn't see his face through the fall of his hair. But she could feel his lips brush across her knuckles. She exhaled sharply.

"It's a pleasure to meet you at last, Ms. Thorn."

Corvin's fingers flexed against her back, and Lux stammered something unintelligible. She could sense the energy shift around them and couldn't say who was at fault. Corvin's shoulders were rigid, while Shaw's appeared to relax, and Lux thought every muscle of her own would likely ache in the morning—if she made it that far. This was precisely why she'd not ever minded spending her time with the dead.

"You as well," she replied and made to tug her hand free.

But Shaw held tight. "I beg of you not to give me reason to hope."

Lux choked at the same moment Corvin intervened. His laugh cutting between them was not at all kind. He made a show of drawing her nearer. "Death to the Devil, don't you work quickly? You'll have to excuse us, Roser. It looks like the mingling portion of this night is ebbing. Dinner is set to arrive. Enjoy the Hallowed Banquet and have a blessed Hallowed Eve."

Corvin turned them both, and she caught the return of Shaw's terrifying grin. She scowled after it, but it was entirely too late. Lux was about to be transported into a sea of riches; she would be lucky just to stay afloat.

Chapter Forty-Six

The second floor's corridor was dim. Even when it opened up onto an inner balcony, the light did not return, feeling instead as if it'd all been siphoned down into a room which glowed coolly with all that it hoarded. She'd not ever entered the ballroom. In truth, she didn't know of its existence until several hours before. A haunting melody rose to greet her at the balustrade; she peered over it.

The room was darkly exquisite with its crowd of sharp coats and expensive gowns. The chandeliers here were comprised of onyx, same as the walls, and their candlelight lit the wooden floor into a syrupy brown. Studious musicians were sat upon a dais at one end of the room; their instruments shone in brilliant silvers and golds. Opposite them were three long tables bare of all adornment but for matching candelabras, thick crystal goblets, and silver dinnerware.

It was a rich, mesmerizing sight; better than anything the dead mayor would have done.

Alcoves lined the perimeter. Lux's gaze skipped over each shadowed space, over every urn spilling with purple dahlias, searching for anything that lurked. Corvin led her to the top of the wide staircase.

The collector's fingertips lifted, trailing along her braids fallen from an attempted chignon, and she couldn't tolerate his nearness anymore. She flinched. His fingers inadvertently dropped to the bare skin of her collarbone.

"Devil—" she gasped, and flung her own fingers to cover the space.

"Something wrong?"

Lux couldn't raise her eyes. If she did, they would give her away. The horrifying dream pulsed around her. The stench of smoke and blood filled her nose.

Saints above, devil below. I might really die here.

Corvin's touch. It wasn't natural. Not at all.

It was cold.

Colder than Riselda. Colder than the mayor.

Colder than those unforgiving *trees*.

Her chin trembled.

"Riselda Grimrook never denied her madness. It is in us, in our blood. We and our mother are the same."

Lux managed not to grab hold of her hair, but it was a near thing. *I am not broken. I am not broken. I am not—*

She braved to look again at Corvin's mouth. Would it be dripping same as the dream?

"I do have a headache after last night," she managed.

She stood beside him still, and when her eyes finally lifted higher to meet his, she searched for some hint of his corruption. Her own soul had once been overgrown with guilt. So had Shaw's. Viktar had been steeped in hopelessness.

If I were to dig inside him, what would I find?

"I hope you've accepted my apology," said Corvin, his expression dipping into a frown. "I let my worry over your safety lead me, and it wasn't the right choice. My philanthropic nature is sometimes a curse in itself."

Vile idiot, she fumed. Worry over her safety?

Never had she been more set on burning something down than in this moment. No, she knew what they really cared for. And it was to see her tied up with strings, and him controlling them.

She had to escape.

"Did I exaggerate the banquet's intrigue?" he asked over her silence, leading her promptly onto the stairs.

Lux drew a slow breath, the music a melancholy thrill that enveloped her. "I see why you look forward to it. This room is like a dream." It was no lie on her part, but she couldn't help adding a second small truth. "Though I still would have preferred to hide away on a balcony than this."

Lux noted every attendant she'd previously overlooked. They stood at the edge of things, and while they were tasked with balancing silver platters of foods, goblets, and flutes—and did it well—the light would not deny the truth. Their eyes were each dulled and lifeless. Behind them, she could find no passion or will. She wanted to tear Corvin's own eyes out for seeing it.

She might have—if she hadn't a part to play.

Corvin laughed at her candor, and Lux's brow furrowed. She struggled to merge all she knew with her experiences. She held onto the arm of a man older than Riselda, though he appeared hardly older than Shaw. A man who'd once shared a very real dream with her and appeared genuine in his appreciation of hers. Even his laugh now was warm and rich. It was hard to fathom that deep inside he'd become as frigid as frost and full of nightmares.

That he was so gifted a liar.

"There's no dancing at this event?" she asked. The question was part curiosity, part wishful distraction. The guests at the base of the stairs were beginning to turn. Beginning to stare.

Because she was unfamiliar to them? Or because of whose arm she was on?

Because they *matched*?

"No, we don't dance. The Hallowed Banquet is an intellectual gathering for Mothlock's Society and investors alike. The ceremony afterward, however"—he winked— "is only for us. Ah, Lux Thorn. Please let me introduce you to one of our longest investors, Ulysses Morrigan, a leading man of industry and Malgorm councilmember."

Lux hardly righted her thoughts before she was arrested by the closeness of the man. Dressed in black satin, he inclined his head toward her. She supposed he could do nothing else wearing such a tight jacket. "A pleasure," he crooned. "I'm always interested in fellow investors. Tell me, what is it you do?"

Lux's lip twitched to lift into a sneer. She could smell the pompous air about him like foul breath, and she nearly told him so. "I'm not an investor."

"Not an investor?" The man's gaze dipped down her luxurious gown. "Then what are you—" His attention snagged. On Corvin's proximity. The way he curved toward her. The man's mouth lifted into a lecherous grin. "Picked a partner at last, have you, Lord Corvin? I'll say it's a good choice at first glance."

His "glance" turned into a thorough perusal. One of those she could feel down to her bones, leaving her wishing to shed her skin to be rid of the sensation. She stepped forward, her teeth nearly bared. "I'm a necromancer, Mr. Morrigan. Tell me, is there anyone you'd like revived? Or are they all better left buried?"

The investor startled. Corvin stiffened. But before anyone could offer any explanation or apology, Mr. Morrigan said, "Glory to the *Saints.* You're quite serious? What a useful little thing you are!" Lux did bare her teeth then. "Say, Alesso. I would be thrilled to borrow her from time to time. Might be a nice trick to have with those who test my limits."

The man laughed uproariously over what was apparently meant in jest, but had Lux ready to slice her hidden dagger down the middle of his clothing to eased the strained fabric. This was so like the Light. So like the late mayor. She could hardly stomach it.

"We will see what the future brings," Corvin replied, his jaw tight. Then he pressed a palm to Lux's lower back and steered her away.

Out of the investor's vicinity, he said, "Sorry for that. Morrigan forgets himself at times. He supports Mothlock's mission, though, so we forgive some transgression."

How unsurprising. She gritted her teeth. "I'm through with further introductions all the same, I think."

Suddenly, a woman stepped into her path. A woman bedecked in an assortment of gemstones and feathers, barely contained hair, and spectacles.

A woman she'd met before.

Mistress Farrentail inclined her head with a soft smile that further creased her eyes. "Happy Hallowed Eve."

"Good evening, Mistress Farrentail. Enjoying your time?"

Lux fought to smooth her own creasing. *The lady who warns me of zealots is here? A vendor and investor both?*

"Mightily, thank you. I've made two new connections, but would love to make it three. Lord Corvin, do introduce me to your lovely young friend."

"Apologies," said Corvin, chuckling. His hand left her to gesture down her person. "This is Lux Thorn. An accomplished necromancer." To Lux, he said, "I swear I'll spare you after this. One cannot deny the year's most celebrated investor."

Lux raised her eyebrow, returning her attention to the vendor. *Most celebrated?*

"Mistress Farrentail supplied us with the tincture enabling our discovery of the nature of these mysterious killings."

Which Lux knew, of course, but she feigned wonderment. "And has the culprit been apprehended?"

Mistress Farrentail blinked owlishly up at Corvin as if she, too, were anxious for this answer.

But Corvin sighed. "Not yet. They're elusive as the Devil it seems. Meanwhile we lost another: discovered too late for your revival."

"Tragic business," moaned the elderly vendor. "Lord Silas should enlist some help instead of taking the investigation all upon himself."

"If he cannot root them out, no one can," said Corvin, and he lifted his gaze to the carved ceiling. "His brilliance is made for this sort of thing."

"How so?" Lux couldn't hide her real interest over the matter. The feeling she experienced around the collector made her want to know everything about the man lest she be on the receiving end of his "gift".

Corvin's attention returned to her. "He can track anything. A natural scent, a perfume. Even blood."

...Cecily.

Lux could hardly focus with her chest's palpitations. Devil take her, she'd promised the girl freedom and had sent her out alone. Cecily could have no idea there was a bloodhound masking as a man inside the manor's walls. "Beastly," she muttered, horrified at her mind's conjured images of Silas skulking through Ravenwood. "But he's taken the evening off, I assume?"

"He has," agreed Corvin. "He's earned it after these relentless few days. For instance, he tracked three scents only this morning. At the cliffsides. And then again, in the cove. Poor Hildred was found drowned there. We entombed her over first Invocation."

Lux's blood chilled fully now, every hair on her body standing on end. But Corvin didn't look at her any longer. He looked at Mistress Farrentail, a pout on her pursed lips. "Oh no! An attendant?"

He nodded. "An awful accident. The staff here have always felt like family to me. We take care of one another in Mothlock. The cliffs are dangerous, but Hildred wasn't new to them. I can't begin to fathom what happened."

Lux could hardly think with her heart thundering. *If he knows it was me...*

"So much loss these days." Mistress Farrentail shook her head full of feathers. "But I almost forgot: Mr. Swallowpeak wished for a word." When Corvin hesitated, she said, "I'll take care of the girl."

His lips quirked. "See that you do." His glance shifted to Lux. "No need to speak to anyone else. I won't be long." Then he weaved through the crowd.

"So rich. So disgustingly wealthy. If we were to bleed them, would their blood be made of diamonds?"

Lux recoiled at the voice, her eyes darting to an alcove where she found clawed fingers gripping either side of an urn, eyes glowing over the lip.

"Draw the dagger. Let's see. Let's see. Let's—"

"I told you not to follow the zealots, you ridiculous girl."

Gone was Mistress Farrentail's sugary voice, and in its stead was a demanding tone, sharply underscored with disappointment. It was a tone she recognized. The Dark Market's claw vendor and her poisoned apples surfaced in Lux's head. Her lips parted in irritation before she hissed back, "And yet *you* did. You told me you didn't know what lifeblood was, and now I know you're a cheat and a liar. You've drunk it, haven't you?"

Unlike the older woman's, Lux's voice was all fury. People were almost always a disappointment to her; she didn't need it to seep into her words.

"Sure, I lied about not knowing what it was, but you couldn't expect me to admit something so volatile in Loxlen. Not to a perfect stranger." Her crooked fingers snatched at Lux's waist, dragging her close. "Why'd you do it then?"

"What? Follow them? Why would I tell you?"

"*Because.* Because this is so much bigger than you, and you did not listen, and now I know what you are, and I am quite literally *shaking* in my *shoes* that you're about to do something foolish."

Lux extracted those gnarled fingers from her gown and smoothed the wrinkled fabric. "Don't preach at me, vendor. I've not done anything." *Yet.*

Mistress Farrentail's eyes abruptly squinted as though she'd heard the word Lux hadn't said aloud. Then she stood on the tips of her toes and peered not into Lux's eyes, but to either side.

"What are you—"

"You didn't wear it! No wonder. It's no wonder! This is the problem with the younger generations: You must spell everything out for them and even then they usually do the opposite out of spite." Mistress Farrentail plucked a familiar yellow feather from her head with hardly a thought. Blood dripped from its end. "You've been *duped.*" Then she grabbed hold of Lux's wrist, warm and strong, and plunged the end into her scalp.

"Devil's tits!"

"Language!" The vendor thwacked her arm before releasing her, and Lux raised that same arm to press the throbbing point of her scalp. Her fingers brushed along the small feather embedded there. "Don't rip it out," the older woman warned. "You need it. You should have had it from the beginning."

But Lux was hardly listening. Because in the back of her head, where a lurking shadow had lingered, was nothing now but her own secrets and buried thoughts. *Where are you?* she thought toward her broken brilliance. Her nightmare. The decaying monster masquerading as her and driving her to the brink of insanity. She peered into the surrounding alcoves and found nothing.

"Welcome to *my* society, girl." The vendor's voice dropped to a whisper. "The minions of Mothlock have been terrifying the towns for over a century. It's time we put a stop to them."

"We? Me and you?"

"Look for the feathers."

Lux was too taken aback by the strange request not to follow through. She glanced around the room. At first, she saw none, but then a woman walked by in an emerald gown with diamond drops in her ears, and in her hair was not only a yellow feather same as hers, but a blue and an orange as well.

"They aren't all the same," said Lux.

"No. That's because they're each for something different. Canary feathers work best to shield against manipulations. Bluebird feathers are good for covering your tracks. An oriole's will keep you grounded so your emotions don't cloud your judgement."

Lux's head spun. "I'm really free? From the nightmare?"

"He put it on you right away, did he? Yes, it's gone. And if he tries to place it again, it'll sting. Birds will warn you of trouble about—if you pay attention."

Lux hadn't allowed herself to feel relief until now. Her shoulders rounded. "Blessed saints."

Mistress Farrentail raised an eyebrow. "Don't tell me they've got you thinking of becoming one of them."

"They've offered," said Lux, scanning for eavesdroppers.

Outside of Shaw, she'd never had an ally in anything; she'd always worked alone. Even partnering with Riselda had been built on using one another without an ounce of trust shared. Lux waited for the feel of resistance to come over her. Instead, an immense weight shed from her shoulders.

"I'd planned to set the place ablaze," she admitted. "Do you have a plan that's better?"

"We do. And it involves you *not* bringing that body underneath us back from the dead."

Lux's eyes widened. "How do you know about that?"

The vendor's nostrils only flared. Her voice changed, settling back into its initial sweetness. "I told you I'd care for the darling."

Corvin's fingertips ran the length of Lux's arm causing her to shiver. She leapt to dig for his corruption, but it was too quick of a touch. He grinned at the vendor and then at Lux. "She's quite interesting, isn't she? And like the loveliest doll in that gown." Lux's mouth fell wide in outrage at the same moment her head alarmed with the dream she'd suffered earlier that day.

Corvin drank from his goblet, and his lips came away stained red. When the music softened, his gaze flicked around the room. "Dinner is about to be served. Lux, would you do me the honor of claiming the seat beside me?"

Collectors and investors moved toward the dark tables, their lacquered surfaces dimly lit. The air she breathed felt heavy. But it was the shadows that bothered her most. They were both too many and too deep. She felt at any moment, something would burst from them and drag her away.

"Of course. Though, I need to excuse myself to the lavatory first."

Mistress Farrentail's small smile and warning eyes was the last Lux saw of her before the vendor melded into the crowd.

She wished the woman wouldn't have gone as Corvin's head lowered near hers, and he said, "Don't tell me you plan to run away."

Lux drew a sharp breath. "No, why would you say that?"

He held out his arm. "Maybe I misread that determined set to your mouth. Come. Sit. Surely, the lavatory can wait until the honoring of all these important minds is through?"

Lux thought about claiming some emergency—a woman's monthly woes to be precise. But seeing Corvin's own determined expression, she felt nearly positive he would have followed her out.

He suspected her.

From the moment he'd spoken of Silas's findings, she knew he did. How much of what she'd done at the cliffs could she blame on a nightmare of his own creation?

Lux had no choice but to take his proffered arm. The tables were arranged into one half of a severed square, open to the floor and the dais of musicians, and her stomach dropped at where he led her.

An attendant drew back a chair at the front table's center. "You may sit," he said, dully.

By the time Lux sat, nearly the entire room had as well. Her breaths quickened and she dropped her eyes. But the stares—they were relentless. She could feel their pricks plain. What had they been told?

Get a hold of yourself, she scolded. *You have a purpose, and you're not alone, no matter what anyone else says.*

When she lifted her eyes again, her gaze met Shaw's. He'd taken a seat farther from her than she'd like, but still her body quieted. *Distract them,* she yearned to mouth. Only, too many paid her attention. She glanced to the mustached man seated beside him.

His stare, acutely familiar, speared her in return, frostlike and hard. A man whom she'd been told was dead. The "brilliant stone mason" possessed irises of the same shade as Corvin's. As Kent's. Even Silas and Artemis.

These collectors.

This society.

She'd not met them all, and most of whom she'd interacted with had been shadowed beneath hoods. But she could see them plain tonight. No one else in her travels had possessed such peculiar eyes: silver with an almost iridescent sheen. A color she recognized now.

The music maintained a mournful presence in the background as Lux stared into irises the exact shade of lifeblood.

Chapter Forty-Seven

She couldn't overcome the jittery feel in her limbs. Her foot couldn't be stilled. A sense of doom encroached. Of time running out. And Lux didn't know what to do.

Mistress Farrentail had said she had a plan. What was it?

Attendants moved toward the tables, carafes steady in their hands. Nausea swirled in Lux's gut as a girl hardly older than Lux herself stopped beside her, tipping a carafe gently above the table. A thin stream of silver poured into a miniature glass set next to her plate; it was barely larger than a thimble.

"Devil take them," she whispered, deadened with rage.

"What was that?" said Corvin, dipping toward her. His breath brushed the shell of her ear.

She leaned away and held up the small glass. "Doesn't seem like enough to last a meal."

Corvin smiled at her, and it did not reach his eyes. "Don't worry, we'll serve you a good dinner wine. That's a tonic for good health and good luck. A tribute to another successful year and for the future ahead."

Lux looked again into the glass. It glistened. Sparkled even. It was what she imagined starlight would be like if she could dip her hand inside their orbs. And she couldn't tell: if this portion of lifeblood was paint or real. It certainly looked real.

Her eyes flicked up when a chair moved back. Farther down from Corvin, Artemis rose. He inclined his head solemnly at the assembly.

"Welcome all to Mothlock Manor. On this divine Hallowed Eve, the Society of Saints is pleased to be hosting yet another Hallowed Banquet. May the nourishment we take now remind us of our collective achievement. Our loyalty. Our faith. To our founding and our futures. May your mastery be limitless."

Here was where Lux could tell they'd done this all before. In a single fluid motion, every person sitting before the tables raised their glasses.

"Cheers," Corvin told her, tapping his against hers. "To our future, you and me."

Death is here, her brilliance said.

And Corvin hardly touched the lifeblood to his lips when a scream ripped through the room.

The fumbled glass fell from his grip, shattering upon the floor. Lux put hers down carefully. All the while she stared aghast at the source of the scream: A woman, shaking, having leapt from her chair, her satin-covered finger pointed.

At a man collapsed over his empty dinnerware. Veins slowly grew stark against his skin.

Lux had seen this ending before.

Verity. The Maidenway Inn. A woman poisoned, a mark on her neck.

And Mothlock. The sanctum. A man beyond her reach.

Silas, that faithful dog, shot to his feet, a shocked rage plain upon his features. And Lux's eyebrows met when a new thought occurred. How hadn't he unearthed the poisoner with his brilliant skill? If he could track three scents outdoors in the wind and sea spray, surely he would have found *something* in a Loxlen townhome.

Unless—

Lux's gaze slid discreetly to Mistress Farrentail. To her head full of feathers, and her mouth a perfect circle, seated beside the dead investor. Her words returned to Lux.

Bluebird feathers are good for covering your tracks.

Silas stalked toward the body while the woman holding tight to the back of her chair cried loud enough to carry throughout the room, "The elixir is poisoned!"

The rising chatter broke into a crescendo. Lux only just realized the music had ceased. All she could hear were indistinct voices and all she could see was Silas, drawing the slumped head aside to run a finger along the body's neck.

His gaze leveled on her afterward, and it confirmed what she'd been certain of. It was the same sort of death as those previous. And she'd no doubt he planned for her to fix it. His eyes slid from her to Corvin. A discreet nod was all the man at her side offered. Then Silas grabbed Mistress Farrentail by her feathered head and pierced her neck in turn.

Everyone screamed.

Even Lux cried out.

She drew her dagger from where she'd buried it in her bodice, ripping the tied cloth from its end. And the society was moving. Lux could pick out each member from the unnatural shine of their eyes.

"It has come to our attention," said Corvin, his voice rising above the din, "traitors have infiltrated this celebration. Traitors who have been systematically murdering Mothlock's good investors for the purpose of sabotaging our sacred purpose." He held up a feather smaller than even the yellow one hidden within Lux's hair.

It twirled between his fingers. "A unique choice, the redwren. But hardly one we wouldn't discover. The society's mastery is *limitless*, after all."

Several more screams were drawn as Silas dispatched another. Lux's breaths grew shallow. *The plan—*

"*Corvin,*" she hissed from the brink of panic. "You cannot—"

"Shh," he soothed. Reaching around her head, he plucked the feather from her scalp. Lux sucked a pained breath, and he said, "Do you think I'm blind to deceit? You may have become accustomed to idiocy in Ghadra, but I am not your demented mayor. I am the Overlord of Mothlock. I read, Necromancer. I read *everything*."

His hand returned to her neck, squeezing tight, and Lux only managed to swipe once with her dagger before Corvin's fingers encircled her wrist in a crushing grip. She cried out.

The screams around her were louder.

"*From sleepless nights and dire days, I call upon your fears.*"

Lux balked at Corvin's sudden incantation; she thrashed in his hold. The plate clattered. Her serving of lifeblood tipped and spilt. The liquid found no grooves in the oiled surface and pooled like the loveliest silver paint.

Corvin only bent nearer like she'd done nothing at all. His lips brushed her neck. "*Unbury your nightmares. Unmask what comes. Chaos divine, let this torture unwind.*"

The apparition returned from the void. Dripping. Insidious. Baring its teeth. It crouched upon the table. Flame-ridden candelabras licked at its unreal skin.

Lux could *feel* his smile.

"*Do not let her go.*"

Chapter Forty-Eight

Corvin screamed. She had never heard him scream before tonight.

When the knife pulled free from his side, he slouched, his hands pressing to the wound. Then he fell to his knees.

Shaw drew back Corvin's head, poised to strike again and end his life, when he hesitated. His eyes found hers. And before Lux could grant or deny the permission he clearly sought, he cried out.

The blade retracted from Corvin's throat when Shaw's opposite hand flung to his shoulder. To the star-shaped bit of glinting metal embedded in his jacket. He bared his teeth and yanked it free.

"Shaw! *Duck.*"

A second flew through the air and burrowed into the wood behind him. Shaw ran to her. Lux grasped his arm when he reached, his longer stride propelling her up the staircase—

"*He will die soon. We can feel it.*"

The apparition scuttled along the banister—a moldering mimic of her. And Lux had no sooner shoved herself away from it when Kent moved into view at the topmost stair.

"The Harvest will not be postponed," he said, a heartbeat before he dodged Shaw's violent swing.

The collector's large fist met Shaw's temple in a sickening crack Lux felt in her soul. He slumped to a heap on the steps and did not move again. "*No!*" she shrieked, but as she lunged, Kent's hand enclosed around her throat, hauling her backward.

"I know you did it," he hissed, when she was pressed against him and unable to move. "I know you revived her. Where has she gone?"

"I don't—" Her lungs squeezed, unable to draw breath. Lux dug her nails into his arm, but found it was not tight against her neck. Panic. She was panicking.

But, bafflingly, her head remained clear.

She attempted a new breath; a choking gasp was all she managed. "What—"

"You wear my creations well," murmured Kent. "I really am sorry to use it against you, but this is far too important."

Lux's attempts to rip at her tightening bodice were thwarted by Kent's changing grip. Her vision was greying. She focused on Shaw. On his unmoving form, his head pressed against the step's edge.

I have to help him. That has to hurt.

But she—could—not—breathe. Her vision darkened, and Kent swept her up, when she, too, would have hit the floor.

Death stole across her skin, pulsed in her chest. Then, she felt nothing at all.

LUX WOKE UPON A throne.

She hardly managed to open her eyes at first. From beyond, she could sense torchlight flickering. A room once large, now feeling very small. Cold air. Goosebumps littered her skin where it touched the unforgiving stone beneath her, and she shivered. She could not focus; her eyes fell shut.

Ahead, voices chanted with a deep and droning cadence. She tried to make out the words but could not; they all streamed together, a seamless link.

It seemed an age before she returned to her body. To acknowledge that though her head felt hollow, her body seemed weighed down like she'd been filled again with enchanted stones. She twitched in sudden fear. But her limbs moved as they should, after all.

It was only the result of whatever they'd done to get her here.

A voice rose, loud and forceful above the chant. It was a familiar voice—a grating, rasping voice—and it said, "On the one hundred and eighty-fifth anniversary this Hallowed Day, we honor the sacrifices made by the Grimrook family. Through their generosity, Mothlock was founded. By blood, it has flourished. May their presence continue to bless our mission and our Harvest."

The chant ended with his words, and at the rasping voice's final uttering, a chorus of assent followed.

"But this night..." A bated quiet descended. "This night, my lords, our society has been granted mercy. Long have we labored. Long have we *suffered*. Our pious road littered with deceit, disloyalty, and even death. *We* are the chosen minds. We are the blessed people. And we will be granted a reward tonight."

Murmurings of affirmations and hiccups of exalted cries had Lux sickened to her core.

The decrepit voice droned on. "Mothlock has long possessed an overlord. And long has it been unbalanced. We feel it every day beneath our feet. The Saints understand our trials. They understand our hearts. And they have sent us a reprieve. A mistress to balance the fates. A Grimrook with the power to harness Death. To reverse the curse upon us all."

Lux grew rigid where she lay, draped over the throne's seat. She opened her eyes again by the barest measure.

The room was a sea of men swathed in black. Black robes. Black hoods. The Collectors of Mothlock formed a wide circle around the ice grave. Standing atop it was a man with arms widespread, his head thrown back and uncovered.

Lux hardly breathed as she beheld the greying skin, the sloughing texture, the pale hair clinging as best it could. It was the voice she'd overheard from the cart that day, but as for the monster it came from, she couldn't identify.

Her heart called for her to look down. Down at the feet of the throne. To a crown of honey-gold hair she would recognize for all her life—and her chest stilled.

Shaw's chin had fallen forward, his head bowed and body slumped, and she waited—painfully long—for any part of him to move. His hand twitched.

Thank fate. He was alive yet.

And she would soon make them regret she was too.

"Our holy quest to Sainthood will no longer rely on glamours and hoods, beholden to weekly doses of lifeblood to render us palatable. Upon this revival, our rest shall be restored. Our health permanently returned. Our final obstacle in grasping perfection will be no more. Rouse our necromancer."

A hooded figure broke from the circle. Lux couldn't be sure, but she guessed it to be the wretched healer. She closed her eyes fully when he neared, stepping around Shaw as though he was nothing more than a rogue bit of furniture. When she breathed next, her nose burned with a horrid scent.

Lux jolted upright. The figure moved back to his place. And while sitting fully upon a cultist's cold throne, holding tight to the carved arms on either side, she stared into a monster's eyes.

A nightmare.

With irises of lifeblood-silver.

The decaying creature held a narrow pitcher in its hand. And when it smiled, Lux found it to be the same one Corvin had worn every time he'd found her amusing. A tongue, black and bloated, ran over a row of rotting teeth.

It said, "We've entered a new day, Lux Thorn. Let there be no more secrets between us."

The voice. It was not in her head. Nor did it sound the same even if it were. It was the voice from the workroom. From moments before. Harsh. Rasping. Old. If she would imagine the voice of the devil, it would sound something like this.

"Corvin," she said, cringing when her voice also rasped up her throat.

How much time had passed?

Hallowed Day, they said. Not eve.

"Don't fret, doll. I know I do not look so attractive to you now in this form. Soon, it will be righted. Soon, we'll be the most powerful Overlord and Mistress of Mothlock." His red-rimmed eyes swept the room. "Nearly two centuries without proper sleep. Our bodies are exhausted."

Revulsion sickened her. "That cannot be why."

He *tsk*'d, and the sagging skin about his mouth shook. "Please don't tell me the why of things. You've barely lived, and you've spent that meager time with the dead. I, however, have lived. Learned. *I* know everything." He turned away from her and, stepping toward the grave, upheld the pitcher. It tipped. A dark liquid ran from the lip, splashing against the ice with an alarming hiss.

Lux folded over her knees. Until her hand could reach Shaw's head. Until she could just run her fingers through his locks. His head lolled backward. The side of his face pressed to her leg, but the other, she could see. And it was blackened and swollen. She seethed. Digging within the confines of her gown, she searched for her dagger and discovered it missing. She found a berry, instead, round and whole.

Her hand retreated when Corvin spoke again. "Bring her here."

Lux shoved herself backward into the throne, drawing her knees up, allowing Shaw's head to fall. Of course, it didn't matter. Collectors flanked her, their ungloved hands reaching—and Lux realized their skin was the same. Grey. Sagging. Nightmarish. She recoiled.

"Don't make this difficult," the one on her left sneered.

Lux's eyes snapped to the shadowed hood. "Silas. Your voice is as ugly as ever."

Silas dragged his hood back, and Lux flinched. He did not smile—he seemed incapable—but his bloodshot eyes appeared pleased by her discomfort. His lips, deeply cracked, moved nearer. From her jaw to her temple, he inhaled her scent. "You killed Hildred, didn't you? I tracked this scent all over the rocks."

Lux's veins iced over, a cold sweat breaking out along her brow. "Get away from me, dog."

His hand gripped the fabric around her middle, and Lux bit her cheek against crying out when he dragged her forward. "Call me that again, Necromancer, and we'll see how far you can run before I *find* you."

"Silas," warned the other. But he, too, reached for her—the one who'd filled her with rocks.

"What?" she hissed. "You don't wish to show off your monstrous looks too?"

In response, the mason shoved back his hood. And he was *old*. So old, his skin hardly seemed attached to his skull. "Is this better, girl?"

Lux stared at his foul face. Recognized its bones from the portrait of Mothlock's founders in the morning room. "No," she said.

She was hauled off the throne before she could say anything else.

"Sew her lips shut for us, Kent," said Silas. "I've been sick of hearing what comes out of them since Verity."

"We'll see," replied Kent, and when he lowered his hood, Lux immediately felt her bodice tighten. She sucked a breath in alarm only to feel the gown release her. He smiled. "Welcome back to the waking world. You lose consciousness so easily—it was almost disappointing."

Lux's breaths blew harsh through her nose. She wanted to lunge at him but knew she'd never make it near enough to put her nails to use. She ground her teeth; at this rate, there would be nothing left of them.

"Enough," rasped Corvin. He did not turn from the dissolving coffin. "Whether our necromancer realizes yet or not, she is tied to the bones of this estate. She will be what settles it. What settles *us*. Show your mistress a modicum of respect."

A low hum of dissent rumbled through the collectors.

Lux's stomach roiled.

"Come. Time to put your brilliance to use." Corvin turned, his hand outstretched.

"You must be deluded," she said, a laugh bordering on hysteria escaping her. "Kill me. I no longer care. I will never revive another for you. I will *never* become any mistress of this saintforsaken place."

"Kill you?" Corvin purred. "Mothlock is a place of preservation. We are not so wasteful here."

She glared at his reach. "Liar. How many have you murdered to prolong your lives? To prolong your *investors'* lives?"

"We do not commit murder, Lux. Not unless it's for the betterment of everyone. It is against our moral code."

Her teeth bared. She'd never felt more like a rabid beast than in this moment. "You know Ghadra quite well, don't you? That city's blood is on your hands. None of what you bought was brought about by natural causes." She couldn't stomach looking at him, but she couldn't stomach looking anywhere else either.

"Did the boy tell you that?" Corvin's expression softened. He looked as he had that first day they'd arrived, taking her in as she took in the sea, nevermind his rotting features. "Maybe I deserve your ire in this instance; we didn't ask how our treatment was harvested. But you must understand me now. The strongest sacrifices are forged in blood; you heard the Grimrook tale. Yes, an ignorant outsider could deem it an evil. But once you examine it, it really is not. Progress is built on these very things you shy away from. It has been throughout all of—"

"Progress! You are a *monstrous*—"

With a hissed crescendo, the last of the ice coffin evaporated. Lux gasped so loudly it should have echoed in the chamber. Her lips parted, her stare collapsing from shock to horror as she looked at the century-old body on the table.

"Come meet my brother. Maybe you will prefer him over me. The rest of your family did."

The body's skin dripped still, bare and unmarked. It was pale and lean and objectively healthy, but when she drew nearer, she saw the mark. A clean cut. From one side of the throat to the other.

"Alixsander Osric Alesso. My esteemed, and much beloved, twin."

Lux felt a numbness come over her. It was almost as if she were floating above them all, even herself. A corporeal form. *This cannot be real.*

"What will you do?" she said, and even her voice sounded numbed and distant. "If he's revived and reverses your curse and all is made right to you? I know it was you who killed him."

"What else do you know?" Corvin replied, a smile in his voice. Then he said, "Tobias. Bring your mistress her tools."

Lux twisted to see the newest collector come forth. In his hands was an onyx tray and upon that tray sat tins, a decanter, and several vials. A black mortar and pestle absorbed the dim light and called to her brilliance. She swallowed. A groaning distracted her next—another member drawing out a hidden fold within the carved table. She now had a workspace. The tray was set upon it, and the collectors retreated to their respective places in the circle.

Corvin walked toward the assortment, his fingers tracing each item with a strange reverence. He lifted the mortar and pestle and turned, settling them in her hands. "Go. Embrace your blessed fate."

With her hands occupied, she could only flinch when his fingers followed the line of her cheekbone, trailing down.

"I am not a Grimrook," she murmured, darkness in her voice.

"A broken branch is still a branch." His rancid breath coated her skin. "Riselda stole *The Risen* from us. She stole even more than that. How did it come to be in your possession? You are *so secluded,* as you say."

"It's gone now."

"Yes. Burned. Mothlock Manor has never seen a fire before your arrival."

Lux was shaking now. Between Corvin's cold, her own adrenaline, and the nightmare's voice in her head.

"Dutiful pet. Always a pet for powerful men. We are nothing if not useful."

She growled up at the apparition's journey across the ceiling. "There is nothing in this for me. Let me go."

"I'm afraid there can be no "letting go". You were meant for the manor. For our society. I knew it from the moment I met you."

"Then you must let him leave. I will do nothing for you if you don't."

Corvin only chuckled harshly beside her. "No, Lux. His betrayal is ours to deal with."

Lux blinked up at him finally, losing her breath to discover him so close. She could track every line of silver in his irises. Like lifeblood had once done to the pad of her fingertip, it'd done the same to each pigmented furrow of his eyes. Her stomach twisted further. "What betrayal? Preventing you from breaking my wrist? You're cured of your wounds already."

"And if I weren't, should he still be allowed to go? He tried to kill me."

"Free him, Corvin."

"No, Lux."

Desperation clawed at every part of her. Her breaths shallowed. "Fine." The mortar clattered onto the table. "Then Alixsander remains as he is."

"You *will* do your part. Or else your beloved interloper becomes another decorated member of our staff. He's a similar height to Manphry. A pair of footmen would be distinguished, I think."

"We will kill him a thousand ways. It's already begun."

"You wouldn't."

"I would," said Corvin, nearly against her lips.

Riselda, you evil witch. You've either died and abandoned us or run and abandoned us. Either way, you've betrayed me. Again.

"Silas—"

"*No.*" Lux could hardly speak through the grit of her teeth, but Corvin raised his hand when the collector readied to break from the circle. "I'll do it. But you will swear to not harvest his soul."

Corvin licked his lips at her agreement. Or maybe it was her demand. But she realized it was neither when he said, "You really are brilliant. I will struggle if you prove to be a failure."

UNBURIED

He gestured her forward.

And Lux, devil take her, could think of nothing else to do but step up. Her fingers moved delicately across the array of ingredients.

She plucked one from the row—

And sealed her fate.

Chapter Forty-Nine

She came to beside the table. Lux blinked at the wide wooden legs as she gathered her wits. She tipped her head back, and Corvin's boot filled her vision. He stood beside her head. In that moment, lying at his feet discarded, she knew she would never be more than a tool to him.

A pet—a doll—for a powerful man.

"Welcome back, Alix. We've missed you greatly."

Lux's eyes widened. It'd worked. How had it actually worked? *Alchemy*, she fumed. Always ruining the order of things.

Corvin's voice was creaking and bitter. A voice of nightmares. But the one that answered was quite the opposite.

"*Corvin?* Death to the Devil! What have you done?"

"Did you see them, Alix? Did you see the Saints in the Beyond?"

Lux slowly pushed onto her knees. Her fingertips buzzed where they met the flagstones.

The society's first overlord cleared his throat. "I can't say. Already, it's faded, and I only recall peace. When did I die? Saints above, Brother, you must tell me what's happened to you. To us."

"You've been gone nearly two centuries."

Silence enveloped the sanctum. And Lux stared upon Corvin's twin as if she didn't belong to herself again. Only for his gaze to slide to hers, to remind her of what she'd done.

His eyes were as raven black as his hair, even in the torchlight. He sat upon the table much the same as Shaw had those months ago in Ghadra. But his fingertips—they weren't the relaxed hold of someone relieved to have been brought back into the presence of family. They blanched in their grip. His gaze flicked from her to Corvin, his features such a replica of his brother's, immediate distrust flooded her chest.

But when his eyes returned to her, they seemed eager to convey something. Something that could not be said aloud. "Congratulations. You've always wanted a necromancer."

The statement reminded Corvin of her, and he glanced down with a flicker of surprise at her kneeling. "A victim of *Mania Malus*. Her brilliance taxes her, but all will be rectified soon enough. We need something from you, Alix."

"Of course you do."

Lux stiffened at the hurt in Alix's voice and glanced back to where Shaw lay upon the dais. He'd shifted at some point during her revival, the back of his head now resting upon the throne, his throat exposed. Her attention landed on the basin. She wished it wouldn't have. A bloom of ice unfurled in her chest.

Her attention jerked from it. Landed once again on Corvin.

At what he held against his hip.

How it glinted in the torchlight.

A syringe—and its needled point.

"There's a problem, you can see. With me. With us all." Corvin gaze swept his brother's form. "I cannot achieve all that I want. I cannot become all that I should be. It's your fault."

Alix laughed, low and humorless and a perfect mirror of his brother. Still, he didn't bother to stand. Like he was perfectly content to remain where he'd been for over a century. "Hasn't it always been?"

"Don't mock me," growled Corvin, and he hovered nearer. "We were never meant to be two."

"Take that up with fate, Brother. I didn't split from you purposefully."

"Trust me that I have." He loomed so that they all were better able to see his face. And in the strange light, Lux thought she really didn't recognize him. A sinister force glowed from his eyes.

He was as wicked as they came. He was the devil on the door. She pushed herself to stand.

"When you died," Corvin said. "I was supposed to be free of your torment. But even in death, you didn't relent. I realized too late that you took what I needed with you to the Beyond."

Alix scoffed. "I took nothing besides my own soul."

"Precisely."

Alix's grip softened. He folded his hands into his lap. His eyes, however, were as dark and hard as the stone around him. "What would you do with it? I think I've given you—all of you—enough."

Corvin's thumb ran the length of the syringe. "A pity you didn't know of our project before your death. Powerful gifts, Alix, are meant for powerful minds. I've been doing what was once an impossible task in your absence, and the collectors have surpassed every expectation. Educating the masses just as you wanted. And bringing peace to the world. All by granting the vast strength of brilliance to those loyal to a common goal. If that isn't worthy of Sainthood, why, I wouldn't know what is."

"Peace—*Corvin*. You're decaying before my eyes!" The horror on Alix's face matched Lux's own. "This is blasphemy. They couldn't have all been in agreement?"

The dark laugh returned. "Do not speak to me of blasphemy—you, a weak believer and maybe even a heretic. This pathway wouldn't have been created if it wasn't meant to be used. Your mission was noble, Brother. But it was a mission rife with faults. People were furthering their brilliances, yes. But it was open to interpretation. It was being put into practice in dangerous ways! Weak, volatile spirits cannot be trusted. I don't understand how you're unable to see that."

"You've lost your mind," Alix whispered.

"That is not my *fault*. You've cursed me in your death; I cannot sleep. All I think of, all I wish for, is to become *more*. Once, I thought that meant you had to be gone. Your soul departed to the Beyond and no longer in my way. But now—"

"*Stop*. You've become something wretched, Brother. I've met no Saints in death, but I can say this, I have felt them. And they do not feel as you do. You've twisted their purpose and will achieve nothing of what you want. If ever a person suffered from *Mania Malus*, it is you!"

That sinister light in Corvin's eyes brightened. Lux was sure there was no blue left now in his irises. He sneered. "*You* are what's wretched. If it weren't for your very existence, I would have been whole from the start. I would not have to do what I now need. And I need your dreams, Alix. Don't worry over me."

"Drain my lifeblood all you like and leave me to the void, but you will never own my dreams."

Corvin laughed outright. "Soon, I will have more than even that."

Lux screamed when the needle plunged into Alix's eye.

Alix twitched, but otherwise did not move. Maybe he couldn't. Corvin held onto the syringe and, carefully, began to draw backward. A liquid like starlight filled the glass chamber.

Lux's shaking grew violent. Her revulsion nearly sent her again to the floor. To remove lifeblood this way...on a living, breathing—

When Corvin pulled away from his brother's eye, Alix groaned. But the society's overlord didn't pause. He plunged the needle again.

After that, Alix made no sound at all. Lux didn't think she'd ever feel well again. She would have rather wished him dead. But as sensitive as she'd become to Death now, she sensed nothing. He lived still.

When Corvin was through and Alix lay slumped and discarded on the table, his silver gaze met hers. "Don't look at me like that." He tapped the starlit glass. "We cannot extract it any other way. I've tried."

As if that were the only part to be horrified over.

Corvin handed the filled syringe to Artemis before making his way to the basin. He knelt. Turning away from the pedestal, he laid his head back and fitted his neck to the groove of the basin's lip. "We must keep them alive, Lux. I know you understand extracting the lifeblood from the dead will sever their ties from this world permanently, their soul unable to return. That drinking it afterward will grant you healing, an additional lifetime. But what we've discovered here—"

Lux's knees weakened when Artemis stepped to Corvin's side. The healer's hand rose, the needled point poised over the soft corner of his overlord's eye. *Wrong, wrong, wrong,* beat her heart.

The needle plunged.

Corvin hissed a pained breath, but he did not move.

And Lux wondered how often he'd done this. How many pilfered souls resided within his rotted body.

Half of the syringe was injected before the needle was removed. Corvin exhaled, long and slow. "To harvest from the living is where true power lies." He laughed this time when his opposite eye was punctured. "He didn't want me to have his dreams? Now I will own his very *soul*."

The needle pulled free. Corvin sat up. Twin trails of scarlet trickled down his face. His eyes found hers, welling red.

Lux wished she could tear him apart. "You are *destroying* people. You have no right."

But Corvin transformed before her. Gone was the grey cast and sloughing skin. In its place, Mothlock's Overlord was again pale, frost-like, and made perfect.

Devil take me.

Around her, every collector lowered their hoods.

"I have *every* right," he bit out, and his voice was his own again. "We are brilliant. We are power. We are *chosen*. How can't you comprehend it is only for humanity's betterment that we do what we do? And I feel it! *Finally*. I have never been more whole than I am now. The curse is lifted, and I am made perfect, Necromancer. I am a *Saint*." He swept nearer to her, his eyes bloodied but eager. "I wish you'd look around you. To realize what a travesty it is to watch brilliances be squandered or used for harm. To see books in the hands of those who cannot begin to understand them. This is my purpose, Lux." His fingers gripped her chin. "I told you so that day on the cliffs."

With the blood still fresh and wet against his skin, he pressed his cheek to hers. Into her ear, he said, "And now you may bear witness to the real extent of my brilliance." When he pulled away, he left behind the scent of iron. Lux swallowed against the rising nausea, swiping at her skin with the back of her hand.

Corvin swept upward and onto the dais, pushing Shaw's head aside before sitting. He eased into the seat. His eyes no longer bled fresh, and the cheek he'd pressed against hers was smeared. He looked maniacal and monstrous, his back pressed against a devilish throne.

"Behold your overlord now! Collectors. Lords. *Doubters*. Have I described enough the perfection that awaits you? I required the soul of my brother, a half stolen from me in the womb. But for you—you need only his blood. Alixsander." Corvin gestured for his twin, and he came dutifully, sliding from the table. The wounds of Alix's eyes were a mirror of his brother's, though the blood on his cheeks was unmarred. When he drew within reach, Corvin gripped his wrist. With the opposite hand, the overlord removed a dagger from his cloak. A black handle—made from a devouring wood.

Lux's teeth clenched.

Corvin drew the dagger's tip shallowly over Alix's palm. Red bloomed and dripped. He didn't flinch.

Lux wanted to lunge at Corvin—to make ribbons of his skin—but all she could focus on was the welling of Alix's hand. Her heart squeezed when Corvin's mouth drifted nearer, and her attention riveted on the horror of it.

His lips pressed over his brother's wound, his eyes on her. Until they weren't.

They rolled back. For a brief moment, white was all she could see, and then his frost-like gaze returned.

And it was gleeful.

Corvin raised his voice and said, "Embrace perfection with me, Lords." He nodded at Alix. "Go to them, Alixsander. Give up your blood. Wipe your blemish from their cursed souls."

When that first collector dropped to his knees and drank, Lux thought this was surely the time she would be sick. Her skin flushed terribly hot. Her mouth filled again. She whipped around so she'd see no more.

She stared instead at the man upon the throne. At his blood-red mouth. He grinned at her and even his teeth were stained. And it was as she sought to look at anything else that she looked at Shaw. To his eyes, heavy-lidded. His breaths, not shallow but deep. Clearly drugged.

And to the syringe, poised as though forgotten beside his head.

Her own snapped up.

"It's time you were mended, Lux. Which is it to be? The artist?" The syringe shifted closer. "Or have you got your eye on another brilliance?"

Everything inside her felt shriveled, cold and dark. *Alone*, beat her heart.

"Except we're not alone. Will never be again. Carve me out or keep me. Either way, I am yours."

Her nightmare sat draped over Corvin, its cracked nails trailing along his features in a horrid caress. Its face—*her* face—ruined as it was, nuzzled into him, inhaling deeply. Lux's stomach turned further at the sight.

"This is the ritual you spoke of?" she said. "This is my cure?"

Corvin gestured widely, the needle glinting in the torchlight. "This is your cure."

"You'd said you were *shattered*."

His laugh wrapped around her, cloyingly sweet. "I'll show you exactly how whole I am now, doll."

A great crash startled them both.

"Another colossal disappointment," a voice boomed.

Kent dragged off his robe in a fury, his banquet finery still underneath. His eyes, when they fixed on her, were the same. As was his decaying body. His mouth, however, was smeared red with Alixsander's blood.

"I have tried to be patient," continued Kent. "I've allowed you your decades of time. Your endless search for a necromancer. Accepting of your promises of a cure. And yet—*disappointment!*" He shook his fist. "I'm convinced now it's all been an elaborate scheme to harvest more power only for yourself. Look at us! Look at *you!* There you sit, an entire soul and no glamour, while we are promised our measly annual portion and a blood debt. This cannot stand."

"That's enough." Corvin's voice came upon them deathly quiet and sinister. "Give it time."

Kent roared, "I have!"

Lux jolted, and so did several collectors: a room of rotting souls and scarlet mouths.

"I am through with it. We will each take a soul tonight." His gaze leveled with her own. "And I will have *hers.*"

"She is not to be harvested. You know as well I that Mothlock wants her. Our harvest has already been chosen."

"*Our?*" Kent barked a laugh. "As you have already taken your lion's share."

Corvin drew to his feet. "You forget yourself, *Lord* Kent. I am Overlord. You are not. I—not you—was destined to become the leader of us. It cannot be a lion's share when you were never entitled to it to begin with."

"Do you hear him? Matthias? Silas? He would keep you as you are. Beholden to Invocation. To lifeblood and glamours and a fraction of a measly harvest. While he is made new again and free of the constraints we still suffer. Who here even knows if we can rest?"

"It is not unheard of," began Artemis, his hands crossed over his abdomen, "for a long-standing curse to take time in lifting."

Kent scoffed. "We're not your uneducated masses, healer. You are spineless. Can't you bend over any farther?"

Color bloomed in Artemis's otherwise grey cheeks, and it was as Lux began to hope the society was finally cracking enough to collapse, Corvin sat back upon his throne.

"You desire proof? Allow me to show you what awaits us now, Lords of Mothlock. I have seen it from the moment I was made whole. Come, Collectors. Meet your dream."

Chapter Fifty

It came upon her in a whirlwind. Lux was so caught off guard, she cried out. The sanctum didn't dissolve, but rather disappeared. In its place sprawled a field of white flowers.

Lux spun a slow circle, trampling blooms beneath her feet. A sweet, subtle fragrance permeated the air. One she couldn't help but to inhale deeply. A calm settled over her heart by its end; her breath eased. She could hear music, but not of any sort familiar to her, and she smiled, bending her ear to the flowers.

"Welcome to the Beyond."

The voice swirled around her, coming from every direction at once. But Lux didn't surge upright as she would have outside the dreamscape. Instead, she rose slowly. Awe replaced everything else, even peace. The strange voice belonged to a figure, tall—inhumanly so—and robed all in white. They stood at the opposite end of the field beneath a violet sky. She couldn't discern a face due to the distance and their hood.

"Are you a Saint?" she called back.

Lux blinked, and the figure crossed the distance.

They stood an arm's length from her now. Pale, unmarked hands reached to lower their hood, and Lux's awe transformed into something else. She looked at herself, standing so tall above, with hair as ebony as it was in life, but shining and long to her hips. Her lips were redder on this face, her cheekbones more pronounced. But it was the eyes that stilled her—eyes entirely silver, not even the slimmest line of green.

"What are you?"

"I am who you could be."

Lux raised her hand to her eyes, ensuring they were open. "Tell me how."

The dreamscape version of her smiled—so lovely, Lux found she couldn't form another thought. *"It is in our grasp. We have been chosen, Lucena Thorn, by the highest power. Rid us of those who would mar our perfection or"*—a crown of thorns materialized on the being's brow— *"damn us to mortal suffering."*

The smallest of feelings disrupted her peace. Enough that she said, "Who is the highest power?"

The Saint's smile grew. *"The Lord of all things. Trust in His guidance. Obey His word. And this"*—the Saint gestured widely at the plain— *"will be yours."*

The dreamscape dissolved. Lux breathed as though she'd nearly drowned. Her vision struggled to adjust, and her knees wobbled. She stood in the sanctum—surrounded by dark walls and dim torchlight. She stood amongst entombed bodies of unwilling, past harvests, and the few overaged and unlucky investors. She looked around the sanctimonious society, at each pair of silver eyes unfocused with rapturous awe. They'd beheld themselves, too, she realized. As what they could be—a saintlike version of themselves, perfect and powerful, in the Beyond.

Several collectors had collapsed to their knees, tearful with triumph, when Corvin, splayed nonchalantly upon his throne, said, "Bring us Cecily Otterbee."

Lux nearly collapsed then too.

The girl was brought forward through the archway in a white robe. Much like the dream, a hood was pulled up and draped low over her face. Lux—if she could have—would have screamed. Cecily was meant to be *gone*.

Attendants gripped her upper arms, and Lux noted the lack of clanking chains. They led her around the gathered collectors until she stood not far from the dais. Lux expected to hear her cries, but the girl was steadfastly silent.

"Considering my natural-born brilliance, I gravitate toward manipulative types; I wanted this soul for us." Corvin nodded toward the girl like she was nothing more than something to be consumed. "I think you will enjoy what manipulating emotions brings you, my Mistress of Mothlock."

Lux's heart beat in her ears. "She doesn't manipulate emotions. She understands them."

"Which makes her underutilized and better off submitted to the society. Come, Lux. I will inject you myself." His tongue licked at his stained teeth. "Once you've had your share, you will never be the same. There is strength in power. Your brilliance will be restored."

He's no different from any twisted revived. All he wants is lifeblood. All he wants is souls.

"And what of her?"

"The harvest? She will continue as she has. An attendant to Mothlock, and all the comfort that ensures. And though her body will age and die as is natural, her soul and brilliance will live on. In us. How wondrous a gift is that?"

"It isn't. I can feel the wrongness like its leaking from the walls. I *refuse*."

He pouted. "After everything? Is it your pride? Stubbornness? If you deny to be amplified, then I suppose I must take it upon myself to do what is best for you. The Saints will understand. Silas."

Lux scrambled backward, awaiting Silas's touch—but it did not come. Instead, she turned and discovered Silas staring at Corvin as though he contemplated doing something much worse.

"*Silas,*" Corvin barked.

"We will not divide the harvest. A fraction of a soul is not enough. Not anymore."

"The Saints—"

"*You* have shown us the true path to Sainthood, and I am through with mortal suffering." He spun, grabbing hold of Cecily's arm. "I will have *my* share."

Silence descended upon the sanctum. Lux waited with bated breath to see who would move first. Then Corvin raised his chin. "Those who feel their portion is not enough, step forward."

At first, it was only Kent who joined Silas. But soon, more stepped up until the majority of collectors had separated from the circle, forming a line in front of the throne.

"The ungratefulness astounds me. Truly, it does. I forged this road you've set yourself upon. I harness *nightmares*. The devastating truths people bury, refusing to acknowledge or study or see. Can you suffer yours without flinching? Show the Saints, then—that you are worthy."

Lux recognized Corvin's incantation now. None of them would be spared his ire.

And she'd no sooner tucked the berry into her mouth when the walls began to melt.

The collectors transformed. Each looked like their most nightmarish version to her, except now their silver eyes glowed, their mouths no longer dried with their earlier feast, but dripping. The torches guttered until she could hardly see. In her head, there was no room for any thought or reaction—all she could hear were screams.

It was worse. Worse than anything she'd ever dreamt or experienced. A torment she couldn't escape. The box she'd reburied in the void burst open, every insecurity, memory, and fear swallowing her up. The walls scuttled with beasts. Each one had her face.

But you are not made up of these bad things, said her heart.

She spun toward the throne. To Corvin. His eyes were wide, and his irises leaked silver, mingling with the blood in his mouth. He licked his lips, satisfied with the chaos he'd toppled them into, and his teeth dripped—a red and silver mix.

His gaze met hers over the madness. His head tilted. And the screams—they quieted to a dull shriek in the background. As Lux lifted her chin and strode forward, the nightmare seemed to ease—just a little—for her.

Corvin's response was immediate. A corner of his mouth rose. "You look like you want something from me, doll."

"I do."

Lux climbed upon the throne.

She *did* want. So many things. But mostly, a future of not being used. Of being free to choose. And though she would never choose this Overlord of Mothlock, this master manipulator of nightmares and dreams, she decided to allow him to believe she wanted only one thing.

Lux licked her lips, coaxed the abundance of want to her eyes, and said, "I've met my future, Corvin. I've faced my truths. Let me prove my worth."

She kissed him.

Corvin startled beneath her. Lux thought he might actually push her away. But when her hands reached upward to grab hold of his robe, he finally seemed to decide she was quite serious. One hand pressed against her chin, angling it higher, and his other cupped her head.

And Lux fell into him. Deeply.

She dove for his soul.

What she found—

Spoiled and ancient.

Rotten, yet powerful.

Corvin's corruption *pulled* at her rather than shutting her out.

She didn't want to touch it. She didn't want to look at it at all. But if she didn't dig farther, she would never know for certain. Lux reached, tentative and slow, and when her fingers clawed and her nails sank deep, Corvin jolted beneath her.

The corruption latched onto her right back.

Her mind stuttered; she could form neither words nor thoughts. Whatever this was, it was not alive in the traditional sense, but that didn't stop it being shoved down her throat. She choked.

And in her drowning was her answer.

Greed. Greed. Greed.

She wanted to scream, but no sound left her. Instead, her lungs seized as they did right before panic set in. And when panic finally came for her, it came in waves bigger than the sea.

She retched and swore saltwater poured from her nose and mouth. This was bigger than corruption—far hungrier—*this* was madness. And it would bury her down here, beneath a crushing weight.

Don't sink.

Her own voice. Not the nightmarish version or the dream's.

You will not be buried.

Because Lucena Thorn fights for those she loves.

In that moment, Lux rejected every foul insecurity, traumatic memory, and overwhelming fear. In its place, she recalled every moment of light she could. Of Shaw. Of her parents. Of majestic mountains, quiet trees, and sea air.

Lux fought to the surface with everything in her.

Corvin's fingers were cold on her skin. His mouth was colder. At some point, he'd pulled her flush against him, his lips moving against hers; she followed him on instinct. When he moaned into her open mouth, she nearly died of disgust. She kissed him all the harder.

Until he shoved her away.

Coughing.

Retching.

Purple saliva dribbling down his chin.

"*What—*"

Lux swiped at her lips as his now moved without sound. "Gorga berries," she whispered so only he could hear. The nightmare dissolved around them. "Did you swallow it? I think you did."

Corvin spat onto the stones but other than a stream of violet liquid, no seed came with it. He lifted his head—and there was murder in his seeping gaze.

"Saints above, devil below." She tutted. "It looks as if your brother's soul hasn't cured you after all." Her fingers came away from the grip she had about his neck, the skin there beginning to grey. "I found *Mania Malus*, Corvin—and it's not eating me. It's eating *you*."

Before Lux could scramble off his lap and off the throne, Corvin lunged.

He was stopped by an old blade to his throat.

Shaw's jaw feathered with a rage that didn't look like it could ever be contained. "*Stay* in your saintforsaken *seat*."

And—laughing wildly—the girl behind Lux lowered her hood.

Chapter Fifty-One

"Devil's *tits*," breathed Lux.

"Unbelievable," growled Shaw.

"Who the Hell are you?" Red-faced and fuming, Kent marched toward the dais.

A blonde braid whipped along with Aline's body. She leveled the end of some contraption upon the collector. "You must be the murderer I've heard so much of. Why don't I shoot you for it?"

"I don't know what you're talking about." But Lux could tell Kent was unnerved. He stared down the barrel of Aline's weapon with healthy suspicion.

"I hate liars. I hate them *so* much. It's over, you know. They're all coming for you."

Lux's brow furrowed, but she asked for no explanation. In case Shaw's sister was lying herself. Whom did they have who would come to their aid?

Kent chuckled menacingly. "You've no idea who you are dealing with, girl. We've survived centuries. Emerged victorious through every trial." He gestured to the collectors converging behind him. "And now we've the key to everlasting power realized at last. We are unstoppable."

Kent's gaze flicked briefly to Lux's own, and before she could register anything purposeful in it, she was dropped to her knees. The *dress*. The bodice shrank upon her form until her ribs screamed. She cried out, dragging at the fabric, but it would not be undone. Her eyes landed on Kent, his hand manipulating a spool of red thread.

No words left his mouth, and soon, none would leave hers again either. She collapsed to her side at the same moment an arm wrapped around her fracturing middle. The brief flash of a blade entered her vision and was gone again. And the pressure—it released. She heaved the loudest breath, there on the ground.

She knew who held her. Knew that knife.

Her bodice had been completely cut through. She could feel it drooping. And she'd no sooner gathered the fabric against her chest, when a horrid crack rent the air.

Lux leapt nearly out of her skin. Her mouth fell wide at the smoke billowing from the end of what Aline held. At the giant of a collector fallen to one knee.

"My leg!" Kent screamed. A small crimson puddle formed around the limb he knelt upon. "What is that weapon!"

But she heard no answer from Aline, only—

"*Lux,*" Shaw managed.

Before her dagger was plunged into his eye.

Lux didn't think, only acted. She dove at Corvin as the remainder of the room erupted. Her dress fell to her feet, and in only a corset and slip, she could finally run freely. She reached the mad overlord in a heartbeat. Gripping the collar of his robe, she dragged her nails across his face. A silent shout came from him, but he didn't release Shaw. Not until she'd punctured him fully.

Corvin swiped out with her dagger. She dodged. And Shaw... Shaw knelt on the flagstones, his hands propping him from collapse. When he surged upright, she hardly recognized him.

His right eye bled so profusely, she couldn't tell if he even had one anymore. Corvin swiped at her again, a snarl on his lips and a rake of scarlet across his face. But his swing was blocked partway.

Shaw tackled him to the floor.

The sanctum descended into chaos.

Artemis knelt beside Kent while another collector stooped to offer his shoulder. "Silas," gasped the large man. "End them."

Sucking his teeth with morbid glee, Silas moved upon Lux. "This has gone on long enough, hasn't it?"

Aline backed into her. Lux gripped her arm and said, "Please tell me that thing can go another round."

"One more for now," muttered Aline out the corner of her mouth.

"We'll have to run after."

"We should have run a *while* ago. What's wrong with his eyes?"

"Your lord and master has lost," Lux hissed. She shifted. Her boot met an object. Bending quickly, she snatched up her dagger. "Leave us be, or end up with a hole somewhere worse than Kent's."

Silas's smile drew wider. "Corvin Alistair Alesso is not *my* master."

She leveled the dagger at his chest when he continued to advance. Lux noted Aline didn't lower her weapon—though her arms looked unsteady.

"Lord Kent has long been the true ruler of Mothlock. Consuming lifeblood while the Alesso boys were just that—*boys*. It was he who taught Corvin how to mutate his brilliance for torture. How to drive each of the Grimrooks mad. Where Corvin too often shied from murder, Kent and I—we saw the vision. We understood that necessity overrules wrongs, and we will not be stifled. Corvin—as useful as his thirst is—was always just a lure for weak souls with strong brilliances. A charismatic monster." Lux did not think his grin could stretch any wider, but it did. "You've been lured here, Necromancer. How does it feel to be *such* a little fool?"

A second crack wracked the chamber. Silas flew backward with an agonized groan, his hand clawing for his shoulder.

"I hate men," said Aline. "Why do they always talk about themselves for ages?"

Lux whipped around to see what had become of Shaw. She found him lashing Corvin to his throne with a pair of blood-red shackles. The collector's head lolled, his face bleeding from multiple lacerations. Her gaze lifted to Alix.

Without further direction from his brother, he stood like a silent sentry beside them. Lastly, she noted the syringe, its glinting end fallen to settle upon the dais.

She darted toward it.

"Go, Aline! We'll be after you."

"But...Lux?"

Lux ignored her. She hadn't meant to, only there was too much else clawing for her attention. Death's near constant embrace. Shaw's mutilated eye. The syringe perfectly positioned and her own new ideas forming. She ran at Shaw. When he raised his face, she ignored the blood, and said, "Is your eye—"

"I don't know," he interrupted, his voice rough and his features fraught. "But it doesn't matter. Go." He gestured ahead of him with the tip of his knife, and Lux saw his fingers were each dipped in red.

He'd painted Corvin in blood.

"Not yet. I've got one more thing to do." She leapt onto the dais and snatched the syringe. To Corvin, his eyes finally focused on her, she said, "You don't deserve his soul."

Lux plunged the needle into the corner of Corvin's eye, relishing the satisfaction. *You deserve this,* she thought, and her mind filled with every face of every attendant she'd met.

Though, while she'd felt the essence of each body she'd revived, she'd never experienced lifeblood like this. For one, there was so *much* of it. It was little wonder Corvin's eyes were sometimes bloodshot with strain.

How did someone sort through such a vat?

"One dark, with a brilliance of dreams," Riselda had said.

...a dreamer's soul.

This. This, perhaps, she could find. And so Lux cast herself once more on a trail only she could see.

Chapter Fifty-Two

A DREAMER EXISTED...TWICE OVER.

Lux reeled, and her fingers on the syringe slipped. Dozens of fractured souls and partial brilliances made up Corvin Alesso. Only two paths were left whole.

And they were the same. He and Alix began the *same*.

He didn't have to use his brilliance to create nightmares—he chose to.

If she'd any doubts over the morality of what she did, they were squashed beneath the revelation. Lux fumed. She gritted her teeth. All it took was the lightest touch to realize which was being consumed and which was untouched. In the end, she didn't need much precision, not at all, when she could see so clearly. Lux drew back the plunger.

She was done by the time the gargantuan statue protecting a madman's throne came fully to life.

"Why does no one ever listen to me!" shouted Aline, grabbing hold of her.

Stumbling backward, Lux knocked into Shaw and his sister. In her hand was the syringe. Its tip glinted like starlight. Her eyes flicked to Corvin's, the fresh blood trailing down his cheeks. He looked murderous, snarling in forced silence. Already, his mouth had reverted to its decay.

And she smiled.

A smile that was wiped clean from her face when the stone saint raised its arms. The wall behind it cracked and crumbled as the limbs broke free from their constraints, and Lux froze in her steps when the faceless being focused on her.

"Destroy the intruders!" the mason shrieked.

Matthias. He'd filled her insides with stones and now he'd have her pulled apart by one.

The sentient giant raised one carved foot—and crushed the pedestal beneath it. Shattered onyx sprayed across Corvin's throne; he tried to cover himself and couldn't. His hands were still secured fast. And already, the sanctum was emptying, leaving them behind to die—Corvin and Alix too. The saint swept out an arm toward them.

Shaw grabbed her around the waist and flung them both toward the empty table. The saint stretched, its head reaching the domed ceiling. The sound of cracking stone reverberated throughout the room, splitting Lux's skull. Her head pounded and her heart raced. The saint's palm splintered the table apart; Lux leapt over a fractured piece.

All this time, she held onto Alix, dragging him along with her.

His eyes, once every shade of darkness, were dulled a lifeless, charcoal grey. "You had better help us fix this when you're *you* again," she growled. Then she shoved the needle beneath his eye.

Alixsander Alesso collapsed against Shaw. Before he could fall, Shaw flung him over his shoulder. With his good eye trained upon her, he said, "Anything else before we go?"

His tone reeked of exasperation, but Lux scanned the room quickly, regardless. They all pressed against the wall when the giant stepped upon the ruined table. Very slowly, it turned toward them. It lowered its head.

"Run," gasped Lux.

Aline sprinted away first, followed by Shaw, and though Lux could have passed by him with his heavy burden, she waited. When the saint lumbered toward the exit, she shifted too. Enough to ensure Corvin remained chained at its back.

Which he was.

But only by one wrist.

No...

The other swung free and, using Shaw's own trick, he painted along the opposite shackle. *Devil below,* they'd harvested the soul of an artist. Stolen their brilliance. And Lux had seen enough. Spinning on her heel, she dodged the swipe of stone fingers and ran out of the sanctum.

Lux knocked into Shaw outside it; it was the same as running into a wall. She ricocheted backward and caught herself at the arched entrance.

"Watch out!" Aline cried.

The guarding statues on either side lunged, but this time, Lux wasn't fast enough. The blow to her cheekbone landed brutally. Something cracked, and she knew it belonged to her.

"Go!" she cried, holding her face as she ran. She could feel it swelling beneath her fingers. Could see Shaw's darting looks to ensure she stayed beside him.

The manor *groaned* at their backs.

The chamber is falling. She hoped it would crush Corvin beneath its weight. She wished it could have crushed Kent and Silas and all the rest too, but nothing for her was ever that simple.

The labyrinth stretched and curved. They passed multiple doors, but Shaw didn't slow and so she didn't either and finally, there was the end—the steep staircase—and they needed only to run up it, through the foyer, and out of Mothlock for good.

Two of those things, they accomplished. But outside Mothlock—

Outside were the dead.

Chapter Fifty-Three

The first body they came upon tripped Aline and nearly Lux. The newest collector, Tobias. His grey skin was pockmarked with wounds, and he lay draped across the steps. Lux's hand fell away from her cheek.

"Devil's..." she trailed, the cacophony overcoming her.

Of shouts, caws, and shrieks.

The crows. They filled the night sky, nearly blocking the moon. And beneath them, in the courtyard, were a mess of silks, suits, and robes.

Some of those were still alive.

Several dove for cover on the garden paths and were immediately latched onto by stems with sharp teeth. Others ran for the gate, clinging to the iron. A single investor attempted to climb; his waistcoat caught on a spire and would not release. None, she noted, were left undisturbed for long.

Meanwhile, robed collectors protected their heads. Using what brilliances they'd harvested, they fought against the creatures bombarding them. Except, what the crows lacked in enchantments, they made up for in numbers and tenacity. They would not be deterred—and the Society of Saints was clearly in peril.

"Why would they come out here?" wondered Lux. "Why don't they hide inside?"

"Because the ground remembers the Grimrooks, and the Grimrooks have returned. The society is no longer safe, inside or out. Look at them. Cowards, the lot, trying to run."

Lux whirled to Riselda standing in the doorframe, perfect and poised in an indigo gown, a soft smile on her mouth as she absorbed the waste laid around her.

"Look at the garden, Lucena. It's blooming."

Lux obeyed, glancing toward the graveyard, to the brambles rising high and arching over the path. The investor and councilman, Ulysses Morrigan, broke free from the birds to barrel down the darkened lane. A stem of teeth found him fast.

Over his scream, Riselda said, "And the vines. Such an exceptional, hardy breed."

Those Lux did not bother with. She whipped back to Riselda. "Where have you been? We've nearly died several times over."

"I've been doing all of this, darling. Awakening the estate. It'd nearly forgotten the touch of a Grimrook, it's been so long. Are you not happy? I did it for you." She leaned away as a crow drew close with its claws. "The birds don't like me much anymore, but—"

Riselda cut off her thought when Lux shied from beating wings. Then a rather heavy weight. A beady, black eye drifted in front of her face to examine her.

"Hello, Crow," she said. "You've been busy."

The animal inclined its head as if pleased she finally understood both their purposes. For once, it didn't peck her, though its claws did dig deep.

"Who's that?" Lux asked. "There's light outside the gate."

"Our reinforcements." Aline eyed the birds with unease. Her fingers wrapped around an orb with thick spikes. Lux had seen a similar invention of the girl's before, and so she became immediately suspicious.

"Reinforcements?" questioned Shaw, setting down his heavy cargo. "Who did you befriend on your absurd journey across the country?"

Aline's eyes narrowed on him. "Cecily."

"Cecily?" Lux startled the crow with her sudden movement, and the bird took flight with an irritated cry. "She's safe?"

"She was the last person we found. Me and the bandits and an old man, along with a few folks from the weird tree town." Aline squinted into the night. "There are quite a few torches out there now."

"Then we should—"

"My goodness, just look at the crows! What a help they've been. Their minds—second only to a few." Mistress Farrentail, bedecked in her feathers, stepped next to Riselda. Behind her came six more women. "It's a shame you've ruined your relationship with the creatures, Riselda; this could have been over before it even began."

Lux looked between the pair. "The vendor didn't die?"

"I can answer for myself, Ms. Thorn, thank *you* very much. No, I didn't die. Though I was severely incapacitated. I have a feeling we were planned additions to Mothlock's staff. I'm happy to say our health was restored before that happy event."

Lux's eyes drifted to Riselda, who'd yet to change her expression. Instead, it was as though she herself had been frozen. Her features were immobile. She didn't blink. She only stared at the body on the ground—the living one.

At Alixsander.

Who had begun to groan.

"What is this naked boy doing on the veranda?" Mistress Farrentail pushed farther out. "Holy saints and devil's tits! That's—"

"*Language*," mimicked Lux, meeting Mistress Farrentail's glare.

"What is the matter with you, girl! I *told* you not to revive him!"

"My choice was either that or something much worse. At any rate, he might not even be lucid. Though at least he has his soul."

Riselda, thawing at last, knelt beside him. "Alix?"

Eyes as dark as a crow's blinked open. The vacant look was gone, and they seemed to focus on Mothlock awhile—until they focused on Riselda. Alix's brow furrowed. Lux looked for any recognition on his part and saw none.

Riselda, noting this too, said, "It is the glamour, I suppose." Without breaking her gaze from his, she reached into her gown. The smallest vial pressed to her lips, and she swallowed the contents. "There, darling. Do you remember me now?"

Alix scrambled away with a cry of alarm. Lux nearly did too, but her legs wouldn't propel her. Riselda turned from his fearful face to find her.

"You see, Lucena? You do not suffer from the madness of brilliance. Because if you did, you would look like this."

Chapter Fifty-Four

Her skin was not sloughing. Her teeth weren't blackened and her tongue remained a usual pink instead of bloated. But Riselda's natural ivory tone was replaced with grey. And her eyes—her eyes were green.

Her hair, no longer lustrous, hung like a dull and brittle curtain about her shoulders. She pushed it back. "I had planned to take this to my grave, but the Grimrooks did value honesty between family."

A pit formed in Lux's gut. "That means I might—"

"No." And now Riselda was stern. "What I suffer from does not follow any bloodline." She glanced at Alix, then toward the bodies collecting on the gravel. "I know vengeance did this. I wanted Ghadra—and everyone in it—to suffer. Because I'd suffered. I wanted Grimrook House returned. For anyone in it to run screaming from my estate. And now...now I want every last one of these traitorous men to die."

She left Alix and drew nearer to Lux. Near enough that Shaw stepped between them. Riselda rolled her eyes, and said around his shoulder, "I realized after a few decades what was happening, when nothing cured me. I had *The Risen*; I understood a necromancer could expunge the madness. But once it came to asking for your assistance in a revival, I simply chose not to."

Riselda cackled so abruptly, Lux startled. "You see, I *like* it." Her finger rose as if she meant to stroke Lux's cheek, the motion meeting only air. "You needed me though, didn't you, darling? And so I did not abandon you."

Lux could hardly stomach Riselda's laugh—it was the phantom reincarnated. And Shaw had had enough.

Low and harsh, he said, "She does not *need* you. She is magnificent *despite* you. And you cannot order her or control her or claim her. She is not *yours*, Riselda."

For a brief moment, Lux thought Riselda was going to lunge at him with her teeth. But the smile upon her face only grew, stretching, wide as it could. "She is magnificent, isn't she? Don't worry, Cockroach. I do not want anything from her anymore." Then she turned and crouched before Alix. "Dear Alix. I loved you like a brother. Why? Why did you betray me? You should have known you would be next."

"Riselda." Lux pushed around Shaw. "Don't kill him. His soul is good. I think he would do good things for Mothlock, if he could."

Riselda's nails twitched beside Alix's face, but she did pull them back. "Well, dearest?"

"I didn't mean to betray you. I only didn't know why you stole and why you ran. You were so secretive and withdrawn from me. I was worried for you, Riselda. Please believe me."

"Because they were taking, Alix. Wasn't it obvious? My family was dying and our estate pilfered piece by piece. How could I trust anyone but myself to fix it? You stole it from me, whether you thought you would do good with it or not." She surveyed the grounds. "It grew sick, even twisted, with our absence."

"I swear I didn't know."

"Ignorance is an excuse I *never* accept."

The danger had returned to Riselda's voice. The vengeance. And Lux shoved aside her discomfort to grab hold of Riselda's bare shoulder. "That's enough—"

Lux didn't mean to. But neither did she stop it. In that moment, she witnessed Riselda's soul—and every bit of its consuming cage.

She surfaced to stunned silence, her fingers removed and now pressed to Riselda's cheek. Green eyes, identical to her own—watched her closely. "Stop. Leave it alone, Vesperine. My Lucena. I am through."

Lux could not break her gaze. "Through with what?"

"My plan. I dare say it was well executed." Dropping Lux's fingers, she rose. "You will listen to her, Alix. More than you ever did to me. She is a Grimrook, and this estate is hers. It knows it too." To Lux, she stretched out her hand and said, "Do not allow *anyone* to steal it again."

Lux stared down at the scroll placed into her palm, dumbstruck. Loose pages lay beneath it. "Riselda—"

"Your blood, darling. It is all you've ever needed. You did not share it with any of Mothlock's traitors, did you?"

Caught off guard, she answered, "No." But then she saw Artemis burrowing his way beneath a body to deter the crows. "Or—I might have. A little."

Riselda's grey skin purpled with irritation. "I taught you better. Curses are mockeries of brilliance—fake gifts with very real consequences which anyone may wield. You had better hope it wasn't kept." Then she strode down the steps and onto the garden path.

She called back, "I will not chop my way out of these, Mr. Roser. No need to follow. Though you may want to head this way eventually. There'll be tonic for your eye and Lucena's cheek in Grimrook House."

Lux, however, was not told to keep back. She leapt after Riselda, to the start of the garden path, and there she watched her—the woman who had both given Lux life and destroyed it—embrace each garden statue. When she pushed into the eager brambles, Lux felt no sympathy, guilt, or sadness.

Maybe it was always how Riselda's life was meant to end. In the graveyard of her family. On her terms.

Mad as they were.

Lux glanced over her shoulder, to Shaw shrugging out of his jacket and handing it off to Alix. To the women who had come down the steps, utilizing their toxic feathers to poison investors who attempted to flee. Aline, fitting her contraption to the gate. And Magda, a guest she'd missed in the mess, sobbing against Manphry, her arms wrapped around his waist.

Lux's fingers tightened on the scroll. On the papers beneath. She moved the deed aside.

The Essence, read that first yellowed page. She shuffled them quickly. To the illustration of an anatomical eye, lifeblood's description alongside.

Not a book of death, but a book of life.

Lux lifted her gaze to peer into Mothlock's dimly lit interior and waited to see if Corvin would come.

She should have been watching other things.

When stone claws snatched her arms, Lux could do no more than shriek and kick before her boots left the ground.

She whipped her head to what held her—thick, stone legs and a beast above that. A gargoyle from the tower. And then down to every upturned face.

An explosion blew the iron gate apart.

Lux was soon in line with the tower's shattered windows, knowing to fall now would find her bones smashed to pieces. She quit her flailing at once; she held onto the gargoyle's feet with all her might.

Matthias! Why isn't he dead?

The beast flapped its wings, soaring over the peak and, for a moment, Lux hung suspended, face to face with the moon. She stared at it, frozen, before a scream ripped up her throat.

The gargoyle dove.

It flew beyond the cliff.

And it was as Lux looked down at the seafoam that it let her go.

Chapter Fifty-Five

The second gargoyle held her much gentler than the first.

Lux could hardly breathe, her heart raced so fast. She stared at the stone beast's body scattered on the cliff's edge and barely knew what to make of what had happened. She'd been dropped by one—only to be rescued by another?

This gargoyle flew less succinctly than the one before. It lurched and sped, then stuttered and slowed, but eventually the lampposts returned, the courtyard visible once again. More chaotic than she'd left it.

For one, with the gate destroyed, there were more bodies than before—including two who ran along the garden path, following her flight.

She couldn't make out their faces until she was nearly upon them. Immediate relief pinged in her chest at seeing Shaw. Along with immediate irritation at seeing Lars.

She cried out when her feet connected with the gravel courtyard, her momentum propelling her forward and into the former's arms.

"*Devil below*," Shaw breathed into her hair and swept her up against him.

"What..." she croaked. "How..."

"That ancient mason is dead. The brambles took him shortly after the gargoyle took you. I made it to the gate but forgot it was locked. Saw you drop."

"Bet you didn't know I have a rare brilliance too, did you?"

Lux turned her head toward Lars, watching him fold his hands into his pockets with a self-satisfied smirk.

"You did that?"

"Course I did." A moment later, his smile fell away. "They did something awful to my father here, didn't they?"

Shaw placed her back on her feet, and they both turned to whom Lars stared. Manphry, sitting on the steps, his head resting against Magda's chest and his eyes blinking but seemingly fixed.

"They took his soul," she said. "Once those who stole it are all gone, he'll go to the Beyond."

I hope.

Suddenly, a girl was at her elbow, grabbing hold of it and dragging her around. "Lux!" exclaimed Cecily. "Lord Kent is still alive. He wants to talk to you."

"Of course he would," Lux said, sickly sweet, and she allowed Cecily to take her to him.

The remaining trio of collectors stood back to back to back. And they were surrounded. By pitchforks, torches, and redwren feathers.

Kent.

Artemis.

Silas.

Lux feared none of them. Not anymore. She strode up to Kent, ignoring Silas's growl but deigning to curl her lip at Artemis.

Artemis, who had told her *she* was mad when really they were—and all by their own doing.

"I hear you had something to say, you moldering troll. What is it?"

The crows circled overhead, appearing satisfied for the moment. They did not bother her or anyone else, opting only to watch.

Kent's colorless lips pursed. "You've made a mistake, Necromancer, doing what you've done. Collectors have minded Mothlock for centuries. We've shaped the country. You must revive them; everything will collapse if you don't."

"I cannot," said Lux, and she pouted. "I've a dark brilliance. Prone to breakage, I'm told."

Kent's eyes narrowed while Artemis's widened. Lux glared at them both.

"This is your last chance, Ms. Thorn." Artemis's stare turned sour. "All the strength of Malgorm will come down on you if you don't do as you're told."

Lux smiled wide. "Let them come meet me by the sea. I'm more than happy to wait."

"You'll stay here?" snorted Silas. "Where I know to find you?"

"Find me? I'm going to keep you here *with* me. Locked in a room with manacles on your ankles. I've a feeling with the number of souls you've taken, *Mania Malus* will see you rotted away by next Hallowed Day." She looked at Kent. "What about this"—she gestured widely at the gathering—"gave you the impression you would be free to go?"

"If we will not be free then you'll not be either," warned Artemis.

Of all things, this struck fear within her. Her attention snapped back to the healer with a snarl—in time to see his nod at something beyond her head.

Lux whirled back. To the doorway, empty. To the tower...

A bloodied, rotting boy—holding a burning torch aloft.

Corvin—

His opposite hand tipped into the flame, and Lux could make no effort in understanding it before she went entirely numb.

Lux didn't move; she stood there, perplexed, as Corvin sneered from his lofty height. And only once Shaw's hand met her elbow, his mouth at her ear, did she realize she couldn't feel him. Not like before.

She turned to stare upon his face.

Nothing.

She felt *nothing*.

"And now you cannot love! What does it feel like, Ms. Thorn?" Artemis ran a grey tongue over matching gums in satisfaction. "I think we should have done it from the start. Let's see where your ambitions take you, now that you've no anchors holding you still."

Lux stumbled forward with the sudden loss of Shaw's support. She heard his fast footfalls in the gravel, but nothing else.

They'd *cursed* her.

Kent's laugh rumbled. "All that effort to save a dangerous little empath when the whole brilliance is better snuffed, and now you're gone and numb. Poetry. Pure and simple." His shoulder knocked Artemis's. "I'd thought Alesso outlived his usefulness, but it seems he can still surprise me."

"Do not *speak* of our overlord in that way."

Kent snorted. Silas laughed harshly.

And then they each began to choke.

Lux stared at each decaying face purpling before her eyes. Then at the deep-green vines extending from the bottoms of their robes. She tracked one between her feet—back to Mothlock.

"I'm sorry," said an old voice. "But maybe the young lady is right, and some things are better off gone."

Lux raised onto her toes and discovered Edgar among the gathered group. How he'd managed to come down from the mountain cabin and all the way to the sea with his arthritic joints, she'd no idea.

"Such a shame about your parts," he continued. "I would have loved to keep them, but I've no use for diseased things. Those are better off burned."

Artemis went to his knees first, followed by Silas. Kent kept her gaze ensnared with his own. He tried to speak, but a croaking noise was all he managed. Though that, too, was cut when he collapsed to the gravel.

The Collectors of Mothlock passed to the Beyond, and Lux knew for certain no saint-like existence awaited them.

She turned away from the scene. She spied Alix first, hovering in his coat that hardly covered anything important. Then Cecily on the stoop offering him comfort. She spotted the bandits, Sven and Viktar, their mirrored horrified expressions, before her glance slid to Aline having come up beside her. All these people arrived to help, and she felt—

Numb.

She was back in Ghadra, consumed by that dark space inside her, caring for nothing and no one.

And that, she could not stand to suffer again.

"Give me that contraption," Lux demanded, holding out her hand.

Aline relinquished it to Lux's palm without preamble. "Pull back on this here. Don't squeeze that until you're sure."

"Simple enough. Will you help the families you brought? Someone will need to round up the staff before I free the last pieces of their souls. I don't want to keep finding their bodies after—" She let the sentence hang.

"We'll get started."

"Thank you. Take Cecily; she's surprisingly fine in a crisis. Leave Alix with Sven."

Aline nodded, and Lux settled the weight of the weapon against her hip. She ran up the steps and into Mothlock.

Chapter Fifty-Six

The ruined frame of Riselda's portrait had been tossed to the ground, revealing the hidden staircase behind it, but it was the newly painted door Lux went through. When she reached the top, she found Shaw with his knife drawn and circling Corvin, attempting to pin the collector's monstrous form against blackened walls.

The Society's Overlord looked worse than ever before. His skin sagged from his cheekbones, and his lips were a necrotic black. He'd bled from multiple cuts along his head; they'd dried in grotesque streaks.

His rabid eyes roved about the room, searching for an escape without success.

He held onto a narrow spear of glass.

Lux looked down at Aline's invention and pulled back where she'd been told. She held it away from her body.

"It's over, Corvin," she announced from across the room. "Your society is finished. Picked apart by crows and the garden and its own greed."

Shaw spun to face her, doing a double take at what she held in her hands; he retreated ever so slightly.

"I think you've misunderstood your own curse," she told the rotting collector. "I can't feel love anymore, you're right. But that doesn't mean I don't *remember* it. And if there was anything I would to fight to get back, it'd be that. I'm sorry you don't remember." Her shaking settled as her arms grew accustomed to the weight of the weapon. She leveled it with both hands at Corvin's robed chest.

"Nothing will ever make me turn as cold as you. You stole my blood. Now give me yours."

Corvin edged backward, his front facing her fully and his back to the shattered window. His cheeks deepened to purple; he shouted at her in heavy silence.

"It's honestly pitiful," drawled Shaw. "Seeing you hang on like you have any power still. You have none. Do one decent thing before your spirit rots away."

This, of all things, seemed to give Corvin pause. His features slackened and his head bowed. His hands rose in supplication. Lux did not trust him, and she drew a hesitant breath, waiting for him to spring.

Which he did.

Backwards.

Through the window.

And Lux didn't fire the weapon after all—but dropped it as she lunged.

As a knife, thrown, sank into Corvin's thigh. Though that neither stopped him nor stuck.

She didn't reach him in time—she knew she wouldn't. Corvin tumbled out of the tower. Down to the raging sea below.

"*No!*" she cried. "Shaw! Hurry. We have to find his body. I have to revive him, get his blood. I can't live like—"

Shaw spun her around so quickly, she faltered.

A knife filled her vision, its end glistening crimson and wet. "I hate to say it, Lux," he said, voice rough with disgust and regret. "But open your mouth."

Her stomach immediately resisted; her palms slicked with sweat. But Shaw's hand came up to cradle her head. He gently drew it back. "I'm sorry."

"It's not your fault," she murmured, staring up into his ruined eye and feeling nothing at all but sick. "It was mine for being so desperate to fix myself."

"You're not broken, remember?"

Lux drew a long breath. *I remember.*

She opened her mouth and allowed the drops to coat her tongue.

Lux closed her eyes at once, scrunching them tight. Something clattered to the ground, then Shaw's hand gingerly cradled her bruised and swollen cheek. "Just breathe. You won't be sick. It worked. It has to."

And Lux whispered those same words to herself until her stomach settled. Her breaths too. Until—

"Saints above," she breathed.

"What? Did it reverse?"

Her initial answer was to bury her nose in his chest. To inhale his scent and his warmth and all it brought within her. But eventually, she said, "I used to be scared of my feelings for you becoming irreversible. But I was never more scared when they weren't."

His temple lowered to press against hers. "We've been irreversible from the start, Lux. I knew I was the one to realize it first." She huffed and he kissed her. "Will you keep it? Mothlock, I mean."

"Never. I feel like I see nightmares in every corner." She pulled back, enough to look out the window. "But I might keep one part."

"DANGEROUS? HOW CAN I be dangerous?"

Cecily wrung her hands in Mothlock's kitchen while sitting beside Aline. Aline, who glanced at her discreetly while taking apart the weapon she'd created. Lux hadn't used its last shot, and the girl had deemed it too dangerous to keep together.

"Corvin enjoyed manipulating," Lux explained. "I think he wanted your brilliance so he might control others' feelings. My guess is Kent was worried Corvin would realize his spitefulness and secret wish to usurp him. You're not actually dangerous. But you were dangerous to him."

"Well, *I* think," said Aline, "that some people don't want to feel others' emotions. It's harder to destroy people's lives when you understand the pain."

Lux's gaze dropped. She'd hidden from others' emotions for a long time. Even her own.

Not anymore, soothed her heart, and she accepted the comfort.

She'd unburied it all, well and truly and good this time.

"I would never use my brilliance to manipulate people." Cecily shook her head, a determined set to her mouth.

Lux leaned back, her tea in hand and eyes drifting to the curved stairwell that had once held a nightmare. That first time she'd ever seen it. She said, "That's why, no matter what they did, you would have always possessed more power than them. They were sinking and rotting, being eaten by their brokenness, and they knew it. It's pathetic, really, how hard they clung to something nature said was never meant to be."

"Nature sure said it loud enough at the end," said Cecily, giggling at her own conclusion.

Aline blinked at her with wide eyes, then snorted, trying to keep a laugh at bay. Lux did too, biting her cheek. But both proved useless. As Aline dropped her head, giggling as high and light as Cecily, and Lux pressed her fingers to her eyes, huffing breaths of laughter through her nose, Lux thought, there was no better way to see justice realized than by all the things the Society of Saints had tortured and overlooked.

"Mothlock is a mess," said Lux, her humor slowly fading. "I don't know where to start."

"I think all of Verity would happily clean it up. They hate what became of this place."

"Just ask people for help, Lux," said Aline, rolling her eyes. "It's what I did."

Lux scoffed. "I don't know what you're implying. I've asked for help from you before."

Aline's expression soured. "Don't remind me. I still haven't forgiven either of you for almost dying." She pushed her teacup away. "But other than that one time, have you ever?"

"She's ashamed," said Cecily, then she squeaked at Lux's sharp glare, covering her mouth. "I'm sorry! I'm trying to be better about blurting others' feelings."

Lux's glare remained. "I've asked Shaw for help. I've asked you, Aline. And I agreed for Viktar to take those two carriage drivers to his lumber mill, didn't I? Just because I take care of myself and don't want to endanger anyone else, doesn't mean I'm *ashamed*." She scowled harder at Cecily.

"But you are," said Cecily. "And I think you should stop. Unless you like it. Being alone." Her expression made it known she knew Lux didn't, in fact, like it.

"Not all the time. No," Lux grumbled.

"Good," replied Cecily brightly. Then she stood from the table. "Come on, Aline. Let me show you where to find a bed that didn't have a rotten collector on it."

As they left hand in hand, Lux dropped her head into her own. She massaged her temples, thinking of all that would need to be fixed. Every lending library that had hindered rather than helped. The body of each attendant gone to the Beyond following their soul's departure. The repairs Mothlock required, and Alix Alesso's continued presence.

The mountain of books in Grimrook House.

Grimrook House.

How she already loved its dark rose garden, glass room, and proximity to the sea. How she daydreamed of sitting beside Shaw in front of the fireplace, a cup of tea in her hands.

She thought of it so vividly, she could almost touch it.

Her path.

Her dream.

And Lux did not second-guess it even for a moment. She shoved herself from the table and followed.

Chapter Fifty-Seven

The organization of Grimrook House's many books was going to take a year of her life—Lux was convinced of it. She blew dust from the cover of yet another subject in which she had no interest, and stacked it atop yet another pile. The former bandits were busy reorganizing Mothlock's Manuscripts in Loxlen. She needed to give them more material.

She'd decided the businesses were going to stay open, but managed by a different society. One of feathers rather than fortune. One that wanted to teach instead of trick. As far as the second Alesso—she hadn't been sure he'd accept what she offered, considering the traumas he'd been subjected to, but he'd seemed eager to continue the path he'd set upon two centuries prior. She was more than happy to hand Mothlock Manor over to him.

Grimrook House, however...

Lux stood and stretched, her gaze sweeping the lit hall. She didn't care for shadowed spaces, and had ensured every lamp was alight as soon as the sun began to set. Twilight would not be grey and dark here.

A creaking drew her attention, and Shaw emerged from the staircase. In his hands were two steaming cups.

"You've made a lot of progress," he said, glancing at her stacks. "Care for a break?"

Lux dusted her hands, and started toward him. "It'll take me through the winter," she whined.

"You could have Aline and Cecily help. They're not doing much up at the manor other than getting in Alesso's way."

"That's the opposite of what he says. He told me Aline has built a lamp that's powered by hand instead of fire and oil."

Shaw's eyes, mended and whole, widened. "But does it also explode or blind?"

She shook her head. "Completely nondestructive."

"Who would have thought." He pressed the teacup into her hand.

Lux traced the murder of crows as they beat their wings across the porcelain. She sipped the tea and moaned. "What did you put in this?"

"You like it?" His gaze dipped to her mouth. He wiped a droplet with the pad of his thumb. "Roses from the garden. And honey."

Lux cleared her throat. "How is your project coming?"

"I finished."

"Every room?"

"Even the conservatory. Care to see?"

She frowned at her own project, far from complete. "I could use a break, I suppose."

She stepped, and her toe connected with the protruded spine of a book. Lux glanced down. Her stare narrowed. Then she bent and reached, pulling it out completely. This place really was a mess.

She blew across the cover.

Necromantic Pursuits. Her heart immediately sped. Her gaze dropped to the author. *Archibald Grimrook*.

"Devil's tits." She flipped it over. "It's the necromancer's journal! I wanted it in Loxlen, but it was so expensive and—"

A woeful chime echoed from downstairs.

"Were you expecting someone?"

"No," said Shaw. His gaze flicked to hers. "I'll see who it is."

She watched him walk away for a few heartbeats before following. Neither were naïve; they knew it was likely they would eventually have to answer for what had happened that Hallowed Day. She planned to tell the truth—for the most part.

That the Society of Saints was experimenting on others, particularly the locals. That they were never the rightful owners of the estate but had stolen it for themselves. That they'd been murdered by the very plants they'd twisted and the crows they'd scorned.

Because guardian's leech, according to Edgar Dosem, was indeed a rather parasitic, venomous plant but particular to cold-blooded creatures. Like crabs. By depriving them of their natural food source and instead, feeding them warm, human blood, they'd grown strange and difficult to sate. Edgar had stayed behind an extra week to convince them to return to their regular diet. Between his ministrations and Lux's admonishments, the brambles relaxed. He'd even been able to prune them.

Now, Lux could walk amongst her family graveyard with almost no worry.

She made it to the large curve of the staircase when Shaw opened the door.

"Alesso," he said, and she relaxed.

She shouldn't have.

"Is Lux here? I'm sorry to say we've been brought a student, passed from a carriage accident. Bashed his head on a stone."

Lux could clearly see the distraught profile of Alixsander and wouldn't have been surprised if the body wasn't immediately behind him at his feet. She'd not revived anyone since him. In all honesty, she wasn't sure she would again. It made her sick—and horribly embarrassed—to know she'd faint.

Besides, what if she were making herself worse with every use of her gift?

Shaw's glance slid up and over to hers. Waiting.

"Oh, bring him in," she grumbled.

Shaw nodded and said, "Take him to the conservatory."

Chapter Fifty-Eight

Lux was the last one through the doorway, and she thought her heart might have stopped.

Her eyes landed on the worktable first, dark wood scratched but clean, and the body being laid upon it. Her gaze skipped over to the counter. To *The Risen* propped open upon a stand, the familiar incantation summoning her from across the room. The shelves were wood too, but without any irritating slant, and they were each stocked with all manner of things she would need for a revival and some things she didn't. Like plant clippings and paintbrushes.

That was when she found an easel with a stretched canvas pulled taut over a frame. It faced the cove while Lux would face the open sea. Voices spoke behind the stunned humming in her head.

She walked up to the counter and her fingers reached, gliding along the vials and decanters. The jars with fused lids. She picked up a mortar and pestle—a new one set beside the one she'd long owned. It was larger, heavier, made of a white stone. She placed it back on the counter.

She reached for the bat wings. The moth powder. The lavender and rain water and rattler venom. She inspected the jar of marsh snapper eyes, and the one of wyvern claws. She didn't think she'd need the howler canines, but those she held to the lamplight also.

It was all so organized and welcoming.

It felt like a proper workroom. *Her* workroom.

But instead of smudged glass and an alleyway view, this one gave her the sea. She pressed her fingers to her lips.

"I know I didn't ask, but I thought you should have a space."

Lux turned to face Shaw, his hips leaned against the counter and his stare open and vulnerable. Her glance flicked to the easel and back again. "You mean for us to share it?"

"Ah, well, I figured—"

"You'll stay?"

"I would," he began slowly. "Only if you allow it."

Lux lost her breath.

For once, in a way that did not terrify her.

She hadn't known. She'd been too scared to ask. Same as she'd been too scared to ask he come along with her the day she'd left Ghadra. Rejection had become commonplace during her years alone. She'd thought she could stomach it from anyone.

She'd realized, some time into knowing Shaw, she would have struggled immensely stomaching it from him.

"Are you sure? You might grow bored only painting the sea. Then there's the matter of your mother. And you hate heights. What will—"

His lips met hers, effectively cutting her thoughts. He pulled back enough to say, "There's more to paint than the sea, and my mother would love Verity. I don't like heights, but I can manage them. What I can't manage is being apart from you. I'm irreversibly in love with you, Lux. I want to stay. If you think the proximity is too much, though, I could move into Mothlock and—"

Lux silenced him in turn. Her lips brushed against his still when she said, "Stay at Grimrook House, Shaw. Stay with me."

She felt his smile—

And heard Alix clear his throat.

Her cheeks burned hot as coals when she whirled toward the newly appointed Minder of Mothlock with a scowl. "It isn't coming up on twelve hours, is it? We've got plenty of time."

"I only had some salt in my lungs," replied Alix, a half-smile pulling at his lips.

The expression was such a replica of his twin's, Lux immediately scowled deeper. It would take time, learning to trust others to do the right thing. To help her.

She turned away, placing her ancestor's journal upon the counter. She could get on with it, perform this revival and deal with the consequences, or...

Her fingers drifted across the cover until she lifted it without fully realizing. She thumbed beyond that first signature page. The handwriting was cramped but sweeping, the flourishes rather lavish for plain journal entries. She read,

To those who come after me:

We have been called by Death to connect with Life. To walk a path of darkness to bring back the light. Keep only your own, and give away what is not. Thrilling accomplishments are ahead.

Your journey has only just begun.

Lux chewed at her cheek. "Give away what is not," she muttered.

She thought the author meant the soul at first, but of course she couldn't keep that. She was merely a host for a moment, and it would burn her up. What else could he refer to?

Lux had decided a while ago she'd unbalanced something within herself. Had noticed how Edgar had used the word too. The botanist had described life in that way—all of it, a balance—and she'd seen firsthand what righting it looked like. From a simple pruning to the end of a siphoning monster.

"Devil take me," she whispered. "I've been doing it all wrong."

"What was that?" asked Shaw.

Lux flipped to the next page, skimming over the entry. "I was so lost before, that guiding someone's soul to feel light for a while was like a reprieve from an abyss. Even if it drained me afterward. But now, I'm not lost—and I think the energy of a revival is too much alongside my own. I've been trying to contain it like I always have, to keep it for myself, but I'm not meant to. I'm meant to give it away."

Her eyes lifted to Shaw, where he watched her carefully. She turned back to the journal, closed it, and then closed *The Risen*, too. She stacked the thinner book in front of the larger one and huffed an incredulous laugh.

A perfect match.

A set.

"The Grimrooks were not all terrible," she said.

"Of course they weren't," replied Shaw.

Lux stared a moment more in wonder before she straightened her spine and snipped, "Everyone out. I don't like people watching me work."

Chapter Fifty-Nine

"Bat wings. Black. Wyvern claws...dew only?" Aline snorted, tucking the list into her coat pocket. "If I'd have known it was going to be this particular—and this weird—I wouldn't have volunteered to buy these things in Loxlen for you."

"Yes, you would have," said Lux, nodding at Cecily waiting by the gate. It was a new one, made of red Ravenwood trees, and strong enough to withstand the salt.

She waved away Aline and her grousing, and waved again at Sven in the driver's seat. She turned her back once they'd climbed into the carriage.

Her glance swept over Mothlock, covered in deep-green vines and lit on either side of the doors by Aline's new lamps. The tower had been closed for repairs and so had the sanctum—Lars was a student of masonry and could only do so much on his own. The manor was still imposing, but the foreboding she'd once felt was gone.

She walked along the graveyard path. With the guardian's leech trimmed back, mushrooms had embraced the spring season, rising from around dark rocks. Everything smelled wet and earthy, with a hint of promised warmth and salt. Lux breathed it in.

She paused near the statue of a woman. It wasn't on the path like Granville's and Rosamund's, but off in the garden. Lux pivoted, stepping from the fitted stones onto mossy knolls and rocks. She picked her way among the mushrooms and told the brambles to remember themselves before stopping in front of the carved creation.

RISELDA GRIMROOK
The House of Grimrook

The woman above the name was not filled with melancholy or despair, but a fierceness never to be sated—her eyes staring not at Lux, but upward.

Lux chewed at her lip. She'd debated giving Riselda a statue at all, but in the end, the woman was indeed her family, and Lux did not need to court more bad luck.

She did sneer though, as she said, "I swear I won't clear anything off more than once a year."

A flutter in the breeze announced an arrival. A crow landed upon Riselda's head. Matching Lux's height, it gnashed its beak then began to preen. A sleek, black feather cascaded to Riselda's base.

"Hello, Crow. Don't forget she's the only one you're allowed to perch on."

The crow warbled back at her, some noise she couldn't interpret, but the creature seemed content. It'd not bothered a single soul since that banquet night. She hoped it wouldn't ever again have need to.

Lux left the bird there to attend its business and made her way to the gate. The narrow wooden door opened with only her touch after she'd reclaimed the deed, and she stepped through to the most breathtaking view.

She would never tire of this.

As she walked the path leading her home, she realized something. That feeling in her chest had returned—not the lonely one or the anxious one, but the sense of perfect peace. She would wake again tomorrow ready for a new adventure, even if that adventure was only to drink a cup of tea in the comfiest armchair beside the glow of a hearth.

Lux strode across the bridge and passed the garden wall, where she came upon a small cluster of stinging nettles. The ribbon in her hair was midnight-blue and new, catching in the breeze, and her skirt was blue to match; she used the latter now to clutch the weeds, severing them by the stems. With her dagger, she cut free the seeds. They scattered in the soil.

She thought of her parents, and especially her mother. The woman who'd named her and raised her, and she said to the earth, "We must never take more than we give."

Lux looked up to find Shaw standing in the ivy-covered doorway. With paint smeared on his nose and a teacup in his grip, he held the refurbished door wide for her. He was smiling.

And Lux could not believe that of all the paths her worn boots could have taken, her freedom had allowed her to choose *this*.

She smiled back, completely content, and hurried inside.

ACKNOWLEDGEMENTS

It's over; I can hardly believe it. It feels so bittersweet letting go of these characters and this world. I've heard that writing sequels is hard, and I can now say that's absolutely true. I could picture the exact ending I wanted for Lux in my head, but finding the particular path to get her there sent me on a lot of writing detours. Regardless, I'm so happy her story turned out the way it did, and I hope you've enjoyed it too!

Endless thanks to Tracy, Blair, and Brandi. Your comments, reactions, and words of encouragement keep me going! I'm so grateful to have you all in my corner.

Thank you, Aubrey. Seriously. I don't know what I would do without your ability to see into my head and know exactly where I'm trying to take a book. You get me (and my clueless comma usage), and I'm forever thankful to have you as my editor.

And lastly, the biggest thank you to my readers! Thank you for being here for my first completed series! Your support will always mean the world to me.

ABOUT THE AUTHOR

GLORIA BOTTELMAN IS A fantasy writer and registered nurse. While living in the Midwest (and dreaming of the PNW), she spends her time trying to make sense of her many book ideas and walking in the woods—usually at the same time.

Connect with her at or scan the QR code below!

www.ingramcontent.com/pod-product-compliance
Lightning Source LLC
LaVergne TN
LVHW030313070526
838199LV00069B/6467